OTHER TITLES BY THIS AUTHOR

MYSTERY
Sir Laurence Dies [The "Dies" Series – Book 1]
Dr. Chandrix Dies [The "Dies" Series – Book 2]
SHERLOCK HOLMES: A Scandalous Affair

FANTASY
Songs of the Osirian [Songs of the Osirian – Book 1]
Rise of the Jackal King [Songs of the Osirian – Book 2]
Daughter of Ra [Songs of the Osirian – Book 3]
Citadel of Ra [Songs of the Osirian – Book 4]
Songs of the Osirian: Companion

SUPERNATURAL/HORROR
Progenitor

ANTHOLOGIES
All That Remains
Beast: A New Beginning
Beast: Revelations

HORROR
Escaping Matilda
Revolting Tales: Christopher D. Abbott & Todd A. Curry

This book is dedicated to the following:
Jeffrey Holt, my rock!

Special thanks, in no particular order:
Jeffrey Holt, Richard Sutton, Rob Reddan,
Michael Jan Freidman, Aaron Rosenberg,
and Scott Pearson.

Copyright ©2020 Christopher D. Abbott
Cover by Richard Sutton
Edited by Scott Pearson
ISBN 978-1-939888-19-8
For information address Crazy 8 Press at the official Crazy 8 website:
www.crazy8press.com

CDANABBOTT.COM

First edition

PROGENITOR

CHRISTOPHER D. ABBOTT

CRAZY 8 PRESS

CONTENTS

I would say to the House, as I said to those who have joined this Government: 'I have nothing to offer but blood, toil, tears, and sweat.' We have before us an ordeal of the most grievous kind. We have before us many, many long months of struggle and of suffering. You ask, what is our policy? I will say: It is to wage war, by sea, land and air, with all our might and with all the strength that God can give us; to wage war against a monstrous tyranny, never surpassed in the dark, lamentable catalogue of human crime. That is our policy. You ask, what is our aim? I can answer in one word: It is victory, victory at all costs, victory in spite of all terror, victory, however long and hard the road may be; for without victory, there is no survival.

—Sir Winston Leonard Spencer Churchill
Prime Minister of the United Kingdom

I have seen war. I have seen war on land and sea. I have seen blood running from the wounded.... I have seen the dead in the mud. I have seen cities destroyed.... I have seen children starving. I have seen the agony of mothers and wives. I hate war.

So, first of all, let me assert my firm belief that the only thing we have to fear is... fear itself – nameless, unreasoning, unjustified terror which paralyzes needed efforts to convert retreat into advance. In every dark hour of our national life a leadership of frankness and of vigour has met with that understanding and support of the people themselves which is essential to victory. And I am convinced that you will again give that support to leadership in these critical days.

—Franklin Delano Roosevelt
President of the United States of America

CHAPTER ONE
Friday, August 14, 1942

Washington's sky was on fire...

The car carrying General William Marshall, Chief of Staff of the Army and a member of a new body of joint chiefs established by President Roosevelt, skidded to a halt at the side of the road. General Marshall, and his aide Captain John Keeney, stepped out and surveyed the ruins of the capital in shocked silence.

Plumes of black-grey smoke rose from destroyed historic buildings, feeding a heavy cloud that was choking the light from the city. The engulfing fires below gave the thick sky an ominous glow. Streets, usually busy with traffic, were littered with the rubble of collapsed buildings. Cars stood abandoned where they'd stopped. The intense heat sporadically caught the plumes alight, causing bright flashes and thunder-like rumbles, which turned the sky bright orange. In between those volatile periods of fiery activity, the city became eerily silent, broken only by occasional unrecognisable animal-like noises reverberating through the streets below.

There were no other sounds.

There were no people.

Marshall blinked as the heat and smoke particles washed over him. His face was a roadmap to the ravages of time, and his deep lines and heavy crow's-feet suggested the battle with time was over and he'd lost. Falling ash clung to his close-cropped white hair, and the reddish hue of his age-mottled skin deepened in colour, as he stood watching the sky burn. An acrid odour travelled along the wind. Marshall wiped his blue-grey eyes as the heat induced them to water. He observed Captain Keeney, who leant into the car and turned on the radio. Keeney was a handsome young man in his late twenties, dependable with an excellent grasp of routine that paired well with being an aide to an old forgetful general.

Keeney tuned the radio until a panicked voice cut through the static.

'Turn that up,' General Marshall ordered

'*... it's difficult to make out. There's gunfire, explosions. We're not sure where it's coming from. There are people running in the streets with what looks like animals chasing them. We're just hearing. Hold on. We're hearing that they've attacked the Pentagon. We... We don't know any... Wait, what was that? The building is shaking. There's something in here with us...*'

Marshall fell back against the car. 'The Pentagon?'

Keeney stared into the horizon. 'Bobby,' he muttered.

'Did you hear me? I said turn that up.'

He came back to his senses and adjusted the volume. Muffled screaming replaced the voice, then the station stopped broadcasting.

The young captain found another.

'*... and that's it, stay indoors, barricade yourselves and... wait, what's that? There's something... fuck! The building is shaking, there's something outside... Jesus Christ, what is that? Get out, get out...*'

Marshall looked grim as the voice on the radio gave a hideous scream, and then that station too went dead.

'Are we under attack, General?'

'It looks like it.' General Marshall scanned the street.

'The Germans?'

Marshall's eyes stared unfocused on the heat haze coming from the horizon. 'Could be, or their allies. Hard to believe they made it this far without alerting someone.'

'Where should we go?'

'Let's find a way through and get to the White House,' he said, getting back in the car. 'See if you can find the emergency channel on the radio.'

Captain Keeney spun the wheel and hit the gas. The car jerked at speed, throwing Marshall into the door. He grunted.

'... *homes, barricade yourselves in and wait for further instructions. This is a public service announcement. Stay in your homes, barricade yourselves in and wait for further instructions. This is a public...*'

'Shut it off,' Marshall said.

The car turned into a street and Marshall yelled in warning as chunks of concrete, twisted metal, and glass fell on the road ahead.

'Fuck,' Keeney shouted, shifting into reverse.

Marshall looked behind. 'You're clear.'

Keeney spun the wheel, but the car gave a violent jolt. Marshall's head hit the passenger window, cracking it, and he blacked out.

When General Marshall awoke, he was being dragged along the road. He looked up at Keeney's bloody face and saw his aide's relief. The car was aflame, lying on its side. Keeney helped Marshall up and they both limped away, finding shelter behind a colossal piece of fallen building.

'Are you okay, John?' he asked. His aide nodded.

Marshall was nauseous and dizzy. Rubbing his temple and feeling the wetness there, he looked at his hand and grimaced. It was red with blood. Keeney tore his shirt sleeve, folded it, and wiped Marshall's face.

'What happened?'

'No idea. Something hit us side on. By the time I got out, there was nothing around.'

'Something? Ouch.'

Marshall pushed Keeney away, but the young captain slapped his hand. 'Let me look. You got glass in here.' Keeney removed the visible shards and went to put the cloth against his wound, but the general snatched it away.

'Was it another vehicle?'

'No, it was more like a...'

'What?'

He narrowed his eyes at Keeney's hesitation. His aide's

unblinking eyes just stared at the devastation. Marshall waited for a reply. Keeney's eyes were wide. Panicked. Keeney turned back to him. 'Sorry, I wasn't really paying attention, not until we ended up in the side of that building. Something large knocked the car on its side. General, I don't feel safe. We should find somewhere less exposed.'

Marshall pressed the cloth to his temple and it eased his pain. 'Where do you suggest?'

'Maybe we should head away from the city?'

He shook his head. 'Where are we?'

'I'm not sure. I don't recognise this area. Sorry, I'm not a native.'

'Nor me,' he said standing. 'I'm sure that's Lincoln Park. Look for a street sign.'

They scanned the buildings. Keeney pointed. 'There, Twelfth Street.'

'Good, we'll head to the park.'

'On foot?' Keeney's breathing increased. It was clear the idea frightened him. 'I don't know if that's a good idea, sir.'

'John,' Marshall said, taking his arm, 'look at me.'

His haunted eyes met with the general's.

'We're going to be fine, okay?'

Keeney nodded as a tear fell from his eye. 'Sorry, General. I'm just...' He turned and vomited. 'Fuck,' he said, spitting.

'You feel better?'

'No.' He was shaking.

'Sit for a minute. You're in shock.'

Keeney fell next to him. 'Jesus Christ, I'm a fucking wreck.' His aide leant forward and took in a shuddering breath.

'That's it. Deep breaths. Just keep breathing.'

'Bill,' Keeney's uncustomary use of the general's first name got his attention. 'What happened to all the fucking people?'

'I wondered that too. Maybe they were evacuated? Or perhaps they're hiding?'

'Maybe.'

'How are you feeling?'

Kenney's eyes fell to the road. 'Terrified. Absolutely fucking terrified, and I don't know why. The place is just on fire.

What the fuck could do this? Was it a bomb? Wouldn't we have felt or seen an explosion? None of this makes any sense.'

General Marshall put a hand on his shoulder. 'I feel it too. The silence... I wish I had answers, but we won't get any sitting here. Let's not speculate. They evacuated everyone they could, that's my feeling. I don't see any bodies, do you?'

He shook his head.

'We have to move on. On your feet, soldier.'

His lips compressed as he nodded. 'To the park, sir?'

Marshall let go of Keeney and wiped his brow. 'Yes, then we'll take Independence Avenue.'

'To the White House?'

'Feels like the best choice. At least there we might get answers.'

Keeney swallowed as he ran eyes along the road. 'If it's still standing.'

'Let's hope so.'

The sky rumbled and went dark. They watched a thicker cloud cover what little light they had, turning the world dark and shadowed. It came with a chill wind.

'Great.' Keeney sighed. 'Now rain too?'

'That's not a bad thing, especially if the city is on fire.'

'True,' Keeney said as the first drops fell.

Marshall slapped his arm. 'Come on.'

They saw no one as they made their cautious walk. They passed abandoned cars, some still running. Navigating roads covered and blocked by debris from collapsed buildings. Keeney suggested using a car, but as they moved further along the densely packed, rubble-strewn streets, it was obvious they'd be quicker on foot. They scanned roads, and buildings, hoping to find answers to what had happened. The only evidence of any people they saw was an assortment of discarded articles of clothing, and a few children's toys.

After a thirty-minute hike, they'd made it to Third Street and could go no further. The Library of Congress and the buildings opposite were all destroyed, their debris scattered across the streets.

Keeney looked around. 'Which way now?'

Marshall rubbed his chin. 'We can't go that way,' he said looking up Third Street. 'Let's see if we can get to Pennsylvania Avenue.'

Keeney grabbed Marshall's arm and pulled him behind a pile of wreckage.

'What?'

Keeney pointed. 'Look,' he whispered.

Marshall observed several shadowy four-legged creatures skittering across the ruins. One turned unnaturally luminous blue eyes their way. They ducked, then peered back over. Marshall breathed a sigh of relief as it disappeared into the shadows. The thumping of his heart blocked every other sound.

'Did it see us?' Keeney's whispered breath made Marshall jump.

'Jesus, John, I don't know. I hope not.'

'What are they?'

'Dogs, I think.'

He caught Keeney's sceptical look as it deepened into a frown. 'They didn't look like any dogs I've ever seen.'

Marshall's agitation came in an irritated hiss. 'Well maybe they weren't dogs then.' He rubbed the sweat from his eyes and let out a lengthy breath. 'They've gone now.'

'Did you see which way they went?'

'Further into those ruins. I couldn't see much beyond it. Stop asking stupid questions.'

John Keeney rolled onto his back and covered his face with his hands. Marshall regretted his outburst because he could tell Keeney was just scared.

'I'm sorry.'

Keeney took his hands away. 'Don't be. I *am* asking stupid fucking questions.'

'That feeling you had before.'

'The fear?'

He nodded. 'Can you describe it?'

'Like I want to vomit again. It's in my head. A nagging sense of... dread, I guess.'

'That's how I feel. I can't explain why, but I think those creatures are herding us.'

Keeney rolled onto his front and peered out towards the rubble of buildings ahead. In an unlit space, he thought he saw a pair of luminous eyes, but they disappeared.

'I'm going to say something wild.' His voice was low, measured. 'These things aren't natural.'

'No, they're not.'

'Like... I don't know how to explain it without sounding stupid.'

'Just say it.'

'Monsters. From a horror flick.' He had that expectant look, like a child waiting for a scolding.

Marshall continued to stare into the devastated building. 'That doesn't sound stupid at all.'

They remained lying for a while longer. A heavy foreboding filled the air, along with occasional flashes in the distance lighting the sky. A rumble of thunder reverberated through the ominous air.

'We should probably move on,' Marshall said.

Keeney nodded and pushed himself up, but Marshall grabbed his arm and he lowered back down. Before Keeney could speak, Marshall gave a signal to mute.

Something had heightened his senses.

Something felt wrong.

A block of concrete nearby tremored, shaking off loose stones. A low rumble behind them, followed by the sounds of more rubble falling, made them turn. A mound in the ruins ahead was growing in slow, pulsating jerks. Debris and earth pushed out and up, creating a giant hillock. It captivated them. What little light remained seemed to leave as the darkness intensified.

They were unable to take their eyes from it.

Something skittered nearby.

The heaviness of the air was choking.

'It looks like something is pushing from underneath,' whispered Keeney.

'Something large,' Marshall agreed. He made a quick scan of the area and spotted a place they could hide.

'Over there,' he said, pointing, 'let's get underneath that collapsed wall.'

They scrabbled away. Marshall monitored the growing mound while Keeney dug a space for them to squeeze in.

The mass grew larger and larger. Its slow surging pulses got faster and faster until it grew like a giant anthill. Then it stopped.

General Marshall wiped the grit from his eyes. There was no further movement and he took in a breath.

Keeney poked his head out of the hole. 'What's happening?'

'It stopped growing.'

The sound of something falling caused Marshall to look back. A few stones rolled down the hill and bounced off the rubble.

There was no other movement. An eerie quietness lingered in the air.

Marshall was about to say something, when the ground shuddered. They each read the other's fear. The shuddering intensified and the ground heaved. They were quickly covered in dust.

A rumbling burst of thunder overhead brought with it a deluge of rain, which soaked them. Marshall helped empty the water filling the hole Keeney had dug for them, which was turning into a muddy pit in the torrential rain. A snuffling alerted them to something nearby.

Marshall put a finger to his lips.

Water ran down their faces, into their eyes and ears, but they didn't move. Marshall pointed up, then into the muddy hole. Keeney understood and shuffled in, Marshall squeezing in beside him. They kept their breathing quiet as they heard movement above. General Marshall pulled out his sidearm. The feel of it seemed to comfort him.

A low growl overhead made them freeze. Then, without warning, the ground heaved and lurched from what might have been an explosion nearby. Debris rained down along with dust that turned to mud in the rain.

They waited for a long time before Marshall poked out his head.

'What do you see?'

'The mound is gone. It's a crater now.'

'It exploded?'

'I think so.'

Something in the pit's core stirred. A horrible dread rose from the pits of their stomach into their shaking hands. Marshall could only stare at the monstrous creature awkwardly heaving itself out of its muddy crater. The general inwardly cursed. He'd spent years rejecting religion and its dogma, which was all undone by his first thought, that a demon was escaping from Hell.

The incubus came to full height. Its body a mixture of molten lava and blackened rocks or scales. As it stretched, vast wings unfurled and flapped. Four armoured arms unfolded and lifted and its long-clawed hands flexed. The monster gave off a misty aura as rain turned to steam against the hideous magma of its body. Four giant bug-like eyes opened, burning with blue fire, and its bulbous, blackened horned head lifted towards the sky. An enormous mouth thundered a chorus of hideous screeching and deep roars, and they covered their ears. The monster's first steps shook the ground, causing bigger debris to fall. The power of its thumped footfalls caused foundation-undermined buildings nearby to collapse further.

Marshall caught sight of yipping black doglike creatures as they joined the larger monster from the shadows. It pushed a path away, taking with it the foreboding terrors that had incapacitated them. It didn't take long for them to come to their senses.

In a slow thumping march, it bellowed an unnatural deafening call. In the distance they heard similar in reply. Everything it touched turned to fire.

Both men exchanged glances, but said nothing.

When the creature was a distance away, they emerged from their muddy hiding place. Marshall gave a furtive look, then tugged at Keeney's sleeve, and they made their escape by slipping and sliding down banks of rubble towards the road. The general glanced back at the massive creature as it made a slow plod through ruined buildings, with more than half of it towering above the buildings it had wandered behind. The question of how Washington had been so quickly destroyed was now answered.

Flashes of intense fire billowed from its gigantic head. Not long after, others joined it.

Marshall and Keeney made it towards another mound and ducked down, as they caught sight of yet another giant monster. It appeared to be heading toward the White House. Marshall turned to Keeney and noticed something wrong. He was lying on his back in the mud, his eyes staring at the sky.

'John?' Marshall shook him, but he was unresponsive.

John Keeney could hear yelling, but the voice was far away. His fear had been too much and his body put him into a safe place. A small part of his mind that had been through years of drilling, compelling him to obey orders, fought against the paralysis. He'd experienced this a few times before in his life. Once, when he was nine or ten, he'd been on a hiking trip with his family in Mexico. He'd woken in bed feeling something moving on his leg. When he threw off the covers, the biggest spider he'd ever seen was making a slow crawl along his thigh towards his crotch. He'd got out a strangled whimper before freezing in terror. Fortunately, his father heard the odd sound and recognised something was wrong. In an instant, he'd smacked the thing across the room and smashed it with his shoe. It was so large it took effort to kill. Keeney remained paralysed for some time after. Neither his mother nor father could reach him.

'John, get up.'

Marshall slapped his face. Keeney's eyes focused. Then he flipped and yelled and his eyes rolled into his head as his body convulsed. Marshall held his head as he shook, willing him to stop, to come out of it. A moment or two passed and the tremors slowed. Keeney closed his eyes and his body relaxed.

With no choice, Marshall sat and waited for Keeney to wake. It seemed to take forever, but when he opened his eyes and focused them, the general gave a sigh.

'Welcome back,' he said.

'General?' His speech slurred and his expression was a mix of confusion and disorientation.

'Take a moment. Get your bearings,' Marshall said, as he scanned the area.

Keeney pushed himself up on his elbows. 'What happened...'

'You had a seizure.'

He read the concern in Marshall's eyes.

'Do you have epilepsy, John?'

He looked down. 'When I was a boy.'

'I see. Was it frequent?'

'Occasional. I haven't had an episode—'

'Can you move yet?' Marshall cut him off. 'I'd like to leave.'

'I think so.'

He pushed himself onto his side and with relief, Marshall helped him up.

'We should make for one of those buildings,' Marshall said, pointing. 'They look stable. Come on.'

'Anything to get out of this rain.'

Together they climbed, then slid down banks of muddy rubble onto a path. They crouch-ran toward the ruined building and, under the overhang of concrete, escaped the onslaught of the unrelenting rain.

As they ventured closer, a low voice came from out of the darkness.

'Get inside, quickly.'

It was a British voice. It startled them at first, but they soon obeyed.

In the darkness a huddled group of weary, scared men and women stared as they walked by. A mixture of military and civilians. Out of the shadow came the source of the voice, and it was someone Marshall recognised. For the first time since he and Keeney had stopped the car, he found a smile.

'Bill?' Colonel Charles Bradley said in surprise. 'My dear

fellow, I'm so happy to see you.'

Despite being head to toe in mud, they embraced.

'Braders,' he said, pulling away and looking at him. 'I've never been so pleased to see anyone in my life.'

The British colonel gave him a lopsided grin, then turned to Keeney. 'Hello, John, rough day, eh?'

'I've had better,' Keeney replied with a sigh.

'Yes, I think we all have. We should be safe for a while. When the big ones come, they sort of wander off and draw all the small ones with them.'

'We saw another a little west of here.'

'There's more than two of them. Let's get you checked out,' he said, and called for a medic.

'I want someone to take care of Captain Keeney first. He needs to rest.'

Keeney opened his mouth and Marshall gave him a look. 'Rest, Captain. That's an order.'

Keeney gave a weary nod and found a place to sit. He lay his hands across his knees and dropped his head onto them.

'Is he okay?' Bradley asked.

Marshall took his arm. 'He had a seizure.'

'Why do I get the impression you're not happy about it?'

'A discussion for another time. Have you someone who can look at him?'

When the medic arrived, Colonel Bradley pointed at Keeney. 'See to him, Doc.'

General Marshall turned his back on Captain Keeney and walked away. Colonel Bradley frowned as he looked between them, then followed.

Colonel Bradley was a tall, lean man in his mid-forties. A decorated member of British intelligence and a veteran of high-profile engagements throughout the war. They'd met six months back at an Allied briefing, and the two became friends soon after. The head of intelligence told him Colonel Bradley was a member of the British Joint Intelligence Committee, their highest intelligence body, but when

Marshall asked him Charlie laughed at the suggestion. As their friendship deepened, he realised with a man like Charlie – or Braders as he preferred – you'd never know his full story.

They sat together chatting for a while, then Doc arrived and offered them his flask. 'It's not the good stuff,' he said.

Marshall took a swig and was grateful. 'Best I've tasted today.'

The medic ran expert fingers over the general's head and found the wound he'd sustained earlier. 'This wound needs a clean.'

Marshall took another drink and offered the flask back, but the medic shook his head. 'Keep it, sir.'

While the medic continued to clean Marshall's wound, the general looked to his old friend.

'Braders, tell me you know what's going on?'

Despite Bradley's casual manner, Marshall knew him well enough to see the events of the day had taken their toll. 'I think you already know the answer to that, old boy. I had my eye on you both for a while, although I didn't know it was you until just now. When that beast surfaced, we had no choice but to wait. It's one of maybe fifty we've seen today. And you know there's nothing like it on Earth, don't you?'

Marshall grunted as the medic continued his treatment. 'John said the smaller creatures were like something out of a horror flick.'

'Not a poor description, is it?'

'What do you think we're dealing with?'

'Demons? Aliens? Who knows?'

'Demons?' Marshall frowned. 'Talk sense.'

Bradley laughed. 'Extra-terrestrial life is an easier concept for you to believe in?'

'Seems more plausible than supernatural beings from Hell.'

'I won't argue with you. I can't say I'm thrilled with the prospect of Hell on Earth, yet it does seem that way. Supernatural or otherwise.'

'True. We caught a few things on the radio before it went

dead. Scraps, really. We didn't see any people on our journey. Are they all dead?'

'Not all of them. They herded most away. Initially, those who hadn't escaped tried to fight, but it was futile. There wasn't time to even form a resistance. Several human-looking creatures began herding people away.'

'Where?'

'No idea. I found what people I could and we've been moving ever since.'

Marshall took another sip. It warmed him. 'How did it start?'

'Quickly. Those giants came out of the earth and in a matter of hours turned Washington into what you see now. While this was going on, these gangly armed oblong-headed things emerged from the pits the larger creatures left behind. They herded people into the streets. They're weak. Bullets put them down easy enough... but the smaller creatures? One man called them monkey-dogs, difficult to spot, unless they're on top of you... and once they are? Well... that's it, I'm afraid.'

'We saw those too.'

Bradley rubbed the bridge of his nose. 'People found out pretty quickly bullets didn't stop them. Nothing apparently does.'

'Have you heard from anyone in the White House?'

'Given what I've seen, I have no reason to expect anyone survived. If they did, I'd imagine they suffered the same fate as everyone else. The White House, like most of the buildings, is an enormous pile of rubble now.'

General Marshall lowered his eyes. 'I don't suppose you know if the president got out alive?'

Colonel Bradley shrugged. 'Maybe. They have contingencies for attacks. There was a lot of activity near the harbour. Happy to report several boats got away. I also imagine the navy got their fleet out. I think it's safe to assume, at least for now, you're the man in charge.'

'I'm glad to have you with me.'

Bradley stood. 'Let's see if we can't find you and John some dry clothes.'

'I feel terrible asking, but... do you have anything to eat?'

He nodded. 'We have supplies, and hot food.'

General Marshall smiled, then winced as the medic dabbed something cold into the cuts on his face. Just like the news he'd got from Colonel Bradley, it hurt like hell.

CHAPTER TWO
Thursday, September 3, 1942
Ten Miles North of Washington, D.C.

Mud erupted with a deafening thunder, showering everyone with slurry and rock. Hearing impaired by a high-pitch whistle, and blinded by stone chips, General Marshall staggered into the arms of another. Someone shouted. The air filled with rapid gunfire. He shook his head and tried to clear his blindness. The world focused into a watery haze as his eyes stared at an unnatural blackness above. Marshall was vaguely aware of someone tugging at him. A massive burst of mud and debris flew into the air, covering them all. He watched as the people around him faltered. Forming a protective barrier in front of him. Marshall swallowed as a hellish thing made from rock and fire heaved itself out of a crater. It roared its indignance as the bright flashes of rockets impacted off its monstrous body. His fear turned to surprise. They'd pushed it back just a little. He felt their emboldened enthusiasm as they pushed forward, but that euphoria left when the monster thumped a giant hand into the earth, rocking the ground and knocking down those who were too close. The enormous disjointed hand then grabbed for those scrabbling away. It found one. Marshall cursed as the terrified kicking and screaming man disappeared into a blackened mouth. He couldn't take his eyes off the poor fellow as the monster's hideous teeth bit down. It threw the remains into a small group, knocking them down as if they were bowling pins, covering them in blood and entrails.

General Marshall yelled for them to fall back. Even though he couldn't hear it he knew they had acknowledged his command, because those he could see turned and ran towards him. The daze Marshall felt cleared, even if his hearing hadn't. Other hands joined those pulling him, as the ground continued to shake. They dumped him into a trench next to others, knocking the air from him, and more soon followed. He blinked at the concerned face of the medic they called Doc. Doc was saying something, but the ringing in Marshall's ears hadn't eased enough for him to understand the words. The sounds of the battle then burst into his head and he could hear Doc's words more clearly.

Doc waved a light in his eyes and Marshall pushed it away. 'I'm alive.'

'General?'

He coughed. 'What's left of him, Doc.'

Doc relaxed. 'You had me worried for a minute,' he said, helping Marshall up.

Marshall took the water bottle offered and drank. He caught sight of his distorted reflection in the door mirror of the transport. His white hair matted with mud and blood.

The air filled with a horrifying screeching roar. They covered their ears.

'Pull the men back, now.'

They called a retreat. Those still attempting to fight were swift to respond.

General Marshall counted as the men funnelled passed, cursing at how few returned. Colonel Bradley approached. His fatigued face thick with mud and sweat.

'That monster's half out. Nothing we've hit it with has any effect.'

Marshall nodded. 'Do we have any artillery munition left?'

Bradley shook his head. 'Bill, it's time to go.'

Marshall cursed. He looked back at the monster and sighed. 'Take what vehicles we can and get everyone to the safety zone.'

'We only have three fuelled.'

'I hate to leave anything behind, but we have no choice. At least tell me we secured the supplies?'

Despite their dire predicament, and his fatigue, Bradley

grinned. 'John found what we needed. He's heading back to HQ now.'

Another bellowed roar came and the ground shook as the hideous beast heaved itself fully out from its pit.

'Okay then, time to go,' Marshall said.

Colonel Bradley began issuing commands.

Marshall was the last to enter the troop carrier. He stared back at the monster as the vehicle flew away. It stood taller than the church it had emerged beside. Huge wings unfurled and its blackened body burst alight in orange-blue flames. When it roared into the sky, the same fire erupted from its mouth. It stomped toward them, but soon lost interest as their transports headed away. Marshall pulled the blanket tighter around him and scanned the faces of his frightened men. He smiled but, despite his best effort, they didn't seem very encouraged.

An hour later the vehicles pulled into the old factory compound they'd set as their HQ, and a group of men closed and locked a set of heavy iron gates. The general exited and dropped to the ground, helping tired, demoralised men to disembark. There was a foreboding blanket of darkness where the sun should have been, and Marshall gave a weary sigh as he rubbed his eyes.

'General?'

He looked up as Captain Keeney joined him. 'A real clusterfuck, huh?'

Marshall waited until the last of the men passed him. 'We've had better days, Captain.'

Keeney nodded.

'How'd we do with the supply run?'

'We emptied as many stores as we could. It's a good haul.'

'Tell me there's bourbon?'

'There is. A few cases.'

Marshall found a smile. 'Good. I want to talk to the men. Have them assembled in the church and bring a few bottles with you.'

'Into God's house?' He seemed to disapprove.

'If God has a problem with it, Captain,' – he poked Keeney in the chest – 'let him come and tell me Himself.'

'I'm sorry, sir, I didn't mean...'

'Dismissed, Captain.'

Keeney came to attention and saluted, then turned away.

The general thrust his hands into his pockets and made a slow march to the church. As he passed the front of the trucks, Colonel Bradley joined him.

'You're still mad at him?'

Marshall gave him a sideways look. 'I said it was a discussion for another time.'

Colonel Bradley stopped him. 'Now would seem a good time.' Marshall couldn't miss the edge in his voice. It was out of character and not something the general was used to.

'I value your experience and input, Braders. The issue I have with Keeney isn't open for conversation.'

'I've known you too long, Bill. Harbouring this... grudge? That isn't your style, and it's also pointless given our situation.'

'Colonel, you're crossing a line.'

'Fine. You want this formal? I don't work for you, General. I've tagged along because it suits my interests.' His tone was icy. 'The poor boy is depressed and drinking himself to sleep at night. Whatever the issue is needs fixing. Or we might wake up one morning and find him dead.'

'You're being ridiculous.'

Colonel Bradley laughed. 'I am?'

Marshalled growled. 'Okay, fine. He lied.'

'About what?'

'About his epilepsy.'

Bradley stared at him. 'So?'

General Marshall's face turned red. 'You're right. I'm angry. No... I'm furious. Not disclosing that information put people's lives at risk. Put my life at risk. How can I trust him to lead others into dangerous situations knowing he might have another seizure at any moment? He's a ticking time bomb.'

'You're not wrong. Still...'

'Respectfully, old friend. Please drop it.' Marshall walked away.

They remained silent as they passed a number of men working on vehicles. Marshall glanced at Bradley; a sigh slipped through his lips. 'John's drinking?'

Bradley nodded. 'Heavily.'

'Monitor it, please.'

'As you wish.'

The general touched his shoulder. 'Thank you.'

Bradley then said, 'All this talk of drinking is making me thirsty.'

Marshall smiled. 'Same.'

'We're safe for now. Time to kick off our shoes and relax.'

Marshall chuckled. 'Don't you ever feel the burden of misery?'

'Rarely,' Bradley said. 'At least, not that I show.'

'That British optimism of yours is gonna wear thin after a while.'

'Stiff upper lip and all that? But you might be right.' He gave a heavy sigh. 'Today's encounter was another reminder of how dangerous things have got. I'd hoped, the further away we moved from the city, we'd see less of these monsters.'

Marshall clasped his hands behind his back. 'They must have weaknesses.'

'You're right, but nothing we've tried seems to make a bloody difference.' Bradley ran a hand through his mouse-coloured hair. 'What's our next move?'

'We can't fight these things, and we're wasting munitions and men trying.'

'We're moving on again, then?'

Marshall glanced at him. 'Do we have a choice?'

'I suppose not,' Bradley said. 'We should consider our strategy. It's clear we need better intelligence if we're to win this war.'

'Intelligence? Gathered from where?' Marshall asked, frowning.

'You'd be surprised at what I can dig up.'

Marshall smirked, despite his mood. 'I believe you. But be realistic. We lost the war.'

They reached the side entrance to the church, and Marshall

stopped. 'Braders, listen. We've no defence against these monsters and no way of predicting when or where the damn things might come at us. I'm tired of losing.'

Bradley met his gaze. 'Fair point. We should consider heading north.'

'It is less populated.'

Colonel Bradley nodded. 'Assuming these things are only interested in cities, we might see fewer in open country.'

'So, we're agreed?'

Bradley nodded.

'You were right,' Marshall said. 'This is a war, but we're not fighting these monsters because we can't.'

'What are we fighting for, Bill?'

'Our lives.'

General Marshall stepped onto the platform and stood underneath the giant cross of Christ. The room was awash with murmured conversation. Colonel Bradley and Captain Keeney stood to one side. Marshall clasped his hands behind his back as he paced. There were maybe fifty men seated. He remembered when the murmuring would have been difficult to speak above. Not anymore.

'We learned more about these creatures today,' he said. 'Nothing we've tried affects them and our weapons are useless.'

The room was silent. He gave a lengthy pause. 'I had a clear strategy for the fight, but...' He paused to look at dirty weary faces. 'It's time we accept the truth. We've lost.'

The murmuring began and Marshall put up a hand. 'Sixteen men died today. Sixteen.' The room was silent. 'We've moved from town to town. Each time we settle, they come. We've seen our countrymen herded like cattle and taken off to god knows where.'

He paused, then chuckled. 'Not much of a rousing speech, huh? I guess you already know I'm not too good with words.'

A few laughs filtered through the men.

'We've had our share of horrors. We miss our friends, our families. These monsters have taken away our freedom, and we fight daily for what little we can maintain. But it's not enough, and I think you know it. There's only one thing left to do. Survive. I know you were hoping this would be our last move, but we can't stay. You gave oaths when you joined the service, to protect this country. I gave that oath too.' He turned to Captain Keeney, who dropped a box onto the stage.

'The sad truth is, right now, we can't protect it. I'm proud of each one of you. Tomorrow we're going to head north. Before we do so, it's time to make new oaths together.' Keeney handed Marshall and Bradley a bottle, and they stepped into a huddle of men, pouring bourbon into cups as they went.

Marshall stood in their midst. 'We swear,' he said, raising his cup, 'to take care of the weak and the helpless. To look out for one another. We swear to survive.'

The murmur wasn't the rousing cheer he'd hoped for.

'We swear,' Bradley said, coming beside Marshall.

'We swear,' Keeney's voice echoed.

One by one they raised their glasses and called out. When the air was no longer filled by rousing oaths, the sombre mood lightened, and then they drank.

'There's plenty of bourbon,' Marshall said. 'Help yourself.'

They shook his hand as he wandered through them. He met up with Bradley and Keeney shortly afterwards.

'Before we move on,' Marshall said, 'I want to gather as many supplies as we can. Split the men into three groups. Rest one, have the other two pack this place up. Rotate them every four hours. John, you rest with group one. Braders, you join group two and I'll be with the third. Questions?'

'Bill,' Bradley said. 'We'll need petrol if we want to get the vehicles running.'

'He means gas,' Keeney said, smirking. 'I might have a solution to that. I scouted gas stations along the town line earlier. I noticed one with an abandoned tanker. It might be full. Even if it's not, we can probably syphon off what's in the pumps and take it with us.'

Marshall smiled. 'First good news I've heard today. Then the priority must be that tanker. Braders, take what mechanics we have and go get it.'

Marshall turned and stepped back into the men.

Bradley turned to Keeney, who met his smile with a scowl. 'I'm going to bed.'

• • •

An hour later, Colonel Bradley leant against a doorframe watching Keeney, who'd stripped down to his shorts and was sitting cross-legged in bed, staring at a photograph. Lost in thought, he didn't notice Bradley come in. A cigarette dangled precariously from his lips, and a half-full bottle of bourbon lay propped against his leg.

'Penny for them.'

John Keeney looked up through eyes wet with tears. Wiping his nose, he stubbed his cigarette into an ashtray, and with a slight slur, he said, 'Sorry, didn't see, Colonel.'

He made to get out of bed, but Bradley put a hand up and sat on the edge.

'Did you speak with the general?'

'I tried. But he's being stubborn. He's angry with you. You know him better. How long does he usually keep this going?'

'I've never known him to hold a grudge before.'

Colonel Bradley held out his hand. 'Can I see that?'

Keeney handed him the photograph, then opened the bottle beside him and took another swig. Bradley watched him for a moment, then turned his eyes to the faded picture of a man in uniform.

'Brother?'

Keeney pulled the bottle away from his lips, wiping a tear from his nose, and shook his head.

Bradley gave a tight smile, then handed the photograph back. 'Ah,' he said. 'There's a complication.'

Keeney lifted the bottle, but the colonel's hand stopped him. Keeney's expression darkened. 'What? I can't drink now?'

The colonel raised an eyebrow. 'Don't you know it's rude not to offer the bottle?'

Keeney's frown lifted as he passed it over. Bradley took a mouthful, then handed it back.

'The man in the photograph,' Bradley said. 'Army man, eh?'

Keeney nodded. 'An instructor.'

'What's his name?'

'Bobby. Captain Bobby Rogers.'

'How'd you two meet?'

'At school. We joined up when we were eighteen.'

'You were drafted?'

'No. We signed up a few years before that. I wanted to join the navy and go to some exotic place, far from home. But Bobby doesn't do good on boats, so the army it was.' Keeney laughed and fell back into his bed. Bradley observed him. There was always something childlike about John Keeney, but alcohol allowed it to properly surface. They continued to pass the bottle. Bradley took another mouthful, while Keeney continued.

'Then the war started and everything changed. He stayed instructing. I got posted to the Pentagon and thanks to the general, I was able to get Bobby transferred not long after.'

Bradley lit two cigarettes and handed him one. 'So, neither of you have seen any active duty?'

Keeney shook his head. 'What about you? What's your story?'

'Me? There's not much to tell. My father was an influential man in the British government, so that gave me a bit of an edge in public life. I lost all three of my brothers in the Great War, it killed my parents. They never recovered. I joined the service just as the war ended. Spent time in France and Germany. Learnt a lot about the cultures, languages, sex... all that fun stuff. Moved from one job or another. When the first rumblings of Hitler's rearmament began, I knew we'd be at war soon enough.'

'I was supposed to be sent to Europe, but the general had other plans for me.'

'You were lucky, then.'

Keeney shrugged. 'I don't feel lucky.'

Bradley smiled and stood. 'You probably want to rest?'

'Oh, please,' Keeney said. 'Don't go yet, and I want to hear more about you.'

'You do, do you?' Bradley chuckled.

'Please?'

'Okay then,' Bradley said, sitting back on the bed. 'Before the new war with Germany started. I had the pick of what I wanted to do. Tried a bit of flying and enjoyed that immensely. An RAF pal took me up in his kite. Such a marvellous feeling being up in the sky. Freeing, you know? I had a taste for the thrill of it and I persuaded him to teach me how to fly. Not long after, Britain declared war on Germany, and that ended all the fun stuff. I was soon sent back to France to pick up my old life and moved around quite a lot. Had a few missions here and there which ended in Poland. I was then recalled to blighty and sent here.'

'You've seen a lot of death then?'

'My fair share.'

Keeney's eyes fell. 'I never saw anyone die before today.'

'It's not something you ever really get used to. So, apart from being an aide to an old grumpy general, what else have you done?'

'Like you, I did flight training for a while. I considered switching to the air force once.'

Bradley chuckled. 'What stopped you?'

Keeney laughed. 'I couldn't get my head around all the instruments.' He took another long drink and eyed Bradley. 'Are you a spy? They say you're a spy, but I don't know if I believe it.'

Bradley leant forward. 'I could be. But I wouldn't be a very good one if I told you, would I? D'you have any family?'

Keeney shrugged. 'Not that I know of. I don't speak with my folks anymore.'

'Because of your relationship with Bobby?'

Keeney looked up at Bradley, his face reddened. 'What do you mean?'

Bradley offered him a smile. 'You're a Kentucky boy, aren't you?'

'How'd you know that?'

'I have a good ear for accents. You're surprised your folks didn't approve? Did you think they ever would?'

Keeney's face flushed a deeper red.

'Look, John, I am not judging you.'

Keeney took another drink. Maybe it was the alcohol, or maybe he felt he could trust Bradley with a secret he'd never spoken out loud in his life. 'I thought my mother might, you know, understand. If I could phrase it right. But my father caught us and went crazy.'

Bradley finished his cigarette. 'Religious type?'

'Yeah.'

'Not surprising, really. Kentucky is in the famed bible belt, isn't it?'

'I don't know where that name came from, but it's accurate,' he sighed. 'I wish...'

'That you knew they were alive?'

He shook his head, a tear fell. 'That I knew Bobby was safe.'

'You must really like him then.'

The boyish captain took another swig of the bottle. 'I don't know why I'm telling you this,' he said, trying to sit up but failing.

'Because you're drunk.'

Keeney laughed then some of his rational thoughts filtered through. 'No one knows, you can't tell anyone, promise you won't.'

'Why would I do that?'

Keeney fell back onto his pillow.

'Listen, John. We're all in a bind. We don't have any information. Maybe Bobby's stuck in some god-awful place like this? Isn't that better thinking than' – Keeney was snoring – 'the alternative.' Bradley chuckled. He took the bottle out of Keeney's hand, pulled the blanket over him, then left.

Outside, Bradley approached Sergeant Hawkinson. 'Hawk, do me a favour. Keep an eye on our young captain for me.'

'Is there a problem, Colonel?'

He handed him the almost empty bottle. 'I'm assuming this was full before he started on it?'

• • •

On a hillock overlooking a destroyed town, General Marshall and Colonel Bradley lay observing a sizeable group of people being led away by a horde of shadowy creatures. They focused through their binoculars on the ragtag group. Men, women, and children trudged defeated under the watchful eyes of larger creatures. Humanoid but not human, they stood at least eight feet tall with oblong heads and long gangly arms. It was by far the largest concentration of them they'd seen.

The sky lightened, if only a little, and because of it there were fewer smaller shadowy creatures. The night was their playtime where they roamed in sizeable groups. During the daylight hours they usually only saw the humanoid creatures, who were slower and easy to kill.

Bradley tapped Marshall's shoulder and pointed. General Marshall trained his glasses on the gigantic monster in the distance. It was a Destroyer. A name they'd assigned to the winged fire-breathing behemoths that tore apart buildings as if they were paper. They'd seen many bursting from underneath the earth. He could just make out the rocky scales along its back, and even through the safety of distance and binoculars, he still felt a strange sense of dread.

'That's the biggest group of people we've seen so far. How many do you think? Two hundred?' Bradley asked.

'Maybe more,' Marshall replied.

'We don't have the manpower to mount a rescue of this size.'

Marshall sighed. 'That's becoming our biggest issue, isn't it?'

'Picking who to liberate?'

Marshall nodded. 'Smaller numbers make for less risk, but I hate to just abandon them.'

The colonel returned to his binoculars. 'I wonder where they take them?'

'And why,' Marshall said.

Colonel Bradley grimaced. 'I don't think I want to know.'

'One thing is obvious. We can't stay here.'

'And there I was thinking we'd finally found a place to settle, at least for a while.'

'It's been almost a month since we lost radio contact with the other military cells. I'd hoped we'd see a military presence here, or something to suggest we were mounting a response, but there's nothing.' Marshall cursed. 'We still don't understand what caused this and what these things are.'

'Demons, according to Father Doyle.'

The general grunted. 'I'm more inclined to look for a less supernatural answer.'

'Me too, but you have to admit, they fit the profile.'

Marshall made no reply.

'I wonder how they subdue the people?' Bradley murmured.

'I wondered that too.'

'We hardly ever see anyone fighting back. I can't believe everyone they grab goes quietly. I wouldn't.'

'Nor would I. Maybe they're just scared. When one of the big ones gets close, it terrifies me.'

'It's got to be something they give off, you know? Pheromones maybe? I've learnt to suppress fear, yet around them, I get lost in it too.'

'Just another unanswered question in our never-ending list.'

'Where should we go?'

Marshall pulled out a map. 'I've been giving that a lot of thought. We can't stay in the open. It's pointless, we've proved that. About thirty miles northwest of here is a military complex, Camp Detrick. We'll head there.' He folded the map and shoved it back into his jacket pocket.

'I don't know it,' Bradley said, flipping on his back and staring up at the oppressive blanket of clouds.

'I'm not surprised, it's new.'

'Why is that your choice?'

'It's the only complex I know large enough to house the people we have and any we find along the way.'

'Is there any reason to think it's still standing?'

Marshall gave a slight shrug. 'No reason to assume it's destroyed either. It's not like other bases. It's mostly underground.'

One of the gangly creatures made a trilling noise.

Colonel Bradley turned and grunted. 'That's our cue.'

'They're on the move,' Marshall said, wrapping up his binoculars.

'What's the plan? Grab everyone and head to this Detrick?'

'Yes. With the creatures concentrated here we should be able to bypass them with relative ease.'

'It'll only take one to sound an alarm,' Bradley cautioned.

'I don't see we have much of a choice, do you?'

'No.'

'Let's head back then.'

They scrambled down the bank, remaining crouched as they headed to the path leading to the vehicle. When they felt safe and far enough away from anything that might see them, they relaxed and slowed. Bradley waved Marshall down.

Ahead, under a mass of overgrowth, they both saw a familiar patch of unnatural shadow.

'You see it?' Bradley whispered.

Marshall nodded.

'We're too exposed here. Let's get back to the vehicle.'

They crept forward, keeping low, approaching the vehicle on the opposite side to the overgrowth. Bradley kept his eyes focused on the darkness, while Marshall slipped around and inside the driver's side. He waited for the prearranged signal, and Marshall soon gave it.

Bradley pulled out a long tube and nodded.

Marshall started the vehicle.

In the darkness, something stirred.

Colonel Bradley stiffened. A set of blue luminous eyes appeared in the depth of the dark, followed by a huffing growl. Bradley pulled the tape off the flare, which burst alight with a hiss, and threw it into the shadow then jumped in the vehicle. 'Go!'

Marshall hit the gas and spun the wheel and the vehicle sped away.

With a roar the monkey-dog creature flew out of the shadows and landed just short of the vehicle, but blinded by the flare and fearful of the daylight, it soon skittered back into the darkness.

CHAPTER THREE
Wednesday, September 16, 1942
Camp Detrick, Maryland

'There.' General Marshall pointed. Bradley turned the wheel and drove towards the extensive buildings surrounded by heavy barbed-wire fencing. Colonel Bradley pulled up some distance from the gatehouse and their extended entourage stopped with them. They'd collected several vehicles along their journey and the number of civilians they'd rescued had increased with each town they'd passed through. A community of around a hundred men, women, and children were now waiting behind them. Marshall and Bradley exited their vehicle. Bradley approached a contingent of men, who'd jumped out the back, and gave them orders. They took up positions as commanded.

Father David Doyle and his sister, Sarah approached them. 'Is this the place?'

Marshall nodded. 'Camp Detrick.'

'What's its purpose?' Father Doyle asked.

'That's classified, Father.'

'Classified?' he remarked with a frown. 'You're sticking to the secretive military nonsense, still?'

General Marshall compressed his lips, his features hard. 'Yes.'

Sarah put a hand on his arm but at the look he tossed back at her, she withdrew it. Father Doyle turned back to Marshall. 'I see,' he said, with a slight shake of his head.

Marshall relaxed a little. 'Look, with any luck, they'll have room for us.'

'If there's anyone left running it,' Doyle replied.

'True. Braders and I will see if there's a military presence here.'

'If there is, will they take us in?' Sarah asked.

Marshall smiled at her. 'I don't see why not.'

Father Doyle didn't seem convinced. 'And if they don't, what then?'

Marshall shrugged. 'We'll move on, what else can we do?'

Father Doyle looked over at the nondescript building. 'Let's hope we can stay. Lord knows, we need a place to rest.'

'Let's go and check on the boys.' Sarah took his arm and he smiled as they wandered back to the vehicles.

'He's right,' Bradley said, as he followed Sarah and the old priest with his eyes. 'What can you tell me about this place?'

'This facility is probably one of the most fortified in the country. What they do, or did, is top secret. It's one of nine set up by FDR to plan and coordinate responses to major disasters.'

'Like this one?'

'I'm hoping so.'

Bradley ran his eyes around the compound. 'Even if this place is operational and manned, they may not want the civilians.'

'Well, it's lucky I have all these stars on my shoulders then, isn't it?'

Bradley nodded. 'What's the plan, General?'

'Let's see if anyone's here first. Come on.'

The answer came in the form of approaching MPs, who brandished weapons at them. When the lieutenant who commanded the MPs saw the general's uniform, he lowered his sidearm, saluted, and issued the orders to stand down.

'General Marshall?' the lieutenant said. 'It's good to see you're alive.'

He returned the salute. 'What's your name, son?'

'Lieutenant Dawson, sir. Bruce Dawson.'

'This is Colonel Bradley, British intelligence. I have men and civilians who all need shelter. Are you able to accommodate us?'

'Easily. You're not the first we've taken in. The CO opened up sections of the compound to house civilians. We'll see to their safety.'

'Is Lieutenant-Colonel Baldwin still in command?'

'Yes, sir.'

'Well, that's a relief.'

Lieutenant Dawson turned to the sergeant beside him. 'Mark, let the colonel know we've got top brass coming and get some men out here to bring in those civilians.'

The sergeant took the MPs and returned to their sentry post. Lieutenant Dawson pointed to the tanker. 'Is that thing full?'

Marshall nodded. 'We've been keeping it topped up as we've gone along.'

'The colonel will love that,' he said, grinning. 'We've been operating on rationed supplies. Half our vehicles aren't working so this is a huge boost.'

Dawson led them alongside a building towards an entrance. 'How far have you come?'

'From Washington,' Marshall replied. 'You have any comms working?'

Dawson shook his head. 'Radio and TV stopped broadcasting a few weeks back. We were getting bits of news, but not anymore.'

Bradley looked along the building and out to an airfield. It was oddly quiet with an eeriness that made him shudder. The usual noises of life, birds, industry, man were replaced with foreboding silence.

'Interesting design,' Bradley remarked. 'Quite a fortress.'

'We had a major overhaul about a year back,' Dawson said. He then looked sideways at Marshall. 'Sir, if I might ask. How bad is it out there?'

Marshall's face turned grim. 'Bad doesn't describe it, Lieutenant. I can't say how the rest of the country is doing, but most of the cities and towns along our route were destroyed. We headed to Baltimore first, but it's like someone just scooped it up.'

'And the people?'

'Those with us are the only survivors we came across.'

Dawson's eyes were wet. 'I've not heard a word from my folks.'

'You're from Texas?' Bradley asked.

Dawson nodded. 'My folks live there, but my brother is here though.'

'Be thankful for that,' Marshall said, patting his shoulder.

Dawson smiled, then turned to Colonel Bradley. 'What about you, sir? Have you been able to get any news of home?'

'I'm stuck here, for now.' Bradley eyed the airfield. 'You have working aircraft?'

'We have several. Can you fly, Colonel?'

Colonel Bradley smiled. 'If I need to.'

They followed Lieutenant Dawson through a doorway, along a corridor, and up a flight of stairs into an enormous room busy with staff. Uniformed men and women, along with civilians, turned as they entered. Someone brought the room to attention as General Marshall came forward. Lieutenant-Colonel Ira Baldwin saluted, then extended his hand.

'General, I'm very glad to see you.'

'It's good to be here, Colonel. I've a few men, mostly civilians. With your permission, I'm looking to house them somewhere more permanent.'

'You're all welcome. We're already taking care of your people. I have a price though.'

'My tanker?'

Baldwin chuckled. 'Yes, and your fleet of vehicles.'

'Some of them are owned by the civilians, so I can't hand them over, but any military vehicles are yours.'

Colonel Baldwin's features hardened. 'There's no personal ownership of anything, General, not anymore. We all have to chip in to survive. But that's a discussion for another time.' His expression softened, and he extended his hand to Colonel Bradley.

Marshall introduced him.

Baldwin crossed his arms. 'British intelligence? Isn't that an oxymoron?'

Bradley said nothing.

'Why don't we go to my office? Lieutenant, once we settle the civilians, initiate protocol Beta-Five.'

'Right away, sir.'

He saluted and left.

'Beta-Five? I'm not familiar with that protocol,' Marshall said with a frown.

Colonel Baldwin gestured to his office and they followed him in. Bradley and Marshall took seats while Baldwin poured three glasses of whiskey. With the door closed, Colonel Baldwin relaxed.

'It is good to have some friendly faces, especially yours, Bill. You came from Washington?'

Marshall took a glass. 'Barely escaped. Found Braders with a few men and got the hell out. It's all gone Ira, they destroyed Washington. It took a week to find a route we could drive through. They tore the cities apart. Baltimore is a crater. There's nothing left of it. We travelled by day, found refuge at night. That's when it's worse. But once we made it through the cities, we saw less of the bigger monsters. This was the one place I thought might still have a chance of being active.'

Colonel Baldwin sipped his drink. 'I have a similar story. Most of the destruction happened early on. Comms went silent a few weeks ago. We rescued a few state government workers, policemen, and a few politicians, but they knew very little. There's been nothing since the Pentagon went silent, although we have had chatter from a few ships that made it out.'

'That's good to know.'

They were quiet for a time, then Baldwin said, 'At least you survived.'

Marshall looked at Bradley. 'I was just lucky.'

'Lucky is good. As more and more people came, and I had no new orders to follow, I implemented my own protocols.'

'Like Beta-Five?'

Baldwin nodded. 'Beta-Five is an inventory protocol for background checks. We need engineers, scientists, educators, doctors, nurses. We've been lucky, especially on the more academic front. Still, locking up a bunch of civilians from all walks of life has presented its own challenges.'

'I can imagine.'

'Maintaining order has been difficult. That's something you might help with. There's a mix of resentment and adulation which swings daily. We've had to deal with several instances of criminal activity. We also had to deal with issues of violence towards civilians who aren't white. As if my job isn't hard enough.'

Marshall shook his head. 'I'm sorry.'

'The local PD ex-chief, a man named Todd Stevens, has been keeping order down there. But his people have a tendency to get heavy handed.'

'You want me to talk with them?' Bradley asked.

'Talk with them, get to know them, befriend them,' he laughed. 'Anything will do.'

'Absolutely. Anything else you need help with?'

Baldwin shook his head. 'No, thank you Colonel. I appreciate your offer, but we're a class-three biological warfare lab. One of nine commissioned with far-reaching protocols, specifically for situations like the one we're in.'

Marshall said, 'FDR himself set those protocols.'

Baldwin nodded.

'I see,' Bradley said. 'It's a security issue then?'

Baldwin looked at Marshall then back at Bradley. 'That's right, Colonel.'

Colonel Bradley swallowed his whiskey. 'I understand. How did this facility avoid the destruction?'

'We almost didn't. Those winged monsters ransacked half the state. Legislative and local government buildings seemed to be their first targets. We suddenly found ourselves with an influx of people and little time to prepare. As numbers grew, we began organising rescue teams to look for survivors during daylight, but we didn't find many. We think they're all dead.'

Marshall shook his head. 'No, they aren't. The monsters take them.'

'Take them? Where?'

'We don't know,' Bradley replied. 'They seem to go with hardly any resistance.'

'Interesting. That suggests they're more organised and intelligent than we thought.'

'Aren't you concerned they might find this place?' Bradley asked.

'Of course. It overshadows everything we're doing here. But we have generators and fuel supplies. With your resources, we've tripled our reserve. We're managing. The scientists are continuing their work, while we do our best to keep this place running and protect the civilians. A group of power employees are working to get all the remaining transfer stations' power redistributed here.' Baldwin leant forward. 'We've discovered a few things. Electricity and noise attract the bigger monsters. The smaller things that live in the shadows, they come and go frequently but don't seem interested in us. We haven't been idle. My scientists have discovered they have a weakness.'

Marshall raised his eyebrows. 'Really?'

'Yes, it's sunlight.'

Colonel Bradley rubbed his chin in thought. 'Makes sense. They don't venture out of the shadows during the day, unless they have to. We've managed to avoid them because they're slower, but we haven't seen the sun in weeks. How are they affected?'

'Ultraviolet is harmful to them, even filtered through clouds. We've several spotlights out front fitted with UV. We shut down power after dark and switch to batteries for critical systems. We've equipped every flashlight with UV filters, because they'll do more damage than bullets. Early on, a creature found its way into a storage building and got trapped in some netting. Initially we thought it was dead. When we began an autopsy, it woke up and killed three of my people before they could raise an alarm. Not long after we fit the labs with UV lights.'

'Fascinating,' Bradley murmured. 'I didn't realise these shadow things had a physical form.'

'When they're incapacitated, yes,' Baldwin said, rotating

the glass in his hands. 'Even when not, they have some presence in the world. Interestingly, the thing we caught used to be a dog.'

Marshall raised an eyebrow. 'Used to be?'

'The word we're using is *mutation*. Its bloodwork comes back as canine. We don't believe it's a new species. The current thinking is they've somehow mutated. If that's so, it might be possible to undo it.'

'We've seen many creatures,' Marshall remarked. 'Some more humanoid than others. A few you can kill, but most you can't. At least not conventionally.'

'They're intelligent. They have a rudimentary means of communication, like many animals, but there's no evidence to suggest that's anything more than an instinct, that's what Doctor Grunner says. Your experiences will enhance our data, so let's compare notes later.'

Bradley said, 'You really think we can transform these monsters back?'

'That's the current theory.'

'Can we see it?' Marshall asked

'Sadly, no. It forced us to put it down.' He paused while he contemplated the next thing on his mind. 'General, we should probably address the elephant in the room.'

Marshall straightened in his chair. 'Indeed. What do you suggest?'

'I'll be blunt. You outrank me, but my position as commander of this facility is by presidential appointment. Despite your seniority, I am not obliged to hand command over to you.'

General Marshall pursed his lips. 'Every member of the armed services in this facility, including you Colonel, come under my direct authority. Your presidential appointment doesn't remove you from the chain of command.'

'You're correct and in normal situations I would serve two masters. But there cannot be two masters here. I was appointed based on my experience and scientific expertise. There's a complexity of work being handled here that, with respect, you aren't qualified to command.'

Bradley looked between them, but kept his mouth shut.

Marshall however inclined his head. 'The choice is out of my hands. I am not in a position to circumvent a presidential order. But Baldwin,' he said, his face hard, 'I expect to be kept in the loop.'

Colonel Baldwin relaxed. 'Without question. Well, perhaps you'd like to rest? You'll have to share for a while until I can make fresh arrangements. We weren't expecting VIPs. I'll make sure you're comfortable. The accommodation isn't too awful.'

'After months on the road, we'll take whatever you have,' Marshall said.

'How big is this place?' Bradley asked.

'We've six floors beneath this one. Nearly all of it is underground. We're far safer down there, believe me. I leave a small guard above after dark.' Baldwin turned to Marshall. 'General, I'd like to integrate your men and officers with ours. No sense in splitting them up. Agreed?'

'Agreed.'

'We set up civilian habitats on the lower level. The military are all on floors above them. We consider the civilians the most vulnerable.'

Colonel Bradley asked, 'Baldwin, do you think we caused what's going on outside? With chemicals and so on? Is that what makes animals turn into monsters?'

'I don't suppose it helped, but no,' Colonel Baldwin said. 'There's something coming from within the Earth, something we haven't seen before. A substance we think might be causing the mutations I spoke of. We've seen it in vegetation and animals.'

'This substance, does it affect us too?' Marshall asked, throwing a look at Bradley.

'Absolutely. It has many effects. Not everyone reacts the same, but the most common seems to make people docile, and easily suggestible.'

'Which explains how they've taken people away with no resistance,' Bradley remarked.

Baldwin stood and they both followed him.

'Let's find you both a room.'

Colonel Baldwin took them through the compound. They followed along corridors lined with thick windows. Marshall observed groups of people in cubicles on the opposite side, dressed in protective equipment from head to toe. There were laboratories with a mixture of instruments neither recognised. Each cubical seemed laid out for a specific task. Marshall stopped to observe three people working around a vat. He noticed they had coloured bands around their arms.

'What's going on in here?' Marshall asked.

Baldwin came beside him. 'High-containment hazard lab. This is where we work on biological components.'

Colonel Bradley pointed. 'Is that why they're wearing coloured armbands?'

'Yes, for decontamination reasons. Shall we?'

Marshall stared for a moment longer, then followed as Baldwin led them further down the corridor. They continued on, passing laboratories and offices, until they reached an elevator and got in.

'The elevators will only go to certain levels, depending on your key clearance. Without a key, they won't work at all.' Colonel Baldwin inserted his key into the panel and four buttons lit. He pressed one and the doors closed.

With a slight bump, the car came to a halt and the door opened. They followed Baldwin into a similar bright corridor.

'We converted this floor to living quarters. Most of it's a giant barracks. There are comforts,' Baldwin said, as he took them towards a large dining area. 'This is the centre of the barracks. The mess is here. If you look at the doors, you'll see they're colour coded. The red doors lead to recreation rooms and a gym.'

He pointed. 'At the end of that corridor are the medical bays. Blue are lounges and bars.'

Baldwin then indicated the opposite side of the room. 'Yellow, you'll find the officers' mess and rec room. There's a library. It's stocked pretty well. A few of the civilians maintain it. Green you'll find sleeping quarters, that's where we're going.'

Baldwin led them through the green double doors into a

room that held around a hundred beds. Each had a compact space and curtain. Those occupied had pulled theirs closed for privacy.

'It looks like a hospital ward,' Bradley said.

'It was. We converted it into living spaces. It's just for sleeping, but we've allowed them to personalise their space and the curtains provide a little privacy. We have quiet rooms they can book, if they require more.'

Marshall frowned. 'For what?'

Baldwin looked sideways at him. 'Whatever they need. Sex, prayer, personal isolation. You look surprised, Bill? It's fairly obvious we could be here a long time. This is their home now.'

They passed through the barracks into another corridor with doors off either side. Marshall poked his head through a doorway Baldwin had stopped at. He observed three cots, seating around a table, a sink, a couple of bookshelves, and lockers. It wasn't luxurious, by any means.

Baldwin led them inside. 'At the end of the corridor are the showers. Will this do?'

Marshall nodded. 'This'll be fine. We'll be comfortable in here.'

'I'll find you a more permanent home soon, General. Something a little larger.'

'I'd appreciate that.'

Colonel Bradley said, 'There's three cots. John can stay with us.'

'John?'

'Captain Keeney,' Bradley said.

Baldwin nodded. 'That's not an issue, it's a three-man room.'

Marshall crossed his arms and looked hard at Bradley. 'No, that's unnecessary.'

'He's your aide, Bill.'

Marshall ignored him. 'I'm sure a captain of his calibre could be of use, Baldwin?'

Colonel Baldwin looked between them. 'I am sure I can find him a new position, if that's what you would prefer?'

'No,' Bradley said.

'Yes, thank you,' Marshall countered. 'He has a head for figures and he's methodical.'

'Bill...'

Marshall glared at Bradley. 'Enough.'

Bradley pulled out a packet of cigarettes and offered one to Baldwin. He shook his head. 'It's a terrible habit.'

Baldwin then turned his attention back to the general. 'Look, it's none of my business, but you both seem a little at odds over this officer. Is there something I should know?'

General Marshall shook his head. Colonel Bradley lit his cigarette, but said nothing.

Baldwin narrowed his eyes. 'Very well then. I'll put Captain Keeney in the command staff, since he's been your aide.'

Marshall waved a hand. 'You can distribute him and the rest of those under my command as you see fit.'

'Is there anything more I can do to make you comfortable?'

Marshall shook his head. 'Braders?'

'Sure. Where can I get cigarettes and a decent glass of Scotch?'

Baldwin chuckled. 'I'll have the duty sergeant take care of that for you. Lunch is served at noon. The duty sergeant will brief you both on procedures for nightfall, how to get around, keys for elevators. I'll settle your man into his bunk.'

They nodded.

Marshall extended his hand. 'Thank you, Ira.'

Colonel Ira Baldwin gave a slight nod. 'General,' he said. 'I'll meet you both in the mess for lunch.'

He left them to settle. Colonel Bradley blew out a puff of smoke as Marshall turned and walked into the bathroom. When he'd finished and exited, he found Bradley sitting against the table. His expression unreadable.

'Save it,' Marshall said.

'I haven't said anything.'

'I can read you like a book.'

Colonel Bradley lifted his head and for the first time, General Marshall saw something unkind in his eyes. 'No,' he said, stubbing out his cigarette. 'You can't.'

'Look, Braders, I'm exhausted. I don't want to argue about

it. John will be fine with Ira and besides, it's not as though I need an aide, is it?'

Colonel Bradley's expression softened. 'I don't like the idea of us splitting up, that's all.'

Marshall smiled. 'I know you don't. But it's for the best.'

'You're probably right. By the way. Did you notice what those scientists were working on in the labs?'

'No, did you?'

He lit another cigarette. 'They were organs.'

'Didn't Ira say they're working on researching these creatures?'

'He did. But they weren't dog organs, Bill. They were human.'

• • •

'I'm putting you in with Barrette. He'll get you situated in no time.' Colonel Baldwin said, knocking on and opening the door. The occupant, who had been snoozing on his bed, jumped up and stood to attention. Keeney couldn't help admire his physique, since he was only wearing a pair of white shorts.

Colonel Baldwin waved at him. 'At ease. Captain Paul Barrette meet Captain John Keeney. Former aide to General William Marshall. We get the privilege of his expertise. Show him the ropes.'

'Yes, sir,' was his deadpan response.

Keeney sensed a tension between them, but that thought was lost when Baldwin turned and extended his hand. 'Good to have you with us, Captain. I'll see you at oh-six hundred tomorrow.'

Keeney took his hand. 'Thank you, sir.'

Colonel Baldwin glanced back at Barrette, nodded, then left and closed the door.

John Keeney dumped his bag on the empty bed as Barrette came beside him.

'Welcome bunkmate,' he said. His expression had changed from unreadable to a full-on toothy smile. It was a friendly smile, Keeney thought.

• • •

It had been several weeks since they'd settled in. General Marshall's men were content within the new regime. He'd seen little of Baldwin as the days went by, but he knew running such a facility was an enormous job. They got together at least once a week for dinner, where Baldwin would chat about things that Bill found no interest in. Baldwin didn't seem to eat breakfast or lunch or use any of the recreation facilities.

Marshall had completed his daily gym routine and was heading to the shower. He stripped and hung his towel on a peg. The water was running, so he knew he wasn't alone. He entered the communal shower and found the lieutenant he'd met on their arrival.

'It's Dawson, isn't it?' he said.

The young officer nodded. 'Yes, General. Or Bruce, if you prefer,' he said, snapping to attention.

Marshall chuckled. 'At ease, Bruce. There's no need to be so formal. Especially when we're both naked, and you're covered in soap.'

The young man chuckled. Marshall hit the button and warm water fell over his body. He turned a few times and lathered himself. Dawson was washing his hair. Marshall took the opportunity to observe him. Late twenties, fair haired, a little under six feet, defined and muscular, with grey eyes. Not unlike his son's.

Marshall inwardly sighed. *To be young and look like that again*, he thought.

Dawson faced the wall, his back now visible, and Marshall couldn't help stare at the scars running from his neck over his buttocks, and down to the back of knees.

'That's some nasty scarring you've got there,' he said.

Lieutenant Dawson wiped the soap from his face as he turned. 'Pretty, huh?'

'How'd you get them?'

Dawson let the water run over his shoulders, his head hung forward. 'Oh, when the shit hit the fan, a monster got me.' He turned off the water and grabbed his towel.

'Looks like you had a lucky escape?'

He dried his hair then let the towel hang around his neck. 'Lost a lot of brothers. I guess I wasn't that lucky.'

'No,' Marshall agreed.

'Can I ask you something, sir?'

Marshall was rinsing the lather off his hair. 'Go ahead.'

'Do you believe in the devil?'

He wiped his eyes. 'What?'

'The devil, sir. Do you believe he's real?'

'I suppose I should. It would answer a lot of questions, wouldn't it? I take it you do?'

Dawson clasped the cross, hanging off his necklace. 'I think he's walking amongst us.'

Marshall thought back to the monsters they'd seen. 'You might be right.'

'Who else can turn the clouds against us? Those creatures out there... You know what my father would say they are? Demons, sir. Demons from the depths of Hell.'

Marshall turned off his water. Dawson was sitting on the bench, drying his legs. 'My father was a pastor. He'd probably say this was all predicted.'

'*Is* a pastor,' Marshall corrected.

'There's no reason to believe he's still alive, sir.'

Marshall sat beside him. 'It's an enormous country, there's no reason to believe all of it is like this.'

'I suppose. What about your family?'

Marshall let out a breath. 'My son is serving in Turkey. I've had no news. I don't have any other family.'

'You don't know for sure if he's alive either?'

'I'm not giving up on him,' Marshall said firmly. 'And you shouldn't give up on your folks either.'

Dawson nodded then they both stood and dressed. Marshall slipped his pants on. 'What about your brother?' he asked, as he pulled the tee shirt over his head.

'Sir?' Dawson was frowning.

'Your brother? I thought you said he was here with you?'

Lieutenant Dawson gave Marshall an odd look. 'I don't have a brother, sir.'

'Are you sure?'

'I think I'd remember if I had a brother, sir.'

'Well that's damn peculiar, because I recall when Colonel Bradley and I met you at the gate. You mentioned a brother?'

'At the gate, sir? I don't work the gate. I work on level three.' At Marshall's perplexed look he added, 'Maybe you're confusing me with someone else?'

'Maybe I am,' Marshall said. 'I'm getting old. My memory must be playing tricks on me.'

Dawson threw his towel in the basket. 'If you don't mind me saying so, sir. You're in good shape.'

'Well now you *have* cheered me up.'

Lieutenant Dawson gave a wide smile. 'Thanks for the company.'

Marshall nodded. 'Maybe I'll see you at lunch?'

'I hope so, sir.' Dawson nodded and left.

Marshall stood for some time in thought. His mind going over the first conversation he'd had with Dawson, back when he and Bradley first arrived. It *was* the same man. Why the hell didn't he remember their meeting? Why would he say he had a brother, then deny it? It bothered him. Marshall turned and went looking for Bradley.

● ● ●

Colonel Bradley was leaning against the doorframe as Doctor Kate Husk looked over her sheet. She smiled and put it down. The thing he'd noticed most about Kate Husk, when they'd first met a few weeks past, was her mouth. She had a pretty mouth. The second thing was her eyes. They were a stunning shade of emerald green. As she came under the light, they sparkled. Mid-thirties, he decided, and looking good for it. He liked the fact she hardly wore any makeup. She had that typical mixture of soap and chemical odour. It wasn't unpleasant.

'Blood looks good. Results are where they should be. As far as I can see, you're healthy,' she said.

'You sound almost disappointed,' he remarked with a grin.

She smiled. 'There are a few tests I haven't done, but they're not invasive.'

'Now I'm disappointed.'

Her facial features remained neutral. She walked towards the door and he stepped back to allow her to pass.

'Follow me, Colonel.'

'We're being formal today are we, Doctor?'

'Yes, we are.'

'Fair enough.'

She led him to an examination room, turned the occupied lock on the door, and pulled the curtain across the window. 'If you could just strip down to your underwear, please.'

Doctor Husk cleaned her hands in a sink, while he did as she instructed. After drying them, she pulled a stethoscope from the small drawer.

Coming behind him she said, 'Take a deep breath and hold it, please.'

He felt her moving the scope around his back. Its cold touch made him shiver.

'Now let it out.'

She came around him and put it on his chest.

'Deep breath... and let it out.'

Taking the stethoscope out of her ears, she dropped it into her coat pocket, and felt around his neck.

'Turn your head to the left. Good... now to the right. Well, that's all good. Drop your shorts please.'

She reached down and he kept his eyes forward.

'Cough.'

Colonel Bradley coughed. But after a few seconds he realised she hadn't removed her hand. He looked at her with a frown. 'Is... is everything all right down there?'

Doctor Husk released him and stood. 'Yes. I was checking for abnormalities, why?'

'Oh, you know...' His eyes fell down and she followed them, then looked up raising an eyebrow.

'It seems to work as it should.' She turned away.

'You're not going to leave me like this, are you?'

Kate Husk laughed. 'And just what are you suggesting?'

He grabbed her and pulled her close. She felt him rub into her. He observed her cheeks change hue and eyes dilate. 'You know exactly what I'm suggesting, you minx.'

Disentangling from his arms she looked down again, a half smile sat on her face, but she shook her head. 'Not here, Charlie,' she whispered, 'It's unprofessional.'

He mimicked her sigh. 'Fine. But I want you to know that this,' he murmured, taking her hand and placing it on his penis, 'is all your fault.'

She removed her hand. 'How is that my fault? You need to learn to control yourself.'

He leant in, giving soft kisses along her neck. She quivered, but pushed him away. 'Stop it. You're terrible. Get dressed, now.'

He picked up his underwear. 'Yes, Doctor. Your office then?'

'No.'

'Bah. When do you get off work?'

'Same time as yesterday.'

He pulled up his underwear and slipped his pants on. Doctor Husk couldn't help staring at his crotch. When her eyes found his, she looked away.

'Do I need to bring dinner?'

Her hand found the handle of the door and opened it.

'Only if you're hungry.'

'I'm always hungry,' he said, following her out.

CHAPTER FOUR

After his shower, General Marshall went back to his room but found it empty. He walked through the barracks, nodding to several men playing cards around a table, and entered the officers' mess. Lunch was being served, but he'd lost his appetite. He grabbed a cup of strong black coffee and found a comfortable seat. There were a few junior officers eating together, but no sign of Keeney. It wasn't long before Colonel Bradley came and sat beside him.

Marshall checked his watch. 'You're late.'

Bradley fell into a chair. 'I've had an exhausting morning. Almost didn't make it for lunch.'

'Really, what have you been doing?'

Bradley's lips curled into a smile Marshall recognised. 'What's her name?'

'Kate Husk,' Bradley said, his eyes on the officers eating at the table.

'The doctor?'

Bradley smiled.

'Isn't that unethical?'

'Probably.'

Marshall shook his head. 'You're terrible. Just be careful.'

'I'm always careful.'

'You look tired.'

Bradley rubbed his eyes. 'I've not been sleeping well, so I'm avoiding it. It's making me irritable.'

'You'd better get yourself some food, they're closing.'

'I'm not hungry. Is the coffee good?'

'No.' Marshall chuckled.

'You want a top up?'

Marshall handed him his cup. Bradley soon returned with two fresh cups and sat next to him. 'There's something I want to discuss.'

'I was about to say the same.'

'Rank has its privileges,' Bradley said, taking a sip.

'Do you remember when we first got here, that young lieutenant we met at the gate?'

'The Texan boy? Dawson?'

Marshall nodded. 'I had a long chat with him today, in the shower.'

Bradley chuckled. 'Did you, by Jove?'

'What do you make of him?'

Bradley rested his cup on the arm of the chair. 'He's a bright fellow. A little queer in his beliefs. A loner from what I've observed. Doesn't play the field, and hardly ever interacts socially with anyone. He's what I would call a routine loner. Not much for games, well, except poker. There he excels. He's a card counter, and a bloody good one. Religious on account of his father, I suppose. Loyal. Handsome.'

Marshall laughed. 'How could you know all that?'

Bradley raised an eyebrow. 'It's what I do.'

'I keep forgetting you're an intelligence officer.'

'What's this all about, anyway?'

'Do you remember what we talked about when we met?'

Bradley tilted his head. 'Not the exact conversation, no.'

'He said he had a brother. Do you remember that?'

'Yes, you made some comment about him being thankful for having him here, right?'

Marshall seemed relieved. 'Then I'm not going mad.'

At Bradley's frown, Marshall leant closer and lowered his voice. 'He told me he didn't have a brother.'

'Why would he lie about it?'

'I don't know, but it gets worse. He also denied ever meeting us. Said he didn't work the gate, something about only working on level three?'

Colonel Bradley rubbed his chin. 'That's what I wanted to talk to you about.'

'What?'

'Level three. Have you been there?'

'No, why, have you?'

Bradley shook his head. 'It's restricted. I haven't been able to gain access and I've been going around in circles trying to. Still, I've found someone who might get me there.'

'Ah,' Marshall said, with a chuckle. 'Kate Husk?'

'With any luck. She is very obliging.'

'You want me to talk to Ira?'

Bradley took a mouthful of coffee. 'Not yet. Let me do a bit of digging because something isn't right here.'

Marshall finished his coffee. 'What do you mean?'

'You haven't noticed?'

'Noticed what?'

'The lack of people? This facility should have a staff of two thousand. So, where are they?'

Marshall's brow creased. 'Ira said he lost a lot of men, surely that accounts for it?'

'But it's doesn't account for the barracks. There's what? Ten dorm rooms on this level? Each with around a hundred beds? Where's the rest of them?'

The general's eyes widened. 'You're right, I hadn't thought about that. What do you think?'

'I think your friend Ira isn't being honest. Many people here aren't.'

'What about your doctor friend?'

'I'm not sure.' Bradley lifted the cup and ran it across his lips, then took a drink. 'She knows more than she's letting on, but it's too early to say if she's deliberately lying. There's a strange quietness here I don't like.'

'It's entirely possible there's another floor like this one, wouldn't that account for the missing men? Perhaps that floor is at capacity and this one isn't?'

Bradley shrugged. 'Even if that's true, why haven't we seen or heard about it?'

'Is it possible that Ira lost more people than he's letting

on? I don't know him well enough to form an opinion on his honesty.'

'Bill, it's my job to discover things and I'm good at it. I know when people are lying. I also know how to read behaviour. Nothing here reads right.'

Marshall remained thoughtful. 'It's been a few days since I went to the civilian level. I'll have a wander, make a few discreet enquiries. Maybe our people have seen or know something?'

Bradley finished his coffee. 'That's not an awful idea. Just be careful what you say, because if Ira is lying, he might have spies there.'

'I still find it hard to believe...'

'That he might be telling you what he thinks you want to hear?'

'It's possible. But what about Dawson?'

'It's damn peculiar. Another strange thing, amongst others. Have you met any of the scientists?'

Marshall shook his head.

'Well I have, and trust me, they aren't doing what Ira said they were.'

'What have they told you?'

'It's what they haven't told me,' he said, cradling his cup. 'Oh, and something else occurred to me today. Something inexplicable.'

'What?'

'The elevator.'

Marshall rubbed his temple. He had a headache. 'What about the elevator?'

'There were only four buttons.'

'So?'

Bradley stood. 'Didn't Ira say this compound had *six* levels?'

• • •

General Marshall weighed up what Bradley had said. He left the officers' mess and headed for the elevator. Closing the door, he pulled out his key, slotted it into the lock, and turned.

He ran a hand over the panel. There were only four buttons, and nothing to show any hidden others. He hit the lowest one. When the car came to a halt, he removed the key and exited. The layout of the civilian floor was much the same as his, so navigating it wasn't an issue. Unlike his floor, this one was full of people, the noise level higher. He came into the large dining facility and collided with four children who were chasing each other.

'Sorry,' a boy said.

Marshall smiled at him. He looked around at the various people and spotted a face he recognised.

'Father?'

Father David Doyle beamed. 'Look who it is! We haven't seen you in days, how's life on the upper levels?'

'Not much different to here, I should imagine.'

A group of men laughed. Children squealed as they played.

Doyle shooed them away. 'Let's find somewhere quiet, shall we?'

Marshall followed him to the chapel. The old priest made the sign of the cross to the altar and lowered his head, then gestured for Marshall to sit in the pew.

'Is something wrong, Father?'

'Possibly,' Doyle said frowning, 'and I don't want to seem ungrateful, but well... there's been unrest.'

'Among your flock?' Marshall regretted the tone the moment he spoke.

'You don't like me much, do you?'

'It's not you, Father. I don't care for who you represent.'

'I understand. You blame God for what has happened?'

'I blame him for doing nothing while it happened.'

The priest nodded. 'You're not alone. Many people here have lost their faith, and to tell you the truth, perhaps I have too.'

'You?'

'It surprises you? I may be a man of God, but I'm still a man.'

The general rubbed his face. 'At least here we're safe.'

'Are we?'

Marshall frowned. 'What do you mean by that?'

'Safety is relative, General. It's true, here we have shelter, companionship, access to food, and medicines. In every sense we're better off, yet what we've lost trumps that.'

'What is it you think you've lost?'

'Freedom, General. Freedom to make our own choices.'

'You can't be serious.'

'I am serious. You might not see it as a military man, because you're used to being set a schedule to follow. These people aren't. We're fed when the kitchen opens. Eat what little is prepared. Have no say in the variety of it. We work as directed, sleep when told to. We've lost our individuality.'

'You think it would be better out there, with monsters in every shadow?' He scowled.

'I don't, but others are questioning coming here. They feel caged, General. Like animals.' He rubbed the bridge of his nose. 'The atmosphere's oppressive. Haven't you felt it?'

'Colonel Baldwin took us in, and he's given us a fighting chance. You know what it's like outside.'

'Hell on Earth?'

'I couldn't have said it better, Father.'

'I will do my best to help transition them, but I have a request. The ex-police officers feel useless. They have limited authority. Nothing more than glorified security guards, that's what Todd says. We're just not used to being under military control. Can you speak to the colonel about giving them some autonomy? It might help to relieve the tensions between them and the less desirable elements.'

'Less desirable? Do you mean criminal?'

'I wouldn't say that. Not all of us *civilians*, as we're commonly referred to, are happy. There's a lot of agitation and Todd's officers are taking the brunt of it.'

'I had no idea, I'm sorry.'

'You were once a member of the joint chiefs, so I'm told. Surely you have authority to make these changes?'

He shook his head. 'Colonel Baldwin is in command. I'll speak to him.'

'Order him! Some general you are,' he huffed.

'I understand your agitation, Father, believe me. As far as we know, the government fell. The president we assume is dead. It's time for everyone to adapt and grow up a little.'

'General...'

'Bill, Father.'

Doyle smiled. 'Bill, these people are existing, not living. If this is to be our permanent home, things need to change.'

Marshall lent forwards, eyeing the cross on the altar. 'I'll see what I can do. But we do it my way. I'll talk to operations and have them increase the food variety and quantities, okay?'

He patted the general's hand. 'I would appreciate anything you can do.'

Marshall nodded.

'Before you go,' the priest said. 'There is one other thing I'd like to bring to your attention.'

'Name it.'

'It might be nothing, but it appears we're missing a few people.'

'How many?'

'Six, including Sarah.'

Marshall gave a concerned look. 'Sarah? When did you last see her?'

'Yesterday. She went to her assigned job but didn't return with the others.'

'Did any of them say they'd seen her?'

Doyle shook his head. 'They were on different assignments. It seems she was working with another group, but none of them returned. I noticed she was missing at dinner, and no one has seen her. I'm worried.'

'David, this should have been your first concern.'

'I'm a leader of faith in this community, I have to look to all, not just one.'

'She's your sister.'

Father Doyle lowered his eyes. Marshall gave him a reassuring squeeze of the shoulder. 'I'm sure she's fine. You know Sarah, she gets caught up in work.'

'True,' Doyle said, nodding. 'Still, if you could ask after her?'

'I will. Has there been anything else you might consider... odd?'

'Nothing other than what I've told you.'

'I need you to do something for me. Listen to people.'

Father Doyle chuckled. 'That *is* what I do, Bill.'

'No, not in that way. I mean listen to their conversations, when they're eating, in recreation, in the shower, wherever... when they think they *aren't* being listened too.'

'You mean spy on them?'

'I should have just said that.'

Doyle narrowed his eyes. 'What's going on?'

'I don't know, but before I say or do anything that back-fires on any of us, I need more information.'

'What am I listening for, exactly?'

'Anything unusual, fishy.'

Father Doyle frowned. 'Fishy?'

'Out of the ordinary, I don't know how to direct you,' – he then smiled – 'but I know a man who can.'

'Ah, you mean our British spy?'

'He's good at what he does. I'll have him come and brief you.'

Doyle raised an eyebrow. 'Provided, of course, you can find out whose bed he's in first?'

Marshall said nothing.

Doyle stood. 'I'll do what you ask.'

'Thank you. I'll make enquiries regarding Sarah.'

'And the others,' Doyle reminded him, listing their names.

'Yes, of course.' Marshall left Father Doyle kneeling at the altar in prayer.

• • •

A telephone rang and Lieutenant-Colonel Baldwin answered.

'Baldwin.'

The colonel's facial muscles stiffened. 'When? No. Do noth-ing. Seal off the compartment and go to Beta-Two with imme-diate effect. Wait there for me.'

He replaced the handset, stood, and left his office. When

Baldwin reached the elevator, he pulled out his key. There was a slight tremor in his hand as he inserted and turned it. The car reached its floor and the doors opened. Two MPs came and greeted him.

'Come with me,' Baldwin said, his expression unreadable. They followed along the corridors until they arrived at the heavy outer door of a lab. He inserted a large key into the lock. They heard an audible clunk as it turned. Baldwin span the wheel in the door's centre until the loud clacking sound stopped, and pushed it open. He turned to the MPs. 'Stay here. Close this door behind me and let no one in.'

'Understood, sir.'

Baldwin didn't move. 'I mean no one at all.'

They looked at each other. 'Including the general?'

'Especially the general. Oh, and one more thing. If anyone other than me tries to exit through this door, you are under orders to shoot them, is that clear?'

They nodded. Baldwin maintained eye contact for a moment longer, then disappeared inside.

• • •

Colonel Bradley made a quick note on his sleeve and slipped along the corridor with practiced silence. As he neared a doorway, he hugged a shadow and waited. With no obvious signs of movement, he tested the door. As expected, it was locked. Making another scan of the corridor, he pulled a small set of keys from out of his pocket, selected one, and unlocked and entered the room.

It was dark. With just enough light to see the rows of cabinets, he opened a drawer on one and ran his fingers along the files until he found what he was looking for. He slipped the file out and began flicking through the pages, pausing at one in particular. He took the sheet and folded it, then slipped the file back into the drawer and closed it. He shoved the folded page into his pocket and made his way over to the door, opening it a crack. Bradley saw no movement in the corridor and deftly exited and locked the door.

• • •

An alarm was going off in the airlock just before Baldwin slipped inside. He found Doctor Grunner standing beside the young man's bed. From his position, he could see that the man's face had turned an unnatural shade of white. There was a lattice of black lines underneath his skin, and they were spreading along his jaw, rising into his cheeks. Both his eyes were bloodshot.

Baldwin sealed the door behind him as Grunner turned, his face visible through his isolations suit.

'What happened?' Baldwin asked.

'He was stable not ten minutes ago. Assist me,' Doctor Grunner said.

'What did you do?'

'This was not of my doing. Tilt his head back, I need to get a breathing tube in.'

Baldwin grabbed the young man's head, but the rubber gloves slipped off the blood seeping through his skin. He wiped them on the sheet and tried again, tilting the head as Grunner instructed. The German lubricated a tube and eased it into the man's throat, then grunted and frowned.

'Is something wrong?'

'It's hitting an obstruction.'

The man bucked and Baldwin lost his grip.

'Hold his head back further...' The man's chest heaved. He made gagging sounds. Blood was leaking onto the bed. Baldwin could hear his heart beating from inside his isolation mask. Doctor Grunner continued working and gave an audible sigh as the tube finally slipped in.

'Stand back,' he said, as dense black fluid spouted out the tube. He continued to work, twisting and repositioning the tube, until at last they heard rasping as the man sucked in much-needed oxygen. Grunner relaxed. He grabbed swabs and handed them to Baldwin. They cleaned the man's face. His eyelids fluttered, then shut, and Grunner attached the tube to a breathing apparatus.

'The machine will keep his brain alive.'

'Will you please tell me what the hell happened.'

Grunner cleaned his gloves. 'He became exposed. It was quick. I had limited time to make observations and gather the data. Once we got him in here, all seemed calm. Except...'

'Except what?'

Grunner turned. 'I think we should assume we've breached containment.'

Baldwin's face turned white. He looked down at the young unconscious scientist. 'Why should we assume that?'

'Because the sample in the lab broke free.'

'What do you mean?'

'While they were working, the vat fell and the sample escaped.'

'It fell?'

Grunner nodded.

'How?'

'The answer lays unconscious beside you. A foolish accident by an imbecile.'

Baldwin stared at Grunner. 'That's a little harsh. The poor fellow's fighting for his life.'

'No, he is dead. At least, he soon will be.'

'What?'

'He lives for the moment only. Once I have gathered my data, he will have served his purpose.'

Baldwin's expression of concern was hidden beneath his mask. 'I won't let you harm him, Doctor. We've already been...'

'You misunderstand. He was dead the moment the sample attacked. What we have done to stabilise him might seem humane, but actually it is not. The kindness will come by allowing him to die with what little dignity he has left. Which isn't much.'

'You're a monster, Grunner.'

'I've heard this before,' the German replied, leaning over the man and drawing symbols on his face. 'If it makes you feel better, the data I gather upon his death will elevate him from his unremarkable and mostly mediocre life.' He looked up. 'That is something to be cheerful for, no?'

Baldwin ignored the question. 'How did this happen?'

'The sample became active, once this idiot left it unsecured.'
'Are you trying to say the sample caused the accident?'
'That *is* what I'm saying.'
'Were there others?'
'Oh yes, there were others.'
'What happened to them?'

Doctor Grunner moved to a curtain and drew it open. They looked through the window.

'Dear God,' Baldwin murmured.

Seven men and women lay dead. Corpses sprawled across tables, corpses propped against walls, corpses curled up in corners, arms stiffening around their folded knees as if balling themselves up could stave off death. As they watched, blood seeped from them forming into a slow-moving red blanket. From out of the broken vat, a viscous black liquid slipped out to meet it.

CHAPTER FIVE

Captain John Keeney wandered the corridors of the military level alone. It was cold. A strange mix of overlapping whispered voices filled the air, which were almost lyrical. A scuffling sound nearby caused Keeney to stop. His heart rate increased, the sound of it heavy in his ears. Keeney couldn't pinpoint the source of the voices. They seemed everywhere. He wiped the sweat from his face and looked down at his shaking hand.

A louder sound alerted him, and he looked up. 'Who's there?'

Something nearby gave a chuckle, and Keeney reached for his sidearm, then cursed when he remembered he'd replaced it with a UV flashlight.

Keeney kept moving, trying hard to ignore the nagging itch spreading across the skin of his chest and neck. The whispering increased in volume, and he felt a sudden dread rise from deep in the pit of his stomach. He turned a corner and stopped dead. Ahead of him corpses littered the corridor and the carpet was sodden with blood. For the longest time he stared at the bodies, paralysed, then found the courage to approach. Keeney made a deliberate footing through them, grimacing at the squelch his boots made when they came into contact with the blood. A putrid stench of decaying corpses reached him and he held his breath. His pace becoming more urgent.

There was an empty path ahead but the skin around his

neck itched worse and he stopped to scratch it. A spike of sharp pain made him curse. He stared in horrified fascination at the lump of fleshy fat that fell from his fingers, leaving a deep hole where blood gushed. It ran down his neck, under his shirt. He clamped a hand on his neck in shock. The hot slick fluid continued seeping through his fingers, soaking his shirt and underwear, dripping down a leg into his boot.

Keeney staggered forward. Panic driven, he tripped on the leg, or arm, of a corpse. His free hand went to the wall, but slick with blood, it slid off, dropping him face first into a pile of dismembered remains. An ashen severed head rolled to face him, and Keeney let out a cry. There was something familiar in the aged lines of its mottled, pallid skin. He sucked in a shocked breath. It was General Marshall's head. Maggots slipped from the empty eye sockets and he scrabbled backwards in alarm. In his haste, Keeney removed the hand protecting his neck and an arc of blood hit the wall.

All the bodies were people he knew. Friends and family. He backed away in terror, the hammering of his heart his only companion. Again, he lost his footing, landing on his back. Panic took him, which jumped to another level when more scuffling sounded nearby. He froze. The only thing he dared move were his eyes. They found the shadowy corner and locked with the luminous blue eyes that were staring back. With a roar, something black came at him... and he screamed.

Keeney's cry woke him up. He blinked several times, coming down from the terror of another nightmare. He put a hand to his neck. It was wet and he looked at it, expecting to see blood, but the moisture was just sweat. It plastered his hair to his brow and stuck his shorts to his skin. The only part of his body that wasn't wet was the inside of his mouth, which was bone dry.

Paul Barrette rubbed his eyes and yawned as he sat up from his bed. 'Another nightmare?'

Keeney pulled the sheets back and sat on the edge of the bed. He cupped his head into his hands and remained silent. Barrette shuffled across and sat beside him, a look of concern crossing his face. 'Hey, it was just a dream.'

'Yeah,' Keeney said, his voice shaky. 'Just another dream.'

This dream, Keeney mused, was more vivid than the previous ones. He shuddered as the images continued to flash through his mind. Barrette was right. It was just a dream. Keeney let out his breath, composed himself, then left the bed and headed for the bathroom. While he relieved himself, he checked his neck in the mirror. Still lost in the dream's imagery, he didn't notice Barrette enter behind him.

'You soaked your bed again.'

Startled, he lost control of his aim and cursed. 'Jesus Christ, Paul. Don't sneak up on me like that.'

Barrette chuckled. 'You better clean that seat.'

'Fuck off,' he said, finishing.

'Don't flush.'

Barrette replaced him at the toilet. 'And don't forget the colonel wants to see you later.'

'Which one?'

'The asshole,' Barrette said, rocking on his feet. It was a routine he'd used ever since he was a boy. It helped him to pee after sleeping.

'That could be either,' Keeney said, further checking himself in the mirror.

'You know who I'm talking about.'

'What does he want?'

'He doesn't tell me shit,' he said, flushing.

'That's because you won't talk to him.' He took a washcloth and cleaned his face. 'Any chance you two might work things out?'

Barrette gave him a look.

Keeney put up his hands. 'I'm just asking. You might have noticed the world is fucking crazy. Maybe it's time to...'

'Don't even say. I told you what he did.'

'I'm sorry.'

Barrette came closer to him. 'Can we leave it?'

'Sure,' he said, as Barrette's fingers ran across his muscular chest. They remained eye to eye as Barrette traced his muscles, down to his navel. He made a light brush against the outside of Keeney's shorts. It had the desired effect. A guttural growl slipped from Keeney's throat as he pushed Barrette against the sink, kissing him hard. When they broke for air, they simultaneously pulled each other's shorts off. Barrette turned, and Keeney leant into his back, kissing the nape of his neck. The mixture of hot breath and light kisses against Barrette's neck made his knees weaken. The sensations caused him to shudder, and he grabbed the sink for support. Barrette smirked as Keeney's lascivious eyes reflected back at him through the mirror.

An hour later they lay on the beds they'd pushed together, both sweat covered, smoking a cigarette.

Paul Barrette turned on his side and stared at Keeney, who was lying with his feet crossed and one arm behind his head. His eyes found Barrette's as he finished his smoke. 'What?'

'Nothing,' he said, handing him the ashtray. 'It's just... I'm glad you're here.'

Keeney sat up. 'I can't take lying in this wet bed any longer.'

'You do sweat a lot.'

'It's not my fault they keep it so hot here,' Keeney said, sighing. 'Come on. Let's put these beds back, then hit the shower.'

After the beds were back to their customary places, Barrette grabbed clean underwear from the closet. He threw a pair at Keeney, who'd picked up the towels and then followed him out.

• • •

Colonel Bradley found Bill Marshall sleeping and let out an irritated breath. He tapped the general's foot and his eyes opened. With a yawn, Marshall threw his legs over the bed, and sat up.

'You're not going to like this,' Bradley said, handing him a sheet of paper. Marshall took and read it.

'Dawson *has* a brother?'

'Had,' Bradley corrected.

'Why wouldn't he just tell me that?'

'I don't know. There are many files like this. I was only interested in Bruce's, so I didn't bother with the others.'

'What does it mean?'

'I've got some ideas. Bill' – Bradley gave him a hard look – 'I think we should consider leaving.'

'And go where?'

'Outside.'

'With the monsters?'

'Monster out there, monsters in here.' He shrugged. 'Take your pick.'

The general frowned. 'You're serious?'

'Deadly. They're doing something terrible here, I can feel it.'

'I'll confront Ira.'

Colonel Bradley shook his head. 'I think that's unwise.'

'I outrank him, he'll do as I say.' Marshall's face turned pink as his anger rose.

The colonel kept his voice neutral. 'Bill, you're a general as long as he lets you be. What are you going to do if he refuses, hmm? If his men ignore your orders we're done for. All of us.'

Marshall wasn't ready to let it go. 'You don't know the men here won't follow my orders. They know who I am.'

'You're right. I don't. But I know we haven't got the evidence necessary to act.'

'And how would that help? Who would we present it to if we did? There's no oversight committee here. Ira runs this show under the authority of a presidential appointment.'

'Yes, he likes to rub that in your face, doesn't he? Listen, if you assert your authority and take command, what do you imagine will happen?'

'Best case? We'll be in a better place to discover what's going on.'

'And worst case, you'll likely disappear. But at least I'll have my suspicions confirmed.'

Marshall sank into his bed, defeated. 'Damned if we do...'

Colonel Bradley nodded. 'We should continue our recon. Keep up the pretence. With respect, General, it's time you got off that bloody bed and did something useful.'

Marshall threw him an angry look. 'Didn't we just establish that was pointless?'

'Not in the least. We need information. Being on friendly terms with all concerned might get us that.'

'You're right, of course,' Marshall said, his features softening.

Bradley allowed a smile to play across his face as he sat beside Marshall. 'All you need to do is keep the friendship going. Deepen it if you can. He respects you, as far as I can tell, and as long as you don't threaten him, I suspect he'll be more open with you than anyone else.'

Marshall then said, 'I almost forgot to tell you. Father Doyle said six people are missing, including his sister.'

'Sarah?'

'No one has seen them since yesterday.'

Colonel Bradley looked sideways at him.

'What?'

'I hate to bring this up, because I don't want to cause an argument, but I haven't seen John for a few days either, have you?'

Marshall's expression changed. 'No, and actually I've been thinking about...'

'How poorly you've been treating him?'

The general met his eyes but said nothing.

'Are you angry because he lied? Or because he lied to you?'

'Probably the latter,' Marshall admitted.

'You know I lie for a living?'

'It's not the same.'

'Why? Because my lies are often done for the benefits of others? You think I don't lie to benefit myself? There are things I've done that would shock you. You want to know what I think?'

'Not really.'

'I think you made him a substitute for your son.'

General Marshall looked hard. 'Don't you dare...'

Bradley held his ground. 'Don't deny it. It's written all over your face. He lied and you reacted...'

'You made your point,' Marshall snapped.

'I hope so.'

'Fine. I'll find him and we can talk.' Marshall compressed his lips as he stared at the paper. The silence made him look up. 'I said I'll talk to him.'

'Good man. Now, let's decide what we're going to do next.'

'I've asked Father Doyle to keep his ears open, but he could use some direction on that front. You're the intelligence officer, what do *you* think we should do?'

Colonel Bradley crossed his arms. 'I'll talk to Doyle while you visit Ira and play friends. Agreed?'

Marshall swung off his bed and stood. 'I'll go pay him a visit right now.'

• • •

General Marshall made a slow march through the corridor towards the main elevator and waited for the door to open. When it did, a grizzled-haired older man in a lab coat stood staring through small round spectacles at him. His expression seemed annoyed, but only for a moment, as Marshall stepped in beside him.

'You must be General Marshall?' His German accent was light, but noticeable.

'That's right, and I'm sorry, you are?'

'Grunner, General. Doctor Hans Grunner.'

Marshall extended a hand. Grunner ignored it. 'Where is it you are going to?'

'To see Colonel Baldwin.'

Grunner inserted and turned his key, then hit the top button. 'How are you settling in?'

'Very well. We're all grateful, especially for beds and hot meals.'

'The food here is awful,' Grunner remarked.

'At least we *have* food?'

Grunner grunted.

'What is it that you do here, Doctor?'

'I am chief scientist,' he replied.

'That must present its challenges?'

'As you say.'

Marshall studied him. Grunner wasn't much for small talk, he discovered. 'How is your work progressing?'

Grunner held a permanently etched frown on his little round face. 'What work are you referring to?'

'Biological research, isn't it? Counteracting those monsters' abilities?'

'No,' he said, 'to both questions.'

'I see. Then what are you doing instead?'

Grunner adjusted his glasses. 'Several things.'

'Throw me a bone, Doc,' Marshall said, with a chuckle.

'A bone?' Grunner held him under the focus of his suspicious beady eyes. 'Are you a *dog*, General?'

General Marshall stood lost for words. Before he could form a reply, the door opened and Grunner gestured. 'Your floor, I think?'

'It would appear so. Well,' he said, stepping out, 'it was a pleasure, Doctor.'

'No doubt.'

Grunner kept his unblinking eyes trained on him until the doors closed. General Marshall blew out his cheeks and shook his head as he walked away.

When Marshall reached the stairs that led to the command centre, he checked his uniform. Satisfied, he ascended and entered. A few men saluted as he passed. A captain he hadn't met before greeted him.

'Is there something I can do for you, General?' Captain Paul Barrette asked.

'I was looking for Colonel Baldwin. Is he around?'

'I'm sorry, sir. The colonel is in a meeting. You can wait if you like or I'll have someone let you know when he's free?'

'I'll wait.'

'Would you like a coffee, sir?'

'Yes, black and sweet.' He spotted Lieutenant Dawson seated with headphones on and smiled. 'Excuse me.'

Marshall tapped his shoulder.

'Oh, hello, General.' He removed the headphones and

adjusted a knob on his screen.

'Anything happening?'

Dawson shook his head. 'It's daylight. We won't get much activity, unless more people come.'

'But doesn't the radar only show metallic objects?'

Dawson shook his head. 'It'll show anything solid, sir.'

Marshall regarded the screen. 'I'm not up on this new stuff, how does it work?'

'It's simple, really. Radio waves go out from an antenna in pulses and reflect off anything they hit. By timing them on this scope, I can determine their range and direction.'

'Amazing. It can even see those shadow things?'

'Yes, even though they hide in shadows, they still have mass.'

'Do they?' he said, his smile broad.

Captain Barrette returned with a cup of coffee and smiled as Marshall thanked him. Marshall sat next to Dawson and cradled the cup as the young man gave an animated explanation about the improvements of radar.

'General,' Colonel Baldwin said, coming forward to meet him. 'So sorry to keep you.'

Marshall stood. 'Not a problem. I kept Lieutenant Dawson busy.'

Colonel Baldwin smiled. 'Shall we go to my office?'

Marshall followed. When they entered, Baldwin closed the door. 'Sorry, I've been a poor host.'

'You're a busy man, I understand completely.'

'Better than anyone else here,' Baldwin said, as he sat in the seat next to him. 'What can I do for you?'

'I've come across some minor issues. I don't think they need your direct intervention, but because of my rank, if I say something without talking to you first, it might appear as though I'm undermining you.'

'I appreciate that, Bill. What's on your mind?'

'I visited the civilian floor and Father Doyle raised some concerns.'

'Yes, he's quite the vocal sort. Go on.'

'They're just not used to how we do things. They're used to more freedom with food and so on.'

Baldwin nodded. 'But the world isn't free anymore, is it? It's full of monsters who took our way of life away. Everyone needs to adapt.'

'I agree. But perhaps I could recommend a compromise?'

'By all means.'

'There are several chefs within the civilian populations and they want to work. Couldn't you put them into the kitchens? Doyle asked for more variety, I can't help thinking if they have their own chefs, they'll feel less under military scrutiny.'

'That's actually an excellent suggestion,' Baldwin said. 'I've been looking at ways of using the civilians to run their own affairs.'

Marshall smiled. 'They'll appreciate it.'

'But it can't be a free-for-all. We have to manage our limited resources.'

'There's a way you can manage that without burdening your staff.'

Baldwin frowned. 'How?'

'You have law enforcement down there with nothing to do. Give them control of managing security. You can cut a lot of your own personnel, freeing them for other tasks. One officer can lead it, that way you'll still keep control.'

Colonel Baldwin nodded. 'Agreed. Would you like to tell them?'

Marshall shook his head. 'I think it should come from one of the duty officers. Make it appear as though it's a routine review. You have a system and it works. If they think it came through me, they'll always be looking to buck that system.'

'Bill,' Baldwin said, leaning forward. 'Having someone to talk with that understands bigger issues is a relief.'

'I'm here for anything you need, Ira. There is one other thing. It seems a few people are missing.'

Baldwin sank back into his chair. 'I've been dealing with that all morning.'

'One of them is Father Doyle's sister, Sarah. He's worried, and frankly, so am I.'

'I got the report first thing. We scheduled four groups to gather supplies. One hasn't returned. I despatched a search party as soon as they briefed me.'

Marshall grimaced. 'Does this happen often?'

'No, but it's dangerous out there. Sometimes people don't come back.'

'Yes, I know, but it's still a blow,' Marshall said, staring into his coffee.

'It's a bigger blow than you think. All gathering parties are one to one. There's twelve people missing, you understand?'

Marshall nodded. 'Yes, I see, I'm sorry.'

'We haven't given up hope of finding them.'

Marshall finished his coffee. 'That's something.'

'Would you mind explaining this to Doyle?'

Marshall nodded.

'I appreciate it.'

'Is John around?'

Colonel Baldwin's eyes narrowed ever so slightly. 'He's working on an assignment, why?'

'There's something I need to discuss with him.' Marshall met his gaze. 'Is it an issue?'

'He's not your man anymore, General. You made that very clear when you assigned him to me. If it's a military matter, then I respectfully request that all such conversations come through me first.'

Marshall gave a tight smile. 'It's nothing like that. It's Braders' birthday coming up, John had some ideas. But it can wait until he finishes whatever it is you've assigned him.'

Baldwin relaxed. 'I'm sorry. I shouldn't have jumped to conclusions. I will let him know, of course. Was there anything else?'

General Marshall stood. 'That's it. I'll talk with Doyle and if you hear anything?'

'I'll let you know.'

Marshall left, closing the door behind him.

CHAPTER SIX

Father David Doyle finished his sermon. When the last parishioner had left, he removed his ecclesiastical vestments and hung them on their customary hook. The lesson he'd delivered on tolerance seemed to go over well, but the distraction wasn't enough to keep him from thinking about Sarah. The door opened and General Marshall came down the aisle. Doyle smiled, but he read something in his face, and that smile fell.

'This isn't a bad time, is it, David?'

He shook his head. 'There's news, then?'

'Why don't we have a seat?'

Father Doyle gestured and they sat. Marshall noticed Doyle's tight posture.

'I take it the news you have, isn't good?'

'It's not great,' Marshall replied. 'Sarah was with one of four groups on a resource gathering trip. Hers didn't return.'

Father Doyle sagged. 'She's dead, isn't she?'

'We don't know that. There's a team out there now, looking for them. I know it's hard but try to keep positive. There could be many reasons why they didn't return.'

'But the likelihood is, she's dead?'

Marshall rubbed his face. 'It is a possibility.'

'I see. Thank you for being frank about it.'

'Colonel Baldwin hasn't given up and neither have I.'

'I will pray for strength,' he said.

'Regarding the issues of food, a solution is being looked at.'

Father Doyle smiled. 'That's something. Thank you, Bill.'

General Marshall was about to say more when they heard yelling. They both went to the door and Marshall opened it. A small crowd formed around two men engaged in a fierce fight. A few tried to break it up, but the brawl pushed them back into the crowd.

'Stay here, Father.'

Marshall pushed through the crowd just as two sizeable men emerged ahead of him. They pulled the two apart. It didn't stop them kicking and screaming, and the strain it took to restrain them was clear. Others interceded and they pinned one down, who continued to yell and buck. It almost dislodged the men holding him but Marshall added his own weight and the man finally stopped.

'What was that about?' Marshall asked.

'You got me, Captain,' the man who held him said.

'General,' Marshall replied.

'Oh, right. Sorry.'

Marshall looked over as the other combatant was being subdued. The level of violence and anger being displayed by both men seemed unusual. He continued to kick and scream as the two men finally shoved him down.

Four MPs dispersed the crowed. A sergeant came forward. 'General?'

He stood and brushed himself down. 'We're good.'

The MPs hauled the man up. His fight had gone and he looked confused. 'What happened?'

'Why were you fighting?' Marshall asked.

'Fighting?' His frown deepened. 'I don't remember fighting anyone.'

'Come on,' the MP said. 'Let's see if a few hours in detention will loosen your tongue.' They led him away.

General Marshall approached the other who was pinned under two sets of knees. The gruff-looking men were each pulling an arm back, and both were panting. Their hold on him eased as MPs came beside them. Marshall recognised their control technique.

'You're both ex-police?'

'We're still police,' the larger corrected, with a scowl.

'I apologise. Can you lift him please?'

When they hauled him up, it wasn't with kindness or care.

'Take it easy,' Marshall's stern tone caught their attention. 'He's just a kid.'

The first thing that struck Marshall, when the boy was lifted up, was his eyes. They were black. It was as though each pupil had expanded over the iris. He was young, mid to late teens, and he didn't blink. His struggling came in sporadic bursts. Marshall waved a hand across his eyes, but he didn't respond.

'What's wrong with him?' an MP asked.

'I don't know.' Marshall examined him closer. 'Does anyone know his name?'

'It's Jake Matthews,' a boy said, pushing through those crowded. His face full of worry. 'He's my brother.'

Marshall knelt. 'What's your name, son?'

'Ciaran Matthews, sir.' He wiped his nose with the back of his hand. He couldn't have been any older than eight or nine.

'A good Irish name,' Marshall said, smiling. 'Do you know why your brother was fighting?'

He shook his head. 'It's not like him, sir. He don't fight with no one.'

The general ruffled his shaggy hair, then stood and turned to the older boy. He called his name, but Jake didn't respond. Marshall then shook him by the shoulders. Jake's head made a slow, unnatural tilt. His blacked eyes stared through him. The general noticed Jake still hadn't blinked.

'He's awake but not aware.'

Marshall pinched the skin on Jake's arm hard. He jolted and the blackness over his irises retracted. Jake's eyes returned to a normal-looking blue grey, along with his awareness. Jake's expression took on a mixture of panic and pain.

'Hey, fuck...,' he yelled. 'Get off, you're hurting me.'

Marshall took him by the shoulders and the officers released their hold.

'It's okay. We're not going to hurt you.' Jake's eyes rolled into this head and he sagged into Marshall's arms. Marshall lowered him to the ground. 'Get a stretcher,' Marshall yelled to the MPs. 'We'll take him straight to the infirmary.'

They scrambled away.

General Marshall felt a tap on his shoulder and he turned to find Ciaran's wide eyes staring at him.

'Is he dead?' The colour drained from his face and his lip wobbled. His eyes brimmed with tears.

Marshall took him by the arms. 'No, no.' He offered a reassuring smile. 'Jake's just a little tired. He'll be fine after a rest, but we'll take him to the doctor to make sure. Where are your parents?'

'They died.' Ciaran's anguish broke as he burst into tears. Instinct fuelled the old general's response and he grabbed the little boy into a hug.

'I'm sorry, don't cry. Everything will be okay.'

Ciaran's sobs slowed into hiccups. Marshall felt relief as Father Doyle came and took the boy from him.

'Come on, let's get some ice cream.'

Marshall mouthed him a *thank you* as Father Doyle led the boy away.

When the MPs arrived with the stretcher, they lifted Jake and took him to the infirmary.

• • •

Inside their yellow isolation suits four scientists, under Doctor Grunner's direction, sealed the last corpse into a heavy clear body bag and dropped it into a cart. With care, they wheeled that cart to the opposite side of the room.

'Now,' Grunner said, 'secure the sample.'

They nodded and turned their attention to the thick, black tar-like mass rolled into a ball in one corner of the lab.

'Careful,' Grunner cautioned. 'Bring the container closer.'

Two of them pushed the drum nearer and unlocked it, while the other two took their shovels and stood ready to lift the sample in. When they got close, Grunner thought he saw it retract. They paused, looking back for instructions.

The German seemed irritated. 'We are ready, yes?'

The smaller of the four looked amongst them. She said, 'We're ready, Doctor.'

Grunner then gave a dismissive wave and backed up to the door.

'Be quick,' he commanded.

They pushed the shovels under. When it sat between them, they made a slow coordinated lift as the drum was positioned underneath. They nodded to each other and tipped their shovels. The sample dropped inside with a wet thud, and they stepped away, placing the shovels onto a bench.

Grunner let out his breath. 'Seal it.'

The heavy lid came down and they each flipped up a large screw, fastening them with a heavy bolt. They fumbled with thick gloves on and were sweating inside their suits. It ran into their eyes. All they could do was shake their heads to clear their vision. It didn't work. After an agonizing number of minutes went by, they finished. Doctor Grunner observed them relax. Two pushed the drum towards the walk-in freezer. While one unlocked and pulled open the door, the others attempted to push the drum over the threshold.

It wouldn't go over.

One of them looked down and cursed. 'We'll need to give it a good shove.'

They positioned to manoeuvre it and then stopped. A heavy thud came from inside the drum.

Doctor Grunner made a slight tilt to his head. 'What was that?'

Before they could answer, another thump came. It was stronger than the first. The force made the drum jolt.

Grunner's eyes widened. 'Push it in, quickly.'

Another jolt heaved the drum sideways. The four scientists lost their hold. Grunner saw one lower his head and run a hand over the drum's exterior. When the next thump came, a bulge appeared in its metal surface and he fell back. Doctor Evelyn Parker turned, but Grunner was no longer there.

'Get it inside,' Evelyn said, cursing. They strained as they pushed, but the wheels kept hitting the threshold and wouldn't go over. 'We need to lift it.'

They attempted that but the surface was too smooth. There was nothing to grip. It thudded and this time a larger bulge appeared, the force knocking the drum from their control. It rolled away, but one of them caught it and pushed it back.

'Two of you get down and lift. Carl, push with me. On three... ready?'

'One.'

The two men took hold.

'Two.'

Gritting their teeth, they took the strain.

'Three.'

In coordination they lifted and pulled. The drum made it over the threshold and inside the freezer, and they wheeled it to a cage, securing it with restraining ties. A few minutes later, they'd locked it in place and began packing bags of ice around the drum, until it was no longer visible.

It thudded again.

A bag dislodged.

Evelyn pulled at them. 'It's secure enough. Let's go.'

She turned and they followed her. When they reached the door, they heard and felt a bigger thud, followed by an exploding crash. The floor was awash with skidding, spinning, ice-cubes. They moved to the drum, but she stopped them and pointed to the gaping hole in its side.

'Out!' she yelled.

They ran.

Carl fell with a cry of surprise. A black tendril had tightened around his ankle. Evelyn turned to help but slipped on the ice and landed on her back next to him. Before she could get up, Carl screamed as he was wrenched back in. The others scrambled out towards the lab.

'Close the fucking door,' a male panicked voiced yelled.

'No, wait. We can't leave, we have to help Carl,' she admonished.

One of them grabbed her arm and yanked her so hard, she fell onto the floor. The other then slammed the door shut.

Evelyn scrambled up, attempting to stop them, but they shoved her aside.

'Open the door. Now,' she yelled.

They ignored her.

When they'd finished securing it, they ran.

Evelyn cursed, but then Carl appeared against the door's small window. She watched as he banged his fists against it. His screams unheard through the thick door and isolation suit. She scrabbled to open it, but they'd removed the handle and taken it with them.

No matter what she did, Evelyn couldn't open it.

'Someone, please, help me.'

Her frustration came in curses while she watched in helpless agony, as Carl continued to scream and thump against the inside window. The look in Carl's eyes turned to panic, as he read the terror in hers, when she backed away.

Carl turned. A black mass was rising behind him. He returned to hammering, pleading, begging. The terror on his face made her cry.

Time froze. Their eyes locked.

Evelyn jumped as something pulled him away.

The window was empty.

Evelyn peered into the gloom. As she got close, Carl hit the window with a bang. She jumped. Carl's silent screams looked different. The action was distorting his face. His eyes were bulged and his tongue poked out unnaturally. The strain on his face went beyond fear.

Carl's mouth turned red and blood seeped from his nostrils, as his eyes haemorrhaged. His face was then obscured as blood covered the inside of the isolation mask. The monster lifted him into the air. His arms flailed. It looked to Evelyn as if Carl was trying to reach behind him. Then both his arms shot out, and his entire body quivered. The isolation suit went taut as his chest thrust forward. Evelyn imagined she heard Carl's scream as his chest burst outward, splattering blood everywhere, exposing smashed ribs and a still beating heart.

He remained dangling, his arms and legs giving spas-modic twitches. In frozen horror she watched his heart give its last few beats as it exsanguinated. The black monstrous mass then slowly enveloped what remained.

Evelyn let out an agonised cry as someone pulled her away.

• • •

General Marshall entered the infirmary as the MPs trans-ferred Jake from the stretcher to a bed. They left as the nurse began her preliminary observations. Marshall gave a brief report of the incident to Doctor Husk. In the waiting room, Marshall picked up an old automobile magazine and began flicking through. It wasn't long before Doctor Husk returned.

'Thanks for waiting,' she said.

He put down the magazine as she sat beside him.

'How is he?'

'Still unconscious. His vitals are normal. We can't find anything to account for his condition.'

'Did you look at his eyes?'

Her expression remained neutral. 'There wasn't anything out of the ordinary. Nothing to account for what you saw. There's no immediate cause for why he remains unconscious. For now, he's stable. We'll wait for the blood work to come back before we do anything else.'

Marshall nodded. 'How long will that take?'

'Not long. We'll move him to an isolation room and keep him under observation. Once he's awake, we'll do a physical. I've made a report, but Colonel Baldwin is dealing with some-thing and he said to liaise with you.'

'He has a young brother. I don't think they have any family.'

'Ciaran? I know him. They lost their parents. He can stay here if he wants to.'

'Thank you, Doctor.'

'Kate, General.'

She had a soft, pleasant voice and a charming bedside manner. Her wide smile seemed genuine. He understood why Bradley enjoyed her company. He thought for a moment, then tested the waters. 'Kate, can I ask you something?'

'Of course,' she replied.

'In confidence?'

'What's on your mind.'

'Have you noticed anything... odd going on?'

Husk's brow turned to a slight frown as she responded. 'You'd need to define odd.'

'I can't. I haven't been here long enough to know what might seem odd to you. But you have. Have you or your staff experienced any out of the ordinary situations?'

She was thoughtful. 'I can give you a generalisation since I won't breach patient confidentiality. Aside from some behavioural changes and a marginal increase in cold and flu cases, I'd say, no, not really.'

'Behavioural changes?'

'A few cases of increased aggression, typical of today's situation. Depression, emotional issues. These things are normal in environments of isolation. Everyone is dealing with loss, despair, loneliness, uncertainty. People aren't used to being locked up together for extended periods, and it's worse when there's no end in sight.'

'That's true.'

She shrugged. 'Sometimes we need to let off a little steam. It's normal. But no one is immune. We've lost our homes, our families, everything we held dear. Something as basic as a routine. Getting up, going for coffee before work... actually being able to *leave* work,' she sighed. 'You were a member of the joint chiefs. Yet here you are rubbing shoulders with ordinary people. Knowing just as much as they do about the state of things on the surface. Aren't you feeling the effects of that?'

'Yes.' Her straightforwardness was refreshing. 'A lot more than I care to admit.'

'None of us signed up for this.' Her soft expression hardened a little. 'I didn't choose the constant scrutiny of maniacal scientists or their inflexible military masters, who think just because they have a rank, they somehow know what's best for everyone when they don't. No offence.'

'None taken.'

'Sorry. There, you see? I'm affected too. Do you have a family, Bill?'

'A son, he's serving in Turkey.'

She touched his shoulder. 'We all have people we're mourning for.'

'I'm not mourning him,' he replied, a little gruffer than he'd meant to. 'I'm choosing to believe he's alive. Why not, I am?'

She shook her head. 'I didn't mean mourning his *life*. I mean the loss of contact. Isn't that worse? It is for me. My parents, my sister? I have no idea if they're alive or dead. And actually, knowing they were dead would be a little better than this uncertainty. At least I could grieve and move on.'

He stared at the floor through unfocused eyes and she gave a sympathetic rub to his shoulder.

'I'll have Ciaran brought to stay with Jake,' she said. 'And if there's any change, I'll have someone get you.'

They stood. 'Thank you, Kate.'

She tilted her head. 'I'm curious about one thing,' she said. 'Why add a confidential caveat to our discussion?'

'Testing the waters,' he replied.

She narrowed her eyes. 'Is there something else going on?'

He shrugged. 'It's probably nothing.'

'Oh no you don't,' she said. 'You're investigating this place, aren't you?'

'I'm taking an interest.'

Doctor Husk chewed her lip, then her features softened and she found his eyes. 'Can I trust you, Bill?'

'Do you trust Colonel Bradley?'

Kate's expression changed. 'I hardly know him.'

'But well enough to... you know?'

Her face turned a shade of pink. 'That's none of your business.'

'You know a lot more than you're letting on. If you trust Braders then you can trust me.'

'You shouldn't pay any attention to what he's been telling you.'

'I didn't mean to offend. I can see I was wrong to bring it up, forgive me.'

Marshall made a move to leave.

'Wait,' Husk said, much louder than she'd meant. 'Sorry. You're not wrong.'

'Something piqued your interest, didn't it?'

'Something,' she repeated. 'Bill, I want to trust you. I just need to know I can.'

'Wise,' Marshall remarked. 'What can I do to gain that trust?'

'I'll think about it. In the meantime, there are some files you should look at. I'll bring them to you when my shift ends.'

CHAPTER SEVEN

Two hours later General Marshall ran the water and waited for it to get hot. After testing it, he cupped his hands and leant over the sink and splashed a little onto his face. The warmth was soothing, but it didn't invigorate him as he'd hoped. As he looked up at the mirror, Marshall caught his reflection glaring back. The coldness of his aged eyes annoyed him and he looked away. The general grabbed a towel from the bar and dabbed his face dry, hoping the eyes of the man he hardly recognised looking back would seem kinder. They didn't.

'When did I get so old?'

A light tap pulled him from his reverie. 'Come in.'

The door opened and with a practiced smile he beckoned Kate Husk in. She closed the door behind her and came towards a table.

'I'm not disturbing you, am I?'

Marshall hung up the towel. 'No. How's Jake doing?'

Husk stuffed her free hand into her lab coat. The other gripped a manila file close to her breast. 'He's still unconscious. I'm concerned, honestly.'

'Is he in any danger?'

She shook her head. 'Not physically, at least not that I can tell. We'll have a clearer understanding when the test results come back. For now, he's just asleep. It's perplexing. Ciaran is with him. When I left, he was reading Jake a story. Oh, your Father Doyle said he'd come by and check on the boys later.

I'm happy he's taken an interest in their well-being.'

'Me too. David could use a distraction.'

'Why?'

'His sister went missing.'

Marshall noted Husk's pained expression as she dropped the file on the table. But when she didn't articulate whatever was on her mind, he gestured to a seat and they sat next to each other.

General Marshall turned the file, but she placed a hand on it before he could open the cover.

'General, Bill, you must understand I'm taking an enormous risk showing you this.'

'I appreciate it. I know I haven't earned your trust, but I promise whatever is in here will stay between the three of us.'

'Three?' He read the concern in her eyes.

'Yes. Colonel Bradley. He's my partner and friend. It's full disclosure or none.' He tapped the file a few times, then crossed his arms. 'You decide.'

She regarded him for a moment. The corner of her mouth lifted. 'You have an unwavering faith in a man you hardly know.'

Marshall remained impassive. 'I know him well enough. Colonel Bradley is dependable and righteous. We've been through a lot together.'

'Military comradery, is that it?'

He shook his head. 'Have you been outside lately?'

Her uncertain look answered his question.

'You don't understand what we've been through, Kate.' His eyes dropped. 'What we've seen, what we've escaped.' When he lifted them, she saw the resolve set there.

'I didn't mean to suggest otherwise, I'm sorry.'

He nodded. 'I know his methods can seem a little unsavoury.'

Husk laughed. 'A little?'

'Okay, a lot then. But I know I can rely on him. My hope is the same can be said of you.'

Doctor Husk nodded. 'I've been in this facility a while now. I've seen my share of senior officials, government stooges, politicians. But you're not like any general I've met.'

'Good,' he said, and turned to the file.

'It wasn't a compliment.'

Marshall looked back at her. 'Self-expression doesn't seem to be a problem for you.'

With a slight shrug she said, 'I work in a field dominated by men. Men who justify their superiority by perpetuating the view that my medical doctorate, one I spent just as long attaining, is somehow worth less than theirs. Self-expression is self-preservation.'

'Fair point.'

'Look, General...'

'Bill, Kate. I like the people I work with to have strength of character. As long as they do a good job, I don't regard gender as an obstacle.'

'Really,' Husk said, drawing out the word. 'And how many female officers, aside from low-ranking secretaries, are in your army?'

Marshall put up a hand. 'You're right. But it's not something I have any control over and you know it.'

'Until they made you head of the army?'

'I suppose we could spend our time debating the subject of political misogyny but what would be the point? We can't be sure we even have a system of government. Going forward is all that matters. Can we agree on that?'

'Like I said before, you're not like any general I've ever met.'

'And while you don't consider that a compliment,' he said, with a chuckle, 'I really do. Now, can we move on?'

'Yes, I think so.'

'Good. Now, about this file.'

'Before you look inside...'

The door opened, interrupting her. Colonel Bradley walked in and eyed them with a smile. He closed the door.

'Private party?'

'No,' Marshall said, kicking out a chair. Bradley straddled it and leant onto its back.

Kate Husk crossed her arms. 'Did you find what you were looking for in the archives?'

Bradley raised an eyebrow. When he spoke, there was a touch of surprise in his voice. 'And I thought I was the player here?'

She held out a hand and he dropped her keys into it. Husk pocketed them and turned back to the file. 'Since I have some idea of what you wish to discuss, why don't you tell me what you know and I'll see if I can fill in any blanks?'

Colonel Bradley pulled out a cigarette and lit it. 'How do we know you're not gathering information for Colonel Baldwin?'

'You don't.' She met his gaze. 'You'll just have to trust me, won't you?'

'It's your call, Bill,' Bradley said, exhaling a cloud of smoke.

'There are odd things happening,' Marshall said. 'Taken in isolation they might be the result of an over-active imagination. Let me give you an example. Do you know Lieutenant Bruce Dawson?'

She nodded. 'I've treated him a few times.'

'Can you tell me what for?'

'No.' The finality of her answer made Marshall frown.

Colonel Bradley leant forward. 'Has he had a mental breakdown recently?'

Husk clucked her tongue. 'What part of *no* did I not make clear, Charlie?'

'Come on, Kate.'

Doctor Husk met his hard eyes with steel of her own. 'Listen, both of you. I have no issue breaking the secrecy clause I signed, but I won't violate patient confidentiality.'

Colonel Bradley had more to say, but Marshall cut him off. 'I respect your ethics, Kate. Let's turn to the facility. Aside from biochemical research, do you know what they're doing on level three?'

Husk avoided Bradley's eyes and shook her head. 'Whatever it is, requires a level of clearance beyond anything I have.'

Bradley let his irritation go. 'Is it connected to the disappearances we've talked about?'

'I can't be sure, but I suspect so,' she said, grateful that his look had softened, 'and they're becoming frequent.'

Marshall rubbed his chin. 'We know of at least twelve

missing people. Ira told me they were lost gathering supplies.'

Husk didn't hide her scepticism. 'There are silos of supplies on the base. We could survive for decades on the resources we have. Colonel Baldwin isn't sending anyone on supply runs.'

'How do you know?' Marshall asked.

'Because our friendly colonel has a protocol for everything. Health checks before and after excursion off the base. It all stopped a week before you arrived.'

Marshall frowned. 'So why would he tell me they're continuing?'

'It's obvious, isn't it?' Bradley said.

'Not to me,' Marshall replied.

'Maybe to explain away any disappearances?' Husk answered.

'Exactly,' Bradley said, 'and with no accountability he can do just that.' He sat in thought for some time, then nodded. 'I've been doing some checking, and I'm reasonably sure human experimentations are being conducted on level three.'

Marshall and Husk both gasped.

'I can't believe Ira would allow that,' Marshall replied. The way his expression changed showed how appalled he was at the suggestion.

Bradley met his gaze. 'He has a Nazi doctor working for him.'

'A German doctor,' Husk corrected. 'There's no reason to suspect he's a Nazi.'

'There's every reason,' Bradley countered hotly. 'Kate, just before we found ourselves in this situation, when we had actual jobs, both Bill and I received regular intelligence reports from our allies. The Soviets liberated a facility in Poland. They thought it was a POW camp, but what they found was something far worse. Inside were thousands of people from all nations in terrible physical condition. The Germans evacuated in a hurry. In their haste they left many incriminating documents behind. Not long after the Soviets discovered it, the full extent of the horrors surfaced. We now know it was an extermination camp and it seems there are more like it. Kate, there were piles of bodies. Men, women, and children. The

Soviets couldn't give an accurate count. Upwards of a million, that's their official number. Although, more conservative elements put it far lower. The sad truth is we might never know.'

Husk couldn't hide her incredulity. 'How could anyone be so... inhumane?'

'With its discovery, the fullness of the Nazi's agenda became clear,' Marshall added. 'I received regular briefings, as did the president, from the heads of the Allied intelligence service. John and I were returning from one when whatever happened to the world happened.'

Husk sat quietly. Shock etched on her face. 'Millions of people,' she breathed. 'And you think there are more of these camps?'

Colonel Bradley's expression remained grim. 'We *know* there are more.'

'Doctor Grunner is an arrogant man, but I hadn't pegged him as a mass murderer,' Husk said, rubbing at her forehead.

Bradley touched her hand. 'I'm sorry if we've upset you.'

She responded to his light touch with a smile.

'But how does this relate to Grunner being a Nazi?' Marshall asked.

Colonel Bradley's contemplative expression suggested he was wrestling with an answer. His face smoothed out once he'd organised his thoughts.

'I know he's a Nazi,' Bradley said. 'Listen, both of you. I was the British liaison when the Americans met with the Soviets. Doctor Hans Grunner isn't his name. It's Albert Hans Grunner-Fischer. He's an ex-SS doctor of medicine, anthropology, and eugenics. Under interrogation he bartered for his life, and that of his brother, Heinz, the little weasel that followed with him. The information they gave up led to the capture of several prominent members of the SS. I *know* Grunner was complicit in human experimentation, but we couldn't prove it. There were no documents pertaining to Grunner or Heinz, which was convenient. Anyway, despite huge opposition, the U.S. government agreed to take him. They gave Grunner and Heinz immunity from prosecution, a change of identity, and here they are.'

Bradley ground his teeth for a moment. 'Perhaps now you can understand why my perspective is different? Whatever is happening here, I guarantee you Grunner *is* behind it. Colonel Ira Baldwin is also complicit.'

Bradley read the sceptical look on General Marshall's face. 'I didn't know any of that, so maybe Baldwin doesn't either?'

Colonel Bradley shrugged. 'All right, let's say that's true. Let's imagine he has no knowledge of Grunner's background. Baldwin is still covering up disappearances, isn't he? That alone makes him a suspect.'

'Fair point. He lied directly about that.'

Bradley stood and stretched out his back. 'What's in the file?'

'It's a list of people I've treated in the infirmary over the last seven months. Dates, clinical observations, treatments, and so on,' Husk said.

'Forgive my confusion,' Marshall said, a slight frown creasing his brow. 'A moment ago, you were fierce with your declaration on patient confidentiality.'

'And believe me I stick to my principles. But in this case, I don't believe I'm in danger of violating them.'

'Why?' Bradley asked.

She pulled a number of papers out and flicked through. 'It's my handwriting. The problem is I don't recall having written it and I don't know who most of these people are. There are three names in here that might interest you though.'

Marshall frowned. 'Whose?'

She turned the page towards him. 'Yours, Charlie's, and a Captain John Keeney.'

• • •

Doctor Grunner stood with his arms crossed as he stared through the small window at the blackened mass on the opposite side. He rubbed his index finger against his bottom lip in thought. With the lab freezer sealed, and the bodies removed, he continued his observations uninterrupted. The monstrous black mass hadn't moved at all. A noise alerted him and he turned. From the doorway, Colonel Baldwin ran his eyes around the lab.

'Grunner?'

Doctor Grunner gestured him in. 'It is safe.'

'Safe seems to have two distinct definitions. Yours and mine.'

The German chuckled. 'Be assured I would not be here if I thought my life was in *any* danger.'

'That's true enough.'

Grunner turned back to the window as Colonel Baldwin came alongside.

'It is most remarkable,' the German said. Baldwin followed his eyes to the window.

'What's remarkable to me, Doctor, is that not twenty minutes ago a man you thought highly of was killed, and yet you don't seem upset about it.'

'Highly?' Grunner shook his head. 'Doctor Morgan is dead. I see no reason to morn. It won't bring him back.'

'How cold.'

'There is no place for emotion or sentiment in science. We embarked on this project knowing we may cause harm to a few, to save many.'

'I was hoping the precautions we put in place would mitigate against... this,' he sighed. 'Where are we now?'

Grunner smiled. It was a horrible smile. 'A stage further, I think.'

Baldwin stared through the glass at the creature beyond. 'It's grown.'

'The sample's mass increased after it absorbed Doctor Morgan. I cannot say for certain by how much, but from a visual inspection it would appear to be, perhaps, a thirty percent increase.'

'Did it consume him?'

Doctor Grunner rubbed his lip again. 'I'm not sure consumed is correct. Assimilated or absorbed would be more accurate.'

'You said in earlier tests, you thought the sample could mimic the form of the subject.'

'And now we have conclusive proof that is so.'

'I'd have preferred a less horrific way of discovering it.'

Doctor Grunner turned his beady eyes on him. 'Are you getting cold feet, Colonel?'

Baldwin sighed. 'I'm just concerned we're going down the wrong path, that's all. Animals were one thing, but we're moving into dangerous territory with this.'

'Animals are of no use to me,' Grunner said, nonchalantly. 'We are passed these longwinded data-gathering exercises. I need to see its growth. I must understand how it converts tissue and organic matter into its own structure. These explanations can only come from the victims, as they are consumed. How will a mouse help with that?'

'That's monstrous.'

He shrugged. 'It's science. Do not forget, your president has given his seal of approval. Any actions taken are on his shoulders. He has freed you of all moral implications. We must find a cure for this virus. And we are even closer now. And besides,' Grunner said, poking him in the chest. 'This was an accident. There is nothing to be done to save Doctor Morgan. We will not waste this opportunity with sentiment.'

Baldwin stared at him. 'What about the effect Morgan's death might have on the others?'

Grunner shrugged. 'I will need a replacement.'

Baldwin closed his eyes. Grunner regarded him. 'The work is all that matters, Colonel. Keep your emotions and weak stomach under control.'

'Remember who you're talking to,' Baldwin said, pointing at finger him. 'This is my facility. I can pull the plug anytime I choose.'

Doctor Grunner smiled. 'Good. This is the man I prefer. Now let us leave and decide our next steps.' He gestured to the door. Baldwin gave a brief look at the thing standing in the freezer, then followed him out.

When they stepped out of the lab and into the corridor, Baldwin asked, 'What of Doctor Parker?'

Grunner frowned. 'What of her?'

'How is she dealing with the loss of her colleague?'

'Ah,' he shrugged. 'Do not concern yourself. She is under sedation.'

'She'll be traumatised when she comes out. They were close, I understand?'

Grunner shook his head. 'That is not true.'

'They weren't close?'

'No, the trauma you describe. I suspect she'll have a brief memory of it only.'

'I don't understand.'

Grunner gave him that thin smile. 'It appears that Doctor Parker has been experimenting with psychotropic drugs in her free time.'

'Is that true?'

Grunner's expression remained neutral. 'It will be,' he said.

Baldwin opened his mouth, but something in the way Grunner was staring down the corridor made him stop. 'What?'

Grunner's eyes narrowed. 'We should talk elsewhere. I think we have been overheard.'

Baldwin took a quick look in both directions. 'There's no one here, Hans. Are you sure you aren't being a little paranoid?'

'It's not paranoia, if it's true.'

● ● ●

Jake thrashed in his bed, his head going side to side. Ciaran jumped from his seat and approached, holding his dirty teddy bear to his chest. The attending nurse looked up as Ciaran came to his brother's bedside. She read his fear and smiled.

'Don't look so worried. He's just having a bad dream.'

Ciaran held his bear a little tighter.

Jake screamed as his eyes flicked open. Drenched in sweat and breathing fast, Jake shook as he focused on the room and onto the nurse who smiled at him.

'Jake, it's okay, you're safe.'

Jake shook his head and rubbed his eyes. 'Where am I?'

The door opened and Doctor Husk approached. 'Ah, you're awake.' She winked at Ciaran who was standing close by.

'How are you feeling?'

'Confused,' he croaked. 'Thirsty.'

'I'll get some water,' the nurse said.

Doctor Husk sat on the edge of his bed as Jake rubbed his eyes. 'Did I do something bad?'

'What do you remember?'

He pushed himself up and grimaced. The bed was wet. Jake looked under the sheet and then back up at her. 'Nothing. I was having dinner, then... I woke up. Why am I in a hospital?'

'You were in a fight. You've been asleep for a while.'

'I had bad dreams.'

Husk put her hand on his forehead. 'Well, you're hot.' She pulled out her thermometer and put it under his tongue. After a while she took it out. 'Slight fever. Nothing to worry about.'

The nurse returned with a glass of water, a sandwich, and a small bowl of canned mixed fruit. He picked up the water and drank.

She took his pulse. 'That's all good. How are you feeling now?'

'Much better,' he said, tucking into the sandwich.

There was a shuffle behind and Husk turned. Ciaran was still standing there.

'Do I have to stay here?' Jake asked.

Doctor Husk nodded. 'You're in a bit of trouble. I suspect General Marshall will be by to talk to you.'

He looked concerned. 'General? Why? Because I had a fight? I don't remember anything.'

She flicked a loose hair from his eye. 'Don't worry. I think it's more to do with the fact that he was the one who helped you.'

'Oh.'

'Anyway,' she said standing, 'I'll leave you both alone.'

Ciaran Matthews felt his throat tighten. He was miserably sure he would cry. Ciaran missed his mom, and he was scared. It hadn't been long since his family had been together, but now things were horrible.

'Hey,' Jake said. He beckoned him. 'Come here you.'

Ciaran climbed onto the bed and Jake took a sheet and

wiped his brother's face off, as the first tears emerging ran down over his chin.

'I thought you were gonna die,' Ciaran said, trying unsuccessfully to hold back further tears.

'Don't be silly,' Jake said. 'Why would you think that?'

Ciaran couldn't answer. He put his face against his brother's chest and gave him a fierce hug. Jake hugged back. 'Hey, it's okay.'

'Jake?' Ciaran whispered.

'Yeah?'

'I miss Mom,' he sobbed.

'Yeah,' Jake said, squeezing him. 'I miss her too.'

CHAPTER EIGHT

A nurse tapped Doctor Husk on the shoulder as General Marshall entered the infirmary. She put down her pen and went to greet him. 'Thank you for coming, Bill.' To the nurse Husk said, 'Mary, give us a minute?'

'Do you want me to check on the lab results?'

She nodded. 'Update Colonel Baldwin on Jake's condition, too, please.'

'Certainly.'

Husk turned to Marshall. 'He's awake and in fine health.'

'Can I talk to him?'

'You can, but go easy. Jake's a little nervous about you, and his brother is, well, terrified.'

'Of me?'

'I'm not sure. Of something. I've not been able to detach him from Jake's bedside.'

'I'll be careful,' Marshall said.

She led him to the room and Jake looked up as they stepped in. Ciaran was sleeping on Jake's chest.

'Hello,' Marshall said, as they both entered. 'Sorry to disturb you, Jake, isn't it?'

'Yes, sir,' Jake replied in a soft voice. He attempted to sit up, but Ciaran snuggled against. 'Sorry, I can't really move.'

'That's okay.' Marshall took a chair and positioned it beside the bed. 'I just wanted to see how you were? Is that okay?'

Jake nodded and Marshall read the concern in his face.

'Am I in trouble?'

The general shook his head. 'What do you remember of your fight?'

'Nothing, sir. I don't remember even having a fight.'

'That's okay. What do you remember before waking up here, anything?'

'It's hazy. I remember having lunch. A man sat next to me. He smelled funny.'

'Can you describe the smell?'

'It was like chemicals.'

'Had you smelled it before?' Marshall asked, looking back at the doctor.

Jake shook his head. 'Everyone smells funny, maybe it's the soap they give us? But his smell was different, stronger, bitter. I remember I didn't like it.'

'What else?'

Jake adjusted Ciaran's head and pushed back into the pillow. 'Nothing, really. I'm sorry.'

'Don't be. I'm just glad you're feeling better.'

'Do I have to stay here?'

Marshall smiled. 'That's up to the doctor.'

'I'll keep you one more day,' Doctor Husk said, 'just to be safe, then you can go home.'

Jake gave a bitter laugh. 'Home? You mean to a room full of beds? It's not home.'

Ciaran was sleeping soundly as Jake stroked his hair. Marshall put a hand on his shoulder. 'It's not ideal, I know. But it's better than being out there... and I think you know that.'

He looked up, eyes brimming. 'Yeah.'

General Marshall squeezed his shoulder then turned to leave.

'Wait...'

'What is it?' Marshall asked.

'He was hot.'

Doctor Husk frowned. 'Hot?'

'Yeah, hot. I remember I could feel the heat coming from him.'

She nodded. 'That's very useful, thank you. General?'

'Get some rest. Father Doyle will swing by later and see how you're both doing.'

Jake nodded through his tears. 'We'd like that.'

'Good.'

When they were back in the main infirmary, Marshall rubbed his chin. 'Have you examined the other man?'

Doctor Husk shook her head. 'No, the MPs never brought him here.'

'I think perhaps you should. If he was hot enough for Jake to feel it...'

'He could have a temperature,' she finished. 'I'll speak with the MPs.'

She frowned as she looked back at the room.

'Is there something more?'

'I'm having an idea and not liking it.'

'What is it?'

'Jake remembers nothing after he came in contact with the man he fought. A man possibly running a high temperature. Something affected both their behaviours.'

'Yes, and Jake didn't remember the event. If the other man didn't either, what could that mean?'

'I'm not sure. I've never seen anyone affected this way before. Whatever it was, it took a bit of time to leave his system.'

'Some form of virus?'

She shrugged. 'Possibly. If his blood results are strange, they'll want him up on the isolation ward. We'll just have to wait and see. This is a little out of my expertise.' Doctor Husk was thoughtful. 'If it's a virus, which one passed it to the other?'

● ● ●

'I see. I appreciate the update, Mary.' Colonel Baldwin smiled at the nurse. 'Tell Doctor Husk I'll come down and see her in the morning, would you?'

'I will, Colonel,' she said, then left. When the door closed, he turned to Grunner.

'What do you make of it?'

The German took off his spectacles and cleaned them with a hanky. 'I don't think I can give you an answer, not without examining the boy.'

'That's not going to happen, not with Marshall taking an interest.'

'But what about this other man? The one in confinement.'

Baldwin picked up the receiver on his desk. 'Could you find Paul and have him come see me? Thank you.'

Doctor Grunner slipped his glasses on and stood. 'I will be on level three then, should you need me?'

Captain Barrette knocked, then opened the door. 'You wanted to see me, Colonel?'

'Paul,' he said, gesturing to a chair. 'Sit.'

The captain looked at the chair, then back at him. 'Thank you, sir. But if it's all the same...'

'Sit,' he said, 'please.'

Barrette sat in the chair, and Baldwin came beside and perched on the edge of his desk. 'Don't you think it's time we had this out?'

'Had it out?'

'Discussed it, man to man? It's been almost ten years.'

'Ten years is long enough for you... sir?'

'Cut the *sir* crap and talk to me.'

Barrette's cheeks turned red. 'What do you want me to say?'

'You're an adult. With life experience. I want you to look me in the eye and tell me you understand.'

'But I don't understand. She was dying. And you were fucking some whore...'

Baldwin shook his head. 'That's not fair. Marcia wasn't a whore.'

'Jesus, Dad.' He stood. 'I don't care what her fucking name was.'

'Your mother and I...'

'You were in her bed when your wife, my mom, killed herself. She did it because of you.'

They remained eye to eye for some time, then Barrette said, 'Was there something you needed from me, Colonel?'

Colonel Baldwin stood. 'Yes, Captain. There was a fight this morning between two of the civilians. One is being held in solitary. The other is in the infirmary. Have the man in solitary transferred to level three, please.'

'Yes sir, I'll have a man do it now.'

'Actually,' Baldwin said, 'I'd prefer it if *you* took care of it.'

He ground his teeth. 'Yes, sir.'

'Then you're dismissed,' he said. Captain Barrette saluted and walked towards the door.

'Paul,' Baldwin said, his voice softer. 'I loved your mother.'

Barrette paused as he took the door handle, then looked over his shoulder. 'Not enough.'

• • •

John Keeney came off duty with a weary sigh. He turned into a corridor and a shuffling noise sent the hairs on the back of his neck up. He stopped to look around, but there was no one there. As he walked further, a sense of dread rose from his stomach. He could feel his heart pounding in his neck. Things were happening as they did at the start of every nightmare.

'Hello, John,' Colonel Bradley said, slipping in beside him.

Keeney jumped. 'For Christ's sake,' he yelled. 'What's with you fucking people sneaking up on me?'

Bradley frowned at his outburst. It was uncharacteristic. 'Sorry, old man. Didn't mean to startle you.'

Keeney rubbed his brow, then gave a nervous laugh. 'This place will be the death of me.'

'Let's hope not,' Bradley put an arm on his shoulder. 'Why so jumpy?'

Keeney looked down the corridor. It seemed to stretch out in front of him, getting longer, twisting. He felt hot.

'John?' Bradley asked.

'Eh? I'm not feeling good.'

Colonel Bradley turned toward him and looked in his eyes. They were unfocused and he was perspiring.

'Come on,' he said, slipping an arm around his back. 'Put your weight on me.' Keeney's eyes were heavy, and his feet didn't seem to want to obey. The colonel cursed as he took Keeney's weight.

'Focus, John. You have to walk.'

With immense effort, Keeney lifted his legs. They made it to the elevator and Bradley strained to keep Keeney upright and insert his key. At length, he activated the elevator, and the car descended. Keeney slumped against him.

Bradley struggled to lift him. 'Stay with me.'

Keeney's eyes fluttered open. 'I... I don't know... I'm so tired.'

'You can rest when we get to the infirmary.'

The car opened and Bradley lumbered out. Keeney, now dead-weight, slumped forward in his grasp. Bradley made it to the infirmary door. Keeney was out cold. With his strength leaving, Bradley looked through the windows and saw Doctor Husk and Marshall talking.

'Help,' he yelled. They both came and Marshall took Keeney's weight on one side.

Bradley gave a long sigh. 'Thanks.'

'What happened?' Husk said, opening Keeney's eyes and flashing a light over them.

'Kate... I'm losing my strength,' Bradley said, his face red.

'Get him in here,' she opened the door and they staggered over to a bed and dropped him on it.

Bradley fell into a chair and shuddered. 'He's a heavy boy,' he said, getting his breath back.

Marshall stripped off Keeney's shirt while she took his vitals. 'Tell me what happened, Charlie.'

'He was heading to the elevator. Seemed to be just staring down the corridor. I scared him, although I wasn't trying to. Then he lost his colour and began perspiring. I kept him conscious for as long as I could, but when we got to elevator, he just went out.'

'His pupils are responding, but he's burning up.'

She went to a drawer and pulled out a bunch of heavy-duty yellow bags. She dumped them between Marshall and Bradley.

'Bill get his clothes off and bag them. Then I want you to strip, bag yours, and get in that shower. Wash yourself, head to toe, and don't stop until I tell you.'

She turned to Bradley. 'You too.'

'What?'

'Do as I say. Get a bag, take all your clothes off and get in that shower, now!' He'd never heard that tone from her before. Mixed with the concern she was displaying, he obeyed.

When Keeney was down to his shorts, Marshall hesitated. 'These too?'

'All his clothes, Bill. Don't be squeamish, he's got nothing you haven't seen before.'

'I haven't seen *his*,' Marshall muttered, as he pulled Keeney's underwear off and piled his clothes into a hazard bag as directed. He and Bradley then stripped, filled the bags, and got in a shower.

As nurse Mary came in Doctor Husk said, 'Hazard protocol.'

Mary hit a large button, the doors shut and locked, and the ever-present sound of air fans ceased.

She went to the wall and picked up a phone. 'Code-red hazard in infirmary.'

'Gown up,' Doctor Husk said, stripping her clothes. 'Wash this man while I shower.'

They heard a door open and she gave a sharp turn. 'Stay in that room, Jake.'

Jake looked scared. 'What's going on?'

Doctor Husk swallowed her fear and put on her practised smile. 'It'll be okay, we have a sick man here. Stay inside, don't come out until I tell you, okay?'

Jake said, 'Ciaran needs to pee.'

'If he can't hold it,' Husk said, thinking quickly, 'bunch up a sheet and have him pee on that. No go back inside, please.'

Jake nodded and closed the door.

Doctor Husk removed the rest of her clothes and covered herself with a towel, as she met Bradley and Marshall at the shower cubicle. When she was satisfied, she ordered them out and took Bradley's place in the cubicle.

Bradley grabbed fresh towels and handed one to Marshall

and they dried themselves off. While Doctor Husk continued to shower, Bradley grabbed some loose-fitting garments from the storage room and handed a set to Marshall, leaving a set for Husk. She joined them shortly after.

'What happens now?' Marshall asked.

'Now we wait for the hazard team. Why don't you both go and keep the boys company?'

Bradley gave a look of concern. 'What about you?'

'I have a patient. What's his name?'

'John,' Marshall said. 'John Keeney.'

She gave a tight smile. 'Go,' she said, shooing them away.

'Come on, Braders,' Marshall said.

He remained. 'Kate...'

She met his eyes.

'Go, I can't have you here, you're a distraction.'

Bradley nodded and he and Marshall walked away.

Doctor Husk joined the nurse. 'How is he?'

'Breathing is laboured. His temperature is a hundred and six point two.'

'Get some lukewarm water and a sponge.'

'Yes, Doctor.'

She began an investigation of his body, top to bottom and found nothing abnormal. She put her stethoscope against his back just as Mary arrived with the water. 'Use the sponge and start dousing him.' Husk said, then continued listening to his breathing whilst checking the clock.

'He's presenting tachypnoea and there's fluid in his lungs.' She took his pulse, while the nurse bathed him. 'He's tachy-cardic,' Husk looked up. 'Where the hell is that response team?'

'This isn't reducing his temperature quickly enough,' Mary said.

'Let's try an ice pack, wrap it in a pillowcase and put it on his...'

They both looked up at movement at the door. The doctor went to an intercom and pressed the button.

'Doctor Grunner,' she said. 'Thank god.'

'What is the situation?'

'My patient has developed a dangerous fever, tachycardia and tachypnoea, progressive respiratory distress, and hypotension.'

'You have initiated a hazard lockdown, why?'

She frowned. 'Because he presented with some form of virus.'

'Really? You could determine this, how?'

'Through experience and observations, Doctor.'

He raised an eyebrow. 'We should be thankful then. Unlike others, including myself, you don't appear to need scientific equipment to come to this diagnosis? Remarkable, really.'

'Look, Hans. I was erring on the side of caution.'

He stared through his spectacles. 'You may have erred, but for now we follow protocol. Here is what will happen. You and your nurse will stand away. My team will come and take him. Is that clear?'

'I'd like to go with him. He's my patient.'

Grunner shook his head. 'Not anymore. Since you have determined a hazard situation, following none of the protocols, you and whomever is with you will now isolate until I decide otherwise. Is that clear, Doctor?'

She gave a tight-lipped nod.

'Good,' he said. 'Go to your office and close the door.'

She sighed and turned to Mary. 'Let's go.'

When they were in, the main door opened and two people in protective suits came and covered Keeney's bed in a clear tent. They then wheeled him away.

The intercom in her office buzzed.

'Yes?'

'How many are in here?' Grunner asked.

'Six,' she responded.

'You, your nurse, the two boys. Who are the others?'

'General Marshall and Colonel Bradley.'

There was a pause. 'Very well, we will have food and water brought to you. There are MPs outside. I am sure I do not need to explain why?'

She sighed. 'No, you don't.'

'When this is over, you and I will have a long talk about following the proper procedures.'

The intercom went quiet.

The door opened and Marshall and Bradley looked up as Doctor Husk entered. Jake and Ciaran were playing cards. Marshall came to her.

'How is he?'

She scratched her head. 'Not well, Bill. Grunner has him now.'

Colonel Bradley stood. 'What?'

'It's protocol. They'll transfer Captain Keeney to a hazard-containment facility on level three and the doctors there will help him.'

Bradley looked terrible. 'We have to stop him.'

Marshall nodded to the door and they excused themselves from the boys' room. When they were in Husk's office, Bradley paced the room.

'What's wrong?' she asked.

He stopped and looked at her. 'Do you know a Doctor Parker?'

'Evelyn? Yes, what of her?'

'I overheard Grunner and Baldwin talking earlier today, they were saying something about how she was dealing with the loss of someone she was close to.'

Kate frowned. 'She wasn't dating, as far as I know. I wonder who it was? Poor Evelyn.'

'Never mind that,' he snapped. 'Someone just died, and the way Grunner and Baldwin were discussing it, I think it happened in the lab.'

Marshall said, 'You think John's in danger?'

'Mortal danger,' Bradley replied.

'Then let's go,' Marshall said, pushing away from the desk he was leant against.

Kate stepped in front of them. 'You can't.'

'What?' Marshall frowned at her.

'I'm sorry, but you won't be allowed to leave. We're in isolation. Grunner has put us in effective lockdown.'

'You just try to stop us,' Marshall said.

'It won't be me,' she said, pointing. 'He's stationed MPs outside the infirmary.'

Marshall looked between them. 'He has us trapped in here?'

'Yes.' Doctor Husk looked down. 'It's all my fault, he's doing it to punish all of us because I called in a hazard.'

Marshall released some of his anger. 'Don't blame yourself.'

'He's right. It's not your fault,' Bradley said, his jaw clenched. 'I think this is deliberate.'

Doctor Husk met his narrowing eyes. 'How so?'

He was staring out the window, his eyes fixed on the nurse. 'The three of us begin secretly investigating and just as we start, we're put in a lockdown? That's not a coincidence.'

'Mary?' she remarked, her eyes now watching her too. 'You think she's in on it?'

'Don't you?'

Neither had a reply.

'And you want to know something else?' Bradley turned to them. 'I think someone infected John on purpose, to put us all together.'

'If that's true, we need a plan to get out of here,' Marshall said.

Colonel Bradley gave him a smile. 'You think I didn't put something in motion, just in case?'

Doctor Husk looked sceptical. 'In case we were put in lock down?'

Bradley winked.

She smiled. 'I knew there was a reason I liked you.'

Marshall interrupted them. 'What about Mary?'

'We'll need to find a way of removing her,' Bradley said.

'That's not going to work. She can't leave, Charlie. None of us can.'

'Not of our own volition, I agree.'

Marshall shook his head. 'Then we're back to square one.'

'I wouldn't say that.' The twinkle in Bradley's eye made Marshall chuckle.

'You have a plan, I take it?'

Bradley stared out at the MPs. 'The beginnings of one, at any rate.'

CHAPTER NINE

7 p.m.

The lockdown was in full force, as the buzz of activity amongst the MPs and other military staff came to a head. The immediate enforcement caused several personnel changes in quick succession. Outside the infirmary, four MPs finished a routine handover and were relieved. Fresh staff then took up positions by the doors as a junior kitchen aide came through the interconnecting doors, wheeling a large cart toward them. One of the MPs stopped him to inspect it. When he seemed satisfied, he pressed the intercom and spoke.

'Evening meal, Doctor. Standard procedures, please.'

Doctor Husk's voice burst through the speaker. 'We're ready.'

The MPs relieved the aide of his cart and sent him on his way, then opened the door and wheeled the cart in, positioning it just passed the threshold. Acknowledging Doctor Husk's thank you through the intercom, he locked the doors.

'That's impressive.' Doctor Husk rubbed her hands with enthusiasm. 'They don't want us to starve.' She lifted the cover and sighed. Underneath was a sandwich and fruit selection. 'Then again...' Husk opened the bottom doors, but the large compartment below was empty. 'I take it back.' She peered sadly at the meagre meal. 'They could have brought this on a tray.'

General Marshall looked out at the MPs guarding the door, then smiled. 'I think I know why.' He turned to Bradley. 'Your doing?'

'Indeed. Both of you, follow my lead.'

Doctor Husk looked between them. 'What's happening?'

Marshall said, 'Trust us.'

Bradley pulled out a small pouch that had been secured with tape on the inside of the cart and opened it. 'Kate, call for Mary.'

Doctor Husk nodded, and nurse Mary came out from the boy's room. 'Oh, it's dinnertime already?' She said, as she approached the cart.

Doctor Husk smiled. 'Take a plate to the boys, would you?'

Nurse Mary nodded but before she could do as instructed, she gave a muffled squeal as Bradley clamped a handkerchief over her face.

'What the hell are you doing?' Doctor Husk said. Her attempt to render aid to Mary was thwarted by Marshall's strong grip. 'Let go of me,' she cried, but Marshall held her back. Nurse Mary then sagged into Bradley's arms and he lowered her down.

Marshall released Doctor Husk, who knelt beside the unconscious Mary and checked her. She looked up at Bradley, her anger palpable. 'Chloroform?' He nodded.

'I'm sorry,' he said, kneeling beside her. 'It was the only way.'

'I don't approve,' Husk said, but the anger left her eyes.

'What do we do with her?' Marshall asked.

Bradley stood and moved to the intercom. 'I say, chaps. Nurse Mary has taken ill.'

The door soon opened and one of the MPs, Sergeant Hawkinson, came to them. General Marshall squeezed his shoulder, and the younger man grinned. 'Good job, Hawk.'

'They're your men,' Doctor Husk said, in sudden realisation. 'How did you manage that?'

Colonel Bradley took a sandwich and bit into it. 'I've had an escape plan ready from the moment we got here. They may have split our men up, but do you imagine for a moment I didn't influence where they all went?'

'But when Mary wakes up, she'll just tell them she was attacked, won't she?'

Bradley shook his head. 'Chloroform affects short term memory. She'll not remember. Trust me, this isn't the first time I've done this.'

'Don't worry, Doctor,' Hawkinson said. 'They have a protocol for people who get sick. I'll call it in, they're not taking any chances. She'll end up going to level three. Even if she seems fine, they'll not release her for at least twenty-four hours.' He stood and turned to Bradley. 'That enough time, Colonel?'

'Plenty. Good work. Make sure your boys are vigilant. These people here are now your priority.'

'Well, let's get her up off the floor at least,' Husk said. Marshall and Bradley carefully lifted Mary and put her into a bed.

'She won't be out long,' Husk said, heading to a cabinet. 'It goes against all my medical ethics, but I'll give her a sedative to keep her asleep.'

'Thank you, Kate,' Bradley said.

'General, Doctor, when the team comes, remain in the office,' Hawkinson said. 'I'll make sure there's no reason to check who's actually in here.'

'What do you mean?' Doctor Husk said, confusion and concern crossing her face.

Bradley touched her shoulder. 'It's time for me to sneak out for a bit.'

Hawkinson opened the cart doors. 'It won't be comfortable, but it was the only way I could think of getting you out.'

'This will do fine.'

Marshall took Bradley's arm. 'John.'

'Number-one priority, Bill.'

Sergeant Hawkinson took the plate of sandwiches off the tray and handed them to Husk. 'We'll bring some proper food once the hazard team collects Mary,' he said.

'Something hot, please,' Marshall said, 'and bring ice cream.'

Hawkinson chuckled.

'It's for the boys.'

'Of course it is, sir.' Hawkinson continued to chuckle as he assisted Colonel Bradley, who was trying to get into the bottom of the cart. Once Colonel Bradley was secure inside, he looked up at Marshall.

'Don't wait up.' He tapped the side then pulled the doors closed, and Hawk pushed the cart outside.

'Ice cream?' Husk said, raising an eyebrow at him.

'What? I like ice cream.'

• • •

Captain Paul Barrette rubbed his neck and yawned. He pulled off his shoes with a sigh and rubbed his feet. It had been a long shift and he was glad to be off duty. He slipped out of his pants and shirt, then grabbed the towel hanging on the door and headed for the shower. It was late. Barrette preferred to shower after everyone else had settled into their night activities. Finding it empty, he hung his towel on a hook and slipped off his underwear.

The water ran for a while and a heavy steam filled the room. He closed his eyes as he allowed the water to wash over him. Leaning his forehead against the wall, he sighed.

'I can see why John took an interest in you,' a voice said. It made him jump.

Barrette turned to see Colonel Bradley sitting on the bench opposite. His legs crossed, right hand holding a revolver, pointing at Barrette's crotch.

'Marvellous view,' Bradley said.

'You shouldn't be here,' Barrette said, stepping forward.

Bradley waved the revolver. 'Now, now, don't be silly. I'm an excellent shot. And it would be such a shame to lose what I'm aiming at.'

Captain Barrette stared at him. 'Why are you pointing a revolver at me, Colonel?'

'I'm trying to decide whether I should kill you, or just fuck you.'

Barrette kept his eyes on the revolver. 'If I get a choice, I'd pick the latter.'

Colonel Bradley tilted his head and smiled.

'What's this all about?'

'I need some answers,' Bradley said, 'and you're going to give them to me.'

Barrette shivered. 'Do you mind if I at least get a towel?'

'No towel for you, not until you've answered my questions.'

There was something cold in that usually warm British voice. It was obvious the colonel wasn't fooling around. Captain Barrette felt fear in his core. He stood shivering from a mixture of fear, and the spray of the water running stone cold behind him.

'What do you want to know?' he asked, through chattering teeth.

Bradley put both feet on the floor and leant forward. 'Everything. Tell me, what's really going on here?'

'And what if I have nothing of value to tell?'

Bradley pulled out a long tube and screwed it to the revolver's muzzle. 'I shouldn't recommend that.'

Barrette's face drained of colour. 'Interesting firearm, is it British?'

'French, actually. Société d'Applications Générales d'Electricité et de Mécanique. SAGEM. They modified this one for me. It's a very useful tool, perfect for just such occasions. I've only ever used it on Germans. Lots of Germans, a few deserters, and an ex-wife, but that's a lengthy story. What I'm trying to say is, it's very good. It's also quiet.'

Barrette's mouth had gone dry. 'Look...'

'Let's start with what's happening on level three, and go from there, shall we?'

'This is a communal shower, Colonel. If you let that thing off, someone will hear.'

Bradley frowned. 'Oh... we didn't get off to a good start, did we?' He lifted the revolver and fired.

Barrette screamed and fell, grabbing his thigh. Colonel Bradley sat back and crossed his legs, waiting for him to stop yelling.

'You fucking shot me?' he cried, blood trickling through his fingers, mixing with the water on the tiled floor. Barrette examined his leg but recognised it was a light skin tear. His pride was wounded worse.

Colonel Bradley stood, grabbed a wash cloth and tossed it to him. 'Here,' he said. 'Clean yourself up.'

Captain Barrette winced as he dabbed the wound.

'Oh relax, it's just a flesh wound.' Bradley crouched and pointed the revolver at his crotch. 'The next one won't be. Start talking.'

'What the fuck do you want to know?'

'How old are you, twenty?'

'Twenty-three,' Barrette spat.

'Just a boy... Start with John Keeney.' He pushed the silencer into the flesh of Barrette's genitals. If it was possible for Paul Barrette to lose any more colour from his face, he did.

'What are you talking about? John came off shift four hours before I did. We were going to meet for dinner. That's all, I swear.'

'What duties did he have today?'

'Same as every day, he supervises the mechanics who keep the air pumps working.' He kept his eyes on the weapon. 'Please... Colonel. I...'

'Did he leave his post for any reason?'

Barrette shook his head.

Bradley read his fear, and something else. 'Are you in love with him?'

'That's none of your fucking business.'

Bradley narrowed his eyes and prodded him. 'Don't play games with me.'

'Fuck you,' he said, shivering and helpless. 'Shoot me then, fuck you.'

'How did John become infected?'

Barrette took in a breath. His expression changed. 'What?'

'How did John become infected?'

'That's not possible. He can't have been.'

Colonel Bradley raised an eyebrow. 'That's an interesting response.'

'It's the truth.'

'How many people are infected?'

'You don't know?'

Bradley growled. Barrette felt the gun push deeper.

'Hey, hey... I assumed you knew. Lots of people. But they're working on a cure.'

'What is this infection?'

Barrette looked him in the eye. 'I don't know. I was told some people got infected by a virus, but they were in the labs. John never worked in the labs because it would be me who put him there. Don't you get it? I wouldn't put him there because... I fucking care about him, okay? Jesus...'

Colonel Bradley continued to stare for a moment longer, then removed the weapon and extended his hand, helping him up. When he was seated, Bradley grabbed a towel and wrapped it around him. He then pulled out a first-aid kit and dressed his wound. It wasn't deep.

'Thanks,' Barrette said. 'You're a fucking psychopath, you know that?'

'I have heard that a few times during my life. Can you walk?'

He nodded.

'Let's go back to your room and talk.'

'You could have just asked me,' Barrette said, with a growl.

Colonel Bradley handed him his underwear.

When they reached Barrette's room, Bradley sat at their table while he dressed in silence. Barrette pulled out a bottle of whiskey and two glasses, pouring a little in each as he sat.

'How did you know?'

Bradley swallowed the entire pour and Barrette replenished it.

'About you and John?'

'Yes.'

He shrugged. 'I didn't.'

Barrette frowned.

'I knew before you'd said a word.' Bradley took another sip. 'This is rather good, Scotch?'

'Irish.'

'Oh... my tastes have been sullied by bourbon.'

'What do you mean before I said a word?'

'It has been my observation when a man prefers the company of other men, he's more inhibited than those who prefer the company of women. Especially amongst others in a communal activity. Isn't that why you shower alone?'

'I'm just shy being around a load of naked men, that's all.'

'I'd believe that if you'd attempted to cover yourself. You didn't.'

Barrette reddened. 'I'd never thought too deeply about it.'

'Liar,' Bradley said, smirking.

Barrette threw him a scowl and drank his whiskey. 'Look, we tried to keep it quiet.'

Colonel Bradley finished his drink. 'What you and John get up to is no business of mine. I'm only concerned with saving John from a monster.'

'You mean Grunner?'

Bradley nodded. 'We're on the same page then.'

CHAPTER TEN

9 p.m.

Colonel Bradley drummed his fingers on the table, while Barrette finished in the bathroom. When he emerged, he sat next to the colonel.

'Everything okay?'

'Aside from a bullet wound in my leg, you mean?'

Bradley's expression remained neutral. 'I'm sure you've had worse.'

Barrette grunted. 'Let's just get one thing clear, Colonel,' he said. 'If you ever point a firearm at me again, I'll kill you.'

Colonel Bradley laughed. 'No, you won't.'

'I'm serious.'

'I believe you. But let me make something equally clear. If the situation had been in reverse, you'd already be dead.'

They stared at each other, then Barrette said, 'I'm only helping you because of John.'

'You're only alive because of John,' he countered. 'Are you done whining, Captain?'

Barrette nodded.

'Good, let's move on to more productive conversation.'

'So how did you escape the lockdown, anyway?'

'Why don't we stick to me asking questions, and you answering them?'

'If that's how you want to play it.'

'Tell me about the infections.'

'It happened about a month before you arrived. We rescued an enormous group of civilians, including the governor and his staff. We brought them in and split them up, the civilians housed on the lowest level and the governor with his people housed with the military. There was a bit of a power struggle with the governor, because he wanted to transfer his base of operations here, but Colonel Baldwin shut him down. They agreed the governor would keep control of the civilians, and Baldwin the military, and that kind of worked, at least for a while.

'About a week in, several people in the governor's staff came down with colds, but as no one bothers treating that, they just took care of themselves. Then more got sick, including some military. Grunner and Baldwin isolated those who had symptoms. This base is one big isolation centre because of the biological hazards we work with. Apart from the labs, the rest of us share a central air system. There was a concern if it got airborne it might affect everyone. The governor agreed and they took anyone who felt sick to an isolated section of the facility.'

Captain Barrette sighed. 'And everything was fine until the people in isolation started getting worse. Then the medical staff treating them fell ill too. Grunner and the colonel decided on full lockdown after that.'

Bradley nodded. 'That all seems reasonable and hardly warrants the level of secrecy I've seen. So, what aren't you telling me?'

'Back then, I wasn't in the position I am now. Actually, I shouldn't even be here. Anyway... I worked with the scientists a lot more. All I know is, things started getting worse after they found a creature and had it taken to a research lab. I got friendly with the people I worked with, and they liked to gossip about stuff, or tell me how clever they were. One morning, Mitch Reynolds was acting like he'd discovered how to make gold or something. Kept going on about cells and light and how the creature had the ability to bend it. He kept saying they might replicate it.

'The next day, it attacked him and Doctor Berger. Mitch died, but Berger survived. Grunner put him in isolation. It didn't take long for him to recover, but soon after he changed.'

'Changed how?'

'At first he became aggressive. Not to the point he was dangerous, not then. He was quick to get irritated, anyway, so it wasn't noticeable right away. Berger helped the sick but started forgetting things. Names, conversations, people he'd treated. They pulled him off and he got into a fight with the governor. Bit him in the face. They hauled him into solitary and a few hours later he died. That's what I was told. The governor seemed unaffected and then something remarkable happened. He got better. After a day he showed no signs of the illness. Baldwin and Grunner removed him from isolation. They were looking at his blood to see if they could make an antidote. Everyone was excited. It seemed like they'd found their answer.'

'So, what happened?'

'A few days later the governor murdered Colonel Baldwin's wife.'

'Good grief,' Bradley murmured. 'How long ago was this?'

'A few months back.'

Bradley frowned. 'I underestimated him. He's much better at hiding his feelings than I thought.'

'You have no idea what that man is capable of, trust me,' he said deadpan. 'But it's not the first wife he's had. Probably won't be the last.'

Colonel Bradley smiled. 'Apparently I underestimated you as well. You don't like him much, do you?'

Barrette shrugged. 'I have my reasons.'

'Care to share?'

'No.'

'Fair enough. Go on with your story.'

'The governor was sitting in the colonel's room. There wasn't much left to identify her. He'd ripped her apart and was just sitting in the remains. The colonel went fucking crazy. Emptied his revolver into him. Just kept firing. Even after the clip had emptied, he just kept firing. I still hear that sound. Click. Click. Click. Grunner took Berger's body and her remains to the labs. Later they found out she was pregnant. About two weeks before you came, the people in isolation died, including all the medical staff. They autopsied everyone and found they'd drowned.'

'That was the official cause death?'

Barrette shrugged. 'No idea. All I know is, they had some weird fluid in their lungs.'

Colonel Bradley rubbed his chin. 'What were the initial symptoms?'

'High fever, difficulty breathing.'

Bradley's face set firm.

'Does John have those symptoms?'

Bradley nodded.

Captain Barrette looked terrible. 'Then he's fucked, and so are we.'

'I don't believe that. It sounds to me like Grunner and his people are trying to find a cure.'

'You misunderstand. If he has the illness, it's spread from isolation. We'll all get it now.'

'Let's not jump to conclusions.'

He backed away. 'You might have it.'

'I might,' he nodded. 'But if it's that virulent, you probably already have it.'

Barrette sat on his bed and put his head in his hands. 'We're fucked....' he kept repeating.

'Stop that.' Colonel Bradley's tone was firm. 'I need you focused.'

Barrette looked through scared eyes.

'Don't make me shoot you again,' Bradley said, with a smirk.

'You're hilarious.'

'Come on,' Bradley said, standing. 'Let's go.'

With a sigh, Barrette followed him out and closed the door.

• • •

The last eight remaining people from the first batch of infected had now died. Doctor Grunner observed their tortured, twisted bodies as Heinz led a disposal team to pack them into containers filled with ice. Once the work was completed, he gave Heinz instructions to sterilize the lab then went back to his office. Grunner ran an eye over a report and made a few notes, then put it into a file and locked it away in his bureau. The symptoms they'd displayed were similar to the others, except for one difference. These subjects appeared to have coughed themselves to death. Like the others, they expressed a disorientated wildness at the end. Throwing themselves into walls, or doors, in what appeared to be an attempt to escape. Most balled themselves up and rocked until they expired. Those they removed and cremated. The three who'd pulled out their own eyes just before the end were transferred to lab sixteen.

Grunner left his office and visited with Baldwin to make his report.

When Grunner had finished his report, Baldwin took the paper he'd handed over and slid it into his drawer. 'What about the thing in the lab?'

'It is as it was. The cold temperature has it subdued.'

'Have you discovered anything about its purpose?'

Grunner shook his head. 'There is nothing to suggest it is intelligent, beyond its design.'

'It consumed a man and took his shape, that seems intelligent to me.'

Again, Grunner shook his head. 'You mistake instinct for intelligence. We already knew the sample had metamorphic abilities. It is my belief we are dealing with a therianthrope.'

'I have no idea what that means.'

'Something that identifies as animalistic. An entity capable of controlling its own evolution.'

Colonel Baldwin looked confused. 'You suggested before it was a mutation from those creatures out there.'

'My opinion has changed with the data. I am now leaning towards a pre-prehistoric creature. A thing that can shift forms when necessary.'

Baldwin laughed. 'Ridiculous.'

'Why?'

'How haven't we seen it before now?'

'Just because we haven't seen it, doesn't mean it is something new. The industry of the twentieth century may hold the answers. As a species, we're drilling into the Earth far more than ever before.'

'Are you saying the monsters out there are... dinosaurs?'

'No. I believe they are far older. Something from the Palaeozoic Era, possibly.'

'When was that?'

'Around five or six hundred million years ago.'

Baldwin shook his head. 'You must be joking?'

'We shall see,' he said. 'I've had something of a minor success regarding our more immediate concerns,' Grunner offered. 'Perhaps it will improve your mood?'

'What?'

'I believe we've discovered a link that might explain why patient zero's condition improved.'

'A cure?'

Grunner shook his head. 'I wouldn't go that far. But it's encouraging.'

'How will you know if it works? It seems to me you're running out of people with the sickness to test it on.'

'That isn't true. There are plenty of subjects in the second batch isolation unit. We will test...'

'People,' Baldwin corrected. 'Not subjects.'

Grunner gave a tight smile. 'Of course. With your permission, we will start testing.'

'What about Captain Keeney?'

'Yes, Captain Keeney,' Grunner said, his left eye twitching ever so slightly. 'Interesting case. He appears to display an additional set of symptoms.'

'Is it possible it's nonrelated?' Baldwin asked, hope filtering into his tone.

'Unlikely,' Grunner said. 'We have him stabilised. I will update you on his condition.'

'We need to handle this. Marshall isn't an idiot, despite what you think. He's probably beginning to suspect something's going on.'

'He would have to be a moron not to,' Grunner remarked.

'But for now, he and his associates are contained. How long they stay this way is a matter for you.'

'We can't keep them locked up indefinitely. We must come up with a story.'

'Why not just explain what we are doing?'

Baldwin scoffed. 'You're crazy.'

Grunner shrugged. 'It is, of course, your call. But I think you should be frank with him.'

'And let him pull rank, again? No thanks.'

'Ah,' Grunner nodded. 'His more senior position remains a constant source of anxiety for you. I understand. What then do you suggest?'

Baldwin suppressed the irritation creeping into his thoughts. 'Do you think it has breached our containment again?'

Grunner remained thoughtful. 'I do not see how. Our precautions have improved since then.'

'When did John get infected?'

'His symptoms are different. It is possible he arrived with this particular illness.'

'Well, if that's true,' mused Baldwin. 'It might help with how I spin it. This isn't the first time we've been through this with Marshall, and you know how it usually goes?'

'Indeed. Then you must change your tactics this time around.'

'I know. I'll think of something.'

'You had better. It infects his captain, his friend. That increases the risk of his involvement. If you aren't planning to let him...'

'You worry about your work, Grunner. I'll take care of Marshall.' Colonel Baldwin's tone suggested the conversation was closed.

Grunner inclined his head. 'Very well. What should we do about Doctor Husk?'

Baldwin frowned. 'What do you mean?'

'I think we should find a replacement.'

'Why?'

'I do not trust her.'

'You don't trust anyone or anything,' Baldwin said.

'Not so. I had trust in the visions of der Führer.'

Baldwin chuckled. 'And look where that got you.'

Grunner leant forward. 'It got me here, where I could continue that vision, with your support.'

'And all it took was betraying him to do so.'

Doctor Grunner trained his beady eyes on him. 'Your accusation isn't without merit. However, Hitler understood the work's importance rose above petty concerns like friendships or loyalty. You are much alike.'

'I'm nothing like him,' Baldwin spat, appalled at the notion.

'Aren't you?' Grunner asked. Before Baldwin could reply he clicked his heals and gave a sharp tip of his head.

'*Oberst*,' he said, leaving Baldwin to fume.

• • •

'Where are we going?' Captain Barrette asked.

'Down a level.'

'Why?'

'I need to talk with a few people. I don't want to be seen, for obvious reasons.'

'You never explained how you escaped hazard containment.'

Colonel Bradley checked the corridor and beckoned him in. 'I know.'

Captain Barrette grunted as they slipped into the elevator. 'Look, I'm helping you, aren't I? When are you going to start trusting me?'

'When you prove I can.'

Barrette crossed his arms. 'I didn't give you away, did I?'

'I haven't given you an opportunity to.'

'You know it won't be long before they notice you're missing?'

'Who are they?' he asked, pressing a button.

'The MPs.'

'Ah,' he nodded. 'The MPs stationed outside the infirmary are forbidden under hazard protocol to go inside.'

'That's true, but if they lift the containment, then they'll know.'

'Oh, don't worry,' he said, as the car slowed. 'I'll be back inside long before that happens.'

'You have an answer for everything.'

'I try to.'

Barrette rolled his eyes.

When the doors opened, Barrette followed as he weaved in and out of civilians into the private rooms beyond the dining area.

'What are we doing here?' Barrette asked.

'Adding a little muscle to our bag.'

'Bag of what?'

'Friends,' he said, stopping at a door and giving it a light tap. 'No more questions now.'

The door opened and Barrette followed him inside.

Captain Barrette appraised the man who'd closed the door behind them and joined five others seated around a table. A tough-looking group, all playing cards, who stopped and eyed him with suspicion.

'Charlie,' an older man with short cropped hair said. 'Who is this?'

'Captain Barrette, Chief. Don't panic. He's sound.'

'Chief?' Barrette said, frowning.

'Yes,' he replied, '*chief*. As in Chief of Police.' He turned his eyes back to the colonel. 'Why is he here?'

'Long story.' He put up a hand. 'Be a good chap and stop asking questions. I have something I need you to do.'

'I wasn't aware I was one of *your* men, Charlie. Besides, we don't have any function here,' he said, turning to the cards. 'In case you forgot.'

'Todd, how many of your officers are here?'

He placed a card down. 'Ten or so.' He looked up. 'Why?'

'Get word to them, quietly. You'll have a function soon.'

'Oh?'

'Ready to serve and protect again, Chief?'

The police chief looked between the men seated, then said, 'What did you have in mind?'

CHAPTER ELEVEN

10 p.m.

Father Doyle was lost in prayer. He opened his eyes at the sound of the door opening and finished his last words before looking around. There was no one there. He got up, walked towards the door, and put his head out, but the immediate area was empty, so he shrugged went back inside. When he turned to the altar, he noticed someone was sitting in a pew. Doyle wasn't sure how he'd missed them. He moved forward and came alongside a woman whom often attended his Mass. A youth in her early twenties. Scruffy black hair, blue eyes. Heavy makeup and bright pink lipstick. She sat in dirty sweatpants and white tee shirt, a black scarf over her shoulders.

Father Doyle's eyes wandered over her slender form. He licked his lips.

'Service has ended, child,' he said.

She gave a thin smile. 'I know, Father. That's not why I'm here.'

'Was there something else you needed then?'

She stood and put a hand on his arm.

'Something,' she said, rubbing her nose with the back of her other hand. 'Can we go somewhere private?'

He gave her an inquiring look.

'Todd sent me.'

Doyle looked at the door, then back at her, and a slow smile spread across his face. 'I see. What's your name?'

'Names aren't important, are they?'

Doyle shook his head. 'I suppose not. Follow me then.'

They went into a side room and Doyle closed the door. She stood by it, waiting.

'And what was it you needed?'

'I was told you could give me a little pick-me-up?'

'Ah,' he nodded. 'Something stronger than spiritual advice?'

She nodded, twisting her hair with nervous fingers.

'This is your fist time?'

Again, she nodded.

Father Doyle opened a box on a table and pulled out a small paper envelope. He studied it for a time, then sat on the bench and motioned for her to sit with him.

'Don't be nervous. Here.' He held out the bag. She took it and sat next to him.

'Aren't you worried you might get caught?'

'No. I supply Todd's substances and he supplies me with what I want. It's a mutual agreement that benefits all of us.'

She gave a slow nod. 'Just between you, me, and God?'

'Exactly. You're not going to tell on me, are you?'

'No,' she said, opening up the small packet and dipping a finger inside. She withdrew and tasted it. Her eyes lit. 'Perfect,' she muttered.

Doyle let his hand fall on her thigh. 'All we need to do now is discuss payment.'

She pushed the envelope into her pants pocket. 'I'm sure I can think of something.' She dropped to her knees in front of him.

'What did you have in mind?'

She slipped her hands along the inside of his thighs, meeting at his crotch. He spread his legs further apart. Doyle's eyes followed her fingers as she undid his fly. Those same fingers brushing against his exposed underwear, and he quivered as her expert hand slipped inside.

She read the lust in his eyes. 'You like that, Father?'

Sweat formed on his lip. His usual calm expression changed to something darker. His breathing quickened. 'Corruptness spews from you, like Hell's fire.'

Doyle stood and undid his belt, dropping his pants. 'We must ask God to forgive your immorality,' he said.

She pulled down his underwear. 'I don't care about God. I just want the magic powder. If I have to suck you off to get it, call me all the names you want, Father. I'm not interested in being saved.'

He gripped her hair and pulled her head back. 'I shall douse your evil with my holy seed. Start using that black mouth to pray for your sinful soul, Satan's whore.'

She took hold on his hips and shuffled forward. Father Doyle grabbed her head in both hands. He let out a guttural groan and began thrusting hard into her face.

'You wicked, wicked child.'

• • •

Bradley sipped his drink and puffed on his cigar as they played their hand.

Paul Barrette sat to one side, looking more uncomfortable than ever. He couldn't fail to notice the looks the burly ex-cops were throwing his way. 'You have a bathroom I can use?' he asked.

Chief Todd Stevens took the cigar from his mouth and pointed. Barrette nodded and went inside. He grimaced as the smell of stale urine hit him. The toilet, stained yellow, was thick with grim. No one had flushed it from the last use.

'Fucking pigs,' he muttered.

Barrette unzipped and began to empty his bladder. He turned at the sound of shuffling behind. A giant dark-skinned man came in beside him, a cigarette hanging loose in his lips. Before Barrette could protest, the guy unzipped and started peeing next to him. Most of it went down the side and over the seat. Barrette kept his eyes front and zipped up as soon as he was able, moving to the sink. It looked dirtier than the toilet. The newcomer finished and walked out. Barrette let out his breath and chose not to wash his hands. When he came out, the card game was almost over.

His eyes found the man who'd just left the bathroom. With a large grin, he stepped into Barrette's space. 'So, you're a captain, huh?'

Barrette took a step back. 'That's right.'

'What do you do, Captain?'

'I'm a liaison between the command centre and the scientists who work in the labs.'

The giant seemed interested. His expression was less gruff than the others. He was well over six foot and muscular. He wore a nice pair of jeans and a white V-neck tee. Unlike the others whose clothes looked grubby, his were immaculate.

'You got a name, Captain?'

'Paul Barrette.'

The giant smiled and extended his hand. 'Tony. Tony King,' he said.

King motioned him to a smaller table away from the others and they sat. 'You want something to drink?'

'What you got?'

He shrugged. 'Whiskey and vodka mainly.'

'There's gin too,' the chief said over his shoulder. 'Give him the good stuff, Tony.'

'Good stuff?' Barrette asked.

'Rocket fuel,' King replied, grinning. 'You wanna try that?'

'Sure, why not?'

King pulled out a green bottle and gave a broad grin. The others chuckled.

'One chip says he pukes,' Stevens said.

Colonel Bradley stared through a haze of smoke at Captain Barrette. 'I say he's a lot stronger than you think. I'll take that bet, but let's make it more interesting. Paul?'

'Yeah?'

'Anything in here take your fancy?' he said, raising his eyebrows.

Barrette's face reddened. 'Fuck you.'

Todd laughed. 'Damn, I like this kid.'

'I think I'm beginning to, as well.' Bradley opened up the cigar box and took one out. 'Hey,' he said. Barrette scowled as Bradley threw something.

Barrette caught it, then frowned. 'A cigar?'

Bradley winked. 'Figured I owed you that, at least.'

'Yeah, you fucking maniac,' he said, and lit it.

'Kid smokes Cubans too? Shit. I really like him now.'

King arrived with a green bottle and two glasses and poured out a clear fluid into each one.

Bradley dealt the cards, smoke flowing over his head. Through the cloud he never took his eyes off Barrette.

Barrette picked up the glass and sniffed it. 'Jesus,' he said. 'It smells like dog shit.'

The room burst into laughter.

Stevens turned in his chair. 'You got to down it, son. You try to sip that, you'll taste dog shit for a month.'

'What the fuck is it?' Barrette said, moving the glass closer to his lips.

'Home brew. Bit of this, bit of that.'

They watched him.

Barrette was aware the room had fallen silent. He shrugged and threw the drink back and swallowed, then gagged. 'Fuck,' he said. 'It tastes like, ugh...'

King laughed as he poured him another and Barrette threw that one back too. King looked over at Stevens, who gave a slight shake of his head.

'Jet fuel, huh? You should think of another name,' he said with a hiccup. 'Because that...'

Stevens nudged Bradley. 'Three... two...'

'Ugh...' The colour drained from Barrette's face.

'Shit,' Bradley said with a sigh.

Barrette grabbed his stomach and ran to the bathroom.

Stevens nodded to King. 'Make sure he's okay.'

The colonel stood. 'How much did you give him?'

They could hear him vomiting. King pulled the door closed.

'Just enough. Don't worry, he won't puke his asshole up. But he's gonna be sick for a while. Go, we'll take care of him. You like this kid?'

'I think so. But don't tell him I said that. Keep him safe for me. I owe you one, Todd.'

'You owe me more than one, limey.'

Colonel Bradley grinned and left.

Todd Stevens shuffled the cards and was part way through

dealing when the door bust open. They looked up as another man came in. His expression grim.

'Jim? What is it?' Stevens asked.

'It's Father Doyle. You'd better come, Chief.'

• • •

Stevens knelt next to Father Doyle's body. The chief put a hand over his mouth as he examined the corpse. Doyle's cranial vault was sheared through. A dense scarlet stain filled with gristle and bone spread outwards from his exposed skull. His pants and underwear around his ankles. Fluid ran down his thighs. As Decker was a forensics guy, Stevens let him take the lead.

Decker pointed to the fluid. 'We know what that is,' he said.

'Who did this?' Stevens asked, ignoring his attempts at humour.

'Jessie.'

'Jessie?' Stevens felt his anger rise. 'Jessie did this?'

'I guess she didn't get the skinny on Doyle's particular kind of payment,' Decker said with a smirk.

'You see my face,' Stevens said. 'It's not laughing, Jim.'

'Sorry.'

Stevens knelt and examined Doyle's crotch. Decker joined him. 'Oh, what a pretty shade of pink,' he chuckled, then caught himself and turned more serious.

'We'll have to clear this up quickly, but it won't be a problem.'

'It's a fucking huge problem.'

'Well, we can't blame Jessie…'

'She knew the score, Jim. Doyle's a fucking predator, but we had a deal. He's been good, ever since the last incident.' His anger mounted. 'This fucking nightmare will bite us, hard. It ain't like we can just make this go away like the others, is it? Doyle's the fucking priest. Oh, that bitch has cost me. We'll have the fucking military cunts all over us now. I want Jessie dealt with.'

Decker looked terrible. 'Come on, boss, she made a mistake.'

Stevens's look made Decker swallow.

'I'll have one of the boys rough her up a little.'

'No.' His jaw set firm. 'Dead. I want you to do it, Jim. No one else.'

Decker nodded. 'What about Doyle?'

Stevens gave him a look. Decker remained staring at Doyle for a moment, then Stevens looked up. 'What the fuck are you still doing here?'

'Sorry,' Decker said, and hastily moved to the door.

'Jim,' Stevens called after him.

He stopped and looked back. 'Yes, boss?'

'I want her to suffer, before the end.'

'Understood,' Decker said, and left.

Something caught Stevens's eye and he looked at Doyle's bloody face. He used his pointer finger to wipe something black and sticky off the exposed skull. Stevens squeezed it between his finger and thumb. It was viscous, tar-like. He watched it stretch and break a few times, then wiped it on his jeans.

CHAPTER TWELVE

11 p.m.

Lieutenant Bruce Dawson had finished his shower and was making his way to the dining room when the duty sergeant approached him. He was a grizzled-looking, hard-faced veteran.

'Lieutenant,' he said, with a nod. 'Busy day?'

'You could say that,' he replied, rubbing his neck. 'Is something on your mind, Sarge?'

'You heard about the new orders?'

Dawson frowned. 'What new orders?'

'We're to implement a distancing protocol now. It's ridiculous.'

'This came from the colonel?'

He shook his head. 'Grunner.'

'I've not heard a thing about it.'

'Well.' He sniffed. 'You have now. Maintain a distance from people and no physical contact. The civilian sector is out of bounds until further notice. The boys' playtime just got quashed. They ain't gonna be happy.' It seemed impossible that his expression could get any fiercer, yet somehow, he managed it.

'I wonder what it's all about?'

The sergeant shrugged. 'You got me. I'm giving you the info. Maybe you could get clarification, the boys would appreciate it?'

Dawson nodded. 'You bet, Sarge.'

'Good boy.' He gave a tight nod and left.

Dawson went to his bunk and slipped into fresh clothes, his thoughts dwelling on the distancing order. He didn't let on to the duty sergeant, but he'd had a good understanding of the distancing protocol. If Grunner wanted physical contact stopped, it meant someone had developed symptoms. He left the dorm and headed to the infirmary.

When he entered the corridor, Sergeant Hawkinson stopped him.

'Sorry, sir, that's as far as you go. Infirmary is on lockdown.'

'Is someone sick?'

Hawkinson stared at him. 'No one comes in or out.'

'I see, well, I have clearance, so you can let me through,' he said, stepping forward.

Hawkinson blocked him, and another came alongside.

'As I said,' – his eyes were hard – 'that's as far as you can go, sir.'

Dawson looked between them. 'I have clearance,' he repeated.

'No, sir, you don't.'

Dawson observed theirs hands moving to sidearms.

'Time for you to leave, Lieutenant.'

'Very well.' Dawson turned and walked away.

The elevator opened, and Lieutenant Dawson stepped out. He made his way down to the offices opposite the level-three lab. It was early evening, so he didn't expect to find many people at their desk. But he knew Doctor Grunner's habits well enough. He approached the door to the doctor's office and gave a light rap and opened it, stepping inside.

Doctor Grunner's office was large but sparse in decoration. He had a pair of worn red leather chairs next to a low coffee table, several cabinets had knickknacks and photographs on the top, and at the far end, a large desk he was sitting at.

'*Leutnant*?' he said, looking up. His black eyes enlarged through his heavy round spectacles. 'Why are you not enjoying your evening?'

'I'm sorry to bother you, Doctor. Do you have a moment to talk?'

Grunner gave him a disarming smile. 'For you? I have many moments. Come, you will have a glass of brandy with me.'

'Thank you, I'd like that.'

Grunner poured two generous glasses and handed him one.

'*Sich setzen*,' he said, indicating toward the chairs.

'I've just been told about the distancing order.'

The German allowed the glass to roll across his bottom lip. 'Regrettable, but necessary.'

'There's been a fresh case then?'

Grunner took a sip. 'Case?' he asked.

'Yes, someone has become sick?'

He studied him. 'Someone has become sick.'

Dawson wasn't sure if he was answering or just repeating his question. He decided it was an answer. 'Is that why the infirmary is on lockdown?'

'A precaution only. What do you know about this sickness? Tell me.'

'Only that it's some kind of virus, like a cold. Nothing more.'

Grunner studied him over the brim of his glass. 'But more than perhaps you should?'

Dawson felt uncomfortable. 'I heard some things, but I assure you, I don't gossip.'

Grunner took a sip and nodded. 'I know this. You are good at your job.'

'Thank you, Doctor.'

'You perhaps wish to learn more about things here? More than a young *leutnant* would know?'

Dawson nodded. 'I would.'

'Well then,' he said, swallowing his brandy. 'Finish up and I will show you.'

They went to the door of the main lab complex. Doctor Grunner opened it and ushered him inside. They went down a series of smaller corridors until they could see labs on each side. Grunner stopped and pointed.

'This is a biohazard area. To go forward, we must wear protective equipment. Come.'

He took Dawson into a compact room, and they dressed in heavy isolation suits. As they adorned the cumbersome suits, another came and checked they were secure. He opened the door and they stepped into an isolation booth.

The door closed behind them.

'We must wait.' The heavy mask muffled Grunner's voice.

The round goggles restricted Dawson's vision. He felt sweat dripping down his neck, inside his shirt.

Water jets came from the ceiling and doused them. When it stopped, the door ahead was opened.

Lieutenant Dawson followed into a bright white room lined with equipment on tables, some of which he couldn't identify. Grunner opened another heavy door and they entered a darker corridor lit by purple ultraviolet light.

'We enter into lab sixteen.'

Lab sixteen differed from the others. It was large, tiled, with many steel tables that looked like they'd come straight from a morgue. They were illuminated by bright bulbs on long cords, and around the room he spotted more UV light. Underneath them were cages of mice and rats.

'What do you do in here?'

He joined Doctor Grunner beside a table.

'The work varies,' he said. 'Here we perform several tests on subjects. These tests have proven successful in providing cures for many illnesses. We have discovered a serum that we believe can cure nearly all forms of viral and bacterial infections.'

'That is an amazing breakthrough, and must be very exciting work.'

Grunner nodded. 'Yes, very.'

He turned to a metal cupboard and pulled out a jar, placing it onto the table.

'This is the source of our success.'

'The serum?'

'No,' he said, unscrewing the top. 'The source is a mystery we may never learn enough to unlock completely. But, given the correct conditions and resources, it is only a matter of time.'

Dawson looked inside. He saw a small amount of black, viscous fluid.

'Some kind of oil?' he asked.

'We thought this at first, but no. It isn't oil. Open cage alpha-one and bring me a subject.'

He did as Grunner instructed. Inside he found several white mice. He grabbed one as best he could in heavy gloves and sealed the cage. He took the mouse to the table. Grunner put a clear container on the surface and at Grunner's instructions, Dawson dropped the mouse inside.

The doctor sealed it with a thick lid that had a small hole in its centre.

Probably to ensure the mouse could breathe, he mused.

'Now I will demonstrate how we develop the serum.' With a pipette, he took a sample of the black substance and Dawson watched as he carefully placed it above the contained. It took Grunner some effort to get a single drop of the viscous substance to come out, but when it eventually did, Dawson watched the heavy droplet fall in fascination. Doctor Grunner then put the pipette back inside the jar and sealed it, placing it away from the container.

Dawson watched as the mouse wandered around. It seemed to avoid the black stuff.

'What now?' Dawson asked.

Grunner came alongside. 'This is where we were paused for many weeks. We know now in these states, it is impossible to integrate the two. If the substance is put onto the subject, it is absorbed, but with no significant effect. If we inject it, the results were the same. Then by chance we found a solution.'

He removed the lid and lifted the mouse, turning it a few times, letting it run over his hands.

'One of these test mice had been injured, despite our care. Regard.' He took a thin back leg between his fingers and snapped it. The mouse gave a squeal. Dawson stared in shock as Gruner then took the other back leg and did the same.

'Was that necessary?' Dawson asked, almost feeling the poor rodent's pain.

'Do not concern yourself, primitive creatures such as these

do not feel pain as we understand. Their response is purely instinctive.'

'I don't know,' Dawson said, still feeling awful. 'It sounds like it was painful.'

Grunner said nothing as he dropped it back into the container and replaced the lid. It seemed to Dawson he did this with a different urgency than before.

'Watch,' he said.

The mouse attempted to drag itself forward, with its back legs broken. It didn't go far. Dawson couldn't help feeling sorry for it. Then something odd happened. The black dot in the container's bottom was moving.

'Is it growing?'

Grunner said, 'Not exactly. Its mass isn't increasing. Continue to observe.'

The black dot formed into a thin tendril that wavered as it manifested. Then it fell in the mouse's direction and slithered towards it. With a speed that made Dawson jump, it grabbed a back leg. The mouse fought against it, but somehow the thin strand was stronger. It pulled the rodent towards it.

'Fascinating, yes?' Grunner asked.

'What am I seeing?'

The mouse was now atop the black substance.

'What now?' Dawson asked.

'Patience.'

Something was happening to the mouse. It was shuddering, quivering. Its tiny body seemed stiff, it bulged its eyes, a tiny tongue poked out of its mouth. Dawson saw its pink eyes go black. He leant forward, then jumped as it burst, hitting the sides of the container with a squelchy thud.

'What the hell?'

'Hell?' Grunner seemed to approve. 'An apt word.'

'It exploded the mouse?'

Grunner shook his head. 'It integrates this way. The sample needs direct access to the heart, so it pushes through and opens the cavity. Once inside, a merging with the remains begins, and something new is born.'

'Something new? A mutant mouse?'

'Yes, in this instance. When the transformation is complete, a sack will develop alongside the salivary gland. It will fill with a venom, which it uses to subdue and possibly kill its prey. We develop an antivenom by harvesting it, using domestic animals as a means to create antibodies. The venom is deadly, but it has other properties. It kills viruses and bacteria. The antivenom loses this in the process. We inject a person with small doses of venom, which kills all other viral and bacterial concerns, then administer the antivenom and a patient is cured.'

'How many mice do you need to make enough? Doesn't seem like you'd get much?'

'Oh, mice aren't useful at all. No, it is simply a means by which we discovered how to extract it. To produce the venom in the quantities we need, a subject must be bigger than a mouse. The interesting thing is, the subject need not be alive once the venom sack is full.'

Grunner picked up the container and watched as the mouse began its slow transformation. He took it to a vat.

'Open this please and be careful. It is liquid nitrogen.'

Dawson obeyed and stepped back. Grunner removed the lid and emptied the contents into the vat. There was an odd lyrical squeal and gurgled fizz, and then it went quiet.

'Seal the vat, please.'

Dawson finished screwing the top down and then returned to the table.

'Was that a good demonstration?'

Dawson nodded. 'Although I felt bad for the mouse.'

'Then let us move on, come.'

Grunner led him to another door and opened it.

'I think you got the wrong room, Doc,' he said. Dawson went to turn, but something hit him and he fell. His world went dark.

When Dawson opened his eyes, he cursed. The pain in his head was hideous. He reached up and found the source, a deep cut in the base of his skull. There was enough light to see the blood on his hand. Dawson realised he wasn't wearing his protective mask. He looked around. It was a circular room, like the inside of a boiler. There was a muffled noise above and he looked up. From a small window, he saw a masked face staring back at him. Dawson made out spectacles within. Disorientated and confused, he groaned at the pounding in his head. A wave of nausea threatened to overwhelm him. As he leant forward, groaning, his eyes fell on something and he frowned. He couldn't make out what it was at first, then his mind cleared enough for him to remember.

He'd seen it before.

The sight froze his heart.

He whimpered.

It was the same black substance Grunner had in the lab, only this was much larger. A tendril began to rise. Ominous and silent. Dawson's attempts to back away were thwarted as he hit the wall.

Tears fell from his terrified, whimpering face.

Dawson's mind was replaying images of the mouse's end. Grunner had made him witness the demise, so he would understand the process as it happened to him. Lieutenant Bruce Dawson's terror eclipsed his ability to speak. When the monstrous black thing had raised itself high enough, it seemed to waiver.

There was a stillness.

A second felt like an hour.

Dawson gave a strangled scream as it grabbed him. He felt other tendrils wrap around his legs, and pressure against his spine. His scream changed pitch as it invaded his body. Chest pushed outwards... blood spraying from his mouth, he felt each rib crack and burst through his skin.

His eyes found Grunner's, who continued to watch long after Dawson was pulled apart.

CHAPTER THIRTEEN

12 a.m.

It had been an almost endless day. Exhausted and feeling every bit his age, Marshall stifled another yawn and stood. They'd played cards with the boys for a few hours, and made sure they weren't feeling too isolated, but when they'd gone to sleep, he slipped away and made himself comfortable. After a shower, he climbed into the bed Doctor Husk made up for him, and with a weariness he hadn't felt in sometime, fell into a sound sleep. A light tap on his arm woke him with a start.

'Bill?'

Marshall turned unfocused to Bradley and yawned.

'You with me?' the colonel whispered.

Marshall blinked a few times and stretched as he sat up. 'I'm awake.'

'Where's Kate?'

'In with the boys.' He rubbed his neck. 'They were having nightmares.'

'Okay, listen, I've got a bit to tell you, and then I have to run. Keep this between us. Doyle is dead.'

'What?' Marshall was awake now. 'How?'

'Turns out, he might not have been the saintly man we all assumed. Someone killed him. Bashed his head in. I found out through a few contacts, although Todd and his men haven't said a bloody word. I suspect they're behind it somehow.'

'Todd?'

'Ex-chief of police, it's a long story. I'll fill you in on him later.'

'What was Doyle doing?'

'I get the impression that he was dealing. Probably Benzedrine or cocaine. From what I've been able to discover, he's a bit of a sexual deviant.'

Marshall shook his head. 'I would never have guessed. You think someone killed him for the drugs?'

'I don't know. I'm really not interested. John is my concern. I've recruited Paul Barrette to help me.'

Marshall gave a look of concern. 'Captain Barrette? Isn't he Ira's man? You're sure we can trust him?'

Bradley smiled.

It was a smile which always worried Marshall. 'Braders? What the hell did you do?'

'Nothing you need concern yourself with. He's on board, and has a vested interest in John's well-being.'

'How so?'

'Let's just say he and John are a little more than friends.'

Marshall raised his eyebrows. 'Oh,' he said. 'Wait... John?'

'Keep that to yourself, Bill.'

'Is everyone here queer?'

Bradley chuckled. 'Our boys outside are keeping anyone away, so we shouldn't get any surprises. But if we do, things might get sticky for me. If it looks like that might happen, they have a plan to cause a bit of disruption.'

'Which is?'

'It's actually a fairly simple plan,' he said.

● ● ●

Colonel Ira Baldwin lifted the fork to his mouth and hesitated. He'd lost his appetite days before, and since the last fatalities, it had diminished further. He wasn't hungry, but knew he should eat. His mind kept repeating recent events, as if to taunt him. Things had been simpler before General Marshall and his men arrived. Not that the old general was giving him any trouble, he mused. If he was poking his nose into things, he'd have to be dealt with. Baldwin frowned as he thought this over. Aware that the fork was still wavering at his mouth, he ate its contents, and dropped the fork onto the plate and pushed it away. His eyes fell on a photograph and he picked it up. Baldwin ran a thumb over the girl's face and his expression hardened.

He stood and straightened his shirt, then poured himself a generous glass of whiskey and downed it. The sound of the clock's second hand seemed louder than usual. It was two a.m., but he was wide awake. Baldwin stared at the clock and relaxed his eyes so they lost focus. The hands and numbers all blurred into one.

A light tap on the door broke him from his thoughts and he went and opened it, then smiled at the woman he found standing there. A large fur coat pulled tight around her. It was an absurd thing to be wearing, but he knew why.

'Sarah?'

'Can I come in?' she asked.

'Yes.' He gestured and closed the door as she passed him and sat on the soft couch. Baldwin went back to the whiskey and flipped another glass, pouring them a shot.

Sarah ran her eye over the half-eaten food. 'Oh, you're still eating?'

Baldwin shook his head and sat beside her. She raised her glass and he clinked it.

'Sarah, you know Marshall and your brother still think you're missing?'

'What did you tell them?'

'That you'd gone out and not returned. I've told several lies for you.'

She remained neutral. 'Is it becoming a problem?'

'Maybe,' he said, looking away.

She took his face and turned it back to her. 'What's wrong?'

'Nothing it's... things are just tough right now.'

'With Paul?'

Baldwin nodded.

'Can I ask you something?'

'Of course,' Baldwin said.

'Why does Paul have a different last name to you?'

'That's easy,' he said. 'Paul took his mother's name when he joined the service.'

'Because of your conflict?'

He nodded. 'As far as he's concerned, his father is dead along with his mother. Anyway, that's enough about that. I'm really rather tired.'

'Do you want me to leave?'

'No, that's not what I'm saying.'

'Talk to me, Ira. Your constant frowning is giving you worry lines.'

He found a smile, but there wasn't much warmth to it. 'Nothing anyone can do about that.'

Sarah looked into his eyes. 'Nothing?'

He kissed her hand. 'There's a lot going on, that's all. Lying about you isn't something I need on top of everything else.'

'I can't go back, Ira.' Her anxiety was clear. 'Please, you know what he'll do.'

Baldwin squeezed her hand. 'I'm sorry, I didn't mean to upset you. It's okay, we'll find a way around this. You won't have to go back. But we can't keep saying you're missing.'

'You're right. What do you say we talk about this another time?'

He finished his drink and put down his glass. Baldwin took her hand and led her to his bedroom.

Her fingers dug into his shoulder blades as he kissed along her neck. She sighed at his touch. Sweat glistened off them both as he spun her. As she straddled him the soft light cast shadows across her breasts. Her eyes never left his. Sarah leant forward and kissed him, while he bucked underneath. His arms holding her tight. With a flurry of thrusts, they fell together in a mutual sigh.

It took a few minutes for their breathing to normalise and he pulled a packet of cigarettes off the nightstand and lit two, passing one to her.

Sarah propped herself up and smoked, dropping ash into the tray he'd laid on his chest.

'You've been quiet tonight,' she said.

He turned to her. 'Have I? Sorry.'

'I'm not complaining,' she said, through a puff of smoke.

He took a long drag and exhaled.

'I just have a lot on my mind, that's all.'

'You always do,' she said, stubbing her cigarette out. 'That rarely stops you.'

Baldwin tossed the pack to her, and she lit another.

'Things have got complicated, Sarah. That's all.'

'With Paul? Or whatever it is you're doing in the lab?'

He remained quiet.

'Which is top secret and none of my business.'

They smoked in silence for a while, then she stubbed out her second cigarette and he removed the ashtray.

'Can we talk about other things?' His arms drew her closer, and she snuggled into him. Her cheek lay on his chest, eyes staring down at his masculine form.

'You have a good body,' she said, tracing a pectoral with a finger. Brushing against his nipple. She felt him quiver and a smile pulled across her face. She turned, head up, so she could see him.

'Shall we fuck again?' he asked.

She grinned as he pinned her onto the bed.

A little while later, Sarah sat fixing her hair in the mirror. She smiled at her reflection and gave a slight flinch. There was something in her eye. She rubbed it, blinking a few times, and it cleared. Sarah leant closer to the mirror and cursed as she noticed it was bloodshot. Her rubbing had made it water. A tear fell, which she caught on her thumb. She gave a brief frown. The fluid wasn't clear, it was blackish, and felt oily. She rubbed it into her fingers and shrugged as it absorbed into the skin.

• • •

The corridor was quiet. Colonel Bradley moved along the wall in a whisper and slipped into the lab's office unchallenged. Once inside, he opened the adjoining door and found the isolation room. His training as an infiltrator of German labs aided his quick thinking. It wasn't long before he found an isolation suit and put it on. His identity covered. He pinned Captain Barrett's identification into his chest pocket, went through the heavy airlock, and stepped into the lab. As he and Captain Barrett were the same height, he felt sure no one would suspect his subterfuge.

Several people were working along benches, but as he surmised, they paid little attention as he passed them. Bradley went into the office at the far end of the lab and closed the door. He went to several file cabinets and poked through, pulling out the odd file and scanning them. Once he finished, he left the office and went through to the next lab airlock. This one was busier. Bradley stepped towards several glass containers, filled with organs. The same ones he'd observed when they'd first arrived. He grabbed a file from a board hanging underneath. A scientist working nearby came close, so he studied the file, waiting to see how they'd react to his presence. They ignored him. His view was restricted from the rounded goggles, but he could observe them easily enough. Their lack of concern suggested they assumed he was another worker. He fell in next to two and made himself look busy as they chatted.

They were working over a metal pot sitting atop a gas burner.

'What's the temp?' a male voice wearing a red armband said, writing notes on papers clipped to a board.

'Ninety-one,' the male working the pot replied, his band yellow.

Colonel Bradley decided red was the scientist in charge.

'Any reactions?' Red asked.

'Nothing yet.'

Yellow made adjustments to instruments hanging from the pot and turned to electronic equipment next to it. 'Wait. There's additional heat coming from the samples,' he remarked. 'I'm reading a two-degree variance and rising.'

'Lower the heat a little, see if it continues to rise.'

Yellow adjusted the burner. 'Still rising. We're at ninety-seven. Not a significant change though.'

Red was beside him in an instant. 'That's interesting. Time?'

'Two minutes and twenty-six seconds.'

'Without the samples it took twice that.'

Yellow continued to monitor. 'Ninety-eight. The samples are activating.'

'Shut off the heat,' Red said, his tone jumped in pitch.

The flame extinguished and they both continued to stare.

'Water temp is dropping, but the sample is at ninety-nine and still rising.'

'Pull them out,' Red said, bringing over a small vat and lifting off the lid. White vapour rolled from it as it made contact with the air. 'Submerge them.'

Yellow lifted a tray of tubes from the pot. Colonel Bradley observed a tar like substance in each, and it appeared to be moving.

'Quickly.' There was new urgency in Red's voice. Once he lowered the samples inside the vat, it gave a plume of vapour which rolled onto the table, and dissipated as Red closed the lid. Bradley saw their posture relax when they sealed it.

'We know the other samples activated at seventy-five degrees, but these didn't until almost at a hundred,' Yellow said.

'Looks like Grunner's theory was right, we can control the activation.' Red lifted the vat onto a small cart. 'The methane-ammonia infusion worked. I only hope it hasn't changed the dormancy values. We won't know that until tomorrow. Good data, I'll take it to Grunner. It's two a.m., I think we should wrap this up, don't you?'

Yellow nodded.

Red looked up, noticing Bradley for the first time. 'The two of you take this back to lab sixteen.'

Bradley nodded and fell in beside Yellow as he pushed the cart toward another airlock.

'Open the door, please,' Yellow said. Bradley turned the wheel and pulled it open. They entered a corridor lit by ultraviolet light. He pushed the cart through as his counterpart sealed the door behind and opened an interconnecting hatch to a lab lit in similar fashion.

'This is lab sixteen?' Bradley asked, in his best American accent.

'No, this is twelve. You've never been to sixteen before?'

He shook his head. 'I'm new. They moved me from section two.'

'Oh. Welcome to hell then.'

'Why d'you say that?'

'You know what we're doing here?' he said.

'Not really, I'm just a military grunt.'

He leant in and looked at Bradley's badge.

'Oh yeah, I see that, Captain Barrette. What are you even doing here? The last I heard, Grunner stopped all military personnel from working in the labs after the accident.'

Bradley shrugged. 'It's a new role. I'm the liaison between the scientists and command. What's your name?'

'Daniel,' he said. 'Doctor Daniel Keswick.'

'MD?'

'Microbiology. We have a liaison? That's new. Usually we give all our data to Grunner.'

'Don't look at me for answers. I got my orders from the colonel direct. Sorry you weren't up to speed with the change.'

Daniel snorted. 'We're used to it. The military brass doesn't tell us much, and nothing about what's going on outside the labs.'

'That's why they gave me the job,' he said, pushing the cart through the doorway.

'We're under strict control,' Daniel said with a sigh. 'Not allowed recreation or contact with anyone outside of the lab. We have our own rooms, which is nice. But it's not much fun being with a bunch of scientists all day and night.'

'Must get boring?'

Daniel laughed. 'You have no idea. I suppose it could be worse. We have everything we need. Since we're stuck here. Still... I'd like a bit of female company, once in a while, know what I mean? We get to spend time with your lot, but the gender pool is a bit lacking, along with intelligent conversation. No offence, Captain.'

'None taken. There are female scientists though, I've seen them.'

Daniel snorted. 'Might just as well be men. New-age women, full of themselves. Far too interested in work than fun.'

'How terrible for you,' Bradley said.

'Yeah well, it's the age we're in. Before it was all about the war. That was bad enough, but since whatever is going on above ground, anxiety and the sense of isolation has really hit home, you know? No one is talking about it. Do you know anything?'

'Not much. We saw some enormous creatures destroying cities and everything in between, and the smaller ones were rounding up survivors. It was like something out of that Orson Welles broadcast.'

'I remember that. *The War of the Worlds*. A lot of fun, actually.'

'Didn't it cause widespread panic?'

Daniel chuckled. 'I'm not convinced. Hard to believe people would think it was true. Martians, for goodness sake.'

'And yet?'

'What? You think those things out there are Martians?'

'You don't?'

Daniel shook his head. 'I work in science, not science fiction. There's nothing otherworldly about them. They're from planet Earth, that's a scientific fact.'

'How can you be sure?'

'Monsters like that couldn't live on Mars. I'm a bit of an amateur astronomer. Mars hardly has any atmosphere, and very little oxygen. These things need oxygen, so they wouldn't have developed that way on Mars. I read the scientific journals. They think the atmosphere is mostly carbon dioxide, much more than Earth. It's damn cold too. Anyway... even if they did come from Mars, how? Strikes me that monsters can't fly rocket ships.'

'Fair point,' Bradley said. 'I heard someone suggest they're demons?'

'That's a load of baloney.'

'Well, let's hope you find the answers and a solution.'

'A solution?'

'Isn't that what you're working on?'

Daniel turned to him. 'Who told you that?'

'I assumed.'

'Well, you know what they say about assumption?'

'Indeed. What are you working on, then?'

'A cure for the virus,' Daniel said.

'Right. Using those samples. How did you get them? From the creature you captured?'

He nodded. 'When it died, its body decayed into this black sludge-like substance. It's volatile and highly adaptive. Even though the mutated dog thing is dead, the stuff it turned into isn't.'

'You mean it's alive?'

'In a manner of speaking, not like us. It's a complex self-replicating organic compound, similar to the primordial soup.'

'Primordial soup?'

'You've never heard of that? It's theorised the precursor to life on Earth may have developed in an amino acid–rich soup, produced by reactions to methane and ammonia in the Earth's early atmosphere. We've been testing the samples using similar atmospheric conditions, while it's in a dormant state. The results are very encouraging.'

'What happens when it's active?'

'I don't think you want to know,' Daniel said.

'Please,' Bradley replied, touching his shoulder. 'I really do.'

'When the sample activates, it invades a body. It penetrates the spine which incapacitates the victim, then pushes through the chest cavity – exposing the heart, which it bursts – absorbs the blood, then consumes what remains.'

'Those tiny samples do that to a person?'

'Not a person,' he said, shaking his head. 'It doesn't have the mass needed for that. I'm talking about mice, Paul.'

'That's a relief. You said you were using it for a cure?'

'We had a nasty respiratory outbreak a while back. A group working on this compound, we call it sample beta, found it could kill viruses. We've been attempting to use it to synthesise a viral antidote ever since.'

They reached another door, and Daniel opened it.

'The sample is native to Earth. Probably been dormant underground for millions of years. Oil drillers pulled it up, no doubt, and released it.'

'The soup?'

'Right. Like I said, it's the building block. A progenitor for life. No doubt it mutated a few things along the way and they multiplied.'

Bradley thought for a moment. 'Like the dogs?'

'Exactly.'

'What about the larger creatures?'

'I don't have all the answers, just theories. Here's one that no one has thought about. What if it doesn't need living tissue to replicate itself?'

'You mean it could come into contact with a fossil and make a dinosaur?'

'If there was trace genetic material, I think it's plausible. More so than Martians and demons.' Daniel sealed the door and they moved on.

'What's so special about lab sixteen?' Bradley said, going through.

'It's an isolation lab.'

'I thought they were all isolated?'

'They are, but this one's different. It's a total isolation zone. Power, air, everything. We keep these samples there. If they activate, we can control the environment and lock them down. Even if we suffer a power failure, lab sixteen remains autonomous. Its temperature must stay below freezing.'

'Yes, I heard you say this soup becomes active at higher temperatures.'

They reached the last door and Daniel chuckled. 'Yeah, and no one wants that.'

'They didn't brief me much,' Bradley said. 'Although I'm suspecting the accident you mentioned is the reason your samples are much smaller?'

'Help me with this seal. It takes two of us.'

Together they opened the door and Daniel held it while

Bradley pushed the cart in. When they were inside, Bradley turned to him. 'I'm right, aren't I?'

'I'm not supposed to talk about it,' Daniel said.

'Come on, Daniel. You've already told me so much. A scientist died. That stuff killed him, I'm right, aren't I?'

He nodded, then put a hand on his arm. 'It's top secret.'

'I have clearance, it's fine.'

'Not from Grunner you don't.'

'The German?'

'Nasty bit of work. There's something about him I don't like. He has a way of leaning into you, like he's about to take a bite out of you, or something. And his ethics are questionable.'

'Surely not?'

'There are rumours about his background. I'm not sure what's true, but I wouldn't want him as my physician. He'd probably infect me with something, just to see the results.'

'He's a highly decorated medical man? I couldn't imagine him doing that.'

'I was there when the accident happened. It was my friend who died. I still have trouble talking about it. That description I gave you about what this stuff can do? I saw it. Grunner just stood there staring. When everyone else was frantic, he just stood there. I swear he was enjoying it. We tried to break in, but he ordered us to lock the door. Poor Evelyn hasn't recovered. After the accident, Grunner had us subdue it with liquid nitrogen. We know at low temperatures it would turn solid. After that, we broke it into smaller samples.'

'These are part of what consumed your friend?'

Daniel nodded.

'I'm so sorry.'

'Ever looked into a man's eyes and seen into their soul? Grunner's evil. Pure evil.'

Colonel Bradley refrained from explaining how he knew that to be true. He just nodded.

Daniel looked down at the vat. 'Help me get it into the freezer.' Once they'd secured it, Bradley looked over at a windowed door. It differed from the others in that it was circular. As if the room was a giant tank. He pointed. 'What's in there?'

Daniel looked over at the door. 'That's a liquid-nitrogen flood tank.'

'What's it for?'

'It's a reserve tank. We converted an old silo. Since we knew we'd need quite a lot of it, we began processing it here. It's easy enough to make.'

He followed Bradley over to the door. They peered inside. With no light, other than what filtered through the window, they could just make out the surface of liquid that filled the room up to the window.

'That's liquid nitrogen?' Bradley asked.

'In the event of a containment breach, it's used to flood the lab. It'll freeze the sample on contact.'

'Along with anyone who happens to be in there with them?'

'If that protocol is active, they're already dead. Come on, it's late, and I'm hungry.' Daniel walked away. Bradley stared at the liquid for a moment longer and turned to join him.

Inside, a black tendril lifted, sending a ripple around the room. It bent as it moved to the window. Black layers pulled back to reveal an eye.

A human eye.

It watched as they exited the lab.

CHAPTER FOURTEEN

3 a.m.

Doctor Kate Husk blinked a few times. The disorientation she felt came with a wave of nausea. The room was full of occupied beds. She didn't know how many, but there were a lot. For the longest time she stood, not sure what it was they meant for her to do. A groan beside her snapped her from the reverie. A man in his early twenties lay in the bed nearest to her. Wearing only underwear and drenched in sweat, he threw his head from side to side as he gave mournful groans. Without hesitation, she was beside him. His eyes vacant, mouth encrusted in vomit running down his neck, soaking the bedsheets. Intuitively she grabbed for the washcloth lying in a bowl of water on a cabinet next to his bed and cleaned his mouth.

'Can you tell me your name?'

His eyes were all over the place. The touch of the damp cloth drew a flicker of response. Those wild eyes soon found hers, and he moaned. His expression was terrible. A tear fell from his eye and she wiped it away. He tried to speak, but the effort was too much.

'It's okay, I'm going to help...'

His eyes upturned and lost their focus again. He arched his back and mucus bubbled from his mouth. Husk cleared it, aware now of the gurgled rasp of his breathing.

He's aspirating, badly, she thought. The aerated fluid that frothed straight from his lungs bubbled out his nose. She attempted to turn him, but then he shot up and gave an inhuman scream.

Husk jumped back, instinctively ducking, throwing both hands up to protect herself. His arms swung wildly at her. She wanted to get him onto his side, but the look in his upturned eyes cautioned her from stepping forward. Husk remained out of reach as his spasming fingers tried again to grab her. She backed further away, her eyes now on the other beds.

A chorus of moans assaulted her, and her heart rate increased.

The man she'd been assisting fell onto his back. His legs and arms jerking spasmodically.

Movement alerted her and she looked up. Focused on her patient, she hadn't noticed two nurses propped against the far wall. They were rising now, in lurching, lumbering advances. As though they had forgotten how to walk. With each step forward they hit beds and other obstacles until they found the bed she was now backing away from. They staggered along each side. Locked in his feverish state, he wasn't aware of them. One nurse, her head held at an odd angle, bent down and almost laid it on his chest, and for a brief moment, she thought the nurse was listening to his heart. But then her pallid face turned into his skin and she started making a snuffling sound, and the other soon joined her.

Husk's frown deepened. Both their faces were hovering close to his chest, making slow jerks along his body, down towards his crotch, heads colliding as they went.

All the time, they were sniffing.

Sniffing.

Sniffing...

Doctor Husk jumped as one of them buried her face into his abdomen. He gave a hideous cry. His body thrashed and his arms flailed. The other then threw her face into his chest, and Husk watched in horror as they bit through his skin and tore chunks of his flesh away, spitting them onto the floor. Their hands holding him down as he thrashed in the agony of their attack. He screamed and writhed as they ripped through his muscles, feasting on his exposed entrails, shoving them into their mouths without bothering to chew. Their faces and hands slick with his blood and filth.

Husk's heart rate increased further as they pulled out organs in their frenzied assault. She didn't know how long she'd been a frozen spectator. Long enough for their victim to cease moving. His dead eyes now locked with hers. She read the accusations they held.

Her breathing came faster. Medical training and obligation were replaced now by a desire to flee. She backed away as they continued, dropping organs onto the floor with wet thuds. Their groans and gurgles in unison. Like a chorus.

She hit against something. There was a crash. Kate saw a tray of instruments scattering on the polished floor. When she looked up, the blood-covered nurse's hazy blue-white fully dilated eyes were on her. With a croaking growl, they lumbered from their victim. Chunks of intestines and excrement fell from their chins.

Husk turned and ran towards the doorway at the far end of the room. She heard the clumsy nurses behind her. When she reached the door, her shaking hands couldn't open it. The nurses shuffled closer.

Closer.

Closer...

Doctor Husk heard their awkward advance and her terror jumped another notch as she twisted and pulled at the useless handle.

But still the door would not open.

Glancing back, she felt her terror increase. It wouldn't be long before they reached her. Their dead, unfocused eyes fixed, with arms outstretched, their intent clear as they began sniffing. Blood dripping from their hands and faces, leaving a slick trail of droplets behind.

Doctor Husk voiced her fear with a whimpered cry. It turned to a scream of frustration, which she directed at the door. But still it would not open.

They were closer still. She knew it wouldn't be long before they reached the door. Husk attacked the handle with renewed desperation, but she recognised if she couldn't open it soon, she would need to abandon it, and run. If they cornered her, they would kill her. But they were slow, clumsy, and unco-ordinated. Walking dead. No, she chastised herself. They weren't in their right minds, that was all. They were sick. It had affected their brains somehow, made them delirious, put them into some kind of waking coma or trance, driven by instinct, maybe? But obviously not dead.

All this and more went through her mind as she calculated how long she would have before it would be too late to evade them, which was rapidly approaching. They'd reached that point she'd decided was too close, and she made to run. But a familiar sound filled her with relief as the door opened, and a strong hand grabbed and pulled her through.

Doctor Husk fell against the now shut door, jumping as the nurses thumped against it on the other side. Feeling safer, her terror subsided. She looked into General Marshall's face and released the fear choking her. She uttered a thankful sigh, then her face froze. There was something wrong with his eyes. They were blue-white hazy eyes, fully dilated, just like the nurses. His head lopsided, tilted, hanging loose as though the weight of it was too great for him to hold up. Husk's fear increased as he staggered towards her.

Marshall backed her into the door. There was nowhere to go and he was too close to evade. His hands reached for her. She tried slapping them away, but he was too strong. When he breached her defences and found her shoulders, he shook them, hard.

The slack, dead-eyed face inched closer.

Doctor Husk screamed as she fought him. His mouth opening, his mucus flying into her face, her mouth.

'Kate!'

Her eyes snapped open.

Marshall was shaking her.

'Kate, wake up,' he said.

Her senses took in the surroundings and her mind cleared. She understood she was waking, and stopped struggling. Her eyes met his. They were grey blue, not dead like the image of him still locked in her mind. His concern clear. She sighed as he released his grip on her shoulders. Doctor Husk sat for a moment, her hands shaking. Shivering from the cold of her sweat-drenched nightclothes.

'Bill?' she said, blinking. The imagery of her dream threatening to overwhelm her.

His happy relief tipped her over the edge, and she burst into tears.

Marshall grabbed and hugged her tight, and she sobbed into his shoulder.

• • •

'How are you feeling?' King asked.

Barrette stared at the mug King placed by his bedside. Barrette rubbed his eyes. His recollection hazy.

'Coffee?' he asked, rubbing his throat and picking up the cup.

'Figured you'd want a pick me up.'

He took a sip and sighed. 'Thanks.'

Barrette looked at Tony King, who sat down in a chair next to his table. In his faded grey sweatpants and muscle shirt, he noticed how muscular King was. His broad shoulders and thick neck were huge, and his biceps were bigger than Barrette's calves. His eyes examined the room as he sipped the coffee. Like his own quarters, it was a three bedroom. But given the small number of personal things dotted around, it seemed there was only a single occupant.

'Mind telling me where I am, and whose bed I'm in?'

'This is my place. You're in my bed, and you're welcome.'

'What time is it?'

'Three-thirty in the morning.'

Barrette lifted the cover and found someone had undressed him to his underwear.

'Where are my fucking clothes?'

King laughed. 'Relax. You vomited all over yourself. Your clothes are being cleaned.'

'Oh,' he said, feeling self-conscious. 'Thanks. I honestly don't remember much.'

King turned back to the table. 'It wasn't your fault.'

Barrette slipped out of the bed and came next to him. It was obvious the larger man wasn't comfortable with him standing so close in just his underwear.

Barrette's expression wasn't happy. 'You put something in my drink?'

'I didn't. But there was something in it.'

Barrette put down his coffee. 'What? And more important than that, why?'

King stood and went to the dresser, pulling open a drawer. He threw a pair of sweatpants over at him. 'Put them on.'

Barrette slipped into the pants and sat. 'Well?'

'Things play out different down here,' he said.

'What does that even mean?'

King gave him a look. 'Don't play dumb. You know what I mean. The rules here aren't the same. Todd is the boss down here. He gives the orders, you understand?'

Barrette sank a little. 'Yeah, I'm beginning to. That British colonel is another fucking lunatic too.'

King chuckled. 'Braders is all right. He has a funny way about him, on account of him being a Brit, I guess. But don't fuck with him, he'll put you down just as soon as look at you. You get me?'

'You know he shot me?' Barrette said, taking a gulp of coffee.

'It's obvious he likes you though.'

'How d'you figure that?'

King shrugged. 'We're talking, aren't we?'

'He works for this Todd?'

'Braders don't work for no one. Him and Todd have a mutual understanding. Like I said before. Just be careful of him, all right? He's a friendly guy, but...'

Barrette finished his coffee. 'But?'

'He's a ruthless brutal killer, and that's coming from Todd.'

'And he'd know?'

King looked grim. 'He was the chief of police here.'

'You say that like it's a bad thing?'

'Look around, tiny. Seen any Blacks, other than me?'

'Now you mention it, no. At least not down here. But we have a mixture within the scientists and military.'

'Well, you won't find none down here. Todd saw to that soon enough.' He closed his eyes and sighed.

'I'm not sure how he thinks he's running the show,' Barrette said. 'This is a military compound. And I'm one of several senior officers. I could have him removed in a heartbeat.'

King regarded him. 'I've been here a little under two months.'

'What's your point?'

King poked him in the chest. 'We ain't clapped eyes on you till today. Don't give me that *I'm in charge* bullshit. You haven't done shit for us.' He was getting angry. 'This is a prison, and the fucking inmates are running it, you get it?' He pushed out of his chair and grabbed a bottle of something from the cabinet beside the dresser.

Barrette compressed his lips. King was right. He'd been down only once since the mass evacuations. And he'd worked in the camp for around six months. He didn't know why either.

'Sorry,' Barrette said.

King took a swig and put the bottle back. 'Forget it.' He regarded Barrette again, then returned to the chair.

'You got any family, Paul?'

'No. My mom killed herself.'

'Shit,' he said, 'I'm sorry.'

'Happened a long time ago.'

'What about your dad?'

'He's dead to me to. What about you?'

King shook his head. 'Not anymore. My kid brother and his whore girlfriend died when one of those monsters smashed our house down. I was lucky, being that I was out back when it happened. Hid till it went and spent the next ten hours digging for them with my bare hands. I suppose I could have left them in the ruins, but I wanted to give them a proper burial, you know?' His eyes brimmed. 'I'd just managed to dig down to where they were buried, when Todd and his cops arrived. We found them still in their bed. Like they was asleep. Todd's cops helped me get them out and I dug their graves in my yard. After that, I joined with them. He don't like Blacks, but I owed him.'

'I'm so sorry. I keep forgetting about what's happening outside. It's been so long since I was out there.'

'Easy to forget when you've been stuck here, I suppose. But not me. I miss him every day. Even that bitch of his.'

Barrette's thoughts had been centred on his mother a lot frequently. Mostly because like a fool, he'd accepted the invitation to meet with the colonel, and shortly after, been stuck with him. It stirred up a lot of horrible thoughts. King touched his arm and he jumped.

'Sorry. I didn't mean to bring up bad memories.'

'It's okay. I was thinking about some friends back in New Jersey. I just assumed they'd be okay.'

'Why?'

'Before the radio's went dead, there was no sign things were happening outside of Washington.'

'Jesus, Paul. That was months ago.'

'I know,' he said. Turning a shade of red. 'I've just been busy. It's not like I can take a week off and go look for them.'

'Why the fuck not?'

'I have a Todd too.'

'I guess you do,' King said, nodding.

They sat in silence for a while, then King exhaled. 'Right, no more of this shit. Time to get dressed and then we have to go meet with Todd.'

Barrette rubbed at the graze on his leg. 'I'm due on duty at eleven. What does Todd want with me, anyway?'

'Braders asked him to keep an eye on you.'

'What does that mean?' Barrette asked, frowning. 'Why?'

'Don't ask me, I just follow what I'm told.'

'Tony, I'm a captain in this facility.'

'Not down here you're not.'

'Where I am doesn't change that fact.'

'I'm surprised a bright young kid like you needs it fucking spelled out,' King said, a touch of menace creeping into his voice. 'You'll learn.'

'I'm not one of his grunts – no offence – and I don't need

a babysitter. I'm gonna head to my room, and get on with my life, and there's nothing Todd or anyone can do to stop me.'

'I wouldn't be so sure.'

'Come on, you're making it sound like I'm a prisoner.'

King slapped his arm. 'Guest, Paul.'

'A guest who can't leave?'

'For his own protection.'

'Really?' he said, crossing his arms. 'Protection from what?'

'Yourself, I suspect.'

'This is crazy. You tell Todd to go fuck himself.' He walked away, but a big hand grabbed his arm, preventing him from leaving.

'I can't do that.'

'Let me fucking go,' he said, struggling to release himself from King's grip.

'Paul,' he said, standing, towering over the smaller man. His grip tightening. 'Let's hit the shower. We'll grab your clothes from the laundry and go see Todd. Then you can tell him to fuck himself, that good with you?'

'Okay, okay, Jesus,' Barrette said as the circulation in his hand cut off. King stared at him for a while longer, then let go. He fell back into the chair, rubbing his arm. Whatever he had to say choked in his throat at the mean expression King was giving him. Barrette realised the seriousness of his predicament, and also that King could snap him in two. He gulped as King turned towards a stack of towels.

'Ready?' he said, holding a couple up.

'Yeah,' Barrette said, flexing the circulation back into his hand. 'Sure.'

• • •

As almost everyone was asleep or in their own space, they could carry Father Doyle's body through the empty kitchen, to the rooms out back, unseen. Kitchen staff took the waste bins every day around nine, and they didn't start work before six, so they'd have plenty of time to prepare the body so no one discovered it. With a grunt, they dropped it onto the table. While one opened a locker, pulling out a set of knives, the other removed the cadaver's clothes. He'd just got to the old priest's underwear, when the body twitched.

'Hey,' the man removing the clothes said in surprise.

'What?' the other asked, coming towards him, meat cleaver in hand.

'It fucking moved.'

'Don't be so jumpy, Henry. The back of his head is missing.'

'Fred, I swear it moved.'

'Look at him? You're just spooked.'

'I ain't going near it.'

'Come here and look.'

Henry came alongside. As he got close Fred shouted *Boo* in his ear, laughing as Henry jumped about ten feet.

'You fucking moron,' Henry yelled.

'Give it a rest. How many times have we done this? No one ever came alive before, did they?'

'No... Sorry,' he said, a hint of embarrassment etching his voice.

'Just get his skivvies off, and I'll start cutting him up.'

Henry pulled the shorts down and threw them in the garbage along with the rest of the clothes.

Fred stood beside the body, still chuckling. 'Fucking moved,' he said shaking his head.

Fred turned the head, so the neck was easier to get at, and raised the cleaver. He swung it down hard. But the blade never reached its target. The cadaver's arm shot out and grabbed his wrist before he could finish the blow. Fred gave a startled cry. It made the jumpy Henry turn, and the colour drained from his face. The naked corpse was rising with one hand on Fred's wrist, and the other around his throat. Its glazed dead eyes looking at nothing.

'Jesus fucking Christ,' Henry yelled, as he backed away in shock.

Fred gurgled as he fought the dead priest's hold. The cadaver gave a sharp flick of its wrist. Henry heard a sickening crack as Fred's body sagged in its grip. The priest dropped him and lumbered off the table. Its hazy eyes looked around the room.

Locked in his terror, Henry couldn't move. His emptying bladder stained his pants as the warm liquid dripped down his legs, pooling between his feet. Frozen, he could only stare at the door. The old priest dropped to the floor like an animal, and began sniffing the air. It skittered to Fred's body, all the time making odd clucking noises. Its head turned this way and that. Cloudy unblinking eyes shifted in constant motion as it ground its teeth. Tears rolled down Henry's cheeks. When the droplets hit the floor, the cadaver snapped its head in his direction.

Again, it sniffed the air, then scooted forward.

When it reached the edge of the puddle seeping from Henry's shoes, it lowered down and examined it. Henry's terror manifested in his throat as a whimper. He tried not to make a sound, but he couldn't stop it from slipping out of his throat. The cadaverous priest shuffled towards him, and Henry's flight response kicked in.

He leapt over the gangly creature and went for the door. With relief he made it to the handle, but that reprieve was lost when something grabbed his ankle and pulled him onto his back. Henry cursed and moaned as his head hit the floor. Dazed, he looked down his body and saw a hideous black tentacle wrapping around his ankle.

Its grip tighter.

Tighter.

His eyes followed it to the creature whose skin was now black. The old priest's body was changing. Pulsating. Expanding. Its arms now tentacles.

Henry uttered a piercing scream as a second tentacle grabbed and slid around his throat, pulling him towards it. Kicking and screaming, he slid along the floor. It lifted him and the tension around his neck cut off any further sound. Struggling in its tight hold, he kicked and bucked. Then his terror intensified, as he felt something moving up his back. It slipped under the collar of his shirt and made a slow crawl along his skin, down his spine.

Then it stopped.

Tension on his neck lessened, and he took a shuddering breath.

Whatever it was on his back began to press against his thoracic vertebrae.

It pushed harder.

Harder...

Henry gave a violent gurgled cry of surprise and pain, his body arched. His face wracked in agony. Tongue poking out in distress, the stress and strain bursting blood vessels under the surface of his eyes and face. And with a sickening wet cracking thump, blood burst from his mouth as his chest ripped apart. The spray from the open cavity hitting the wall and ceiling.

Henry's flailing ceased, replaced by the occasional spasming twitch of his limbs, as the blackened cadaverous priest lost its form and merged with Henry's broken corpse.

When it finished, and Henry was no more, it fell to the floor as a black gelatinous goo. Tendrils collected Fred's body and absorbed it, along with any remaining biological mater in the room. When it was done, it slid along the floor and up the wall, disappearing into a vent in the ceiling.

CHAPTER FIFTEEN

4 a.m.

Colonel Bradley knocked and opened the door. Todd Stevens and Jim Decker looked up as he entered. From their expressions, he decided, what they had to say would not be good. He took a seat next to them.

'Want to tell me what happened to Doyle?' he asked, lighting a cigarette and exhaling.

'How the fuck did you find out about that?' Stevens said, giving Decker a terrible look.

'It wasn't Jim,' Bradley said. 'I have sources, I'm not going to tell you who they are.'

'Well, that makes you a fucking problem then, Charlie,' Stevens said, standing.

Bradley looked up at him. 'Sit down, Todd. Before something bad happens.'

Todd Stevens' face turned a shade of purple. 'Listen you fucking...'

'Sit down,' Bradley said, his face firm. 'I'm not here to argue, nor fight. But believe me,' he said leaning forwards, 'if that's how you want to play this, you'd better have the stomach for it.'

Stevens and Bradley stared at each other, but eventually the Chief sat down.

'You brought a fucked-up priest here, and now I have a mess on my hands.'

'You're blaming me?'

Stevens let out a lengthy sigh, then shook his head. 'No.'

'I don't have intel on everyone we gathered. We picked up a few miscreants on the way, that's life. Don't waste my time with this nonsense, what have you found out?'

Stevens looked to Decker, then waved a hand. 'Jessie killed him.'

'Did she say why?'

'Not really,' Stevens remarked, getting up and grabbing a pot of coffee. He returned and placed it on the table, along with three cups. They each took one and drank.

Decker looked at Stevens, then said, 'Jessie did say, while she was doing the dirty, that Doyle went crazy. She kept babbling on about stuff that made no sense.'

'Like what?'

'That the devil had possessed him.'

'What made her think that?'

'His eyes went black.'

Stevens slurped at his coffee. 'Jessie likes to keep eye contact when she performs.'

Bradley shook his head. 'I suppose it's a good thing Sarah is missing, I'm sure this news will kill her.'

Stevens looked up. 'Sarah's not missing.'

'What?'

Stevens sat back in his chair. A smug look crossing his face. 'Sarah is fucking the colonel.'

Bradley raised an eyebrow. 'Really? That *is* interesting.'

Stevens smiled. 'After my girls service your fellow military friends, they tell me all about it. How d'you think I got these rooms, and those for my boys? By asking nicely?'

'Ah,' he said, with a chuckle. 'Police chief turned pimp, eh?'

Stevens leant forward. 'Everyone works for me, Charlie. Including Sarah.'

Bradley recognised the stony look in his eyes. He'd underestimated Todd Stevens.

'You've done well.'

'Sex sells,' he said, downing the last of his coffee. 'And it always will. I can tell you anything you need to know about the boys upstairs. Their preferences, kinks... some of it will make your toes curl. No one here steps out of line, and that line is fair but enforced when necessary.'

He turned to his colleague. 'Right, Jim?'

Decker nodded. 'It's the only way to keep people in check.'

Stevens smiled as he turned back. 'It's the only way to keep people in check.'

Bradley looked between them. 'Not a pimp... A mobster? I am impressed, Todd.' He paused, lifting his cup. 'I take it Jessie is dead then?'

Stevens shook his head. 'I'd avoid the stew for a couple of days, if I was you.'

'How delightful,' Bradley said, a look of disgust on his face. Then he sighed and rubbed his eyes.

'I recognise that look. What?'

'It's nothing, at least not yet.'

'It's something,' Stevens said, leaning into the table. 'If something bad is going down, I need to know about it.'

Bradley rubbed his chin in thought. 'There's odd stuff happening in the labs, and I mean, odd. I've gathered a little knowledge. It looks like they're working on an inoculation for a strain of flu or something. It has a high mortality rate.'

Stevens chuckled. 'That's old news, they've been working on that since we got here. Still with no idea how it infects so many or how they become infected. It's actually good for us, because with so many people dying off, or disappearing, we can add a few bodies and no one is the wiser.'

'Except Doyle, he's a higher profile.'

'Yeah,' Stevens said, 'that's being taking care of as we speak. So, what's got you worried about the lab people then?'

Bradley expression hardened. 'You ever met the nasty little Nazi doctor?'

'No. But I've heard of him. Grunner, right? He's a Nazi?'

'Yes, and a vile one.'

Decker laughed. 'According to the wireless, they're all fucking vile.'

Bradley stared at him. 'Not all of them. Some are just boys, following orders, doing what they think is right for their country. Children, really.'

'I never thought of them like that. Must be hard when you

look one in the eye and see a child staring back?' Decker said.

'I wouldn't know,' he said with a sniff. 'I usually put their eyes out before they stare back at me.' Something in the way Bradley said that made Decker shudder.

'Grunner is one of the worse ones? One of their leaders?' Stevens asked.

'Yes,' Bradley said.

'Why?'

'Because he has a reputation of human experimentation, that's why.'

Stevens and Decker exchanged looks. 'You think he might be deliberately infecting people?'

Bradley nodded.

'But why?' Decker asked.

'More test subjects for his inoculation, would be my guess. Or maybe he just likes it?'

'That's fucking evil,' Stevens said.

Bradley's expression turned hard. 'Oh, the irony, Todd.'

Todd Stevens smirked, but said nothing.

'In the lab, they have this substance. A sort of prehistoric sludge, they got from one of these dog creatures. They're experimenting on it, under Grunner's watchful eye, but...' He shook off his concerns and his facial features softened. 'It's a puzzle, and I don't have all the pieces, but I'm concerned.'

'You think he plans to infect everyone?'

'It's entirely possible. We should all be worried.' He sighed. 'Just remain vigilant and keep an eye out for anyone acting strange.'

'Like eyes turning black, strange?'

Bradley pulled another cigarette from his pack. 'If anyone acts out of character, even slightly, separate them.'

'And do what?'

Bradley lit the smoke and took a long drag. 'Watch them,' he said.

'You're beginning to worry me,' Stevens said. 'And I don't worry easy.'

'Nor do I.'

'And if they go crazy?'

'You really need me to spell it out for you?'

'No,' Stevens said, his features turned hard.

'What are you going to do about Doyle?' Bradley asked.

'Taken care of. My best men are on it. By the time anyone notices him missing, he'll be gone. We cleaned up the mess. What about your people? How are they holding up?'

'Bill and Kate are fine, they're in lockdown. The boys are with them too. My men are keeping them under surveillance.'

'The Matthews boys? Respectful kids. There aren't a lot of kids here, sadly. I knew their mothers, nice lady. What about your other friend, the one who got sick?'

The colonel put his cup down. 'No news yet, but that will change soon.'

'Because of Captain Barrette?'

Bradley nodded. 'Where is he?'

'Should be here any minute, Tony has him.' Stevens narrowed his eyes. 'Is he a threat?'

'No,' Bradley said, finishing his coffee. 'He's just a boy.'

'Didn't stop you scaring the crap out of him. Do you trust him?'

'No, not yet.' Bradley was thoughtful. 'I think I can use him, though.'

'What if he tries to use you?'

Bradley gave him a look.

Stevens put up his hands. 'What's your plan?'

'Once I've spoken with Paul, I'm going to have this lockdown suspended.'

'How are you going to do that?'

'I'm going to pay Colonel Baldwin a visit,' he said.

The door opened and they looked around. Tony King and Paul Barrette entered, and by the look on the young captain's face, he wasn't happy.

'Good morning,' Stevens said. 'Feeling better?'

Barrette stood with his arms crossed. 'No thanks to you.'

Stevens indicated a chair, and Barrette sat.

'Let's lay our cards out, so we're all on the same page. First off, I'm sorry we drugged you.'

Barrette looked between them. 'Go on,' he said, not acknowledging his apology.

'Captain... Paul, can I call you Paul?'

He nodded.

'Paul, there's some strange stuff going on upstairs. Things we're beginning to see down here. Look, I'm sorry if my precautions have annoyed you, but we need to work together.'

Barrette looked at Bradley. 'I'm sorry if I don't take you at your word, Todd. I've been shot, drugged, and now I'm a prisoner too?'

'Guest,' King mumbled.

'Who can't leave?' Barrette shot back.

Stevens said, 'Tony, get Paul's clothing from the laundry.'

King nodded and left.

'Sorry,' he said, turning back. 'Listen. You can leave once you've heard us out.'

Barrette noticed Colonel Bradley had said nothing.

'Sure, I'll listen.'

'It's about the labs, and what they're doing there,' Stevens said.

Barrette looked at Bradley but said nothing. 'What about it?'

'Charlie can fill you in.'

Colonel Bradley put out his cigarette. 'He already knows everything.'

'Well why didn't you fucking say so?'

'I have my reasons.' He turned to Barrette. 'I have a plan, but I can't do it alone. I need your help. Are you in?'

Paul Barrette sat for a moment in thought. Colonel Bradley pulled out another cigarette, and Barrette watched as the older man struck a match and took in a long drag. He watched it light up as he pulled on it, mesmerised by its orange glow.

'Can I have one of those?'

Bradley chucked him the packet. 'Keep them.'

Barrette lit one and exhaled. It calmed him. 'You must have stockpiled a lot, seeing as how many you smoke.'

Bradley smiled. 'Just enough to kill me.' He waited for Barrette to make a response.

'I don't like you, Colonel,' he said. 'You shot me, and you

had these guys drug me. I don't trust you, and if I thought it would make me feel better, I'd put a fucking bullet between your eyes.'

Bradley inclined his head. 'Fair points, but...?'

'I think you mean well, for a lunatic. So, I guess I'm in,' he said. 'Regarding the lab stuff. It's supposed to be top secret. How you got in to get that information is actually impressive.'

'It's what I do,' Bradley said. 'Oh, you'll probably need this.' He placed Barrette's ID on the table.

Barrette picked it up and laughed. 'You pretended to be me? And they suspected nothing?'

'Disguise is an art form. Convincing people you are some-one else isn't as hard as you might think.'

The young captain turned the ID over a few times. 'You are an interesting man, Colonel,' he said. 'Ruthless and scary, but interesting.'

'You're warming up to me, I can tell.'

'No,' he said, 'I'm really not.'

'Paul, what they're doing is wrong. However well inten-tioned it might have been. People have died. And since they've been working on this sludge stuff, more people have died.'

'A lot more than they've reported, I know because I've seen the bodies,' Barrette offered.

Colonel Bradley gave a slight tilt to his head, 'From the virus?'

'Yes, and when Berger went crazy.'

Stevens and Decker frowned. 'Who's Berger?'

'Scientist,' Barrette said.

Bradley leant forward. 'From the way Paul described it earlier, he said the creature they had in the lab attacked him.'

'That's right, after he bit the governor in the face. I had to deal with the aftermath of that.'

Stevens said, 'Wait. As far as I knew, the governor died from the virus. You're saying it was because Berger took a bite out him?'

'No,' Barrette said. 'He was sick, but after Berger bit him, he got better. When they let him out of confinement, Colonel Baldwin killed him.'

'You fucking guys are no better than me,' Stevens said. 'Why did Baldwin kill him?'

'Because the governor murdered Baldwin's wife.'

Stevens whistled. 'Can't blame him then. I'd have done the same fucking thing. Still. I knew the governor. He was a hard man. Balls of steel, that one. As corrupt as they come. Never pegged him for a murderer, though. Not really his style. You think it had something to do with the virus?'

Barrette shrugged. 'I don't know, probably.'

'The behaviour change, that's the key,' Bradley said. 'It all comes back to the creature. After it attacked Berger, he went crazy. It changed him, but how? Whatever it was gave him the ability to cure himself and others of viruses.'

'You're not wrong. But it died with him.'

Bradley tilted his head. 'How do you know?'

'How do I know what?' Barrette said, irritation creeping into his voice.

'That he died, did you see the body?'

Barrette thought for a moment. 'There were lots of bodies. I don't recall his exactly, but I'm sure...'

'You don't sound very sure,' Stevens said.

Barrette lowered his eyes. 'It was stressful, there were so many. I... he died. He died in solitary, they told me.'

'Who told you?' Bradley said, stubbing out his cigarette.

Barrette's face was red. 'Doctor Grunner.'

'And what do you imagine Doctor Grunner would do if he had the cure all wrapped up in Berger's body?'

They looked at Barrette. 'You think Grunner lied, and is using him to make the antidote?'

'Don't you?'

'But if that's true...'

'Why are they still experimenting on that creature sludge?' Stevens asked.

'Yeah,' Decker said. 'If they have an antidote already, they wouldn't need to.'

'What do you think they're doing with the samples then?' Barrette asked.

'That,' Bradley said. 'Is the question we need answered.'

• • •

King leant into the giant drum of the dryer and pulled out the clothes and folded them. It was almost five. He decided he'd check on Henry and Fred, then drop the clothes off. As he turned to leave, a strange sound made him pause and look up.

CHAPTER SIXTEEN

4:30 a.m.

John Keeney opened his eyes to a blurred whitewash. It took a few blinks to clear his vision enough to see anything he could understand or recognise. A shadow moved across him as a woman's smiling face greeted him. She was doing something to his arm. He felt tightness and turned to see her pumping a band around his bicep. Her green eyes watching the dial. Ears plugged by the stethoscope, she focused as she slipped the resonator under the band. Keeney's senses were more alert. His muffled hearing and blurred vision cleared. He croaked, but she didn't hear him. When the pressure on his arm eased, she removed the stethoscope and let it hang around her neck.

A light shone into his eyes and he tried to wave it away. As the afterimage of the light faded, he could see her more clearly. An older woman, maybe midfifties. Slightly heavyset, with kind eyes. Her black hair seemed unnatural. She had those lines around her eyes that came from frequent smiling.

'Well,' her masculine voice said, 'that's a good sign. I'm going to give you an injection. You'll feel a small pinch, okay?'

Keeney nodded then grunted.

'All done.' When the needle was removed, she pressed the injection site with a cotton wadding, and then put the syringe on a tray beside her. 'Can you tell me your name?'

Keeney coughed as he tried to speak. His throat was sore and his mouth was too dry to form words. She reached out to a tray beside her and picked up a cup of water, allowing him a few sips. The effect was immediate.

'Better?'

'Much,' he croaked. He gave another dry cough. She let him take more before returning it to the tray.

'Thanks,' he said, rubbing the side of his head.

'Headache?'

'Yeah. I'm used to them.'

'Can you tell me your name?' she asked again.

'Only if you tell me yours,' he replied.

She chuckled. 'I suppose that's fair. It's Margaret. Doctor Margaret Callahan.'

'John Keeney.' He frowned. 'How long have I been here, Margaret?'

'Not long, around ten hours. Do you know where you are?'

Keeney looked around. 'Looks like a hospital?'

'Not quite. It's an isolation ward. Can you tell me what year this is?'

'Nineteen forty-two. Why are you asking me all these questions?'

Her bedside manner disarmed his agitation. 'Nothing to worry about, just making sure you're thinking straight. Do you remember who the president is?'

'Do we still have one?' His expression made her sigh.

'I should take that question out, shouldn't I?'

'What happened to me?'

'Nothing serious. A slight virial infection, but you're fortunate to be here. We've been working on antiviral medication for some time. That was a top up I just gave you.' Margret slipped a thermometer into his mouth. Keeney went to ask a question, but she put a finger to her lips and looked up at the clock. When she pulled it out and read it, she seemed satisfied.

'Normal. What do you remember?'

'Not much.' Keeney rubbed his temple again. 'I'd finished my shift and was heading to my room. I remember feeling tried. Someone helped me then nothing more till I woke up here.'

'You presented with a fever and your blood pressure had spiked. The doctor on the civilian section took care of you until you came here. Actually, she did a good job of dropping your core temperature. But as I said, we're equipped a little better. Your vitals are normalising and you'll be right as rain soon.'

'What made me sick?'

'Difficult to say. The environment here is well controlled. We screen out a lot of these things routinely, but you came from outside. It's probable you came in contact with something before you got here. Then there are the other factors to consider.'

'Such as?'

'A combination of things. A minor head cold, a lot of stress, overwork, lack of sleep, and an over indulgence of alcohol.' She raised an eyebrow. He said nothing. Colour tinged his cheeks, but her smile eased his embarrassment. Margaret sat on the edge of his bed. 'How's your head?'

'Bad,' he said, rubbing it.

'You're used to them? Most mornings, huh?'

He said nothing.

'John, you've been through a trauma. We all have. Lord knows life isn't normal, not anymore, still as a doctor I'm advising you to cut out the alcohol.'

Keeney sighed. His thoughts, as always, turned to Bobby.

'Be honest, how much are you drinking?'

'Just enough to make the pain go, I suppose.'

'How much is that?'

'I don't know.'

'And does it take the pain away?'

'No,' he replied, not meeting her eyes.

She squeezed his hand. 'You've lost someone, haven't you?'

Keeney didn't trust his voice, but his brimming eyes told her what she need to know. She tilted her head and became mock-stern. 'Now then, solider, no one likes a crybaby.' She wiped the tear from his cheek. Keeney's grief broke and he sobbed. He took a shuddering breath as he fought his misery, covering his eyes with his free hand. Margaret remained holding the other. When he'd recovered, he managed a smile.

'Sorry. I don't seem to be able to control it.'

'I'm no shrink,' she said. 'You've got a lot of stuff bottled up in that head of yours. Seems to me you could do with letting some of it out?'

Keeney said nothing.

'Silent type, huh?'

'I'll figure things out on my own.' He regretted his gruffness almost immediately.

'That's fair enough,' she said, unfazed. 'But you won't find the answers in a bottle, John. Trust me, I know.'

She handed him a washcloth. He wiped his face. 'You lost someone too?'

'Haven't we all?' She stood and picked up a bottle of pills, shaking two out and handing them to him.

'Take these, they'll help with your head.'

Keeney swallowed them and finished the water.

'Are you hungry?'

'A little,' he replied, handing her the empty cup.

'I'll have something light made up.'

She collected the bottle and other smaller instruments and dropped them into her coat pockets.

'When can I leave?'

'It's four-thirty in the morning. Not until I say so.'

Doctor Margaret Callahan straightened his bedsheets.

'Thanks,' he said.

'You're welcome. Get some rest. I'll come check on you in an hour.'

Keeney laid his head back down and drifted off to sleep.

As she approached the nursing station the ward sister looked up. 'How is he?'

Margaret picked up a file and made some notes. 'Responding well, his vitals are good. He's a strong boy,' she said. 'Looks like this new serum of Grunner's worked just fine.'

'I'm sure Doctor Grunner will be pleased,' the sister remarked.

'We'll need to observe him. Check his vitals every thirty minutes and get him a sandwich or something? He's hungry.'

'I'll see to it, Doctor.'

'Thank you, Sister. I'll be in my office if you need me.'

• • •

Captain Barrette rubbed his eyes and yawned. Colonel Bradley and Todd Stevens stood discussing several things he'd lost interest in, and he filtered them out. Only when Jim Decker returned to the table with more coffee, did he focus on anything but how tired he was.

'Where the hell is Tony?' Decker said.

Stevens frowned. 'That's a good question.'

Almost on cue, the door opened, and King walked in carrying Barrette's clothes.

'You took your sweet time.' Stevens eyed him. 'We were just about to send a fucking search party.'

'Sorry, boss, I got side-tracked.'

King handed the folded clothes over, and Barrette took them to the bathroom.

'Everything all right?' Decker asked.

'Why wouldn't it be?' King's snapped response was uncharacteristic.

Decker raised an eyebrow. 'Easy there, big fella.'

'Sorry,' King muttered.

'You seem spooked, Tony. What's wrong?' Stevens remarked.

'Ah,' he waved his hand. 'It's nothing.' Tony tried to shake himself free of concerns. 'I heard strange noises in the laundry and it set my mind wandering. This place is getting to me, that's all.'

'You're not the only one,' Bradley leant forward. 'You said strange noises, can you describe them?'

'It's silly.' He looked between them. When they remained silent, he sighed. 'I thought... well, there might have been an animal in there.'

'In the laundry?' Bradley asked.

King shook his head. 'Sounded more like it was above me, in the panels.'

'In the ventilation ducts?' Decker asked.

'I suppose so. I probably imagined it. It's like you said, boss, I just got spooked.'

Stevens nodded. 'Did you check on Henry and Fred?'

'I did. They weren't there.'

Stevens's head snapped around. 'What?'

'The place was spotless. And I mean spotless.'

Decker looked at Stevens. 'Maybe they haven't started?'

Stevens shook his head. 'Unlikely. Henry loves his job too much.' He turned to King. 'Any sign they'd been there?'

'The priest's clothing was all in the garbage. Looks to me like they'd taken care of things quick. It was a good job.'

'They're professionals,' Decker offered.

Stevens's frown deepened.

'Professional at what?' Bradley interjected.

'Disposing of bodies, Charlie. Henry and Fred are the best in the business. You want a body gone, they're like fucking magicians. You'll never find a trace and you'll never pin it on them either. Henry came from a family of butchers who all worked for the mob, and worked mostly with his father. It took years to even realise they'd had any part of the crimes we were investigating. Once we fingered them, we thought it only a matter of time, but they outsmarted us at every turn. Then one day Jim and I went on a random drug bust and there they were, right in the middle of carving some guy up. Caught red-fucking-handed. I mean, the irony. Years we'd spent trying to get those bastards and boom. I couldn't believe my fucking luck. They turned informant quick once we applied suitable pressure, of course.'

'Of course,' Bradley nodded. 'Now they do the same for you?'

Stevens rubbed his chin. 'When necessary. It seems they're a lot more efficient now.'

'Practice makes perfect,' Bradley said.

'It does. Still—' He looked to Decker. 'Go make sure it *is* efficient, and find out why they haven't reported back.'

Decker nodded then turned. 'Let's go, big guy.' King followed Decker out.

Bradley folded his arms. 'Now it's you who looks spooked.'

Stevens narrowed his eyes. 'Have you ever cut up a body, Charlie?'

'No,' he remarked. 'But I can imagine, with the right tool, it wouldn't take much.'

Stevens shook his head. 'Henry could cut up a body in no time, but thirty minutes to do that, clean the room and dispose of it? That's a stretch.'

'Could they have started earlier?'

'It's possible. But even if that were the case, and they finished the job, there's no way they wouldn't have let me know.'

'I'm sure Jim will get to the bottom of it,' he said.

Barrette came from the bathroom dressed in his uniform.

'There you are,' Bradley said, beaming. 'Suits you better than those sweatpants.'

'What's the plan, Colonel?'

'It's four forty-five. Here's what we're going to do.'

• • •

Lieutenant Colonel Ira Baldwin opened his eyes and yawned. He pulled the bedside clock to his blurred eyes and sighed. Five fifteen a.m. Two hours too early. Sarah stirred beside him and he pulled the sheet over her and slipped out. As a young man, Baldwin never slept naked, but when he hit his forties, he found he could no longer sleep in anything but his skin. He made a quiet exit and entered the bathroom. Groggy from the booze and lack of sleep – they'd continued their lovemaking till way into the small hours – he stood and relieved himself. Checking his profile in the mirror.

Baldwin entered the small kitchenette and opened the refrigerator, his body bathed in the interior light. He took a jug of water, poured a glass, and drank. Satisfied, he closed the door and entered the living room. As he stepped towards the table, the sound of a striking match made him freeze. In a darkened corner where the soft light of the kitchenette didn't reach, he saw the shadowy form of someone sitting in his chair. And he was smoking.

Baldwin stared for a moment, the fog of sleep slipping from his brain. The figure lent forward, and to his annoyance, he saw it was Colonel Bradley.

'What the hell,' he cursed.

The light next to Colonel Bradley switched on, and Baldwin saw he was sitting crossed legged, flicking ash into a mug beside him. Baldwin snarled, but it stayed in his throat as he caught sight of the weapon balancing on Bradley's leg. Bradley's eye looked Baldwin over as he put the cigarette butt into the mug and picked up the weapon. Baldwin couldn't help admiring his tenacity, nor the elegant design of the pistol pointing at his chest.

'A French SAGEM 1935-S M1, if I'm not mistaken,' Baldwin said. 'But with what looks like a modified barrel. The seven point six-five millimetre?'

Bradley smiled. 'Impressive. You know your pistols, Colonel.'

'It's a hobby of mine. Why are you pointing it at me?'

Colonel Bradley uncrossed his legs and leant forward. 'Why does anyone point a weapon at another person?'

Baldwin gave a slight tilt to his head. Showing no outward emotion, he asked, 'Did you come to kill me?'

Colonel Bradley was also unreadable. 'Not right away. I thought I'd get as much information as I could, if you're agreeable?'

'Would you mind if I put some clothes on?'

'And give you a chance to arm yourself? Oh no, I like you just as you are. Besides,' he said with a brief glance to the bedroom door, 'we wouldn't want to wake Sarah now, would we?'

Baldwin wasn't the easy-to-intimidate type, but in Colonel Bradley he recognised a steel resolve that meant he'd have to rethink his strategy. He trained for this exact scenario, but he didn't believe standard responses would work on a man like Bradley. What little he knew he'd gained through conversations with John Keeney. And although it wasn't much, one thing Keeney made clear. Colonel Bradley spent time as a covert operative in France and Germany, which made him much more dangerous.

'Do you mind if I sit, or would you prefer I remain standing?'

'You can sit,' he said. Baldwin moved towards the couch, but Bradley shook his head. 'On the floor. There's a good chap. Right here, in front of me.'

Baldwin sat. 'I underestimated you,' he said. 'I'm sorry for that.'

'It happens. I'm not offended,' Colonel Bradley remarked.

'I can assure you...'

The pistol waved. 'No, no. Let's not get off on the wrong foot.'

Baldwin lips thinned as he nodded. 'Let's cut to the chase then. What is it you want?'

'Information,' he said, then raised the pistol. Baldwin stared at it.

'I'll ask some questions,' Bradley said. 'Questions I may, or may not have the answers to. If I think you're lying, I'll shoot your right foot. If I know you're lying, it'll be the kneecap. Is that clear?'

'Crystal.'

'Good.' Bradley shifted forward in his chair. 'Why don't we start with Doctor Grunner?'

● ● ●

Tony King followed Jim Decker through the dorms out into the private complex, where they housed the call girls, next to rooms for those in senior positions within Stevens's organisation. Ex-police and gangsters alike, which amounted to the same thing in King's book. Henry and Fred shared a room, but when they opened the door, it was empty. Decker frowned and darted away. King made a quick sidestep to be out of his way. When Decker reached the next room, he threw open the door and turned on the light. Two sleeping grizzled-looking men yelled and cursed but changed their murderous expressions when they saw Decker.

'What's wrong?' one said.

'Have either of you seen Henry or Fred this morning?'

They shook their heads, both stifling yawns.

'Get dressed,' he said.

The two hefty men sighed as they threw themselves out of bed.

'Tony, fill them in,' Decker said, gesturing. 'I'll go let the boss know what's happening. I'll join you later.'

King nodded and Decker left.

CHAPTER SEVENTEEN

5:25 a.m.

'Give me one of those,' Baldwin said, as Colonel Bradley lit another cigarette.

Bradley stood and passed it then lit another. 'I thought you said it was a terrible habit?'

Colonel Baldwin took a long drag and exhaled. 'It is.'

They smoked in silence. Bradley crossed his legs, laying the revolver in his lap. Baldwin flicked ash onto the table beside the chair. Bradley put out his cigarette.

'You're performing human experiments here, aren't you?'

Baldwin was silent a long time. Eventually he said, 'Yes, we are. I have a question, though.'

'I'm listening.'

'Have you been conducting investigations and breaching my security?'

'I have.'

'Under whose authority? Not General Marshall's. If he'd had the balls to take action, he'd have done it before now.'

'It's an independent investigation.'

'To what end?'

'To expose you.'

'I see. Thank you.'

Colonel Bradley's eyes narrowed. 'You're being very calm considering I might shoot you.'

'No, you won't.'

Bradley chuckled. 'I'm superb at poker, Baldwin. I hardly ever lose. Do you know why?'

'I imagine because you're good at spotting a bluff.'

'Exactly. I also don't overbid my hand.'

'Then you should be able to read me. Look at me. I'm not concerned and have no reason to be.'

'Let me explain something to you. For three years I worked undercover in France and Germany. In the name of my profession and under authority of the British government. They prepared me to do whatever it took to survive. I've shot and killed many men like you, Colonel. Men who believed themselves above the scrutiny of others.'

'You make it sound like you're a gun for hire, but I know that's not true.'

'What do you know?'

Baldwin stubbed out his cigarette on the table. 'That you're a highly trained British Secret Service operative. Despite your roguishness, you're also an honourable soldier who follows orders.'

Colonel Bradley maintained a neutral expression. 'Appealing to my vanity won't aid you.'

'Actually, I was appealing to your patriotism. Assuming that the British still recognise such things?'

Bradley ground his teeth. 'You're responsible for the deaths of many.'

'I am. And so are you. These are things we do in war time.'

Colonel Bradley laughed. 'Please. You're attempting to hide atrocities behind platitudes you think I'll understand. And I would have, had you not been working with a Nazi doctor.'

'Ah,' – he nodded – 'you're aware of Grunner's past I see.'

'Aware? I was there. I saw the results of his handy work.'

'Not his, at least not directly. He was a junior member of the SS.'

'Don't,' Bradley rumbled, his face reddening. 'Don't you dare try to justify...'

'I'm sorry,' Baldwin said, and it looked like he meant it. 'Poor choice of words. I wasn't trying to justify anything. But the truth is, right now, I need him. We all do.'

'You're no better than he is. Conducting experiments on people? Oh yes, I know all about it.'

'Do you?' Baldwin leant forward. 'Tell me what it is you think I'm guilty of.'

'Murder.'

'Murder,' he repeated in a whisper. He then looked to Bradley. 'You're right. I am. But not through choice.'

'I'm done going around in circles with you,' Bradley spat. 'You'd better start explaining what you're doing here, or I'll shoot you and find out for myself.'

'You'd really shoot a naked unarmed man?'

'I'd shoot my mother if it got me what I needed.'

Baldwin couldn't help but smile. 'Interesting. That makes you no better than me. But you have overlooked one thing.'

'You murdering people for nefarious reasons? No, I don't think I have.'

'I'm under orders.'

Bradley frowned. 'What?'

'That's right. This facility is under a direct order and they sanction the work happening. I have full autonomy from the president of the United States.'

'That's the best you can come up with?' Colonel Bradley gave him a sad look. 'I'm disappointed.'

'I recognise it must seem a stretch, given what you think you know, but I assure you it is true.'

'It's a shame you can't prove it.'

'Actually, I can. If you'll permit?'

His frown deepened as he nodded. Baldwin crossed the room to a bureau and pulled open a drawer. He paused at the sound of Bradley's revolver cocking. 'Be very careful,' Bradley said.

Lieutenant-Colonel Ira Baldwin turned side on and pulled an envelope from the drawer. Watching the revolver pointed at him. With his free hand he closed it and returned to the floor. Baldwin handed over the letter, but Bradley waved the revolver at him.

'Open it and show me.'

He pulled out a letter and unfolded it, turning it so Bradley could see. At the top was the unmistakable embossed presidential seal. 'This is a presidential executive order. It empowers me to make any choices necessary to find a cure for a virus that has infected millions. Would you like to read its contents?'

'In a moment. Tell me about Berger and the governor.'

Baldwin's smile thinned. 'I have a feeling you already know.'

'Is Berger dead?'

Baldwin shook his head. 'He's the source of the antivirus.'

'Why would you let people think he was dead?'

'I don't believe we have.' Baldwin frowned. 'Someone told you he'd died?'

Bradley rubbed his chin. 'Never mind that. What happened to the governor?'

'Before or after I killed him?'

'After.'

Baldwin gave him a tight smile. 'His body was disposed of like all the others that were infected.'

'Cremation?'

'Something like that.'

'Let's talk about the sample.'

Baldwin raised an eyebrow. 'How *did* you learn about that?'

'I infiltrated your labs, it wasn't difficult.'

'You impress me.'

'What is this sample?'

'We don't know exactly what it is. We think it's a progenitor for the monsters outside.'

'When one of those creatures dies, it reverts to this stuff?'

'No. We think our UV lights caused it in the one we captured. We didn't take the right precautions because we thought it was just, well, goo. We know better now. It's alive and it killed several people.'

'Including many scientists?'

Baldwin nodded. 'Some survived. Most didn't. But before any of that, people were coming here sick. We isolated them and that's when we heard how widespread the virus was.'

Colonel Bradley frowned. 'We didn't see evidence of viruses or even people when we made it out of Washington.'

Baldwin said, 'That's because you were infected too.'

'This is the first I've heard of it,' Bradley said.

'It isn't. You've just forgotten.'

'You're not making any sense.'

Baldwin leant forward. 'Look at me, Colonel. This isn't the first time we've had this conversation. You're a clever man. My hope is at some point you'll begin to recognise the truth.'

'What truth?'

'That you, John, and General Marshall arrived here infected and we treated you.'

Bradley laughed. 'Mind games won't save you.'

'Have you been having nightmares?'

'What?'

'Nightmares. Have you?'

'Yes.'

Baldwin nodded and sat back into his chair. 'Headaches?'

'Those too.'

'It's the side effects of the drugs. The virus attacks certain parts of the brain, specifically long-term memory, reasoning centres, and the hypothalamus. The drug developed here by Doctor Grunner kills the virus, but we've never been able to stop these side effects. On balance, I'd rather have bad dreams and a few lost memories, than the alternative.'

'Which is?'

'I suppose the best way to describe it would be somewhere between living and dead.'

'Why is John sick? Who infected him?'

'No one infected him. As I told you, he was already infected. He's being treated now and I'm told he'll make a full recovery. The dose of the drug doesn't always kill the virus completely. From what I've been told, it can sit dormant in the hypothalamus. The area that regulates body temp and sleep, amongst other things.'

'I don't believe any of this.'

Baldwin looked him in the eyes. 'I think you do.'

Bradley held out a hand and Ira Baldwin passed him the letter. He scanned through it. When he'd finished reading, he pulled a face. 'There's no way to know if it's genuine.'

'There is. Take it to Bill Marshall he'll verify its authenticity.

He and FDR are close friends.'

Bradley read it again, then a thought occurred, and he looked up. '*Are* friends? You meant *were*.'

'President Roosevelt is alive and well.'

Colonel Bradley didn't hide his astonishment. 'You're in communication?'

Baldwin took back the letter and nodded.

'Where is he?'

'The last time we spoke he was heading north.'

'How are they moving?'

'By sea.' Baldwin stood and adjusted himself. 'Unless you intend to carry through with your threat to shoot me, I'm going to put some pants on.'

Colonel Bradley was thoughtful. 'None of what you say changes what you've done. Orders or not, you've killed people, that's not okay.'

Baldwin flashed him an irritated look. It was the first time his cool broke. 'You think I don't know that? You think I had a choice? Mr President, please don't pick me for this assignment. You have no idea the mental agony I've suffered over the choices I've had to make. The losses I've endured. A bullet would be welcome, but we both know there's a much bigger issue that needs controlling.'

'Grunner?'

'Grunner.'

Bradley slipped his revolver into his pocket. 'I don't trust you, Colonel, and I'd advise you not to do anything to give me reason to kill you, because you know I'll do it.'

'Yes, I do.'

'Fine. Get dressed. We're going to see Bill.'

'We have to remove the quarantine order first.'

'You can do that when we get there.'

Lieutenant-Colonel Baldwin nodded and entered his bedroom while Bradley stood mulling over what he'd learnt. Less than five minutes later he returned dressed.

'Are you ready to go?'

Colonel Bradley gestured to the door.

'After you.'

• • •

6 a.m.

The server pulled up a hatch as people started joining the queue for breakfast. Several men passed cups around and conversed, filling them with coffee and orange juice, then took a plate and grabbed some breakfast. The noise level increased as they found empty seats around tables, and the morning ritual started like any other day.

It wasn't long before the dining area was full. King waited in quiet contemplation for his plate to be filled, observing the activity of the surrounding people. Stevens's crew never ate in the dining room. They had their own private area. When King's plate was full, he passed through the crowd to the separate room and joined them.

'Tony,' Decker said. 'We need more coffee.'

He put his plate down and nodded.

'Grab some juice too, will you?' Stevens said, between mouthfuls of powdered eggs.

Stevens smiled as King left. 'He's a good guy.'

'For a blacky,' Decker remarked. The men seated next to him snickered.

Stevens laughed.

When King returned, he dropped a jug of juice and a pot of coffee on the table, and sat.

Decker ran the last of his juice around his mouth and swallowed, pushing his plate away. 'Boy, did I need that.'

'It's swill,' a large red-faced man complained.

'He's not wrong,' said another.

'It's hot and fills you up, so stop complaining,' Stevens barked, staring at each.

They lowered their heads and continued their breakfast in quiet.

'Any news on... you know?' Decker said, lighting a cigarette.

Stevens finished his coffee and poured more.

'Nothing.' He leant forward. 'It's bothering me, Jim. We

need to find Fred and Henry. We're the ones who make people disappear down here.'

'You think it has anything to do with what Braders was talking about?'

Stevens leant back in his chair. 'Maybe. Either way, I need answers. No one but us knew what they were doing. Not even Charlie. Either they made themselves disappear, or...'

'Someone else did.'

'Right.'

'Or something else did,' King added.

Stevens turned to him. 'Something? You still on about animals in the ventilation?'

King shrugged as he dug into his eggs.

● ● ●

Colonel Bradley and Ira Baldwin walked in silence through the corridor towards the elevator.

'Lieutenant Dawson,' Bradley said.

'What about him?'

'When we met, he said he had a brother.'

Baldwin gave him a sad look. 'A twin, yes. He was one of the unlucky ones.'

'Bill said Dawson didn't remember having a brother, and didn't recall meeting us when we arrived. He was treated with this drug too?'

'Good, you're starting to believe.'

'I wouldn't go that far.' They stood in silence for a while, then Bradley said, 'We've been here longer than we think, haven't we?'

Baldwin nodded. 'A lot longer.'

When the doors opened, they stepped out and made their way through the morning crowds and up to the infirmary. An MP tapped Sergeant Hawkinson's shoulder, and they stood, saluting at the approach of the senior officers.

'At ease,' Baldwin said.

They remained rigid. Both with hands on their sidearms. Hawkinson said, 'Colonel?'

Baldwin regarded him. 'I said, at ease.'

'I wasn't talking to you, sir,' he said. Baldwin looked back at Colonel Bradley, who gave a slight nod.

'Colonel Baldwin has lifted the quarantine, Hawk,' Bradley said. 'Why don't you get yourself some breakfast? There's no need for you to remain. Isn't that so, Colonel?'

'Yes,' Baldwin remarked.

'Very good, sir. I have the boys breakfast down here. That way they'll be in calling distance, should you need them.' Hawkinson saluted and walked away.

When they'd passed, Baldwin said, 'Your men?'

'Indeed. Shall we?'

Bradley slipped a key into the sealed door lock and they entered. Marshall and Doctor Husk came out from her office.

'Bill,' Bradley said. 'Ira has some things he would like to discuss with you.'

General Marshall stepped back into Husk's office and held the door open for Ira Baldwin, who walked in. Doctor Husk went to follow, but Colonel Bradley caught her arm.

'Let's give them a little privacy, Kate.'

She nodded and smiled, but he saw something in her eyes. She seemed unsettled. 'What's wrong?'

'Oh,' she waved a hand. 'It's silly. I had a nightmare, that's all.'

He took her hand and led her to a set of chairs, where they sat.

'Tell me about it.'

While General Marshall paced, reading the letter for the third time, Colonel Baldwin sat on the edge of Husk's desk and waited.

Marshall looked at him. It wasn't a kind look. 'You son of a bitch.'

'I've been called worse.'

'You knew. You knew all this time and said nothing.'

'As you can see, I was under orders, Bill.'

'General,' he snapped.

Baldwin stood. 'General, I understand you're angry...'

'Angry,' he spat the word at him. 'Angry doesn't begin to express how I feel.'

'I understand, but please hear me out.'

'Sit,' he said, pointing to a chair. 'And start from the beginning. Don't you dare leave a thing out or I'll have Braders shoot you.'

Ira Baldwin sat. 'Why don't you just do it yourself?'

'One perk of being a fucking general,' he snarled. 'Start talking, Colonel.'

• • •

'And then Bill woke me up.' Husk rubbed her eyes as she finishing her story.

'I'm sorry. No doubt this place is getting to you, as it is for all of us.'

'I thought about that. But Jake said he'd also had nightmares. When he described them... Charlie, they were the same.'

'We're all in a place of confinement, it's natural we'll share similar experiences that might translate into dreams.'

'No,' she said, touching his hand. 'He had the same dream. The details were almost identical.'

'That is a little different,' he agreed. 'But look, I've had them too.'

'You have? Bad dreams?'

'Terrifying,' he said. 'I almost stopped trying to sleep because of it.' He took her hand and kissed it. 'But then I remembered that they're just dreams, Katie.'

She smiled. 'I haven't been called Katie in a long time.'

'Does it annoy you?'

She shook her head. 'I like it.'

'Good,' he said. Bradley was about to say more, when the raised voices from the office caught their attention.

'What's that all about?' Husk asked.

'Our friend Ira is confessing his sins to the general.'

'Well it looks like Bill might end up hurting him. Maybe we should go in?'

Colonel Bradley pulled her onto his lap. It startled her.

'What are you doing,' she said, in a low voice.

'Listen to me, Katie. It might become necessary to leave this place...'

She opened her mouth to speak, but he cut her off.

'Just listen. I have an awful feeling something terrible will happen. Call it a premonition, call it what you like. I've only had this feeling twice before. Once when a car hit and killed my uncle when I was a boy, the other recently in France. The first time it happened I was six or seven. I didn't understand it then. But the next time it happened I was older. It's my internal warning system. It saved me from a German infiltrator who'd murdered six members of the French Resistance. I trust this feeling, Katie.'

'You're scaring me.'

'Good, because I'm scared too.' He ran his thumb over her eyebrow. 'If I ask you to leave, will you go with me?'

She frowned. 'I can't abandon these people.'

'That's not an answer.' He took and kissed her hand.

Husk's cheeks turned pinkish. 'Will you stop that,' she admonished.

'I don't think I can.'

'You're terrible.' They looked at the office window as Marshall's yelling increased.

'I'd have thought he'd be all yelled out by now?'

Bradley took her head in both hands and kissed her, taking her weight as she sagged into him. When he broke the kiss, she looked into his eyes.

'I thought I was just a bit of fun, for a man like you,' she said, straightening her hair.

'A man like me?'

'Yes. You don't seem the type to stick around.'

'It's not an unfair assessment.' He rubbed a smudge of grime from her cheek. 'But lately, I've begun to realise something.'

'What?'

'There's something more than fun between us.'

She laughed. 'That's presumptuous.'

'If you don't feel the same way, Katie, tell me now.'

She looked at the office, then back. 'Fine,' she said. 'I like you, but I can't leave these people behind.'

'Because of your oath as a doctor?'

She nodded. 'They need me.'

Colonel Bradley regarded her. 'I understand. When the time comes for me to leave, I'll give you the option again.'

'I doubt my response will be any different.'

'We'll see.'

• • •

The dining room was almost to capacity when the last of the breakfasts were served. The chef finished consolidating the leftovers and sent his servers to eat. He had his ritual for cleaning, which he never passed onto others. He nodded in satisfaction at the surfaces he'd just wiped down, noting the sparkle under the bright hanging lights. Turning them off, he had picked up a plate of his own when a clattering sound above made him look up. One of the ceiling tiles had fallen, exposing the ducting above. He put the plate down and bent to pick it up. At that moment, something cold hit his neck. Instinct made him rub at it.

He took his hand and studied it. Not water as he'd first thought, but tar, or grease, or something similar. With a frown, he rubbed it between his fingers. The viscous substance didn't absorb. Wiping it off onto a towel, he picked up the tile, when another drop hit his head. Growling, he looked. Something large and black then fell with a wet thud in front of him, and he jumped back in alarm.

It took a few seconds to calm his nerves. He crept forward and knelt down, pulling a pencil from his pocket, and poked at it. It wasn't like anything he'd seen before. It was a large blob of thick jelly substance, almost slug-like, and very sticky. When he poked again, it seemed to react.

'What the hell are you?'

As he bent closer a tendril shot out and grabbed his throat. Another quickly filled his mouth. He fell, flipping like a fish out of water. He pawed at the sticky substance filling his mouth, as it pushed its way down his throat. With his airway blocked, it wasn't long before his eyes fluttered and rolled into his head, and not long after that he stopped moving. The substance left a slick trail on the floor as it continued into his mouth, until the last piece disappeared inside him.

• • •

Todd Stevens and his crew had finished breakfast and now consumed a third pot of coffee. Decker had outlined the plans for the day, while the others listened and groaned at the various tasks they'd been assigned. King cleared plates and cutlery into the cart as they talked, then sat down beside Decker.

Stevens was about to add something, when a hideous commotion from the dining area made them turn.

'What the fuck was that?' Stevens asked.

The sounds of crashing made them leap to the door. Just as they opened it, the first sets of screams began.

• • •

Doctor Husk's hands were shoved into her lab-coat pockets. She's been observing General Marshall and Colonel Baldwin since they'd stopped yelling at each other. Now they appeared to be talking, and she was pleased. The noise had motivated a curious Ciaran and Jake to come from their room, who were now sitting with Charlie. Ciaran on his lap, Jake in the chair beside them. She wasn't aware of their conversation. Her attention was focused on Marshall and Baldwin.

She turned as Ciaran's giggle cut through her thoughts. Something Charlie said made them laugh. It made her smile too. Charlie was good with the boys. They liked him and he seemed to like them too. She wandered over and ruffled Jake's hair.

A crash made them jump. Two MPs burst through the doors, panting. They were scared.

Bradley lifted Ciaran off and sat him down, then approached the MPs. 'What's wrong?'

'Something's happened,' one said, his face as white as a sheet.

'Boys,' Bradley commanded, 'back to your room, now.'

Jake took Carian's hand and they made a quick exit.

• • •

General Marshall had finished yelling and was now rubbing his temple. Ira Baldwin approached him.

'Headache?'

The older man sighed. 'No thanks to you.'

'Frequent?'

'What are you my doctor now?'

Baldwin's eyes met his. 'Humour me. Are they frequent?'

General Marshall frowned. 'I suppose so, why?'

'Any nightmares?'

'What?'

'Bill... General, it's important. Have you been having nightmares?'

He nodded.

'And each time you have one, do you also get a searing headache that sits above your eyes?'

'Sounds like I'm not the only one?'

Baldwin shook his head. 'I'm going to ask you something. It's going to sound strange, and you'll probably think I've lost my mind. Here it is. How long have you been here?'

'That's a stupid question, since we both know exactly how long I've been here.'

'I know, but I want to hear it from you.'

He was irritated. 'About two weeks, give or take a day. I haven't been ticking off a calendar, Ira.'

'Bill, this may come as a bit of a shock, but you've been here longer than two weeks.'

He shrugged. 'So? I've lost a few days. What are you driving at?'

'Bill, I'll try and explain...' He frowned as something caught his attention in the infirmary. 'What's going on out there?'

• • •

The second MP staggered into Doctor Husk. Covered in blood, he slipped from her hold as he collapsed in the doorway, taking her with him. She attempted to turn him onto his side.

'Charlie help me.'

Together they pulled him further in to the room and began removing his uniform jacket.

'It's not his,' the other said, his unfocused eyes stared through them.

'What's not his?' Husk asked, observing his pallor.

'It's not his blood.'

'Whose is it?'

He just stared. Colonel Bradley took him by the shoulders. 'For god's sake, man, snap out of it. What the hell happened.'

'Blood, so much blood...' His eyes fluttered and the colonel caught and lowered him. Marshall and Baldwin came from the office. The general reaching them first.

'What's going on?'

'We don't know, Bill. These two came in shouting something about blood and then they passed out. This one is covered in it.'

His eyes ran over Husk as she attended to the MP on the floor. 'Kate, you're bleeding too?'

She looked at her coat and hands which were crimson. 'It's not mine and it isn't his either, as far as I can tell.' Husk wiped her hands on a section of coat that wasn't already soaked. She checked the MP's eyes.

'His pupils are dilating, that's good.'

Baldwin and Marshall knelt beside them. 'Will they be okay?' Baldwin asked.

'They're just in shock,' she said. 'Something frightened them into an almost catatonic...'

Her sentence was interrupted by sounds of crashing, and blood-curdling screams, from somewhere down the corridor.

Lots of screams.

'What the hell was that?' Husk said, poking her head out the door. Bradley pulled her back in.

'Stay here,' he said, then looked back at Marshall. 'Bill?'

General Marshall pulled a sidearm from one of the MPs. 'I'm with you, let's go. Ira, stay with Kate.'

Both men then left the infirmary.

CHAPTER EIGHTEEN

7 a.m.

Colonel Bradley tiptoed along the corridor towards the double doors separating him from the dining area, with General Marshall following close behind, their weapons drawn. Marshall paused as Bradley made a slow slide along the wall, stopping at a door. He peered through its circular window. Bradley pointed to the floor, and then the wall, and Marshall ducked and flattened himself opposite.

They stood for some time waiting and listening. The only sound was the slow whine of air moving through fans somewhere above them. A bead of sweat ran from Marshall's forehead, disappearing into the fabric of his shirt. The dining area beyond the heavy doors was dark. The lighting now replaced by the sporadic flickers of dying bulbs, which highlighted Bradley's hawkish features through the window.

'What do you see?' Marshall whispered.

'Take a look.'

Marshall slid along the wall until he reached the door on his side and looked through. His perspective was limited. An occasional flicker from a random assortment of bulbs illuminated upturned tables and bodies. Lots of bodies. Sprawled everywhere.

'Good god,' Marshall muttered. 'What the hell happened?'

'A good question. Are you feeling brave enough to find out?'

Marshall's expression betrayed him. 'You want to go in there?'

'We need answers. If you like, you can go back to the infirmary? There's no reason for us both to be in danger.'

Their eyes met. Bradley's suggestion had been an obtuse one, but it had the desired effect as Marshall shook his head. Colonel Bradley then offered him a reassuring smile. 'Before we go in, there's something I want to say. I'm beginning to suspect I was wrong about Ira.'

'Oh?'

'Did he tell you about the virus that's infecting people above ground?'

'I think he was going to, but then we were interrupted. I didn't give him much of an opportunity to talk, to be fair.'

'I heard,' Bradley chuckled. 'He suggested to me we came infected. We had a treatment created by Grunner and it may have affected our memories.'

Marshall frowned. 'I don't believe my memories have been affected. Have yours?'

'I'm not sure.'

'Do you believe him?'

Bradley nodded. 'Bill, we've seen the evidence that might prove it.'

'Kate's file? She didn't remember writing it.'

Bradley continued to stare through the window. 'Exactly, and don't forget young Dawson.'

'That's right, he didn't remember his brother or meeting us. But if we were wrong about Ira, maybe we're wrong about Grunner too?'

Bradley turned to Marshall, and the look on his face was not kind. 'No, not him.'

'But if he made the treatment, surely...?'

'I have no answer for Grunner's motives. It seems to me, on the balance of evidence, Grunner may have stumbled upon the cure by accident.'

'You're saying he has an ulterior motive? One Ira isn't aware of? That he's carrying on from where he left off in those awful death camps?'

'I think Nazi doctors don't stop their evil work just because they aren't in Germany.'

'What is it he's doing?'

Bradley indicated the window with his head. 'I think we're about to find that out. Stay behind me. If things go south, I want you back at the infirmary. Understood?'

'No,' he said, with a frown. 'I'll not leave you.'

The colonel took his arm. 'I appreciate that, Bill, truly, but listen. I can take care of myself, but not both of us. Someone has to ensure Kate and the boys are safe. If it's not going to be me, it better damn well be you.'

The general looked through the window, then back at him.

Bradley squeezed his arm. 'Agreed?'

Marshall sighed and nodded. Bradley gave a tight smile. 'Thank you. Are you ready?'

'No. Are you?'

'Come on.'

After checking his weapon, Marshall stepped back as Bradley put his hand on the door. He made a slow push and exposed a crack of darkness and a good view of the room beyond. Marshall saw his eyes darting as he paused, watching.

'Looks like maybe thirty bodies,' Bradley breathed, 'possibly more. It's difficult to tell. Some are in pieces.'

Bradley opened the door further and stepped through, steadying himself on the door as his foot slid on something. They both recognised the distinctive metallic odour of blood in the air. Bradley put a hand out to stop Marshall and pointed down. 'Watch your step.'

The floor was slick with blood.

'What's the plan?' Bill asked, as they made further careful entry.

'I don't have one. I'm running on adrenaline. Let's look at a body, maybe that will help.'

'Help with what?'

'I don't know.' Bradley's curt response cut off any further questions.

General Marshall followed to the nearest body, which wasn't too far in. It looked like the poor fellow had been trying to drag himself away from something. From the limited light,

Marshall couldn't see much. He was shirtless, face down. He could just make out a hole in his back. Too big for a standard revolver. Looked more like a 9mm.

'Keep watch while I take a look,' Bradley whispered. He dropped and begun examining the body, while Marshall scanned the room. The limited light didn't penetrate the depth of darkness. With his loss of the room's perspective, he felt his disorientation increase. There was no way to know where in the room they were. He looked back to the door they'd come through, and found comfort in the light from its little round windows. The silence in the room was eerie.

Bradley flipped the poor fellow over, and after what felt like an eternity, he stood.

'Well?'

The colonel's face was grim. 'Something ripped his chest open. From what I can tell, his heart is missing.'

'Was that a gunshot wound on his back?'

Bradley shook his head. 'Something pierced his back and burst his chest open, but it doesn't look like any gunshot wound I've ever seen. The fracture patterns on the bones suggest the ribs were broken from the inside. And they're clean breaks along the sternum.'

'Some exit wounds are bigger,' Marshall persisted, 'and it would explain his heart being missing.'

'But it wouldn't explain the lack of gunshot sounds, would it?' Bradley whispered.

'Good point. Who do you think would be capable of doing this?'

'Not who, what.' Bradley eyed the room. Marshall had never seen him so alert. The skin on Bradley's face was tight, and his entire body was like a coiled spring. He put his hand on Marshall's arm, and it was shaking. 'We're in real danger.'

'From what?'

'Something we might not survive. A predator.'

Marshall felt fear rise from the pit of his stomach. 'If you wanted me scared, you're succeeding.'

'I'm scared too.'

'Is it a monster from outside? Did it get in and is now loose?'

'More likely a homegrown monster from the lab. I have an idea, but we can discuss it later. Let's move in a little more.'

'Lead on.'

The colonel made a careful tread around each body, Marshall following in his footsteps as best he could. Once they'd ventured further, and penetrated deeper into the darkness, Marshall almost collided with Bradley, who'd stopped. His posture was stiff. He gave a gesture and they dropped.

'What?' Marshall whispered.

'We're not alone. We're being watched,' came the hushed response. Even though their eyes had grown accustomed to the low light, there were areas they couldn't see into. Bradley pointed to one. The gloom seemed almost darker there.

'I saw something move, over there. It's hidden, but it knows I saw it.'

'Are you sure? I don't see anything.'

'Trust me,' he said. His eyes scanning, searching. 'It's there.'

'Maybe a survivor?'

Bradley's eyes narrowed as he shook his head. 'Oh, I don't think so. I told you, it's a predator. And now, it has our scent.'

Marshall gripped his revolver. 'Let it come.'

'Be careful what you ask for. Whatever it is, it killed all these people. Doesn't look like they gave it much of a fight, does it?'

'No,' he breathed. 'But they weren't armed.'

'I'm not sure that will help.'

'You don't know that.'

The sound of something metallic clattered along the floor, followed by an odd gurgling moan filling the air. It stopped their conversation. Marshall gripped Bradley's arm. 'What the hell was that?'

The flickering light illuminated the colonel's blank expression. His unblinking eyes never leaving the darkness. 'It's playing with us.'

Marshall squinted, trying to see whatever it was lurking in the darkness.

'D'you feel it, Bill? That odd sense of dread working its way along your spine?'

He said nothing.

'Come on,' Bradley whispered. 'The longer we stay here the less safe I feel.'

They continued the journey at a crouch. Navigating though bodies and entrails had been difficult, but soon they reached a wall opposite from where they'd come in, and Bradley breathed a sigh of relief. 'I've lost myself. Aren't we near Doyle's little church setup?'

'No,' Marshall whispered, 'if memory serves, we should be close to the rec room.'

'Yes, I recognise it now. How far would you say?'

'Fifty or sixty feet, maybe? If we stay along this wall, it should be the first door we hit.'

'Good memory. We'll make for the nearest one. Ready?'

Crouching low, they followed the wall. It wasn't long before they found the first of the double doors.

Colonel Bradley checked his weapon, then looked back at Marshall. 'Stay here. I'll make sure it's safe.'

Bradley then slipped over to the other door. He stood, his revolver in hand, and gave the door a little push. It swung in a little, then settled back. Satisfied, Bradley nodded to the general, and pushed it open. They locked eyes and Marshall gave a nod. Bradley pushed the door further open, stepping forward, and Marshall jumped, as something yanked Bradley through.

• • •

Colonel Baldwin put the phone down and sat staring at it for a few moments, then stood and went back to the infirmary. Baldwin had attempted to get the MPs to describe what they'd witnessed, but what they said made little or no sense. From the way they'd described things, it sounded almost like a sample had escaped into the civilian population. But that was impossible. Grunner had just assured him that wasn't the case. All the samples were accounted for. Grunner even sounded surprised by what the MPs had said, but in his cold way, he assured Baldwin that whatever was happening was unrelated to their work. After Grunner said he'd send a response team, Baldwin had hung up. The doctor's platitudes didn't stop a gnawing feeling of doubt in the pit of Baldwin's stomach.

Baldwin pondered on things. How truthful was Grunner being? How had he let things go as far as they had? And how would he explain any of this to Marshall, and regain his trust or respect? He looked through the window at Husk who was attending Ciaran and Jake. He sighed and rose, leaving the office.

'When will the response team be here?' Husk asked.

Baldwin crossed his arms and lowered his chin onto his chest. 'Soon.'

'Good. I need to check on my patients.'

Baldwin watched as the older boy came forward, his younger brother standing close but a little behind. 'Sir?'

The colonel smiled. 'It's Jake, isn't it?'

He nodded.

'Well then, Jake. You have a question?'

The boy looked at his younger brother, then back. His teenage face trying to mask the fear obvious to anyone who could read it. 'Are we going to die?'

Baldwin knelt down. 'Not if I can help it,' he said, looking over at the younger boy. 'I know this must seem frightening, but trust me. When the team comes, we'll all be out of here safe and sound.'

The smile he gave seemed to reassure them. Jake turned to Ciaran. 'See? It's all going to be okay.'

'I'm going to see if Doctor Husk needs my help. Why don't you boys go back to your room?'

'Come on Ciaran, we can play pairs.'

The younger boy looked out from behind Jake's back as Baldwin entered an examination room nearby.

'I don't like him,' Ciaran whispered.

'Why?' Jake said, taking his hand and walking him back to the room.

Ciaran wrinkled his button nose. 'He smells funny.'

Jake chuckled. 'You crack me up.'

They entered the room and Ciaran ran and jumped on the bed. Jake pointed at his feet. 'Get your stompers on.'

'Why?' Ciaran asked, flexing his toes.

'Case we have to leave. Can't have you in your bare feet. Get.'

Ciaran groaned. From the look on Jake's face, he could tell Jake wasn't messing around. The boy slipped off the bed and found his shoes. 'Fat-head,' he murmured.

Doctor Husk was finishing her examination of the MPs as Baldwin stood in the doorway. The two men were asleep on their beds.

'How are they?' he asked.

Husk looked round. 'Sleeping,' she said, in a hushed tone.

Baldwin put up his hands, then moved aside to let her pass. She pointed to her office and he followed behind. When they entered, she closed the door.

'I would like some answers.'

Baldwin sat in the chair opposite. 'Ask. I'll answer if I'm able.'

'You know what that thing they saw is, don't you?'

'No,' he said, meeting her gaze. 'Not exactly.'

'Is it going to be like that?'

'May I call you Kate?'

'I'd prefer Doctor, actually.'

He said nothing.

She stared at him. 'Charlie has been investigating, you know. He tells me everything.'

'Between the sheets?'

Crossing her arms, she said, 'Was that necessary?'

Baldwin sat forward and looked down. 'No. I apologise.'

'Thank you.' She waited. 'Well?'

'Well, what?'

'Aren't you going to tell me anything?'

'Didn't you just say Colonel Bradley tells you everything? What do you need to hear from me then?'

She turned and pulled a file out of her tray and passed it to him. 'Maybe start by explaining this.'

He opened it and flicked through the pages. 'You'll need to be more specific.'

She regarded him. 'You don't like to answer questions, do you?'

'Well, it's a lot more fun asking them I'll admit.'

'How come there's data in that file, in my handwriting, that I don't remember writing?'

'The short answer is, the antiviral medicine we administered to you when you were ill has had a detrimental effect on your long-term explicit memory.'

'I don't recall ever having been ill,' she responded.

'Few do. General Marshall certainly doesn't, nor does Bradley. You have the data right here.' He handed the file back. 'Your handwriting, isn't it?'

'Yes,' she breathed. 'But I...'

'Don't remember writing it, I know.'

She stared at him.

'Kate, there's a virus on the surface and it's turning people into, well, monsters. It eats away at certain parts of the brain. When it's done, there's nothing of the person left. Nothing.'

'What parts of the brain?'

'The hypothalamus, and frontal lobe.'

'You found a cure?'

'Of sorts. We can cure the virus, but there are side effects. Early memory loss, bad dreams, headaches. Not everyone manifests these symptoms.'

'I've been having those symptoms.'

'Yes. You'll recognise the difficulty in convincing someone whose memories appear intact and uninterrupted.'

'I do,' she said. 'If I didn't have the evidence of my own notes to back up what you're saying, I'd find it hard to believe too.'

Baldwin rubbed his face and yawned.

'Bill, John, and Charlie were all infected?'

He nodded.

'The boys too?'

'Kate everyone here, aside from a small few, has been or is infected.'

She flipped through her notes as Baldwin sat bouncing his pressed together hands off his lips.

His eyes didn't leave her.

• • •

Resolve replaced General Marshall's sudden fear as he barrelled through the door, weapon pointing, and came face to face with a cursing muscular dark-skinned giant of a man. Colonel Bradley had somehow slipped behind the giant and planted his revolver against the man's right temple, forcing his arm up his back.

'Jesus, Charlie. Lemme go.'

It took a moment for the killer instinct to leave him. Bradley released his arm and stepped back. 'Sorry, old man,' he said.

Rubbing his arm and stepping away, King sighed. 'You nearly gave me a fucking heart attack.' He turned away, looking back into the dim room. 'It's okay, boss. It's just Charlie and some old geezer.'

Marshall scowled. 'Some old geezer?'

King ignored him.

The general put a hand on Bradley's arm, stopping him. 'You know this meathead?'

'Yeah,' Bradley chuckled. 'This bruiser works for Todd Stevens.'

It relieved the general to see a little of Bradley' swagger return. 'Todd Stevens? He's the ex-police chief you told me about, right?'

'Come gangster. A real peach, you'll love him.'

'Sounds like it.'

'Let's go introduce ourselves, shall we?'

Stevens and Decker slipped out of the darkness. Bradley read their fear. It didn't surprise him to find Stevens and Decker alive. Stevens's sense of self-preservation sat above everything, and everyone. It wasn't just good fortune they'd had their own dining room to hide out in, it was design. Stevens had a backup plan for everything. Colonel Bradley thought it was smart, but he could tell by Bill's body language he didn't feel the same way.

'Am I fucking glad to see you, Charlie.' Stevens said.

'Likewise. Todd, Jim, this is General William Marshall.'

'General,' Stevens said, extending a hand. 'Chief Todd Stevens. Wish the circumstances were better.'

General Marshall gave him a politician's smile. 'Likewise, Chief.'

Stevens gestured to his companion. 'This is Jim Decker.'

Decker ignored the outstretched hand. 'General, huh? Nice of you to fucking show up.'

Colonel Bradley stepped forward. Decker turned his angry eyes on him. 'You can fuck off too.'

Marshall put a hand on Bradley's chest as Stevens stepped between them.

'Can that shit. You're scared. We're all fucking scared, but this isn't helping.'

Decker allowed his eyes to drop. 'Sorry.'

Stevens lifted his chin and looked into a terrified face. 'Hey, we've been through plenty, you and me, we'll get through this too.'

'Yeah, true.'

Decker's rudeness hadn't upset Marshall. He sympathized because he felt the same fear.

'General,' Stevens said. 'Why don't you give Jim your side-arm, then you, me, and Charlie can talk?'

'Of course,' Marshall said, handing the revolver and spare ammunition to him.

'Thanks.' He noted Decker's grim expression brightened now he had a weapon. 'And sorry,' he mumbled, looking between them.

Stevens extended a hand and squeezed his shoulder. 'You and Tony keep an eye out by the door, okay? Let us know if you see something.'

'Don't worry,' King said, as they moved away. 'You'll fucking hear us.'

'Sorry about that,' Stevens said, rubbing his eyes.

'Forget it,' Marshall said. 'Can you tell us what happened?'

'We were having breakfast as usual and then all hell broke loose. It's a bit confusing. Something started attacking peo-ple... an animal, maybe? We couldn't tell how many people were out there, but King said the place was fucking packed. It's the one time you can guarantee everyone'll be in the same fucking place.' He sighed. 'It was obvious we couldn't do much to help, so we stayed in here. I've seen some shit in my time, General, sir. Been at more violent crime scenes then I can count, so you can appreciate I've developed a strong stomach, but this... I've seen nothing like it.'

'I have.'

They turned to Colonel Bradley, who was rubbing his lip, lost in thought.

'You have, Charlie?'

'Yes, in France. After a German patrol massacred a bunch of civilians.'

'Oh right,' Stevens said, nodding. 'I keep forgetting there's a war on. It was like this?'

'No,' Bradley said.

Stevens had never seen Charlie Bradley unsettled. That was enough to tell him things were worse than he thought, if that were possible. 'You okay?'

'Not really.'

Stevens understood. 'No, I suppose none of us are.'

Marshall put a hand on Bradley's arm and the colonel patted it. He took in a lengthy breath and exhaled his uncertainty. 'We can't stay in here. Let's decide on our next moves, okay?'

'Sounds like a plan to me.' Stevens said.

General Marshall looked back at the two men huddled by the door.

CHAPTER NINETEEN

8 a.m.

John Keeney threw off the covers, swung his legs over the side, and sat naked at the edge of his bed. The sister had told him twice in not so many hours he'd have to stay, but the second time had been once too many.

Her imperious face met with his. 'And just where do you think you're going? Get back into that bed this instant.'

Keeney didn't care for the condescending way in which the sister spoke to him. He'd never been one to listen to overbearing, stubborn women. She reminded him of his mother and that meant she was already fighting a losing battle.

She stepped closer.

'Did you hear me?'

He thought back to the times he and Bobby had dealt with the arrogance of women like her. Thinking of him bolstered his defiance.

'I heard you.'

Her stern expression made little difference. Keeney had suffered that wrath all his life. At age nine, his mother caught him and the boy next door experimenting. He'd suffered more than wrath for that. From then on, he'd imagined what it might be like to grab the poker she regularly used on his naked backside and turn it on her. Bobby was always the first to remind him, when he fell into his dark place, that his angry thoughts resulted from years of abuse. But Bobby didn't know about the dreams. How he'd wake up sweating with images of his mother's head smashed beyond recognition. The look he flashed the sister must have expressed those thoughts, because her tough exterior faltered.

She softened her hard brow. 'You're not well enough to leave, Captain. And you can't go without the doctor's permission.'

'Go get her then,' he deadpanned.

She made another step forward. 'Only if you get back in that bed.'

Keeney stood fully naked before her. The sight of it made her eye twitch.

'I'm leaving, sister. If I have to walk out like this...'

She put up a hand. 'Fine. At least let me find you something to wear.'

'I'll come with you,' he said.

She looked aghast. 'You'll do no such thing.'

'I don't think you recognise that you're not in control of this situation.' His tone lifted with every word.

'There's no need to shout.' To her credit, she remained cool.

'What's all this ruckus?' Doctor Callahan's voice made them turn. She was standing in the doorway carrying a set of folded clothing.

'Doctor,' the sister said. 'Captain Keeney is insisting on leaving. I tried to explain that he can't, but he belligerently refused to listen.'

Margaret Callahan nodded. 'Thank you, Sister, I'll deal with this.'

She turned hard eyes back at Keeney, then left.

Doctor Callahan dropped the clothes she carried into his hands. The slight smile on her face made Keeney come down from his anger. 'That's the first time I've seen her like that,' she said. 'Sister can be a little domineering, but she means well, you know. You were planning on leaving in your birthday suit?'

Captain Keeney pulled and zipped up his pants. 'If I had to.'

'You're certainly full of spunk. Captain Barrette is here. I asked him to bring some clothes, since you came as you are. Your results are fine, so I'm releasing you.'

He finished dressing. 'Thanks for taking care of me.'

'You're welcome, John.' She headed to the door, then turned. 'You should probably avoid Sister when you leave.'

For the first time that morning, he found a smile.

When Keeney met with Barrette, he felt a twinge of guilt at how happy Barrette looked. After a brief discussion with the nurse, they left the ward and headed out into the corridor. When the door closed, Keeney turned to him. 'Thanks for bringing me some clothes, you're a lifesaver.'

'Don't mention it. How you feeling?'

Keeney shrugged. 'Honestly, I'm not sure. It's all a bit of a blur.'

Barrette made a light touch to his arm and was about to say something, but Keeney moved away. 'Let's get out of here.'

They passed several nurses as they exited. Barrette jogged to keep up with him. 'Hey, would you stop for a minute?'

Keeney stopped and Barrette could tell from his expression he was uncomfortable. 'What's wrong?'

'Nothing.'

'Something, though. Spill.'

'It's just... I think you might have got the wrong impression.'

'About what?'

'Us,' he said, looking up and down the corridor.

'Relax, there's no one here,' he pointed out. The smile spreading across his face made Keeney feel even more uncomfortable. Barrette crossed his arms. 'I think you're reading too much into things.'

'Am I?' Keeney's frown deepened.

'Would you stop already, Jesus.' Barrette leant forward. 'We fucked, John. It was good. Better than good. I won't lie, I'd like to do it again. Tell me you didn't like it too?'

'It's not that,' he said, keeping his voice low. 'Of course, I liked it. It's just...'

Barrette's smile faded as his cheeks displayed the embarrassment of his realisation. 'Oh, you're not into me?'

'I'm still holding out for Bobby,' Keeney said, avoiding his eyes. 'I've been feeling terrible that I... we... you know?'

'Boy, did I read that wrong.'

'I'm sorry.'

'It's fine. I'm okay with it.'

Keeney felt a sense of relief wash over him. 'Are you?'

'Yeah, sure.' The way he answered suggested that wasn't true, but Keeney decided to leave it. There was a moment of uncomfortable silence, then Barrette smiled. It seemed false.

'Anyway. We have to go to the civilian level.' His voice sounded deadpan and it was obvious he was trying to work through his disappointment. 'Come on.'

'Right now?' Keeney groaned. 'I just want to take a shower.'

'You don't smell that bad,' he said, over his shoulder.

'Paul...'

They reached the elevator and waited. Barrette shoved his hands deep into his pockets. 'Something bad happened,' he said as they waited.

'Something bad happened?'

'I don't know much.'

'Is General Marshall okay?'

'As far as I know. He's still in isolation.'

'He's still in isolation?'

'Are you going to repeat everything I'm saying? It's annoying.'

'Sorry. Why is he in isolation?'

'Because of you. Don't you remember?'

Keeney shook his head.

'You got sick. After they took you, they isolated the general, the doctor, and that lunatic Bradley all together in the infirmary.'

Keeney rubbed his eyes. 'I don't even know how I got there.'

'Bradley took you. Sorry your shower's gonna have to wait. That British meathead wants you down there, and I'm afraid if I don't bring you, he'll kill me.'

'Don't be ridiculous,' Keeney said with a laugh. The expression on Barrette's face made him frown. 'You're serious?'

Barrette rubbed at his thigh. A dark expression crossed his otherwise handsome face. It didn't suit him. 'He fucking shot me and had me drugged.'

'What? Why?'

The door opened and they stepped in. 'Because of you.'

'Because of me?'

'You're doing it again,' he sighed.

Keeney put a hand on his arm. 'Why the fuck would he do that?'

'I... I don't want to talk about it.'

'He shot you, and drugged you, and you don't want to talk about it? What the hell?'

Barrette lowered his eyes. 'I don't think you want to hear why he did it.'

Keeney let go of his arm. 'You lied to me, just now, didn't you?'

'Yeah,' he said, stabbing at the button.

They were silent as the doors closed. 'Are you okay?'

Barrette looked back. 'What d'you think?'

'I'm sorry.'

They said nothing more while the car travelled down. When it opened they stepped out.

'This isn't the civilian level,' Keeney said.

'I know, we can't use the elevator. I told you, something bad happened. It's all locked down.'

'You keep saying something bad, but you haven't explained what bad is.'

'I don't know. I told you.' Barrette's irritation grew. 'Jesus. It's been locked down, no one is allowed in or out. That qualifies as bad, doesn't it? Will you quit asking me stupid fucking questions?'

Keeney raised an eyebrow. 'Okay, sorry.'

Barrette's shoulders dropped. 'I'm sorry, it's just... it's been a long day, that's all.'

'It's just after eight in the morning, Paul.'

'Is that all? Feels like much later.'

'Yeah, to me too. Okay, genius, how *are* we going to get down there?'

'I know a way,' Barrette said, a grin spreading across his face.

'I thought you might.'

'Follow me.'

Barrette led Keeney through the corridors into a small electrical room with a metal hatch that opened into a section he'd never been to. It looked unfinished. The lighting above was softer. The corridor floor replaced by sheets of metal mesh, sitting atop thick pipes. Red lights, ducting, and smaller pipes ran along the top and bottom of the walls in neat lines.

'Where are we?'

'Service level,' Barrette said. 'Each floor has one.'

'Why does it look like we stepped into a submarine?'

'It's probably the same setup.'

It was warmer in the service corridor and when Barrette paused to get his bearings, Keeney unbuttoned his shirt and fanned himself. 'Damn, why is it so hot?'

He could see the sweat forming on Barrette's brow. 'The ventilation and electrical equipment for this level generate a lot of heat.'

They rounded a corner and Barrette gave a happy exclamation as he made his way towards a large hatch.

'This is maintenance hatch two, there are three on every level. They run to the lowest level and back up to the surface,' he said, struggling to turn the wheel. Keeney added his strength and the wheel spun easier. 'We can take this down.'

'You said the floor was in lockdown?'

Barrette climbed through onto the ladder. Keeney put his head in and grimaced. The ladder extended in both directions into darkness. Small bulbs fixed at equidistant intervals weren't strong enough to illuminate the shaft.

'Yeah,' Barrette said, moving up a few rungs so Keeney could get on underneath. They pulled the door shut and used a lever to lock it. 'No one in or out.'

'Except in a maintenance hatch?'

Barrette shook his head as they descended. 'The hatch we're going to is a level below the sealed section.'

'There's a level below?'

'Yes,' he grunted, the heat taking its toll on him.

They made careful progress. Keeney had no idea how far up they were. He felt uncomfortable, his hands sweating. Every now and then he cursed as they slipped off a rung. He looked up and saw Barrette struggling, his shirt covered in sweat.

'What's with the heat?'

Barrette's breathing laboured as they remained immersed in the oppressive atmosphere. 'These tunnels vent excess heat... from the service areas.'

'Yeah?' He wiped a hand on his already soaked shirt. 'Well, it's stifling and I'm finding it hard to breathe.'

Barrette wiped his eyes. 'It's a lot hotter than I expected too.'

Sometime later they reached another hatch. Both drenched and breathing hard.

'Tell me this is it?' Keeney breathed, looking up.

Barrette shook his head. 'One more... to go.'

'Ugh,' Keeney sighed.

As they began descending, a strange sound filled the air above. A reverberation that sounded like a screech. They stopped and looked up.

'What was that?' Keeney asked.

The sweat was pouring from Barrette, dropping on Keeney. 'No clue. Probably ventilation.'

'You're dripping on me,' he cursed.

'Stop complaining. You were... just fine with it the... other day,' he said, in quick breaths.

Despite being uncomfortable, and claustrophobic, John Keeney chuckled as they continued their descent.

Muscles aching, and breathing almost impaired, they reached the hatch and sighed. Keeney, unable to speak, just pointed. Barrette nodded. He reached the large handle, but his hands slipped off the lever, and he fell back. His strength gone.

Keeney looked up as the strange noise they'd heard before echoed above. Barrette climbed down beside him and together they opened the door. A blast of cooler air greeted them as they stepped through. With the hatch secured, they slid down and sat against it, taking a moment to breathe. After they'd rested a short while, Barrette stood and extended his hand, pulling Keeney onto his feet.

Keeney pulled his damp shirt away from his body. 'Where to now?'

'If we follow this corridor, it should lead to storage rooms under the kitchen. We'll be able to use the dumbwaiter to go up.'

'Won't it be small?'

'It's industrial sized, we'll both probably fit inside.'

Barrette brushed the slicked mop of hair from Keeney's face and smiled. 'Ready?'

'Lead on.'

Barrette navigated them along service tunnels with lighting that cast eerie shadows across each section as they passed through. The mixture of the pale yellow and red bulbs giving the darkness an ominous feel. They turned a corner and Barrette stopped. Ahead they came to a T-junction.

'Great. Which way?'

Barrette frowned. 'I don't know. I'm a little lost.'

'We should split up.'

He shook his head. 'No. Besides, you don't know what you're looking for.'

'It's a fifty-fifty chance then.'

'We'll go that way,' he said, pointing left.

Barrette entered, Keeney following, but a low whine from somewhere ahead stopped them.

'More ventilation?' Keeney asked.

'Probably, come on.'

It wasn't long before they entered an enormous room with a higher ceiling, filled with large wooden containers. Keeney read the stencilled label on one. 'This looks like an ammo stash.'

Barrette nodded. 'Which means there should be an armoury close by. Let's find it. I would feel better if I had a weapon, wouldn't you?'

Keeney nodded.

They continued on and Keeney pointed to a heavy door. 'That looks hopeful.'

Barrette tried the door, but found it locked. He took a bunch of keys from his pocket, and flicked through them until he found one that fit the lock and turned it. Keeney smiled as he unlocked the door. Inside they found racks of various weapons, along with magazines, and other equipment.

'Doesn't look like anyone's been down here for years,' Keeney said, blowing dust off a rack of maybe a hundred sheathed bolo knives. He picked one up and pulled it from its scabbard, then attached it to his belt and took one to Barrette, who was checking an M1911 pistol. They each took one, and several empty magazines.

'Grab that ammo box,' Barrette said.

Keeney lifted it off the rack and opened it, clipping the bullets into the magazines, while Barrette picked up two holsters and ammo pouches with belts.

'Jackpot.' Keeney looked up. He was finishing filling the magazines when Barrette returned with two flashlights. He turned them on. They gave a soft blueish light.

'UV filters,' he said in answer to Keeney's frown.

'How many are there?'

'Looks like five.'

'Let's take them all.'

When they were stocked and armed, they left and locked the room. Barrette led them down an adjoining corridor and stopping at another T-junction.

'Left, or right?' Keeney said, seeing no obvious answer.

'Left,' Barrette said.

A clattering sound made them jump.

'That wasn't ventilation,' Keeney said, grabbing Barrette's shirt.

'No.' Barrette looked at him. 'It sounded like metal on metal.'

'Maybe we dislodged something?'

Another clatter echoed in the corridor, followed by something spinning along the floor that hit Keeney's shoe. He bent down and picked it up. It was an empty magazine. He turned to Barrette, who had his pistol out.

'We're not alone. Something threw that at us,' Barrette said.

Keeney took his pistol out. 'If someone's down here, let's see if we can find out who.'

'Wait.' Barrette pulled out a flashlight and turned it on. Its blueish light didn't illuminate much. He swung it in an arc until its light hit a patch of shadows. When the ultraviolet passed through it, the shadow became an unidentifiable blackened lump that gave a loud screech, then darted up the wall and disappeared into the clusters of pipes and ductwork above.

'What the fuck was that?' Keeney said, taking a step back.

'Let's not hang around to find out.'

They went left down the corridor and entered a room similar to the one they'd come from. Barrette went to the far wall.

'There,' he said, beaming. 'We found the dumbwaiter.'

'We won't both fit in there,' Keeney said in alarm.

'Shit, it's a bit smaller than I thought.'

Barrette opened the gate and sighed. 'And of course, the fucking thing's in the up position. We'll have to bring it down first.'

He pressed a green button and an electrical whirring noise burst through the quiet. They could hear it coming down. It seemed to take forever, but when the cart reached them, they found it full.

'Jesus Christ,' Keeney said.

Once they'd emptied it, Keeney looked at the cart. 'There's nothing to send it up from inside.'

'Get in,' Barrette said. 'I'll send you up.'

'What about you?'

'When you're out, I'll bring it down. When I'm in, I'll yell, and you can bring me up.'

Keeney nodded, then backed into the cart. It was a tight fit, but he managed to squeeze in.

'You comfy?'

Keeney squirmed. 'No.'

Barrette's eyes met his. 'I'm sorry about earlier.'

'What? Jesus. You sure like to pick your moments...'

Barrette grabbed his face in both hands and kissed him. The passion he displayed and the lustful look in his eyes made Keeney's heart flutter. Before he could think about what just happened, Barrette winked and pulled the door and gate across, then slapped the button. The cart jolted and Keeney waited in cramped agony for it to reach the top. He tasted Barrette's sweat. Despite everything, it made him smile. When it stopped, Keeney slid the gate and door open and came out.

'I'm out,' he yelled.

'Okay,' came Barrette's response up the shaft, 'I'll bring it back down.'

Once it reached the bottom, Keeney heard Barrette open the gate and curse a few times. 'Fuck, it's tight. Okay, I'm ready,' he yelled.

When he heard the gate below close, he pressed the button. As it started its ascent, Keeney heard a heavy thump. 'What's wrong?'

'I dunno,' Barrette said. 'It's juddering.'

'You're probably too heavy,' Keeney shouted.

'Fuck you.'

Keeney chuckled as he scanned the kitchen. He'd noticed the usually bright lighting was out, and only a few bulbs appeared to be working. He also frowned at the lack of people.

'It's quiet up here,' Keeney said. 'It should be full by now.'

There was another thumping from the shaft.

'Paul?'

There was no reply.

'Paul? Are you okay?'

The response was a muffled cry, followed by a thumping, then a blood-curdling scream that made Keeney's heart miss a beat.

Barrette continued to scream. Keeney rushed to the door, yelling his name. Barrette's shrieking grew in intensity as Keeney bashed the button. His concerns and fears manifested in frustrated cursing, but those were soon left in his throat, as the horrible screams worsened.

Keeney stood staring at the door, willing the cart to arrive. The screams suddenly lessened into cries and whimpers. Keeney thumped the door. There was a sudden high-pitched shriek, which made Keeney jump. He heard a ripping crunch, and then there was silence.

When the cart docked, Keeney opened the door and pulled the gate across with a shaking hand and jumped back, as Barrette's bloodied arm flopped out. The inside of the cart awash and dripping in crimson horror. What remained of Barrette's body was no longer identifiable. Keeney tentatively reached out and touched Barrette's hand. He dropped to his knees as anguish took hold of him.

CHAPTER TWENTY

9 a.m.

Doctor Husk was worried about the boys. They weren't talking much, they just sat huddled together in their room, and the worst of it was Colonel Baldwin. He just stood by the main door watching out the window. She chewed on her lips, weighing up the heavy choices before her, and then left the boys to talk again with Baldwin.

He hadn't moved from the door in thirty minutes.

'Where are they?' he mumbled to himself.

Husk knew he wasn't directing the question at her, but she answered anyway. 'Where are who?'

He glanced at her, then turned back to the window. 'Grunner's clean-up team. They should be here by now.'

'You're worried?'

'Things aren't going as I'd hoped.' His moist breath fogged the window.

'I'm worried too. About Charlie, about the boys. Don't you have any idea what's happening?'

He said nothing.

She tried again. 'I'm guessing it's bad?' He remained staring, ignoring her attempts to engage him. Husk was about to say something when movement down the corridor stopped the words from coming. A group of seven people dressed in hazard suits, wearing cylinders on their backs, were heading towards the infirmary.

Baldwin opened the door and greeted them. 'Thank god,' he breathed.

Husk watched though the window as one unhitched a metal gun-like device connected via a hose onto the cylinder he was carrying. Another made a brief check of what she imagined was a regulator valve, then tapped the first one's shoulder twice, and stepped back.

'Where is it?' a muffled voice said through his mask.

Baldwin pointed to the corridor Charlie and Bill had disappeared down an hour earlier.

She frowned at their exchange. *It?* she thought.

'Stay here, we'll sweep the area.'

'It's getting hot,' Baldwin said.

'We know, Grunner had us shut off the ventilation and seal the air ducts. Just in case.'

In case of what, she mused.

'The hotter it gets, the worse...'

'We know,' came a curt voice. 'Colonel, with respect, we trained for this. We know what we're doing. Any other disturbances that you're aware of?'

Baldwin shook his head. 'I think it's localised. What's Grunner doing?'

'Implementing protocols for lockdown in the labs. He's jumpy, but that's nothing new.' He turned to the others and held up a closed fist, then opened his hand. They responded in the same way.

'When we're finished, we'll come let you know.'

'There are two men I want you to look out for,' he said. 'It's important.'

'There are a lot more than two people down here, Colonel. Why are these men more important than the others?'

'They aren't,' Baldwin said, checking himself. 'I just meant they're important to me. Colonel Bradley and General Marshall, keep an eye out for them, please. They went to investigate.'

The masked head nodded. 'Okay, but no guarantees. I don't need to tell you what it does to people.'

She frowned. *It*, again.

'Good luck,' he said, stepping back and allowing them to head away. He came back into the infirmary and closed the door. Doctor Husk stared at him.

'Start talking, you son of a bitch,' she said.

• • •

Doctor Grunner's scientists and many military personnel gathered together in the dining room waiting as he came in to address them. There was a hushed silence as he made an adjustment to his little round spectacles. Behind him stood eight heavily armed men dressed in black coveralls and face masks. Each carrying submachine guns and many other weapons. The assembled military personnel all eyed the men who were standing still behind him.

'We've had an incident.' Grunner made the statement with a calmness no one else felt. 'As a precaution, we have sealed the civilian sections and closed off the ventilation.'

A murmur rippled through those gathered. He waited for them to quieten.

Doctor Evelyn Parker stepped forward. 'What kind of incident?'

'A terrible kind. All work on the samples will cease. Take them to lab sixteen and lock them into containment.'

'What about the serum?'

He regarded her. 'What about it?'

'It contains trace elements of the sample, should we contain that too?'

Doctor Grunner licked his lips. 'Did I say we needed to contain the serum, Doctor Parker?'

'No, I just thought...'

He stepped forward. 'I do not require you to think, Doctor. Just obey my instructions.'

She met his unblinking eyes. 'When should we start?'

'I suggest now,' he said, dismissing her with a wave.

Evelyn turned and the remaining scientists followed. Grunner watched them leave, then turned to the military.

'Who is the senior rank here?'

'That would be me.' A man stepped out of the crowd. 'Captain Williams.'

'I don't care. I want armed guards on all means of access to and from this level. No one in or out. Anyone you find breaching that order, you are to shoot. Is that understood?'

Williams shook his head. 'I'm sorry, sir, but I won't give that order. Not until I understand why.'

Grunner nodded. He held out a hand, and Heinz stepped forward and handed Grunner a revolver. The captain watched the exchange with concern. Grunner then handed the revolver over. 'What is your opinion of this weapon?'

Williams turned it a few times. 'A Browning forty-five automatic. Standard issue.'

'I didn't ask you what it was, Captain. I asked for your opinion of it.'

He tested its weight. 'It's reliable and accurate. There's a reason it's been in service for so long.'

'It does what we ask of it, in fact. Nothing more, nothing less.'

Captain Williams nodded. 'Point and shoot, like most pistols.'

'Thank you,' he said, holding out his hand. The captain handed it to him. Grunner released the safety and before anyone could blink, lifted and shot the captain through his forehead. The men in the room dropped along with the captain's lifeless body.

When they'd recovered, they were facing down eight submachine guns. Grunner passed the revolver back to Heinz, then turned and clasped his hands behind his back.

'Who, now, is the senior rank?'

Another older man pushed through the crowd of angry scared faces, his eyes full of rage. 'That would be me, sir. I'm...'

'I need not know who you are. Only that you understand my instructions.'

He nodded.

Grunner leant forward. 'I'm sorry, I could not hear your reply.'

The officer looked down at the blood pooling from the back of Captain Williams' head.

'I understand,' he said, clenching his teeth.

Doctor Grunner gave a thin smile. 'Excellent.'

'Most of us only have pistols, sir,' he said. 'The armoury is on the floor above.'

'I am aware. But since to leave this floor would mean having you shot, I suggest you all pool resources and double up where weapons and ammunition remain in short supply. Is that clear?'

He gave a tight-lipped nod. Grunner put a hand to his ear and leant forward. 'I'm sorry?'

'Yes, sir, it's clear.'

'Then why are you still standing there?'

• • •

'But did you see what attacked them?' General Marshall asked for the second time. Stevens rubbed his eyes.

'It's like I said before. There was screaming. When we got to the doors the lights went out. It wasn't possible to see anything.'

'So, you retreated to the safety of your upturned desks?' The edge of disgust in Marshall's voice made Stevens growl.

'Hey...' Stevens brought himself to his full six feet. Marshall just stared at him. 'You don't get to judge me, you arrogant old fuck.'

As they stared each other down, Bradley gave a light cough. 'Are you two done? Because I rather think we have more pressing concerns.'

They turned eyes on him.

'Good.' He rubbed at his lip as he thought. 'Now, the first thing we should do is...'

King made a noise loud enough to make them pay attention. They turned to see him gesturing wildly.

'What?' Stevens said, irritated by the summons.

'Movement,' Decker whispered.

Stevens's irritation fell and he knelt beside him. 'You see what it is?'

'No,' Decker remarked.

King cracked open the door a little. Bradley crouched next

to him and touched his shoulder. 'Let me get in there.'

King moved aside and Colonel Bradley peered through, then looked back at Marshall. 'Seven people dressed like they know they're up against.'

Marshall crouched next to him. 'What are they doing?'

'They appear to be spraying something on the bodies. I can see them clearer now they've come a little closer. Yes, they're definitely spraying something.'

'You think they know what's happening?'

'At the very least, they have a better idea then we do.'

'Why the fuck are we just standing here?' Stevens said.

'Wait,' Bradley warned.

Stevens ignored him and pushed through the doors. He yelled and waved to attract their attention. It worked. The nearest turned to his companions and made waving gestures, pointing at them. Decker and King exchanged smiles.

Bradley gripped Marshall's arm. Marshall read the colonel's expression as the colour drained from his face. It was a look he'd never seen in Bradley. It was something beyond fear.

Colonel Bradley backed away from the door, and Marshall found himself dragged along. The tightness of Bradley's grip was beginning to restricted the blood to his hand.

Decker and King kept the doors open while Stevens stood yelling. The newcomers were gesticulating at him, but not being military, he failed to recognise the signals.

'There's a few of us alive over here,' Stevens yelled.

The hazard suits froze in position. One man was making a frantic cutting gesture across his throat. Stevens looked back at Decker with a frown. Repeating the gesture, he asked, 'What's all that nonsense?'

Decker shrugged. 'Charlie, what's that gesture about?'

They turned to find Bradley pulling Marshall back away from the door.

'Charlie?'

'It means,' Marshall said in a cool voice. 'You're making too much noise. Shut up.'

Todd Stevens cool finally broke. 'I've just about had enough of you.' He turned to Decker. 'Gimmie that fucking shooter.'

Decker obeyed, and when Stevens looked back at the general, he found himself staring down the barrel of an odd-looking pistol. 'Put it down,' Bradley commanded.

'Didn't I already explain this to you, Charlie? This is my fucking turf. You don't get to come in here and...'

'I won't tell you again,' Bradley said, his finger finding the first pressure on the trigger.

Stevens knew Charlie would kill him before he could even aim. He dropped the gun and put his hands up.

Bradley stepped forward. 'Kick it to me.'

The gun slid over and Marshall picked it up.

'What is wrong with you two?' Stevens gestured to the group of men outside. 'We're about to be rescued.' He frowned. 'Now why are they doing that?' The response team were all pointing up.

Bradley and Marshall looked at each other.

They all looked up.

Stevens froze in his tracks. 'What's that?'

Decker and King cocked their heads, each had a growing feeling of apprehension. Something overhead made a noise. A soft thudding. Stevens frowned and stepped back towards his men.

The ceiling buckled, twisted, then fell open. Through the hole, Stevens glimpsed a solid mass and gulped. King picked up a piece of broken pipe.

'Get behind me, boss.'

Stevens didn't move. The black thing his eyes locked onto had him paralysed with fear. Decker grabbed his arm, yanking him away.

It fell from the cavity like treacle and pooled on the floor in front of the giant man wielding a pipe.

Marshall felt Bradley's hot whispered breath on his face; it made the hairs on the back of his neck stand. 'Get ready to run,' was his message.

The thing oozing from the ceiling came to a stop and King frowned at the black puddle. He turned back to Decker and Stevens. 'Looks like oil or something, it must have come from the ducting.' He frowned at the look on their faces.

They then backed away.

King turned to find the puddle growing into a vague humanoid shape. It swayed and twisted as it elongated. Thin rings rippled up and down its fluidic body. An appendage formed and reached out toward him. King lifted the pipe and planted his feet on the floor, shifting his weight to his back leg, as though waiting for a pitcher to send him a ball. When it got close, King swung hard and battered it away. The append-age recoiled and he centred himself again, waiting. Sweat fell from him in huge droplets.

Marshall felt Bradley tug at his sleeve and he moved with him. Neither took their eyes off King or the monstrous things he was battling. Bradley manoeuvred them around the back of Decker and Stevens, who were focused on King. The crea-ture sent another tentacled arm, again King knocked it back.

'What's it doing?' Decker asked.

'Playing with him,' came Colonel Bradley's whispered response. It made Decker and Stevens jump. They hadn't noticed he'd circled behind.

'What do we do?' Stevens said, his earlier bravado gone.

'We leave,' Bradley's calm voice said, 'right now.'

King knocked an even thicker arm back. 'Is that all you've got?' he yelled.

In response, the creature sent another. King swung, but a second flew out and snatched the pole from his grip, and the monster's black arm coiled around his neck. He yelled as he fought to remove it. A third found his mouth and forced itself down his throat. While he struggled, it lifted him into the air and turned him. His eyes went wide, but King's strength was good enough to pull the thing from his mouth, and he took in a breath.

'Get it off me, get it off me,' he yelled.

Colonel Bradley ran eyes to the door and then back to the creature. 'Grab something and help him,' he yelled.

Spurred into action Decker and Stevens grabbed their own broken pipes and rushed towards it.

Bradley stopped Marshall from doing the same. 'Bill, let's go.'

The general shook off his hand. 'We can't just leave them.'

'They're all dead already, look.'

The creature changed its response to their attacks. New appendages formed and simultaneously knocked the weapons from their hands and coiled around their arms, pulling them towards it. The strength and speed of its attack surprised them and when they reached its bulky mass, it took hold of their necks, turning and lifting them till their feet were no longer on the ground. They kicked and screamed, pleaded, and cursed.

General Marshall and Colonel Bradley stood as still as they could.

Decker's eyes went wide and then he screamed. It was the worst sound Marshall had ever heard. He made a move, but again, Bradley restrained him.

The horrifying scream continued and Decker's skin went taut. They watched helpless and afraid as each of the victims writhed in tormented agony. The noise of each person's scream became one long chorus. Decker bucked. His crotch darkened as his bladder emptied. Then, unlike the others, he gave an extended shriek that pierced Marshall's soul. Decker's chest burst apart, spraying them with blood, bits of cartilage, and bone, and he fell limp in its hold.

The other two, seeing what had just happened to Decker, began a renewed fight. Each bucking and screaming. Stevens made eye contact with Bradley. 'Charlie...' he managed, eyes pleading.

Colonel Bradley read the request and raised his weapon. Stevens nodded. Despite his agony, and the blood seeping from his nose, he smiled. Bradley fired twice in quick succession, putting a hole in both Todd Stevens and Tony King's foreheads.

General Marshall lowered his eyes.

The creature gave a gurgled, inhuman, cry of outrage and released their bodies. It grew larger, enveloping Decker's remains as it did. It was as if everything inevitable about their future now reared up in front of them.

They ran.

• • •

The sound of someone yelling pulled him out of his misery. Keeney wiped the greasy blood from his hands on his pants and used the back of his hands to wipe away his tears. He scooted forward in a crouch, all the time aware that whatever had killed Barrette could come and kill him too. As he got nearer the heavy steel counters, the man's yelling changed to screaming. Keeney froze. His heart began beating too fast in his chest. The screaming intensified. He willed himself to look over the edge, but he couldn't do it.

Keeney didn't know if he could go through seeing another person in the same condition as Barrette. Two shots in quick succession rang out and the screaming stopped. He found the courage needed to look over the top and relief flooded though him, as he saw Marshall and Bradley running towards a group dressed in hazard suits. Keeney ran around the counter to the door and burst through.

Marshall knew he was the slower of the two, but Bradley always remained behind him. As they cut across the room towards the hazard team, something caught his eye. A door opened and another survivor was running to join them.

No, Marshall realised, not another survivor. It was...

'John!' he yelled. Despite the caution he should have taken, he turned towards him, grabbing him in a tight hug as he got close. When they broke, Marshall could tell he'd been through the ringer.

'You're bleeding?'

He shook his head. 'It's not mine.'

General Marshall took Keeney's youthful face into both hands. 'Jesus, I'm so happy to see you.' Marshall's eyes brimmed as he again pulled Keeney into a hug. 'I'm sorry,' he whispered.

Keeney smiled.

Colonel Bradley came beside them. 'I'm glad to see you safe.'

Keeney released himself from General Marshall's grip and

turned to Bradley. 'You son of a bitch.' He swung his fist into Bradley's right cheek. To his credit, the colonel didn't react. He just stepped back rubbing it in confusion.

Marshall had a tough time restraining him. 'John, what the hell. Stop!'

Keeney breathed hard but regained his control. Colonel Bradley ran eyes along the length of him. Keeney was shaking. There was blood on his shirt and pants, and it was still wet. His puffy raw eyes shouted a personal tragedy that made the young man look twenty years older. Bradley observed how Keeney's anguish was unrestrained. Bradley looked to the many weapons Keeney had somehow gained. He'd come out from the kitchens. Only Barrette's hairbrained plan to use the dumbwaiter from the floor below could have achieved that. And then there was the shirt he was wearing, that had another man's name stitched on the chest.

Bradley closed his eyes. 'John, I'm so sorry.'

'Fuck you,' he screamed. The anguish in his voice almost tipping him back into the misery he felt earlier. 'You don't get to be sorry, not after what you did.'

Marshall frowned and continued restraining him. 'What the hell is going on?'

Bradley said, 'It's okay, Bill, let him go.'

Keeney stared at him. 'Don't come near me, I'll fucking kill you.'

Bradley stepped forward anyway, 'No, you won't.'

Keeney continued to stare. The words he wanted to say ballooning in his throat and dying there, snuffed by the grief boiling inside, stopping his lips from opening and releasing them.

'John, I am so sorry.'

The seal broke on Keeney's control. He fought it, like he wanted to fight Bradley. He wanted to hurt him, curse at him, scream at him, something. But the colonel just stepped right into his space and wrapped his long arms around him, and all the grief and anguish came back as he sagged sobbing into Bradley's shirt.

A moment later, one of the masked men approached. 'General Marshall?'

'What's left of him,' he said.

'You seem intact to me. Any other survivors?'

'None that we've seen.'

The masked man nodded.

'You know what this thing is, don't you?'

He put a hand on Marshall's shoulder. 'I don't have answers to any of your questions, General. It's time for you to leave.'

They heard an echoing, gurgling inhuman cry and Marshall looked back at the room they'd escaped from.

'You're all lucky to be alive, General,' he said, giving the men a hand signal. 'Go back to the infirmary. We'll take it from here.'

He moved away, the others forming into a staggered line beside him at his command. Marshall didn't need telling twice. He found Bradley holding Keeney by the shoulders. They were in quiet conversation. He didn't know what Bradley had done to make Keeney react the way he had, but it looked like they were working it out. He felt terrible interrupting them, but he did so anyway.

'We need to go now,' he said.

They nodded and followed him.

CHAPTER TWENTY-ONE

9:30 a.m.

'I know things seem bad,' Baldwin began. Doctor Husk thew him a terrible look at his attempt to placate her.

'Stop changing the subject,' she said.

He sighed. 'Kate, look, there are things I can't tell you. You of all people should recognise the difficulty of being obliged to withhold information.'

Her eyes were hard. 'That must make this much easier for you.'

'Easier?' He grunted. 'Nothing about this assignment has been easy, Doctor. And if the situation were reversed, you would do exactly the same.'

'I doubt that. Not if it meant putting people at risk, or worse. I have two boys back there,' – she threw her arm towards their room – 'two boys with no parents, no known family. Terrified little boys, Colonel. Does that concern you?'

'Jake is hardly a little boy,' he corrected.

'That's not the point.'

'What is the point, exactly?'

She opened her mouth, but the words caught there as General Marshall entered followed by Charlie and Captain Keeney – the man who'd taken ill and been quarantined – who was covered in blood. Her questions to Baldwin forgotten as she came to greet them. 'I'm so happy to see you all,' she said, her eyes on Bradley. Marshall touched her shoulder as he walked past, heading for Baldwin.

Husk turned to Keeney. 'You probably won't remember

me,' she said, 'but we've met before. John, isn't it?'

He nodded.

'I'm Kate. Are you injured?' She ran an eye over him.

'No.' He managed a smile. 'This isn't my blood.'

Husk nodded and turned to Bradley. 'You're injured,' she said, taking his head and turning it. 'That's a nasty bruise.'

Bradley took her hands. 'It's nothing more than I deserved. How are the boys?'

'They're okay. What happened?'

Marshall looked at Baldwin. 'Care to do some explaining now?'

Baldwin eyed him. 'I'm afraid I'm under orders not...'

General Marshall threw up his hands and yelled at the ceiling. 'For the love of God. I order you to tell me.'

He shook his head. 'You can't. My orders come from the president.'

'Well, I won't tell him if you don't,' Marshall bit back. He turned and rubbed his forehead. Colonel Bradley stood and pulled out his revolver.

Baldwin stared at him. 'You're going to shoot me?'

Husk stood between them. 'No. I won't allow it.'

'Get out of the way, Kate.'

'No. Stop this, right now.'

'Braders,' Marshall said, 'this isn't the way.'

'Oh,' he said, aiming between Baldwin's eyes. 'I think it's the only way.'

Keeney put his hand on Bradley's revolver and shook his head. The colonel's lips thinned. Their eyes met and he lowered his weapon. Baldwin gave a small sigh as Keeney came and took his hand, dropping a set of bloody dog tags in. He looked at Keeney in confusion, then read the name. Much to everyone's surprise, Baldwin let out a dismal groan.

'Paul?' he murmured. His shoulders dropped. His eyes filling with tears. 'No, no!'

'I'm sorry,' Keeney said, his own tears forming. 'What the hell killed him?'

Baldwin put the tags to his forehead and closed his eyes. Everyone stood in silence, watching. The colour left Baldwin's face and Keeney took his arm, leading him to a set of chairs.

Marshall frowned. Baldwin, a man who had stared down the barrel of Bradley' revolver twice, was now... lost.

'Fuck your orders. I want to know.'

Baldwin took in a shuddering breath. He was fighting the emotional response that was threatening to follow. He remained tight lipped. Keeney took his hand. 'If it would help, I can describe every scream...'

Baldwin wrenched his hand away. 'Stop... for God's sake...' His tears falling.

Keeney leant forward. 'You owe it to your son and those who... loved him.'

Husk and Bradley exchanged looks but remained silent.

Marshall felt Keeney knew what he was doing, and left him to it. He watched as Keeney and Baldwin sat crying. Keeney had taken Baldwin's hand again and this time he held onto it. Keeney was saying something into Baldwin's ear, and it made the colonel cry out in more grief. Keeney then spoke loudly enough for them all to hear. 'Please... I want to know what killed him, and how I can kill it.'

Baldwin stared at the tags till his eyes blurred and he could no longer read the words. He rubbed the tears from his nose and nodded.

'That thing is the results of our attempts to make a vaccine for the virus that's killing millions. We call it *the sample*. There are two types. Alpha and beta. Alpha is deadly. A single drop turned a mouse into an uncontrollable abomination and heat mixed with high humidity made it worse. Only cold and ultraviolet can subdue it. Sample beta is not quite as deadly. The monster out there is, I believe, a Beta.'

'Sample alpha attacks the brainstem and other centres before the victim manifests physical changes. Not all these attributes are the same. But one thing we found, almost by accident, is when it starts the transformation it kills off bacterial infections, viruses, cancers, and just about any other maladies and abnormalities you care to mention.'

He looked down at the tags for a moment, then continued.

'Grunner and his team made a serum that we tested on

refugees who arrived here infected. Understand, most of those people could no longer make rational or reasoned decisions. It worked. People who by our own standards of medical knowledge were deemed vegetative, miraculously recovered. We couldn't believe it. It was a breakthrough. It could very well lead to curing all known incurable diseases across the planet. But then we encountered a problem.'

'Once you'd cured everyone there was no one left to test it on?' Bradley said.

He nodded. 'The president was so encouraged he gave us total autonomy to do whatever we needed to do. After that, Grunner extended his research.'

'I bet he did,' Bradley snarled.

'The president sanctioned this?' Marshall asked.

'Bill, the America we knew is almost gone. It's a war. We win or we die.'

'Go on,' Marshall said.

'The rest is simple. I asked members of the military to volunteer, and Grunner and the others began infecting them with diseases and illness. This facility has samples of almost everything. I put my own morals aside, because every single one of them recovered. But then a few people got sick after treatments. Then many people.'

'And they all died?' Keeney said.

Baldwin nodded. 'Horribly.'

Bradley looked at Marshall. 'That's the reason the compliment of military personnel is so low.'

Husk said, 'You said some got sick after initially recovering. Were they all infected with the same thing prior to inoculation?'

'Yes, they were given hepatitis B, I understand.'

'A blood-based virus,' she said, pulling at her lip. 'And only these people regressed?'

'I believe so. But I don't know for certain.'

'Where did you put the bodies?' she asked.

'Most of them are in cold storage.'

'Most of them?' Bradley said.

'During the clean-up, several corpses came alive and killed

any personnel they came into contact with.'

There was a soft intake of breath, and they looked over to find the boys had sneaked out of their room, and were listening behind an examination table.

'You boys shouldn't be listening to this.' Her firm voice was met with a stubborn teenage scowl.

'Why not? It affects us to.'

'It'll give you nightmares,' she said.

'Worse than the ones I already have?'

She paused as his words sunk in. 'Well...'

Colonel Bradley touched her shoulder and then picked up Ciaran and sat him on his lap. 'They should hear it. Go on, Colonel.'

Jake sat next to him.

Doctor Husk chuckled despite everything. The boys really liked him.

'There isn't much more to tell. They turned into monsters and attacked people. We found a way to subdue and kill them. And that was the last of it, at least I thought it was.'

'Until today?'

'No. We had a second incident, not as bad. An officer who displayed no symptoms of any kind, came into the command centre and killed himself. One minute he was alive and chatting with his brother, the next minute he pulled out a revolver and the back of his head and half his brain painted the wall. He had no history of suicidal tendencies. We couldn't work it out. We had to sedate the brother. Grunner felt he might develop similar tendencies, so isolated him with several others suffering from a rare respiratory virus. Many were intubated, and some were in danger of drowning in fluids building up in their lungs. When we extracted those fluids, they were black. We later discovered sample properties in the mucus.'

'This serum contains trace elements of the sample? Correct?' Husk asked.

'That's correct. It is the basis of it.'

'Even in trace form it continued to do what it was designed to do?'

Baldwin frowned. 'I don't believe we can truly understand

what its purpose is, Doctor.'

'How many bodies have you tallied now?' she asked. 'I think it has shown you what its purpose is.'

Marshall rubbed his face. 'Well, as fascinating and gruesome as that story was. How does it affect what's happening now?'

Husk looked at Baldwin. 'He's already answered that.'

'Would someone like to enlighten me?' Marshall said.

Husk crossed her arms. 'We're all ticking time bombs, aren't we?'

Colonel Baldwin nodded.

'Only those who've already been inoculated, I'm assuming? I haven't,' Marshall said.

'I told you before, Bill. You cannot rely on your memories. Almost all of you came infected and were treated and inoculated. Some took months to recover. Others, like John here, were treated more than once.'

'Those men in there,' Bradley asked. 'The ones cleaning up your mess? They were spraying bodies with something.'

'It's concentrated hydrochloric acid.'

'Which does what?' Marshall asked.

'Makes the corpses unpalatable, or indigestible, or something. The creature needs to renew its source of fluids, and it likes the biological kind.'

'The monster eats us?' Ciaran's curious voice made them all turn.

'I think Doctor Grunner would argue it absorbs us.'

'So, a dead body can become one of those monsters?'

Baldwin nodded. 'I'm still struggling to understand where it came from. The labs are locked down, no one here has died, as far as I know.'

Bradley made a face. 'Yes, about that.'

'Did someone die?' Baldwin asked, looking between Bradley and Marshall.

'Father Doyle,' Bradley said. Jake and Ciaran gave him a sad look. 'Sorry, boys.'

Marshall said, 'Is that what happened? Doyle became the thing that killed everyone back there?'

'It's likely,' Baldwin said. 'Did he kill himself?'

'No,' Bradley said. He looked at the boys for a second then said, 'He was in the middle of something intimate, when...'

'When what?'

'Well,' – again he looked at the boys – 'either Jessie bashed his head in, or it just exploded.'

'Charlie!' Husk snapped.

Jake and Ciaran giggled.

Baldwin's misery, however, was now replaced by an urgency he hadn't shown before. 'We're leaving. Now.'

'Is there something different about Doyle's case?' Husk asked.

Baldwin's agitation increased. 'I'll answer all your questions once we're off this level. Please, trust me, we have to go.'

Baldwin and Marshall stared at each other for a second or two, then Marshall turned to Husk. 'Are the MPs okay to move?'

'I... No, I gave them a sedative.'

Baldwin pushed past them towards the door. 'What? Of all the stupid, irresponsible...'

'How was I to know?'

'Leave them then,' Baldwin said.

'We'll do no such thing,' Doctor Husk shot back.

Baldwin sighed. 'How long will it be before we can wake them?'

'An hour?'

Bradley lifted Ciaran as he hopped off the bed. 'I'm sensing that might be too late?'

Marshall turned to Baldwin. 'Can't we carry them to the elevator?'

'No. They're locked down. We can't override them on this level.'

'Then how are we supposed to get out?' Husk asked.

'The service ladders?' Keeney suggested.

Baldwin nodded. 'It's the only way. But we'll never be able to carry two deadweight MPs.'

'Then I'll stay with them,' Keeney said.

Marshall looked shocked. 'Absolutely not.'

'I know how to get to the tunnels. I can get them there. There's no other choice.'

'He's right, Bill,' Bradley said.

The general stepped closer. 'I can't leave him alone down here.' Before Marshall could react, Colonel Bradley deposited Ciaran into his arms. 'He won't be alone. Go with Ira and get Kate and the boys to safety.'

Marshall looked terrible. 'Braders...'

'Jake, go with Kate.'

Jake nodded and stood beside her.

Marshall gave him a look. 'Don't get killed.'

Bradley smiled at him. 'I'll do my best.' He locked eyes with Husk as he took her hand. 'Wait for me,' he said.

'You'd both better make it,' she replied, her eyes brimming. 'Wait for me.'

Husk opened her mouth to speak, but he grabbed and kissed her, hard. When he released her, Colonel Baldwin ushered them out of the infirmary.

General Marshall was the last to leave. He stared at Bradley and Keeney. 'Don't take any risks, boys. Promise me.'

They nodded.

Marshall hefted Ciaran up and followed the others out.

John Keeney sat on the chair he'd positioned next to the beds the two MPs occupied and allowed his eyes to close. But within the darkness of his thoughts, Barrette's terrible screams rang out. He opened his eyes and found Colonel Bradley staring back at him. 'I'll look out, if you want to rest,' he offered.

Keeney shook his head.

Bradley nodded. 'John, I meant what I said before.'

'I know,' he said, going over to a cart he'd spotted against a wall. It still had breakfast on it. Not that he was hungry. He lifted the silver flask and shook it.

'Tell me there's coffee in there?' Bradley said, coming next to him.

'Feels full.' He opened it and the aroma hit him. 'Yeah, and it's still hot.'

Keeney poured two cups and they both drank.

'I hope these guys wake up soon,' Keeney said checking one. 'I really want to get out of here.'

'No arguments here,' Bradley said. 'I'll be happier once we're up a level too.'

'No,' Keeney shook his head. 'I meant out of this facility. I wish we'd never come.'

Colonel Bradley downed the last of his cup. 'Any more coffee?'

Keeney handed him the flask.

'We're no safer out there,' he said, filling his cup and handing the flask back to him. 'You know that.'

'At least out there we knew the rules,' he said, emptying the last of the flask. 'We could protect ourselves.'

'We lost enough to learn it,' Bradley reminded him.

Keeney sighed. 'I just...'

'What?'

'I just want to feel the wind on my skin. I want to see trees, grass... anything but bright lights, and corridors. But most of all...'

'You want to find Bobby?'

His eyes instantly teared. 'Yeah.'

Bradley was thoughtful. 'I have a plan. It's risky. Actually, it's suicidal. But I've been giving it a lot of thought.'

Keeney put down his cup. 'Tell me.'

'Before, when we didn't know if anyone was still alive, we weren't focused on anything but survival.'

'Look where that got us.'

'Right. But since we know now that the president survived, the likelihood that others have as well is high.'

'I was thinking the same. It's given me a lot of hope.'

'Ira said the president was travelling by sea. You said Bobby was at the Pentagon about the time of the... well, whatever, happened?'

He nodded.

'Strikes me that in the event of an attack, they'd have an underground bunker or two.'

Keeney finished his coffee. 'At the Pentagon? Sure.'

'If they got the president to safety, I'm betting they got the

Pentagon staff out as well.' Bradley put his cup on the cart. 'There's a hangar up top, I saw it when we came in.'

Keeney looked hopeful. 'Can you fly an aeroplane?'

'With your help I can. But there are some hard choices to make before that.'

'You mean where we fly to?'

'No,' he said, 'who we take with us.'

CHAPTER TWENTY-TWO

10 a.m.

Colonel Ira Baldwin pointed to a large hatch and they crowded towards it. A heavy chain and a hefty padlock lay across the wheel. He pulled a bunch of keys from his pocket and unlocked it, letting the chain fall to the ground.

'Bill, help me with the door.'

Marshall dropped Ciaran, who stood by Jake and Doctor Husk, and the two men turned the heavy wheel and pulled the hatch open. Husk stood fanning herself, lost in thought, when a small hand found hers. Ciaran didn't look up. He focused on the men pulling on the door, the sweat pouring from them. The air stunk of body odour. Jake slipped off his sweatshirt and tied it around his waist.

'It's hot,' he said.

'And it'll get warmer,' Baldwin said, motioning them forward. He peered through the hatchway. They could feel the heat inside. Baldwin pointed to the ladder. 'It's a bit of a climb, but we need to take this up three levels.'

'Three?' Husk said.

'The level above is likely on lockdown, so they'll have chained it. The level above that is main labs, we've no business going there. Best to go for level two. If they've locked that down, they won't have chained the access hatches. Protocol is different for those levels. They'll have men posted and the entrances locked.' He dangled his keys. 'Ready?'

Marshall nodded. 'Kate, you follow Ira, boys you follow Kate. I'll be behind you.'

'Bill, once you're in, seal the hatch.'

They entered one by one. Marshall then swung the hatch shut.

• • •

'Can I ask you something?' Keeney said, handing back the cigarette to Bradley, exhaling.

'Anything.'

'Why did you shoot Paul?'

Colonel Bradley considered his answer. 'Are you sure you're ready to talk about it?'

He nodded.

'I wanted to frighten him.'

Keeney scowled. 'Well it worked, because he was terrified of you.'

Colonel Bradley continued to smoke. 'I'm not going to apologise again. I knew the two of you were becoming close. I also knew he might get a little attached. You haven't given up on Bobby. When I tested him, it was obvious his feelings for you were strong. If it were just about sex, he'd have responded differently.'

'He liked me.'

Bradley handed him the cigarette.

'I told him I didn't feel the same.'

'How did he take it?'

Keeney looked at him and Bradley just nodded. 'I've thought a lot about things after we found the armoury,' he said, a frown pulling across his face. 'About what would have happened if we'd switched roles, and I'd stayed behind, you know?'

'You'd be dead. I think he knew that.' Bradley took the cigarette back and finished it.

'What? You're saying he sacrificed himself to save me?'

Bradley leant against the door frame. 'A last noble act, maybe? The dumbwaiter idea was his. He knew only one of you would get out. Paul may not have known he would die, but I think it's obvious he wanted you safe first. I might be wrong, but that's how I read it.'

'Me too.'

'Bill was an idiot for treating you so harshly,' Bradley said. 'We've had it out more than once.'

'I don't blame him,' Keeney said. 'But I think he forgives me.'

'What makes you say that?'

'Back when we met up, he said he was sorry. He said it before he knew there was something to be sorry about.'

'It was pretty evident that something horrible had happened, but I do think he's remorseful for his handling of you.'

'I lied on my application, it's an offence. I understand why he was upset.'

Bradley smiled. 'That's not what pissed him off. Honestly, he's treated you more like a son, than an aide. That's not your fault.'

When he didn't reply, Bradley said, 'Paul was Ira's son?'

Keeney nodded.

'You didn't think Bill or I might want to know that?'

'Honestly, an opportunity didn't arise to tell you. And since the general had sent me away. Anyway, he told me in confidence.'

The colonel nodded. 'The secrets we learn in the beds of our lovers, eh?'

Keeney lowered his eyes.

'I'm sorry. That was insensitive.'

'Yeah it was.' He looked up. 'You can give me another smoke as compensation.'

A grin spread across Bradley's face. He opened the packet, pulled one out, lit it, and handed it to Keeney. He then turned and sighed, touching a sleeping MP. 'How much longer before they wake up?'

Keeney shrugged as he smoked. A shout alerted them and he dropped the cigarette and stood on it. 'What was that?'

'Let's find out.'

They left the room and entered the infirmary, their pistols out. There was another shout. A muffled exclaim, nearby. Keeney and Bradley exchanged glances.

'Is it coming from the dining area?' Keeney asked.

The colonel opened the door a crack and peered down the corridor. 'Yes.'

Bradley's eyes never left the doors at the far end. He jumped as a hideous cry filtered towards them. A second blood-curdling scream followed. He looked to Keeney, the colour draining from his face. The door burst open as one of the clean-up team came through. He fell, making a frantic scrabble to get up, but his heavy suit impeded him.

'Stay here,' Bradley said, and ran to help.

When the colonel reached him, he found the fellow flailing. His bulky suit preventing him from righting himself. Bradley grabbed him, and the man screamed. 'It's okay, it's okay,' Bradley reassured him. 'I've got you.'

The man's suit was slippery with blood. Bradley couldn't see any punctures and assumed it was someone else's. He helped him up, but just as they were about to leave, a black tentacle burst through the door and grabbed the man's leg, and he fell onto his back. He screamed as Bradley attempted to stop him being pulled away, but the slickness of blood made it impossible to hold him, and he was yanked out of his grip.

When the doors opened, Bradley's eyes went wide. The creature had more than doubled in size.

He swallowed and stayed as still as he could, filtering out the horrible cries. When the doors swung closed, Bradley turned and ran back to the infirmary. Keeney met him at the door.

'We need to leave,' Bradley said, panting. His eyes remaining on the doors at the far end. 'Right now.'

'What about the MPs? We can't just...'

'We don't have time...' The words fell from him. He saw one of the double doors move, just a twitch – maybe a few inches – then it moved again, this time a little further.

Keeney followed Bradley's eyes. The doors moved again and now the black monstrous shape behind them was visible. It kept poking at the doors.

Keeney and Bradley looked at each other.

'She'll never forgive you,' Keeney said, as they backed away.

'I can live with that. Can you?'

'They're asleep. Maybe it will ignore them?'

'Good point. And they're sedated. If it does eat them, they won't even wake up.'

Keeney stared at him.

'What? It's true.'

The doors opened wider and this time they remained open. A thick black goo began seeping through the crack. Keeney pulled the flashlight off his belt.

'What are you going to do with that?' Bradley breathed.

'It's UV,' Keeney whispered.

'If you turn that thing on, I swear I'll hurt you.'

'But UV will kill it.'

The colonel put a hand on his arm. 'It's much, much bigger now. I think that'll just piss it off. Please put it away.'

The black gloop poured through faster. Keeney lowered the flashlight.

'Yeah... Okay, I think you're right.'

'Please tell me you know where this service area is?'

'Yeah.'

Keeney followed Bradley to the infirmary door.

'Can we go now?' Bradley asked.

'Yeah.'

Keeney turned and ran, Bradley following close behind.

They made it to the end of the corridor and hugged the wall at the intersection. Bradley lay against it and hissed to Keeney, who stopped and hurried back. 'Let's go,' he whispered.

Colonel Bradley put a finger to his lips, then slowly peeked around. He could make out the black puddle at the far end. Just as it had done before, when it fell from the ceiling in Todd's dining room, it began to grow.

Todd. His thoughts drifted momentarily. Todd, Jim, and Tony. He could see their faces, their expressions of pain, the awful cries. He shuddered. Bradley hadn't felt any remorse over Todd and Jim's demise. These men had run an organised mob with an unknown count of faceless victims. For men who'd disposed of those victims by having them cut up on the same kitchen tables they'd later have their breakfast served from, death was appropriate. Although the manner that death had taken would haunt him for some time. His thoughts drifted to Tony. A decent chap who was just trying to fit in, a man of limited intelligence, with a loyalty that had just been misplaced. As far as Bradley had seen, Tony was one of those wrong time and place people. It felt right that he'd spared him a hideous death. He thought about all those men and women lying there dead. Decent people just trying to live their lives as best they could under the rules of a cop turned gangster. But for all Todd's faults, Bradley couldn't lay blame for their demise on him. Grunner, he'd decided, bore that responsibility completely.

Colonel Bradley had seen death at the hands of others and his own. He'd made it a point never to revisit those memories. There was no value in it, unless he wanted to be reminded of how ruthless he could be. Now as he watched the elongating creature growing and forming into a bipedal humanoid shape, his mind's eye ignored years of conditioning, deciding at that moment to play back the images of Jim's last moments, as he was brutally ripped apart. Bradley ground his teeth and focused. Using memorised breathing exercises to calm his fears and force the memory away.

It wasn't long before the rippling monster slowed its upward growth and assumed full size. Bradley observed its thick legs, which formed more in line with those of a theropod than a human, tilting its bulk forward as it settled. It now took on the aspect of a half man, half dinosaur. Keeney's whispered voice snapped him from his reverie, and made him jump. 'What's it doing?'

'Nothing.' Bradley's scowl silenced him. He turned his eyes back to the creature. *Why was it just standing there? It isn't acting the same as before.* Turning to Keeney, he voiced those concerns. 'There's something different about it.'

'Different from what?'

'It's changed. It looks more like one of us.'

'Maybe that came from the last few people it ate?' Keeney's voice was shaking, the fear spilling out of his hushed tone was unmissable. 'I really want to go.'

'Just a minute longer,' Bradley said, his curiosity peeked. 'I want to see what it does.'

'I've seen what it does, and I've...'

Colonel Bradley shushed him. Keeney growled but said no more.

The creature's nondescript head continued to change, to sharpen, until it took on full facial features. It had a definitive nose and mouth, and what looked like a pair of black eyes, that then rolled into two white-yellow eyes. It blinked a few times, then ran those new eyes around the corridor as if it was searching for something. It lifted its arms and studied the long spindly fingers of its hands, which it extended and flexed. Colonel Bradley's face drained of colour and turned back to Keeney.

'Look,' he said, switching places. 'You recognise it?'

The light extenuated Keeney's grim expression, one Colonel Bradley mirrored. 'It looks like one of those monsters we saw herding people in Washington.'

'A lot like it,' he agreed.

'But they were weak and killable,' Keeney reminded him.

'True. I don't suppose we'll get that lucky. It answers the question where they came from.'

'You mean from us?'

Bradley's face came beside his. 'It's not an unreasonable assumption, is it?'

'No.'

It continued to flex its fingers. It seemed mesmerised by the action. 'You think this is what we'll turn into?'

Bradley hot breath hit his right cheek. 'Maybe.'

It looked up. A wet clicking gurgling noise came from the wide opening that Keeney could only describe as a mouth. It lifted a gangly arm and covered its eyes.

'What's it doing now?' Keeney asked.

'I think the light bothers it.'

They watched as it backed away. Its lipless mouth continued to make slapping clicks. It stretched up on powerful legs, raising thin, claw like fingers until it found the light fitting, then ripped it from the ceiling. With a shower of sparks the circuit broke, plunging the corridor into darkness, the creature along with it.

Keeney swallowed. 'We can't see it now.'

Bradley squeezed his shoulder. 'Look sharp.'

The only light came from the infirmary. Keeney stared into the gloom, waiting for his eyes to adjust. He couldn't see anything. Then from the darkness, where the low ambient glow penetrated, he saw it reflect off a pair of yellow eyes.

'I think,' Bradley whispered, 'we can safely say it doesn't like the light.'

'Or perhaps it can see fine in the darkness, and knows we can't.'

'That's not a cheery thought.'

'Please, Braders, I want to go.' Keeney's nervous, sweating hands fumbled with the flashlight he'd been holding. It fell and rolled onto Bradley's foot.

Yellow eyes flicked towards them.

Bradley grabbed the flashlight. 'Agreed. Time to leave.'

• • •

The slow climb up continued in silence. The heat stifling any conversation. Marshall looked up at the back of Jake. The boy was grunting with each step, the back of his shirt wet with sweat and grime. He stopped for a moment as his exhaustion threatened to overwhelm him. Somehow Jake knew he was struggling and stopped to look back at him.

'You okay, General?'

'Oh yes,' he said, waving him up. Finding the inner strength needed, he took in a shuddering breath, and pushed on.

Ciaran's hand missed a rung and he gave a squeal as he misplaced a foot. Jake had slipped in closer behind his little brother and caught him as he fell. Husk looked back. 'Are you okay?'

Jake, with one arm around the ladder and one around Ciaran's waist, nodded. Jake waited for Ciaran to find his footing, letting go of him only when he was steady enough to continue the climb.

Baldwin paused to wipe sweat from his forehead. Not far above he could see the hatch for level three, which meant at the rate they were going, maybe another ten minutes to the one above that. Husk tapped his leg and he looked down. 'How much further?' she breathed, grateful for a moment's rest.

'Not far.' He pointed. 'That's the hatch for the lab. We're around halfway.'

She nodded as he set off above her.

It wasn't long after that Marshall reached the level-three hatch and stopped. The others continued unaware he'd stopped for another rest. The heat was taking its toll. Marshall wasn't a young man and the exertion made him dizzy. As he clung to the ladder, catching his breath, he thought he heard something coming from the other side. Marshall leant towards the heavy door and focused his hearing. He couldn't make out what had attracted his attention. A muffled grinding came from the other side. A sound he recognised yet couldn't place. He knew he'd heard it before and recently. Then it came to him. It was the sound the metal chain made when Baldwin pulled it off the wheel of their hatch. Marshall looked up and sighed. They were a distance above him. If he somehow caught Baldwin's attention, it would mean stopping them all and forcing them to climb back down to him. Marshall stuck to the plan. It was possible that someone on that side had the same idea as them, but if they were attempting to open the hatch, that meant they were breaching the lockdown. He pondered on his choices when another sound made him almost lose his hold on the ladder. It was the unmistakable sound of gunfire.

Jake looked down, calling after him. 'General? Are you okay?'

Marshall reacted to Jake's call. He cupped his mouth with a hand. 'I heard something,' he yelled back. 'Tell Ira. Gunfire.'

Jake relayed the message. There was no way Baldwin could get down to him, not without climbing over Husk and the boys. 'Tell him to get up here,' he called to Jake.

Jake nodded and yelled back down.

The gunfire continued in sustained bursts. Automatic gunfire. The heavy lever on his side of the hatch was juddering. Marshall didn't think twice as he reached it and gave it a yank. His muscles ached as his strength sapped, then it spun free and almost knocked him off. An instant later two things happened. The door to the hatch flew open, and several men came running towards him. They had a look of terror on their faces. Louder gunfire pierced the air, reverberating up the tunnel reaching Baldwin, Husk, and the boys. They made an instinctive crouch.

Marshall tried to catch the eye of one of the men, waving and beckoning. But the man stood some distance from the hatch, his eyes trained on something above it. Marshall called to him, but the soldier couldn't respond. He was fumbling with his weapon. The general put a foot onto the threshold, intending to assist him, when he saw black vine-like strands flow from above and fill the space between them. Distracted by his weapon, the soldier didn't notice the danger.

'Look out,' Marshall yelled. The warning made the soldier look up. A strand flew and he screamed and fired. Marshall ducked as bullets bounced around him. They ricocheted off the ladder and walls, and up the service tunnel. He gave a loud curse and clamped a hand on the blood streaming from his right thigh. The soldier had lost his discipline. He was screaming, indiscriminately firing, and it wasn't long before his weapon went silent. When Marshall looked up, he saw the man hanging upside down. The poor fellow had a terrible look on his face. As Marshall clung to the ladder, he witnessed the man's last moment, as the creature pulled him in two. His bottom half landed some distance into the corridor beyond and the top half spun through the hatch hitting the ladder, spraying blood everywhere, and disappeared down the shaft.

'Bill!' Doctor Husk shouted.

General Marshall remained as still as he could. The pain from his leg was excruciating, but his mind had long since lost interest in processing it. His eyes focused solely on the hatchway, at the black mass forming tentacles that were making a slow reach for him. Above he heard shouting in unison. Urging him to climb. But he couldn't. The bullet to his thigh had crippled him.

Marshall stared in silence as they reached him. Slithering out of the dark, coiling around his legs, his waist, his arms. He looked up at Jake, who was yelling. His young eyes full of tears. Marshall felt one hit his forehead, he reached up and touched the spot. He offered the boy a reassuring smile as the tentacle things tightened.

Marshall closed his eyes and exhaled his fears. His eyes then opened and locked on the anguished faces above, and then he was pulled him from the ladder, and in the blink of an eye, General William Marshall was gone.

CHAPTER TWENTY-THREE

11 a.m.

Doctor Grunner reached his office and began pulling drawers open on his desk. He looked up at his assembled guards and paused. 'You four, secure the corridor. Make sure no one gets near this room. Shoot anyone who tries to interfere with you.' Grunner waited for them to leave before turning to the other armed black-clad men. 'You four stay with me, in case they fail.'

Doctor Grunner returned to his desk, taking several notebooks out of the drawers and carefully placing them into an old leather attaché case. He went to the wall and pulled a painting open which revealed a safe. From inside he removed documents, large bundles of cash, and a metal case which he stuffed in. With a sigh he looked at his younger brother, Heinz. A condition of the agreement he'd reached with the US authorities, Heinz was always by his side. No one had any idea of Heinz's background, so he was able to pass him off as just another German scientist. His talents, however, were far more suited to this current situation. Heinz had recruited others sympathetic to the Nazi cause. Those others now formed his security. His protection. Nothing was more important than that.

After Heinz had issued Grunner's orders, the three remaining men stood by the door. Heinz removed his mask and approached his brother, who put a hand on his chest. 'We were so close,' Grunner sighed. 'So close.'

'Albert,' Heinz said in a thicker German accent, 'it is time for us to go.'

Grunner nodded. 'Yes. You are right.'

'Do you have everything?'

Grunner patted the attaché case. 'Almost. Notes and beta samples. But we must go to lab sixteen because I do not have the alpha samples, and we cannot leave without them.'

'Now that you've released the beta creature from cold storage, what is to stop it coming for us?'

'Do not worry about the betas,' Grunner said, putting a hand on his shoulder. 'I can deal with them.'

'And the alpha?'

'It remains contained within lab sixteen's liquid nitrogen tank. It is safe.'

'What if it escapes?'

Grunner gave him a look. 'Did I not already say it is contained?'

Heinz nodded.

'Stop fretting.'

'Won't the Americans try to stop us?'

'I doubt it. They have two betas to deal with.'

'Do you think they will learn to control the creatures?'

He laughed. 'No. We fear what we do not understand. It is natural. An instinct within us, a drive to be superior above everything else. When we encounter something that threatens this, it is simple. We kill it. No group of men on this planet can claim they would do anything different, and if they did, then they would be liars.'

'Once we have the samples, where shall we go?'

'To the hangar.'

'And what of our men?'

He followed Grunner towards the door. 'We will need them. Let's go.'

• • •

'This is blood,' Bradley said, as his hands slipped off the rung of the ladder

Keeney had just finished sealing the hatch. 'I've seen too much of it.'

'Is the hatch locked?'

'Yeah.' He gave it another turn. 'That thing shouldn't be able to get through.'

'Let's hope not. Come on.'

They ascended and Bradley pointed. 'Look, it's all over this wall. See the pattern? Arterial spray.'

'What do you think happened?'

'I'd say, someone fell down this shaft bleeding out. You weren't joking about the heat.'

'No,' Keeney said. 'Let's go, old man.'

Colonel Bradley chuckled. As they reached the midway point between the two floors, Bradley stopped.

'What is it?' Keeney said, slipping up alongside him.

Bradley put a finger to his lips, then pointed. Keeney could see the hatch above was opened.

'Didn't Ira say that floor was sealed from the other side?' Bradley whispered.

Keeney nodded.

'There's no way Ira could have opened it from this side?'

Keeney shook his head.

'Let's go and see if we can find out who opened it.'

'Wait. What if the monster is waiting there?' His eyes stared at the blackness of the open hatch.

'Given how it has behaved, that seems unlikely.'

'You can't know that,' Keeney said, his eyes still locked on the hatchway. 'That blood came from somewhere... what if...'

Keeney clamped to the ladder. Bradley observed his tightening grip, turning his knuckles white. He recognised Keeney's paralysing fear. It wasn't the first time he'd witnessed terror overwhelm a man. The trauma he'd recently been through may have heightened it. Keeney had lost nearly all his colour. Bradley had seen something like this before, in France. A few men, locked in their own fears, terrified of dying. They would get to a point where it was impossible to calm them, after that, they were useless.

'John, listen to me.' Bradley put a hand on his shoulder. 'We're going to get out of here, okay?'

Keeney's breathing turned rapid. The heat and his anxiety

made sweat pour from him. Calming him now was critical. If Keeney passed out, he'd drop from the ladder and that really would kill him.

'John,' he said in a slow measured voice. 'Look at me, that's it. Listen to the sound of my voice, the cadence of my words. Focus on my mouth, watch my lips moving. Don't think of anything else. Just listen to my voice and watch my lips moving, that's it. Now, take in a deep breath then hold it. There you go. Now let it out. Good man. Just listen to the sound of my voice...'

Bradley repeated himself until Keeney's control of his breathing overcame his terror. Bradley put his hand on the back of Keeney's neck and gave a gentle squeeze. Keeney's eyes refocused.

'How are you feeling?'

'Better,' he said. 'Thank you.'

'Do you trust me, John?'

'I trust you, it's just...'

'You're scared of dying?'

Keeney's cheeks tinged red as his eyes looked down.

'Don't be embarrassed. Who isn't afraid of dying? But here's the kicker. We all die someday. Maybe it'll be today, or perhaps in a month, or even a year for now. There's no certainty to it, but if there's one thing I do know it's that we absolutely can't let our fears control how we respond.'

'Aren't you afraid?'

'I'm terrified.'

'You don't seem it.'

'That's because I know how to control it. It's difficult, it takes a lot of effort and practice.'

Keeney looked down at his pants and grimaced in embarrassment. 'I peed myself.'

Colonel Bradley said nothing for a second, sighed, then winked and pointed down. He had the same stain on the front of his pants too. 'There now, feel better?'

Keeney couldn't help but chuckle. 'You did that for me?'

'I did it because I needed to go. You're not the only one who drank too much coffee.'

'You're a ridiculous man.'

'I am. But more than that, John. I'm your friend.'

Keeney smiled.

'I won't let anything happen to you.'

'You can't promise me that.'

'You're right, I can't. To the best of my abilities, then. Ready to face whatever is waiting?'

'I am. And don't take this the wrong way, but if today is anyone's day to die, I hope it's yours, not mine.'

Colonel Bradley gave a toothy grin. 'That's the spirit. Come on.'

They neared the open hatch and Bradley motioned Keeney to stay put. He then climbed up further, until his eyes were in line with the bottom of the opening, and peered in. It was dark. He couldn't see much beyond where the limited light of the tunnel extended. What he saw made him swallow. The remains of at least three people were illuminated by the sporadic flickering of a light further down the corridor. Colonel Bradley climbed a few more rungs and stopped. It was quiet. Too quiet. Detaching the flashlight from his belt he flicked the switch on, and shone the UV light inside. It hit nothing, so he carefully unscrewed the filter, which allowed the bright beam to showed him more.

Bodies.

Bodies everywhere.

But no sign of anything else.

Keeney had crept up beside him.

'What do you see?'

'What I expected. Hold this.' Bradley handed Keeney the flashlight and leant towards the hatch, took hold of the bar, and yanked it closed and spun the lever. It secured with a ratcheted click. They both let out the breath they'd unconsciously held.

'Well I feel better,' Bradley said, the sweat pouring off him. 'What do you say we catch up with Bill and the others?'

'That sounds like a good idea.'

They continued up the ladder.

• • •

Baldwin, Husk, and the boys sat inside the electrical room against boxes stacked to the ceiling, and listened. Doctor Husk held Jake's hand while Ciaran hugged him. Baldwin looked through the window for the second time in as many minutes, then sat back down. They'd been in the room for maybe ten minutes and the only good thing was Ciaran had stopped crying. The last of the screaming and other noises of death from the far side had stopped, leaving only a vacant silence.

Ciaran's hesitant voice broke it.

'They're all dead. Aren't they?'

Husk calmed her own fear. 'We... We don't know that.'

'Whoever's left alive, they're gone, they left. We're going to die in here too.'

'Stop talking like that,' Baldwin said, his tone sharp.

Ciaran's eyes welled up and he hugged his brother tighter. Jake felt the fear and loss too. His mind's eye playing back the general being pulled off the ladder. The horrible screams he expected would follow, but didn't. Somehow that made it worse. At least if he'd heard the monster hurting him, there would be no reason for his brain to fill in the blanks. He closed his eyes. A tear fell.

'Hey,' Husk said. 'He's a scared little boy, and he's not the only one.'

Baldwin rubbed his eyes. 'I'm... sorry. We're safe in here.' He tried to sound positive. 'For now,' he added, looking back through the window.

'I need to pee,' Ciaran said in a small voice.

'Me too,' Jake echoed.

Baldwin's shoulders dropped. 'Can't you hold it?'

'No,' Ciaran said, standing. 'It's already coming out.'

The colonel rolled his eyes. 'Oh, good grief.'

Husk took his hand. 'Ignore him. Come on, you can pee in this corner. I don't think anyone will mind.' She went to leave, but he grabbed her hand and she met his dark scared eyes. 'Please, don't go,' he said.

'Okay, I won't.'

He relaxed. 'But don't look,' he cautioned her.

'I promise.'

Ciaran turned his back and it wasn't long before he was done. She led him back to the boxes and sat with him, while Jake took his place.

'What's the plan?' Husk asked.

Baldwin shifted his eyes to hers. 'At some point we need to leave this room,' he said.

'Agreed. So, what's the plan?'

'I'm working on it,' came his gruff response.

Doctor Husk wiped grime from Ciaran's face. A metal clunking noise came from the room with the access hatch. She looked at Baldwin, who crouch-walked to the door and peered through.

'What is it?' she asked, coming alongside.

'I think someone is trying to open the hatch from inside the service shaft.'

'The creature?'

Ciaran cried, and Baldwin frowned. 'Shut him up, or he'll get us all killed.'

The boy sobbed harder and Jake turned on the colonel, 'You shut up. It's all your fault, anyway.'

Baldwin took a step towards him, but Kate slapped his arm. 'Will you stop.'

With a sigh, Baldwin turned his attention back to door.

'You're not very good with children, are you?'

Baldwin held the dog tags hanging from his neck and closed his yes. 'No.'

She cursed at her insensitive remark. 'I'm sorry.'

Baldwin opened his mouth to say something more, but a heavy clang made them jump.

'What should we do?'

'We could try to jam it,' he said, looking for something to use. He turned to the boys. 'Jake, see if you can find something like a metal pole, or anything you think might stop the wheel turning.'

Jake nodded and both he and Ciaran began opening crates and boxes.

• • •

'Shouldn't we just open it?' Keeney asked. Bradley shook his head.

'And get Bill's forty-five in the face? No thanks.'

'But the general knows we're coming. I'm surprised they locked it.'

'Bill had no idea how long we'd take to get here. I think since they opened the hatch below, and our friendly monster has worked its way through the people on the lab levels, it's safe to assume they changed their plans.'

'I've been thinking about that.'

'About what?'

'The people on the level below.'

'I wouldn't do that, put it out of your mind,' Bradley said, trying the lever again. It felt stuck.

'No, I mean... how did it get up here before us?'

'It can move faster than we can. You saw how it changes shape. It probably just went thought the ventilation.'

Keeney was quiet.

'What?' Bradley said, frowning.

'There's no easy way for it to do that. Not between levels. Paul told me. The ventilation isn't fixed that way.'

'Okay, then it found some other way up. You and Paul did.'

'Yeah, from the floor below the kitchen. But other than the elevator shaft or this service tunnel, it wouldn't be easy for it to do that.'

Bradley grunted at the effort of moving the bar. 'What are you saying then?'

'I think there's more than one.'

Colonel Bradley blinked a few times, then turned back to the hatch. 'Well, you're just full of cheery thoughts, aren't you, John? This bloody lever is stuck.'

Keeney added his own strength to it and felt it give.

'What do you want to do now?'

Bradley thought for a moment. 'How good is your Morse?'

'Rusty. I think I can do something simple.'

'Get ready with the flashlight, we'll open the hatch a

crack, and you can use it to send a signal.'

'What shall I say?'

'SOS?'

• • •

Husk grabbed Baldwin's arm. 'It moved. The wheel, I saw it.'

Baldwin called out to the boys. 'Any luck?'

Jake shook his head. 'There's nothing in here we could use. It's all just glass and stuff.'

Baldwin pulled out his revolver.

'Will that help?' she asked, eyeing it.

'No, but it will make me feel better if I get a few rounds out before it kills me.'

The colour left her face.

'Kate,' he said, handing her his keys. 'There's been no activity outside for a while. Take the boys and get out of here.'

'Trade one terrible situation for another? No thanks. Not without you.'

'I can buy you some time.'

'You can't. It's suicide. We'd stand a better chance with you alive and showing us where to go, now stop being a martyr and...'

The wheel turned again and this time the hatch opened, just a crack.

'Go,' Baldwin hissed, raising his weapon. The sweat building on his top lip. Doctor Husk backed away, then paused as a beam of light came through the crack. It flashed at regular intervals.

'That's not the monster,' she said, stepping towards it.

Baldwin cursed. 'Get back here, you can't know that.'

'Since when does a monster use a flashlight to send Morse code?'

'You're right. Why didn't I see that?'

Baldwin followed her to the hatch, then motioned her to get behind him. 'Advance and be recognised.'

'It's us,' the unmistakable dulcet British voice said, 'Braders and John. Open the bloody door, we're boiling alive in here.'

'Boys,' Doctor Husk cried. 'It's okay, it's just Charlie and John.'

They rushed to her side. Jake assisted Baldwin as they pulled the hatch open. Colonel Bradley followed by John Keeney stepped through, and they closed it. Bradley caught the boys' eyes and smiled. Ciaran beamed and went to run, but Jake grabbed his arm. He pointed to Husk and made kissing face. Ciaran chuckled.

Baldwin stared at them. 'I'm glad to see you both. What happened to the MPs?'

'They didn't make it,' Bradley said, holding his breath, waiting for the verbal assault he been imaging she'd unleash on him. But instead she threw herself into his arms and held him tight. 'We're fine,' he said with a laugh. Bradley then saw the tears running down her cheeks. They weren't tears of joy.

'What is it?'

'Oh, Charlie,' Husk said, through sobs. 'It's Bill.'

Keeney came beside him. 'What about him?'

'The monster. I'm sorry. It... it took him.'

Keeney put a hand to his mouth and slumped against the wall, sliding down till he was sitting, then buried his head in his hands. Baldwin sat next to him. Colonel Bradley held a sobbing Husk in one arm, and two crying boys in the other.

CHAPTER TWENTY-FOUR

12 p.m.

Doctor Grunner and Heinz crouched by a door. Grunner hugged his leather attaché case close to his chest and only moved when the gunfire along with the terrible screams had stopped. The air was full of the acrid odour of cordite. Heinz, being careful to remain unseen, peered through the window then made a quick duck and crouch-walked back to him. His face was grim.

'Situation?' Grunner asked, adjusting his spectacles.

'The men were unsuccessful in their attempt to stop the creature.'

'I think the entire facility might conclude that from what we just heard. What are our options?'

Heinz sighed. 'It is motionless at the intersection that leads to the upper entrance. I see no way for us to bypass it.'

Grunner sat in thought then turned his eyes on Heinz. 'We must distract it,' he said.

'I agree, but how?'

The doctor stared unblinking through his thick lenses.

Heinz gaped. 'Me?'

'Our choices are limited, so yes, it must be you.'

'But... it will kill me.'

'Not if you follow my instructions.'

Heinz was hesitant. 'I don't know. Can't we just wait?'

Grunner scowled. 'We have a few hours before our window closes. The risk of being seen outside by some errant creature is high, but our odds of survival out there are far higher than if we remain.'

'If only you hadn't released the creature...'

'Be quiet.'

Heinz closed his mouth and looked back at the door.

'There is a risk... but given how important my work is and how valuable I am, you must conclude that this risk can only be yours. Yes?'

Heinz grimaced. 'What must I do?'

'Listen to my instructions and enact them exactly as I say.'

Heinz gave a last look out the window and gave another long sigh.

• • •

'... and then we got the hell out.' When Colonel Bradley finished his story, Baldwin sat rubbing his eyes. 'John and I made it to the ladder and climbed up. It looks like your labs are done for,' Bradley said.

'We lost Bill at that access intersection,' Baldwin said. 'We were a little above. I guess he saw something that made him stop. We were only aware of it when someone started firing through the hatch.'

Colonel Bradley sighed. 'Why didn't he just climb away?'

'There were bullets bouncing all around us, it was lucky none of us were injured, or worse. Jake thinks a bullet hit Bill in the leg. I don't know if that's true. But it would answer your question. Not long after, it took him.'

Colonel Bradley closed his eyes.

'I'm sorry.'

Bradley scowled. 'Sorry? This is all your fucking fault,' he hissed. 'You and that Nazi. If I didn't need your help to get us out of here, you'd be dead.'

Baldwin remained impassive. 'Understandable. I'd feel the same way if I were in your position.'

Colonel Bradley shook his anger away, then turned kinder eyes on him. 'I'm very sorry about your son,' he said.

'Thank you.'

Keeney came through from the other room. 'Everything

seems quiet. Should we consider moving on?'

Colonel Baldwin looked at Bradley. 'Whenever you're ready to go?'

'Just a moment. John suggested something while we were climbing. It wasn't a nice thought. He said there might be more than one creature out there.'

Baldwin considered his answer. 'There are three,' he said.

'Three?' Keeney gasped. 'When were you going to fucking mention that?'

'Sorry,' he said, 'old habits. The creature in our lab's cold storage is something we refer to as a beta. It's a spontaneous awakening. A hybrid mix of the host and trace amounts of the sample used in the vaccine. It's a very rare event. In nine out of ten cases, before the sample could transform the host, a fluid build-up on the lungs incapacitated them. We found the process could be stopped by extracting that fluid. It's a simple procedure. Then there's the one on the civilian level.'

'If it came out of Doyle,' Bradley said, 'Then it did so after he was dead.'

Baldwin sighed. 'I've seen something similar, only once. It was unrelated to anything we were working on. Evelyn thought it was a stage of the virus affecting the people out-side. I told you it attacks areas of the brain. A man arrived before you with symptoms, and died. We later found out he had an undiagnosed brain tumour. Somehow it ruptured and killed him. Not long after, he came alive. We designated it as an AHC. Animated Human Cadaver. We housed it in a controlled environment and witnessed it dissolve the man's tissues and bones down to a puddle. Grunner used that as the basis of his second vaccine, which had fewer side effects. Those given it rarely needed another. The infected man had something in common with Doyle. Neither were treated for any viral-related symptoms by us, they appeared immune already.'

Bradley rubbed his chin. 'You're saying they were infected prior to coming here?'

'Yes. That's exactly what I'm saying.'

'What about the other one?' Keeney said.

'The alpha. It's unique. Adaptive and highly intelligent. It's also probably the single most dangerous thing alive. It's submerged in liquid nitrogen. There is no way for it to escape. I can only conclude the other beta must be loose. My hope is, it somehow found a way to escape cold storage.'

Bradley and Keeney looked at each other.

'You hope it escaped? I don't understand,' Keeney said.

Baldwin shrugged. 'If it didn't, someone let it out. But no one would be foolish enough to do that.'

'No one?' Bradley asked, raising an eyebrow.

'Well,' Baldwin said, 'Perhaps one person might.'

Colonel Bradley's lips curled. 'Grunner.'

Keeney frowned. 'But why would he do that?'

'Because he's a Nazi, that's why. They have no respect for life. To them... we're just... samples.'

Lieutenant-Colonel Baldwin looked between them, but found nothing to say.

'Ira, you said before you knew how to kill it.'

'In theory at any rate.'

'What the hell does that mean?' Bradley snarled.

'It means, we had some success neutralising the beta samples. But it's not like pointing a gun and shooting it, if that's what you're hoping for.'

Keeney sighed. 'Just tell us what we need to do.'

'Okay. We need to electrocute it.'

'Them,' Bradley said, turning to Keeney with a raised eyebrow.

'Apparently,' Keeney murmured.

'I have an idea but it's risky,' Bradley said.

Baldwin stood in the doorway. 'Colonel?'

Bradley looked at Husk then back at Baldwin. 'We're going to get out and make for the hangar.'

'You intend to fly out from here?'

'That's my plan, Colonel. Are the aircraft fuelled?'

'Yes, but we haven't used them for months.'

Doctor Husk, who'd been looking through the window, turned to Baldwin. 'Do you think we can make it outside?'

'Absolutely,' Bradley answered.

Her eyes never left Baldwin's as he gave a slow shake of his head.

• • •

Heinz slipped through the open door and collected his thoughts. The monstrous creature, seemingly unaware of his presence, was directing its focus on the remains spread around it. Tentacle-like appendages pulled apart black survival suits, to get to their meaty contents. Heinz swallowed the bile threatening to erupt from his throat as his eyes caught the chunks of their remains, now splattered along the corridor. Mustering his willpower, the German made a slow crouch-walk a suitable distance away, then stood. Movement at the window caught his eyes. Grunner was staring at him through his thick round spectacles. With his thoughts gathered, and Grunner's instructions fresh in his mind, Heinz shouted in German and then waited. The creature ignored him as it continued ripping through the clothing, absorbing the contents. Heinz looked back at Grunner, who was waving his hands. He shouted again but the creature remained uninterested in Heinz's vocal demands. Again, he tried and still it ignored him.

Heinz then pulled the flashlight from his belt, switched it on, and waved the UV beam along the wall and onto the monster's back. The effect was instantaneous. The black bulk retracted from its touch. The glistening body rippled as it turned. Heinz could see no features to suggest it was facing him, because the bulky thing was just a blob of blackness, but as it had turned, it indicated the thing definitely had a front and back. Heinz touched it again with the UV and this time it made an inhuman cry and slid up the wall. He backed away. Each time the creature surged, he used the flashlight to halt its progress and drew it along the corridor away from Grunner's position.

Doctor Grunner kept his eyes on Heinz until he disappeared from view and switched his attention to the beta, which was rolling itself along the ceiling. As instructed, Heinz used the flashlight anytime it formed an appendage which recoiled back at the touch of the UV beam. When both Heinz and the beta were gone, Grunner grabbed his attaché case and fled in the opposite direction. He navigated through the remains spread around the corridor. Grunner paused and retrieved a flashlight, clasped in the death grip of a severed hand, which he removed and flung aside, then headed further into the complex. At an airlock leading to the labs, he stopped and fumbled with the lock. His eyes fell on the crimson-obscured windows with little emotion.

With the airlock open, and feeling safe within, Grunner took a slow breath and sealed it. The usual spotless controlled laboratory was in disarray. Instruments were smashed, the floor littered with broken glass and other debris, and scattered human remains. Doctor Grunner did not stop to consider the lives lost. He set his focus on reaching lab sixteen and retrieving the alpha samples. Their importance couldn't be exaggerated. But even though those samples would elevate his research, it wasn't Grunner's only priority. His deep-seated desire to maintain personal safety came above all others, and he would – and had – sacrificed everyone and everything alive to ensure he preserved it.

It didn't take long for him to navigate the interconnected labs to the ultraviolet-lit corridor, which ended at the heavy reinforced door to lab sixteen. A whisper caught his attention and he stopped. He narrowed his eyes but could see nothing along the corridor, or in the labs beyond. The intensity of the ultraviolet would incapacitate any beta that found its way in, before it could do him any harm. He shook the feeling off and unlocked the door then stepped in.

Doctor Grunner crossed the floor and opened the safe containing the samples. He retrieved several vials. One by one he encased them within thick metal blocks, being careful not to overtighten the screw caps, and deposited them into his case. He reached inside the safe and stiffened at the sound of a heavy ratcheted click from behind. He turned. Grunner's usual deadpan expression gave a hint of uncharacteristic surprise.

'You?'

• • •

Colonel Bradley made a quick review of the corridor before turning back. 'We'll head through the service area down to the dining room, and make for the stairs up to the command level.'

With no objections, Bradley opened the door. Husk picked up Ciaran and Bradley smiled. 'Baldwin, you know the quickest route, you and John take lead. Kate, Jake, you follow them and I'll take the rear. Are we ready?'

Baldwin and Keeney slipped out. Doctor Husk went to follow but Bradley stopped her.

'Stay with Jake,' he said, ruffling the boy's hair. 'If something happens, the boys are your only priority. You understand?'

She nodded. Bradley checked his revolver, then kissed her. 'Let's go then.'

They followed each other through the service corridor. It wasn't long before the metal walkway flooring and subdued mix of red and white lighting transitioned into a brighter finished corridor. Along the way they navigated through the sickening sources of the horrific screams that lay strewn along their path. Husk whispered to Ciaran and pushed his face into her neck, begging him not to look. Jake observed the carnage through brimming eyes. Despite willing those eyes not to look, he found he couldn't. The smell of death stuck in his nose. Bradley almost bumped into him as he doubled over and vomited.

Bradley knelt beside him. 'You feel better?'

Jake wiped his mouth, the colour gone from his face. 'Not really.'

The colonel took Jake by the shoulders. 'Brave heart,' he said. 'Come on, we're lagging.'

They both walked faster to catch up with the others. Baldwin put up a hand and they stopped, then dropped to a crouch. Bradley scooted alongside them. 'What?'

Baldwin pointed. 'I need to make a quick detour.'

Colonel Bradley frowned. 'Why?'

'What's so important about that room?' Keeney asked.

'It's Baldwin's quarters,' Bradley replied.

'I have to go,' Baldwin said.

Colonel Bradley ground his teeth as he thought.

'She could still be alive,' Baldwin said. 'Please.'

'Sarah?'

'It's a minor detour. I've lost everything, Bradley. If she was smart, she stayed in the room.'

'Ira, that was hours ago.'

'I know...' Bradley read the sadness in his eyes. 'I'm begging you.'

Bradley stared down the corridor. 'Which way to the dining room?'

'Head down here,' Baldwin said, pointing, 'then take the next right. You won't miss it.'

Colonel Bradley sighed. 'Fine. Go, we'll wait for you there.'

Baldwin scooted away.

'You want me to lead, John?'

Keeney shook his head and lifted his hand. They stood and followed. Bradley waited as they passed.

'How long will it take?' She asked, changing the arms she held Ciaran with.

'Don't worry, he'll join us soon. Go on, now.'

Husk carried on and Bradley took up his position behind.

Ira Baldwin entered his room and closed the door. He ran an eye around it, pleased to see it was in the same state he'd left it. The lights were still off and the room was dark. He walked through the living room and into his bedroom, but Sarah was not there. He stared down at the unmade bed and his shoulders dropped. Sarah must have left and there was no telling now if she was alive or....

A muffled whimper froze his thoughts. It was coming from under the bed. Baldwin made a slow crouch and lowered his head and looked under. He found a pair of terrified eyes looking back at him. 'Sarah?'

Her eyes blinked several times before she spoke. 'Ira? Is that you?'

'Oh, Sarah,' he said, extending his hand. She took it and he helped her out. Her cheeks stained with tears. He embraced her as she sobbed into his neck.

When her sobbing ceased, he wiped her eyes. 'We have to leave. Are you fit?'

She wiped her eyes with the back of her hand. 'Yes.'

'Good. We're going to make for the dining room.'

'What is happening? I heard all these terrible screams, and saw a thing, it was... Oh, Ira, there was so much blood. I hid under the bed. I didn't know what else to do...'

He held her again. 'It's okay, it's okay. You're safe now. Let's get out of here.'

Baldwin took her by the hand and tried to lead her to the door, but she didn't move. 'Sarah, we can't stay—'

He wasn't sure what had cut the words from his mouth, but when he felt Sarah's grip tighten, Baldwin's eyes followed hers towards a dark corner. With horror, Baldwin watched as something blacker than the shadows detached itself from the wall.

Keeney led them around the intersection and blew out a sigh of relief at the sight of the dining room entrance ahead. He looked through a window. It seemed like the room had been tipped upside down. Heaped in the centre were several tables. Keeney waved and Bradley came next to him. 'That look like a barricade to you?'

Bradley nodded. 'There might be someone alive in there,' he said. 'Let's be cautious. Scared people can be highly unpredictable.'

'You think I don't know that?'

Colonel Bradley put a hand on his shoulder and winked. 'Lead on, my friend.'

Keeney crouched low and the others followed. When he reached the door, he pushed it open a crack. Before he could go any further, a bullet rang out and splintered through the door an inch above his head.

CHAPTER TWENTY-FIVE

1 p.m.

'You want to throw me that bone now, Doc?'

Doctor Grunner's eyes never left the revolver pointing squarely at his face. He remained motionless as he licked his dry lips. General William Marshall gave a slight tilt to his head as he limped forward.

'If you intended to kill me,' the German said with a sniff, 'you would not have wasted any time with idle conversation.'

'I've had a shitty twenty-four hours. Most of it I understand thanks to you.' He shifted the barrel a few inches and fired. Grunner dropped, clamping his left ear. The bullet hadn't hit him, but it was close. Looking at his hand but finding no blood, he cursed his reaction and stood. 'You made your point,' Grunner remarked in a shaky voice. Marshall couldn't help noticing he held his case a little closer to his chest.

'As I was saying,' Marshall continued. 'I've been incarcerated, subjected to inoculations that have erased my memories, shot... and, oh yes, attacked by a monster you helped create. A monster that has killed so many people. A monster we believed to be utterly evil. But then it let me go. I've pondered on a lot of things, while I searched for you. The conclusion I came up with was, there was only ever one monster here. You. Given that, you can appreciate, I'm sure, how not killing you right now is probably the hardest choice I've faced today.'

Grunner's eyes narrowed. 'What do you mean, it let you go?'

'I thought that might pique your interest.'

'It is vitally important that you tell me exactly what happened.'

'I'm not going to.'

Confusion crossed the German's face. 'I demand you tell me.'

Marshall ignored him, and pointed to a section of the room that looked like it could be a silo. It had a very heavy looking stable door at its bottom, and a thick glass window on the separate door above. 'What do you keep in there?'

Doctor Grunner flicked his eyes in the direction Marshall was pointing. 'It contains many gallons of liquid nitrogen.'

'Why?'

'Why what?'

'Why do you have that much stored in here?'

'I did not design this place,' Grunner said. 'It has always been this way.'

'What would happen if I opened that door?'

'The room would flood with liquid nitrogen. As soon as it hit the air, it would revert to nitrogen vapour.'

'It would freeze us to death?'

'Given the volume of liquid and the speed in which the vapour would fill the room, it is debatable whether we would freeze or asphyxiate. Why? Do you intend to open it?'

Marshall stared at him.

Grunner however waved a hand at him. 'You are a survivor, General. I do not see you intentionally committing suicide.'

'I might open it quick enough to escape.'

Grunner simply shook his head. 'The liquid will flood the area. There is no way you could survive opening that door. But I might make it to the exit before then.'

General Marshall looked over to the door. 'I hadn't thought of that.'

'You see? I like you. You think things through as reasonable men should. Unlike the others, you have wisdom. We may not like each other, General, but we can work together, I think? We can come to a reasonable understanding, yes?'

'You misunderstood,' Marshall said. 'I meant I hadn't thought about you making it out before I could open it.'

Marshall redirected his weapon, a look of regret passing across his face.

'Wait, a moment...'

The shot hit Grunner in the left knee, twisting his shin and ankle in a burst of blood, sending the torn-out kneecap up the wall and over into the corner of the room. His glasses fell and skidded over to the general who bent down and picked them up, while he waited for Grunner's screams to subside.

'You shot me,' the German gasped; his face ashen, disbelief and pain crossed it all at once. 'Why did you do that?'

Marshall crouched next to him.

'Because I want you to suffer.' His voice was as cold as the room. 'I want you to feel unbearable pain and hopelessness. When I leave here, no one will come to save you. You'll just lay here, bleeding. Maybe you'll survive the wound. But locked in here? Alone? How long do you think you'll last?'

'It is inhumane,' he said through gritted teeth.

'Oh, the irony, Doctor.'

'Please,' he said reaching out a hand, 'please I beg you. My work can save humanity. I am its saviour, you must see this?'

General Marshall stood then looked through his glasses. 'You really do have bad sight, don't you?'

'Without them, I am blind. At least leave them for me, so I may read and write.'

Marshall pocketed them and stepped away.

'Won't you grant me a dying wish?' His pain affected the strength of his voice.

Marshall stopped and turned. 'You want to know how I survived?'

Grunner nodded.

'I was unarmed, wounded, and willing to die. When it pulled me off the ladder, I knew I had no chance. There wasn't anything I could, so I closed my eyes and waited for it to kill me. Then it put me down and wandered off.'

'What? No, I refuse.... That... that is nonsense. Its primary instinct is to kill. You are lying.'

'Maybe I wasn't a threat? Maybe its instinct is to defend itself against those trying to harm it. Truthfully, I think it just wants to be left alone. I can understand that.'

Grunner shook his head. 'You are lying, that is the only truth here.'

Marshall shrugged. 'Well, if a creature comes by, I guess you'll get to test that out.' He reached down and picked up the attaché case, then looked over at the silo. 'There was a question I meant to ask, since you were so good answering the others?'

'I will answer on one condition.'

'This should be good.'

'You return to me my spectacles. Agreed?'

Marshall pulled the lenses from his pocket and looked at them. 'All right. Here's my question. Instead of opening the door, what if I just shot a hole though it? What would happen?'

'Much the same. The calibre of bullet would determine the diameter of the hole. We set the labs at a temperature of sixty-eight degrees. The liquid-to-gas expansion ratio at that temperature means the size of the hole would make little to no difference. The end results would be the same. I implore you, General. Do not do it. Liquid nitrogen would be the least of our concerns if you do.'

'Why? Because there's another one of those creatures suspended in it?'

Grunner used his good leg to shuffle backwards so he could rest against the wall. He removed his lab coat, tearing out the lining, tied a rudimentary tourniquet high up his leg, and wrapped the remainder around his knee to stem the blood. The effort made him cry out in pain.

When the pain subsided, he found his voice. 'You are remarkably well informed. I suspect your British friend has something to do with that? I will tell you, since I am at your mercy. It is not one of the creatures loose out there,' he said, with an agonised hiss. 'It is *the* creature. The alpha. If you shoot a hole in that tank, it will escape. No one will be safe if you do. Not in here nor outside. It would kill everything it came in contact with. I do not think even your loathing for me would push you to that? I've answered your questions, return to me my spectacles as agreed.'

Marshall dropped them into his lap and Grunner put them on. When General Marshall came into focus, he was holding Grunner's attaché case. Grunner's eyes were fixed on Marshall's right arm, which he'd extended outwards. The revolver in his hand pointing directly at the silo.

Grunner's eyes went wide. 'Don't.'

Marshall didn't even blink as he squeezed the trigger. The shot hit the silo and a steady stream of liquid poured through the hole, creating an immediate hazy fog.

'Goodbye, Doctor,' Marshall said, as he turned to the exit.

'This is murder.' Grunner continued his screaming in German.

Marshall paused at the door. 'Here,' he said, throwing the revolver to him.

Grunner caught the weapon, pointed it back, and fired. It clicked. He fired again, but nothing happened. He turned it over, continuing his torrid of curses at the missing cartridge clip. Marshall threw the cartridge to him. 'Two rounds,' he said, pocketing the bullets in his hand. 'Just in case you miss with the first one.'

Before Grunner could react, Marshall stepped through the door. Doctor Grunner was fumbling with the cartridge, then yelled in dismay, as the door closed. The steady stream of liquid was growing into a large pool with the gaseous vapour rolling above it. Grunner knew he had little time. Propping himself against the wall, he managed to put his weight onto his right leg. With extraordinary effort he stood and hobbled along towards the door. When he reached it, he pulled on the release lever but it wouldn't make a full turn. He tried again but it would only go so far. With dawning misery, Grunner realised Marshall had jammed something in the wheel. He hammered on the inside window.

General Marshall's face reappeared and Grunner cried in relief. Marshall had meant to scare him, but he was a kind caring man. He could never be so cruel. Marshall was pointing from the opposite side. Grunner shook his head, unable to understand what he was referencing. It was then that Grunner saw Marshall's eyes move from him to something else. Something behind him. Gruner turned and flattened against the door. In the massing pool, a black shape was growing. He turned back to the window in time to see Marshall exiting the corridor through the door at the far end.

A noise behind forced Grunner to turn. The monster had slowed its growth. He watched in fascination as it changed from nebulous to humanoid. Only this time the process didn't stop at a rough approximation. It continued till the physical attributes of a human male were obvious. Eventually its rippling slowed and the blackness of its mass turned pinkish. When it finished a young muscular naked man was standing before him.

A man Grunner recognised.

It was Lieutenant Dawson.

Doctor Grunner raised the revolver and fired. Dawson looked down at the hole in his chest and put a finger inside. He could feel the warmth of his blood flowing from the hole down his body, mixing into his pubic hair, and running down his leg. He tasted his blood, then moved towards Grunner.

The doctor fired again. The bullet passed through Dawson, but it didn't stop his advance. When he reached the terrified German, Dawson snatched the revolver from his hand, and crushed then dropped it.

Dawson put a hand against the door and leant into Grunner's face. 'Mouu muullets.' His voice was sluggish. 'Mouuu,' he said again, then stepped back, rubbing at his mouth.

Grunner's expression changed. His fear subsided. 'You... you can talk?'

Dawson was stretching his face. 'Thhhoo.' He continued to rub his mouth. 'Twwwo.'

'Two? I understand you,' Grunner said. 'Two, yes?'

Dawson nodded.

'Twooo, buullits.'

'Two bullets? Is that what you're trying to say?'

Dawson nodded. His words coming easier now. 'Yesss, two... bullets. Why?'

'I don't know, he just gave me them.' Grunner examined

Dawson's youthful face. 'It's remarkable. You look just like him. You have mastered replication now, it would seem? Amazing.'

'Yes,' he nodded. 'Doorson.'

'You took his form from the matter you absorbed?'

'Yes.' He looked down at the hole in his chest, which was sealing itself. 'I am Bruce Dawson,' he said.

'Well, no, you are not. But we can spend time talking about that.' Grunner said, the pain of his leg caused him to grimace.

'You...' He stopped, as if searching for a word. 'Hurt?'

'I was shot, yes.'

'No... You hurt... me.'

Grunner nodded. 'I thought you would do harm to me, so I shot you.'

'Do you regret it?'

'I did not know you wouldn't harm me. I reacted out of instinct. Something I think you understand, yes?'

'Instinct. I understand.'

'I postulated that your instinct was to harm and now that the data has proved otherwise, so I must change this opinion. Do you understand that?'

'You were wrong?'

Grunner said, 'I suppose it had to happen eventually.' He grimaced as the pain began to assert itself. He slipped down, but Dawson caught and steadied him. Grunner grunted as he thanked him. Dawson held his weight with no effort.

'Doctor... Grunner?'

'Ah, you know me?'

He considered. 'I do. I am Bruce. I have his memory.'

'That's extraordinary.'

'Why did he give you two bullets?'

Grunner frowned. 'For my protection, although why two I don't know. Why does it bother you?'

'It says something,' Dawson said, his words coming fluently. 'About the way you think.'

'Does it?' Grunner asked. 'Your cognitive function improves every second. Are you capable of complex thoughts already?'

'I believe so. It took a second, what with the walking and talking.'

Grunner ran his eyes over Dawson's face. 'Your approximation is perfect. Right down to the colour of his iris. You can survive bullets. That tells me your body isn't in fact biologically the same as ours. You've duplicated the internal organs, and blood, but they don't function as ours would. You have also manifested genitals, but do they serve a purpose, other than the aesthetic?'

Dawson looked down. 'It defines me as male, doesn't it?'

'From a gender-specific position, yes. But there are many biological factors that make up a man. Not just having a penis. I wonder just how deep your approximation goes? Cellular, clearly. But do your organs function? You pump blood, I have seen this. But you do not appear to experience pain. And you are breathing... I wonder if your body even produces waste?'

'You would like to examine me?'

Doctor Grunner was consumed by his own genius. 'Oh yes, without question. You are the pinnacle of every human experiment I have ever performed, and will complete my corpus on the study of anthropological genetics.'

Dawson smiled. 'That would make you the greatest scientist to ever live?'

Grunner's eyes were unfocused. 'Without question. With you, I can solve all the mysteries of human evolution. No one in the scientific community will question my accomplishments ever again.'

'Only one question needs an answer.'

Grunner nodded. 'Where you came from, perhaps? The genesis of your existence, maybe? Are you *the* progenitor? I have so many.'

'I know, but none of these are the question I consider the more important.'

'Which is?'

'Why General Marshall gave you two bullets.'

'Compared to the marvel that is you, it is of no consequence.'

Dawson stared at him. 'You did not consider what those bullets were meant for, did you?'

Grunner frowned. 'I do not understand the relevance.'

'I know you don't,' he said. 'They were meant for you.'

'Me? Why?'

'As mercy.'

'Mercy from what?'

'Me,' he said.

Dawson grabbed Grunner's throat and his eyes bulged. He lifted the German, and Grunner's legs dangled. Grunner used the one good one to kick at Dawson's groin. The German then yelled, as Dawson threw him across the room. He landed with a splash in the pool of liquid nitrogen, and flailed. Doctor Grunner knew the Leidenfrost effect would give him time before the liquid could burn his skin, provided he continued to move to maintain an insulating layer of heat. But as his clothes froze the thought was lost. The stinging sensation radiating from where his clothes bonded against his skin, turned quickly into intense pain, causing him to cry out. With immense effort he flipped from the liquid, screaming as the right side of his body partially froze. The damage to his skin and muscle was extensive but some of the remaining heat from his body helped to counter the numbing effect.

Grunner crawled into a pair of legs. Twisting as best as he could to look up, he saw Dawson drop to a crouch. 'I remember everything,' Dawson said. 'Such an odd sensation. I can recall every aspect of my death. But most of all, I recall your face looking back at me through that window.'

'I am sorry,' he managed to gurgle. 'But it was necessary for my... data.'

The terrified doctor was lifted and dumped onto the only table in the room. With his right side frostbitten and some fingers missing, he could do nothing but lay there whimpering.

Dawson whispered into his left ear. 'There's a moment when the brain can no longer process the overwhelming level of pain impulses being sent to the brainstem,' he said. 'I think that's a good design, don't you?'

Grunner felt pressure on his back. 'Please... please...' he whimpered. 'Please... mercy...'

'Mercy?'

Grunner was slipping into shock, as Dawson continued to put pressure on his spine. 'Don't be afraid, Doctor. This is just data for my research, I'm sure you understand?'

'Please...'

Grunner's eyes then went wide and he screamed as the pressure intensified. That scream soon turned into a gurgled horrific shriek, as Dawson, with inhuman strength, pulled Grunner's spinal column and half his skull from out of his back and dropped it on the floor.

'That was for Bruce,' he murmured, wiping his bloody hands on what remained of Doctor Hans Grunner's body.

Bruce Dawson pulled the lever on the door and the obstruction Marshall pushed through the wheel on the other side sheared in two and fell. The door then opened and he stepped into the UV-lit corridor and smiled up at the purplish light. As he passed through the last door and entered the lab, Dawson paused as he caught site of his naked reflection in a dented metal cabinet. He ran his hands along his body and smiled. 'I need to find some clothes.'

CHAPTER TWENTY-SIX

2 p.m.

John Keeney lay prone, looking through the crack of the door. From his position he determined the shot had come from the barricade, but he'd been unable to see the shooter. Colonel Bradley left Husk and the boys, then crouched along the wall, stopping beside him.

'I can't get a clear view,' Keeney said. 'Any advice on how to proceed?'

Bradley pulled a handkerchief from his pocket and handed it to him. 'Try waving that. It might work.'

Keeney took and slid it through the crack. 'Don't shoot, we're friendly.'

They waited while Keeney waved the white cloth. The wait rewarded them with a scared voice.

'Who is it?'

'It's Captain Keeney. I have some people with me,' he called back.

'What do you want?'

'To get out of this fucking corridor. Can we please come in?'

There was scuffling and scraping and then the door opened. Keeney looked up at the young dishevelled officer, he'd spent the last few weeks working with and smiled. 'Mike?'

'Thank god,' Lieutenant Mike Li said, the relief on his grimy face clear. 'Get everyone in.'

When they'd all entered the dining room, Li sighed. 'Sorry,' he said, ushering them to the safety of his encampment. 'I've taken to shooting first lately.'

'No harm done,' Bradley said. 'How long have you been here?'

'Since the shit hit the fan. I don't really know. A few hours?'

Jake and Ciaran settled next to an upturned table. Lieutenant Li opened up a container. 'You hungry?'

They all nodded.

'I've some Jell-O here.' Li handed them one each. 'Hope you like cherry?'

The boys ripped open their packets and began devouring it. Husk, Bradley, and Keeney took the offered water with thanks and drank.

'What happened?' Li asked.

'The place is done for,' Bradley said. 'I have the awful feeling that aside from us, and maybe a few others, everyone else is dead.'

'How?'

'Experiments, Mike,' Keeney said. 'Nasty experiments created monsters that are killing everyone.'

'The black thing?'

Husk looked at the boys. They'd stopped eating and fear crept across their faces.

'You've seen one?' Bradley asked.

'Yeah,' Li said, swallowing his Jell-O.

'Recently?'

'A little while ago. Two of the guys with me went to check it out, then I heard their...' He looked at the boys and stopped. 'That's why I shot at the door when it opened. I thought it had come back.'

Colonel Bradley grimaced, then looked at Keeney. 'Ira.'

Lieutenant Li looked shocked. 'The colonel, sir. He's alive?'

'He was about fifteen minutes ago.' Bradley turned to Husk. 'I have to warn him.'

She compressed her lips and nodded. 'Don't be long though,' she said, taking his hand.

'I'll be back before you can miss me.' He winked at the boys and turned to Keeney. 'You'll be okay?'

'Why are you wasting time on him? He's the fucking...'

'John,' Bradley said, taking his shoulder. 'I have to.'

'Fine,' he said, sighing. 'Just hurry back.'

Bradley nodded then scooted out the door and was gone.

Keeney turned to Li. 'You got anything stronger than water?'

'Yeah.' Lieutenant Li pulled a flask out of his small container. 'There's some coffee here if you want it?'

Keeney sighed again.

• • •

General Marshall paused against the corridor wall to catch his breath. The pain from his leg came in waves, followed by a nausea he had to fight to stave off. He was hot and a little disorientated. He shook his head and tried to tough it out, but dizziness forced him to stop and sit. Marshall checked the bandage he'd wrapped around the wound and grimaced. It was soaked through with blood and the cause of the sudden onset of his weakened state. When he'd taken care of Grunner, his adrenaline and the pain meds he'd found in an abandoned med-kit had given him strength and dulled his pain, but that strength was now leaving. Fast.

I just need five minutes to catch my breath, that's all.

With his vision tunnelling, some part of Marshall knew he should get up. He should fight. But where that voice had been the louder, it soon became drowned out by those demanding he rest – and they sounded far more reasonable now. Marshall hung his head forward and closed his eyes.

I just need five minutes to catch my breath, that's all.

'General, are you alive?'

A gentle shake reached him and he opened his eyes. It took some time for them to focus, but when they did, he saw the outline of a man kneeling in front of him. He appeared to be checking his wound. Marshall's leg felt hot and he took in a breath from the pain of it, but it wasn't long before his strength returned and his mind cleared.

'I believe I am,' Marshall said, blinking to clear his clouded vision. 'I was just resting my eyes. Bruce?'

'Welcome back.' Dawson beamed at him. 'Thought I'd lost you there for a minute.'

Marshall took his boyish face into both hands. 'Oh, Bruce. I'm so happy to see you.'

'Likewise, General, but we should probably leave.'

Dawson stood and extended his hand. 'It's time to go. Come on, up you get.'

General Marshall shook his head. 'I'm injured. Go on without me, I'll just slow you down. I can barely put any weight on this leg.'

'What are you talking about? It's just a flesh wound.'

The general laughed. 'If saying it would only make it so.'

'General, please, trust me. I changed your bandage while you were sleeping. I stopped the bleeding. It isn't as bad as you think. Come on, please, take my hand.'

The general looked at his leg and noticed a clean bandage over the bloody mess of his pantleg. He took the hand and Dawson pulled him to his feet with a strength that surprised him. The next surprise was that he could put weight on the leg, without searing pain. Dawson picked up and handed him the attaché case, and Marshall put it under his arm.

'Thank you,' he said. 'I told myself I just needed a few minutes to catch my breath. Do you know if anyone else survived?' Marshall followed Dawson as he set off down the corridor.

'On this level? I'm not sure. It looks like everyone is dead.'

Marshall stopped. As if seeing him for the first time, he asked, 'Bruce, is there a reason you're naked?'

'Yeah, sorry. I was in the shower when the monsters came. I hid until it was safe. I was heading to get some clothes when I found you.'

General Marshall frowned. 'Monsters, plural?'

Dawson nodded.

'I see. Let's find you some clothes. Can't have you running about in nothing but your bare skin.'

Dawson pointed. 'The scientists' living quarters are just over here. Bound to be some clothes there.'

'When we're done, we'll head up to the second level. Hopefully, Ira, Kate, and the two boys made it to safety.'

'That's your plan?'

'Well, Braders' plan actually. If he and John made it out of the civilian level. We're all to meet up there.'

'I assume I can join you?'

Marshall put a hand on his shoulder. 'You really have to ask?'

He shrugged.

They came to a door. 'Be wary,' Marshall said in a soft voice. 'Those monsters can sneak up real quick.'

'They're probably a lot closer than we realise,' Dawson said over his shoulder.

'But they aren't the killers we've been led to believe,' Marshall said, as they entered. 'I escaped one.'

'I know,' Dawson said.

'How could you know?'

'You talk in your sleep.'

'I do, do I?'

'Jackpot,' Dawson said, opening a closet. He found a pair of pants and slipped them on. Now he was dressed Marshall felt comfortable looking at him. Dawson was fussing in the closet, his back facing him. It was then Marshall noticed something wrong. A thing different from the last time he'd seen him, back in the shower. Marshall stiffened and stepped away. When Dawson turned, he saw the change in Marshall's posture and frowned.

'You don't like the pants?'

The general's eyes were hard. 'What happened to your scars, Bruce?'

Dawson turned his back to the mirror in the door and looked over his shoulder. 'Damn,' he said. 'You always forget something.'

Marshall backed away until he hit the door behind, and a revolver appeared in his hand. Dawson stared at it.

'General, I'm not your enemy.' His eyes remained on the revolver. 'You don't need that.'

Marshall kept his fears in check. 'You're not Bruce. Who are you?'

'That's a little difficult to explain.'

The general cocked his weapon. 'Try me.'

'It's complicated. I am Bruce. Or I should say I'm every-thing he was.'

'Was?'

Dawson nodded. 'Thanks to Doctor Grunner.'

'What about him?'

'This will sound odd, I know, but... Grunner murdered Bruce.'

'You're not making any sense.'

'I'm trying to, General. But it's...'

'Complicated, yes, I heard you. What are you?'

'The best way I can think of saying it is, we are Bruce.'

The general narrowed his eyes. 'We?'

'General, that weapon won't help you.'

'Immune to bullets, are you?'

With a speed that shocked Marshall, Dawson snatched the weapon from him, then returned to his previous position. They stared at each other, as Dawson raised the revolver. Marshall compressed his lips, waiting for him to follow through, but then he turned the weapon on himself and fired, dropping to a knee with a groan, coughing blood.

'Jesus,' Marshall said, instinctively dropping and catching him as he pitched face first into the floor. The general turned him on his back. 'Why the hell did you do that?'

'To... show you,' he said, the pain evident on his face. He dropped the revolver and Marshall returned it to his holster. Dawson's face was white. Blood seeped out of the wound. Marshall put his hand on it and Dawson clasped it with his own. His shaking slowed and his breathing settled and the colour returned to his face.

'It's okay.' He carefully removed the general's hand. 'Look.'

Marshall examined his chest. The wound was healing right before his eyes. It wasn't long before there was no evidence of the shot. Dawson's strength returned. 'I hope I don't have to make that point again,' he said. 'Help me up.'

'What the hell is going on?' Marshall said, as he pulled Dawson to his feet.

'I'll try to explain. But first, there's something we need to discuss. Two bullets.'

Marshall's eyes widened. 'What did you say?'

'You gave Grunner two bullets. He didn't understand the reference.'

'How could you know that?'

'I was there.'

The realisation dawned on him. 'You're one of those creatures?'

Dawson shook his head. 'The ones out there are abominations. Part of them comes from me, but only a tiny part. They're driven by instinct.'

'To kill?'

Dawson shook his head. 'To survive.'

'By killing,' Marshall snarled.

'It's not their fault.'

'Whose fault is it then?'

'You already know the answer to that.'

'You're the creature Grunner had in the lab?'

'Can you stop calling me the creature?' Dawson said, with slight smile. 'It's kind of rude.'

Marshall looked at the blood on his hands. 'Sorry, I don't know what else to call you.'

'My name is Bruce.' Marshall flinched as Dawson took his hands, but the look in his eyes was kind. 'And thank you.'

'For what?'

'For rescuing me.'

Marshall frowned. 'I did?'

Dawson let his hands go and looked down at his pants. 'I need to find fresh ones. These are ruined.'

The absurdity of it made Marshall laugh.

'You shot the tank and freed me. That was your intention, wasn't it?'

The general remained unreadable. 'I have no idea what you're talking about.'

Dawson gave him a knowing look. 'Don't play dumb, General. You knew he had me in there. Was it because you wanted me to kill him?'

Marshall looked away. 'No, that's not true.'

'Lie to yourself if you wish. You incapacitated him then

left him to die by either being immersed in liquid nitrogen, or by the monster you hoped to unleash on him, or both. Don't deny it.'

'I...' Marshall rubbed his eyes. 'It never occurred to me that anyone would know.'

'Why didn't you just kill him? He deserved it, didn't he?'

Marshall thought for a moment. 'Yes. But that isn't the right way.'

'Why?'

'Because no single man should ever have that kind of power. To be judge, jury, and executioner.'

Dawson smiled. 'Except Braders?'

Marshall relaxed. A chuckled slipped out. 'Well, he is an exception. But even he shouldn't. Did you...?'

'Kill him?'

Marshall nodded.

Dawson pulled out a fresh pair of pants. 'I did. Brutally.'

The general closed his eyes, then opened them at Dawson's light touch.

'Don't feel bad. You know what he did to all those poor people.' Dawson went back to taking out more clothes. 'Grunner was a sadistic megalomaniac. In the camps in Germany, and Poland, he murdered so many innocent people. Women, and children. Especially the children. I see his victims. Their hideous cries. Begging for death. His horrendous experiments here are nothing compared to what he did to those children. You have no idea how those poor people suffered.'

'You talk as if you were there?'

Dawson paused and looked over at Marshall. 'In a way, I was.'

'None of this makes sense. How could you have been?'

'I wasn't physically there. I absorbed part of Grunner's essence before he died. I needed to understand him and now that I have, I wish I hadn't. I don't regret killing him. And I would do it again. You said no man should have the power over life and death?'

'That's correct.'

Dawson slipped out of his pants and put on clean ones. 'I am no man.'

'You look like one to me. What did Grunner do to Bruce, the real...? I mean the other...?'

Dawson's eyes turned sad. 'I remember things from two perspectives. Grunner had been subjecting me to tests, removing samples of my being, hurting and subduing me. There wasn't anything I could do to stop him. Then he put Bruce in the tank. It was instinct, I suppose. I thought all men were like Grunner. I thought he would hurt me, so I attacked and absorbed him. When we merged, I understood that Bruce was as much a victim as me.' A tear brimmed in his eye. Dawson took it on a finger and examined it. 'It's funny. I know what this is, but it's the first time I've ever experienced the conflicting feelings that create it.' Dawson smiled and wiped his eyes and nose. 'There are a lot of things I'm still getting used to. Anyway, to honour the gentle soul I consumed, I gave him back the life I stole. In every sense, I am Bruce.'

Marshall softened his stance. 'If it hadn't been for your lack of scars, I wouldn't have known.'

He pulled out a shirt. 'I can't explain why I made that mistake. What's in the case?'

'This?' Marshall looked down. 'I don't really know.'

'So why are you guarding it?'

'It was important to Grunner. I think there's value in keeping it.'

Dawson checked himself in the mirror. 'What do you think is in there?'

'Given how much importance he put on his work, I'd say it's his research.'

'Do you think this knowledge might be better forgotten, given how he got it?'

'Not if there's a cure to the virus that's infecting the world, no.'

'Ah,' Dawson nodded. 'Yes, I'd forgotten about that.'

'I agree that the way he got the results was questionable...'

Dawson raised an eyebrow. 'Questionable?'

'Unethical then.'

'Have you opened it to see what's inside?'

'No. I didn't get a chance.'

Dawson tucked his shirt in. 'How do you know it's not stuffed with a change of underwear?'

'Good point.' Marshall unlatched and pulled open the flap. 'It looks like notebooks and...'

'Samples?'

Marshall nodded.

'You want them out in the world? Given what happened here?'

'Not really, but maybe someone else could...'

'Pick up where Grunner left off, maybe?'

Marshall stared into the bag. 'The notes will be of value. At least they could point people in a new direction. Who knows, they may have already found a cure.'

Dawson said nothing.

Marshall pulled out the ampules. 'These contain samples of...?'

'They're parts of me.'

The general thought long and hard then handed them to him. 'They are yours, then.'

Dawson unscrewed the caps and one by one, poured the contents into his mouth and swallowed. 'Thank you,' he said.

'Are you ready?'

'Ready for what?'

'To get out of here?'

Dawson frowned. 'To go where? Another place of experimentation? I'd rather stay here.'

General Marshall put a hand on his shoulder. 'Some secrets aren't worth dying for, Bruce.'

'You'd do that' – his expression a mixture of surprise and relief – 'for me?'

'For Bruce, yes.' Marshall met his eyes and said, 'I'm probably making a terrible mistake, but since I should have been dead, at least twice, I'm going with my gut. You could have let me die in that corridor. I don't know what you are, but I do know you're not evil.'

'You can't know that for certain,' Dawson deadpanned.

'I think I can. You said the monsters out there are an abomination?'

He nodded.

'But part of them comes from you?'

'A very small part.'

'Small enough to show mercy when it recognises its victim isn't a threat?'

'I suppose so.'

'That's all I need to know.' Marshall poked his head down the corridor. 'It's all clear. Let's go.'

• • •

Colonel Bradley sneaked back along the corridor towards Baldwin's room when he heard movement ahead. Feeling exposed in the open corridor, he doubled back to a room he'd passed and disappeared inside. He positioned himself so he could see along the corridor and stiffened. From a vent in the ceiling he observed a creature oozing through and pooling onto the floor below. When the last of it had flopped out, it grew itself into a humanoid shape. To Bradley's relief, it trudged along the corridor away from him, back in the stairwell's direction. Away from where Baldwin had gone, but more important than that, away from the dining room.

Bradley slipped out through the open door and made his way towards Baldwin's room, pausing at the intersection and flattening himself against the wall. The creature was down the far end, and as far as Bradley could determine, it hadn't seen him. He waited until it disappeared. With a sigh, he turned and collided with another that had appeared beside him. A black appendage slapped him into a wall, and he fell hard, coughing blood onto the floor.

• • •

General Marshall and Bruce Dawson made their way along a service junction and out through a series of interconnected rooms to the stairwell that would take them to the upper level.

As Marshall entered, Dawson put a hand on his shoulder.

'We're not alone,' he whispered.

'A creature?'

'I can sense it.'

'Any idea where?'

'No.'

Marshall noticed he was scanning the area with eyes that were now just black. They returned to normal when he stopped. 'I can't pinpoint it. But I know it's close.'

'We can't just sit here,' Marshall said. 'We should either go forwards, or find another route up.'

'I shouldn't have come.'

'Stop that,' Marshall commanded.

'Sorry. We're here, we should go forward. But, If I can sense it, it's likely it senses me too. I'm putting you in danger.'

Marshall grunted. 'I've been in danger from monsters ever since I stepped into this godforsaken place. And not all them were grown in a lab.'

Dawson flashed him a grin. 'We have that in common then. Well, General, it's your call.'

Marshall removed his revolver and dropped it. 'Forward then. If we pose no threat, they shouldn't harm us.'

Dawson didn't look so sure. 'Maybe not you,' he said, 'but I suspect my existence might be considered a threat.'

'We'll deal with that when and if we have to. Come on soldier, get moving.' Marshall opened the door and looked in. 'It's clear.'

They ascended the stairs in silence. When they reached the top, Dawson stopped him from opening the door. 'It's here,' he whispered.

'On the other side of the door?' Marshall said.

Dawson shook his head, then slowly looked up. Marshall felt a tightening in his throat as his eyes followed. On the ceiling above, a pool of black rippled as it threw out its hideous tentacles to grab them.

CHAPTER TWENTY-SEVEN

3 p.m.

Colonel Bradley scrabbled along the floor as fast as he could, but the thing grabbed his ankle and jerked him backwards. He cursed as his face smashed into the floor, but he managed to flip onto his back and detach a flashlight from his belt as the monstrous thing jerked him closer. Its grip on his ankle tightened and the colonel cried out as he felt the bone crack. His foot was now jutting out at the wrong angle.

Focusing on his nervous fingers, ignoring the pain threatening to overwhelm him, he fumbled with the flashlight's switch. When it came on, Bradley directed the UV to the appendage and it retracted. The monster gurgled and another appendage flew, but again the UV stopped it. With the creature momentarily confused, Bradley detached a second flashlight and turned it towards the blacked thing's bulk. With two sources of UV now concentrated together, Bradley noted with satisfaction the area it hit seemed to smoulder. The creature roared and bent away, but he continued waving them in an arc that confused the thing long enough to use his good leg to slide further away.

Another appendage came faster than the colonel could react. It took his wrist and squeezed until his hand could no longer hold the flashlight and it tumbled to the floor. Another appendage knocked it away. Bradley turned the remaining UV onto his held wrist, shoving the lens directly onto the tentacle wrapped around it. He yelled, as the thing tightened its hold, bearing the pain the UV caused. Eventually the UV won out and the appendage retracted.

Bradley looked for the other flashlight and grimaced. It was on the other side of the corridor. There was no way he could chance going for it, not with his ankle broken. He had to keep the thing at a distance. Stop it from pulling him close enough to kill him. The great mass stood there, rippling. Colonel Bradley could almost feel its indignation. He wondered how long he could hold it off before it took him. The feeling returned to his left hand and he switched the flashlight over. He pulled his revolver out with his right hand. Bradley knew bullets wouldn't hurt the monster, but he'd decided early in the war if he was going out it would be by his hand. He raised the revolver to his head... then someone yelled.

The creature turned and appeared to quiver as it let out a gurgled shriek. Bradley dropped the revolver and rolled to the other flashlight, tears forming from the agony he felt. Through gritted teeth he concentrated two beams on its back. The monster gave a terrible shriek then turned itself into a funnel and shot towards the ceiling, disappearing into a ventilation panel. Colonel Bradley retrieved his revolver and breathed. The source of the yelling rushed towards him. It was Colonel Baldwin and Sarah Doyle. Baldwin was carrying a much bigger flashlight and a bundle of files.

Colonel Bradley lay on his back and concentrated on his breathing. The pain pulsing through his ankle and his wrist had deadened a little. 'I never thought I'd be so happy to see you,' Bradley said.

'It's been a strange day,' Baldwin deadpanned. 'Can you stand?'

'Not unaided.'

Baldwin switched the flashlight to his right hand and he examined Bradley's foot.

Bradley said, 'How is it?'

'It doesn't look that bad.'

'You're a terrible liar, Baldwin.'

'Actually,' he said with a genuine smile, 'I'm an excellent liar. Take my arm.'

Baldwin helped him to stand, and Bradley cried out as pain

wracked his body. The colour slipped from his face and his eyes drooped.

'Hey,' Baldwin said, slapping his face. 'Stay awake.'

'Trying,' Bradley breathed. He looked at the scared woman and smiled. 'Hello, Sarah.'

'Charlie,' she said.

'You've been in Ira's room this whole time?'

'We can chat about that and anything else later,' she admonished.

'Sarah, help me,' Baldwin said. She took Bradley's other arm over her shoulder. 'That's not good,' she said, averting her eyes from his foot. It was wobbling like there wasn't much holding it on.

'I've had worse,' he said, attempting a smile that never fully formed.

'Grab his leg,' Baldwin said, 'we'll carry him.'

'I can hop,' came Bradley's indignant response.

'Ready?' Baldwin said, ignoring him.

She nodded.

'I said I can hop. Put me down this instant.'

'Let's get him to the dining room.' They continued ignoring Bradley's demands to be put down.

• • •

'Run!' Dawson shoved him and Marshall fell back with a gasp. Dawson lost his form and became a blacked thing, like the one attacking them. He'd burst through his clothes and pulled the monster off the ceiling. Marshall scrabbled back from them as they wrestled. In their fight, they merged a number of times. It was difficult for him to distinguish between them. An appendage shot out and Marshall ducked. He watched the battle rage until they separated. One twisted and flew down the stairs, leaving the other standing above him. Marshall had no idea which it was, then it shrunk and reformed into Dawson, who extended his hand and helped him up.

'You're naked again.'

Dawson just sighed.

'You can go to all the trouble of turning yourself into a person, but you can't make clothes?'

'It doesn't work like that.'

'I'm sure we can find you more. It's gone. Let's get moving.'

Dawson looked down the stairwell, his features grim. 'I can't go with you.'

'Why?'

'It's mutating. I got a sense of its purpose, and it knows what I do.' He turned back to Marshall. 'I have to stop them.'

'I want to help you.'

'You can't. You said before that they wouldn't attack you if they didn't feel you were a threat. Well, that was true before, but they've adapted now.'

'What do you mean?'

'They're a hybrid mutation and they're dying.'

Marshall frowned. 'That sounds like a good thing to me?'

'It makes them far more deadly. Everything is a threat to them now. They've maintained themselves by consuming the remains of the people here. Thanks to me, they know that source is running dry. They'll either wither and die, or...'

'Go looking for more.'

'General, I have to stop them. When we merged, it recognised itself in me, but also knew I was a threat. If I come with you, they'll get out into the world and then they'll be unstoppable.'

Marshall took his shoulders. 'I don't want to leave you. I won't leave you.'

'Believe me I'd rather go with you, but they can't be allowed to continue to kill everything just to stay alive. You can't stop them. Only I can.'

'We'll wait for you.'

Dawson shook his head. 'Bruce died. Perhaps he should just stay dead. You're the only person who knows about me. You said before that a secret was worth dying for. I say a secret is also worth living for.'

'What will you do?'

'There are others here,' he said.

'Others?'

'Scattered here and there. In the civilian levels, in the

infirmary, the isolations wards. I can save them.'

'How?'

'I'll think of something?'

'Then what?'

'I'll think about that afterwards too.'

General Marshall took him into an embrace. Dawson lay his head on the older man's neck. Then they parted.

'I'm glad I got to know you. Both of you.'

'And me. Oh,' he said, as a thought occurred. 'The creatures in the world, they're part of the source I'm from. We're old. Far older than you know. They're acting on instinct, but they're capable of adapting, of being shaped to become more than just, well, monsters. Do you understand?'

'You mean they're like you?'

'They're from me and I'm from them,' he said. 'Now I think you know what you have to do?'

Marshall nodded. 'How widespread is it?'

'It's difficult for me to know, I'm not connected with them. But I imagine most of America, at least as far as Canada. You should head north.'

'Why?'

'We don't like the cold.' Dawson said. 'Your friends are waiting in the dining room. Through that door, follow the corridor and make a left. One of them is injured. Do you have a container in that case?'

Marshall riffled through and pulled out a hip flask. 'Only this.'

'Perfect.' He unscrewed the cap and took a long drink, then put a finger over the opening and dropped in a small amount of black fluid, then replaced the cap and handed it back. 'Make him drink this. It'll heal him.'

'Like you healed me?'

Dawson smiled.

'Thank you, Bruce.'

'Thank you,' he said, 'for showing me friendship, even knowing what I am. I know that not all people are like Grunner. It will be a lot of work, but you can coexist peacefully with my kind, if you choose to. The choice is really up to you.'

General Marshall nodded. 'Will we ever meet again?'

'I do hope so.'

Dawson leant forward and kissed him, swirled himself into a funnel, and disappeared down the stairs.

• • •

Keeney shot up and ran to the door, as Baldwin and Sarah helped Bradley through. Bradley's face was white and taut with agony. He took Bradley's weight off Sarah and he and Baldwin helped him up onto a table that Doctor Husk and Lieutenant Li had put the right way up.

Bradley let out a strangled cry as they lowered him on. She ran her hands along his leg, towards his mangled foot. The boys huddled close, but backed away as he screamed and bucked at her ministrations.

'Hold him,' she said. 'I need to get this shoe off.' Doctor Husk pulled at the laces but stopped as his terrible cries increased. She looked at him, his eyes finding hers.

'How bad is it?' he managed to say.

'Bad.' She pulled his trouser leg up and examined the purple swollen ankle. 'Looks like multiple breaks.'

'Ugh,' he sighed. 'Just... give me a minute to get my breath.'

Doctor Husk turned to Baldwin. 'Give me your belt.'

Baldwin unlatched it and handed it to her. She then turned to Li. 'You too.' He obeyed and she took it.

'I need something to use as a splint,' she pointed to a chair. 'The back of that chair, the spindles. Can you break me off a couple?'

Li pulled out a knife and turned it, using the top saw to cut them out. Kate looked up at the woman. 'I don't know your name?'

'Sarah,' she said.

'Great, Sarah. Get me some water, as cold as possible. There's a sink behind that serving hatch.'

'I'll go with you,' Keeney said. 'I'll see if there's any ice.'

They left and Husk turned to Bradley. 'Charlie, I have to get this shoe off.'

He shook his head. 'Leave it.'

'Listen to me, I know you're in pain. But you'll lose that foot if I don't.'

Bradley blinked a few times, then nodded. She handed Baldwin a belt. 'Give him this to chew on, and hold him.'

Husk went to his shoe, then looked up. His teeth biting the leather.

'After three.'

He nodded.

'One, two—' She pulled the off the shoe. Bradley screamed as Baldwin held him. His foot was yellow and black. When he had calmed enough, Baldwin removed the belt.

'You said on three,' Bradley said, his voice almost a whisper.

'I know, sorry.'

'How does it look?'

'Terrible. It's the worst injury I've seen. There's no blood flow going to your toes and your ankle is swelling. I'm almost certain you'll lose the foot, but if we don't drain your ankle, we could have a bigger problem.'

'Then it's a good thing I came along when I did,' a voice said from the doorway.

They each looked over.

'Bill!' Husk said, her shock mixed with happiness. 'You're alive!'

Bradley's eyes turned. 'I'm delirious.'

Jake and Ciaran, who'd remained quiet and to one side, ran and grabbed him, almost knocking him over. He kissed their heads and wiped tears from their dirty faces, then came to the table. 'I can't leave you alone for a second, can I?'

Despite his agony, Colonel Bradley laughed. 'You old devil.'

General Marshall pulled out a flask. 'Fancy a drink, *old boy*?'

'Bill,' Husk said, 'if that's alcohol, I'll need it. As much as I want to hug you, I need to think about amputating this foot and I'll need that to help sterilise...'

Marshall shook his head. 'Trust me, Kate. I have the solution, right here.'

Doctor Husk frowned as he opened the flask and carefully

tipped the contents into Bradley's mouth. The colonel swallowed and Marshall put a hand on his forehead. 'You'll feel better in no time.'

'I hate brandy,' he said, and then his eyes widened. 'What...'

The pain in his foot lessened. Husk couldn't believe her eyes. The swelling in his ankle visibly reduced, and the colour returned to his foot. Somehow, whatever Bill had given him, it was healing him – bones and all. Bradley sat up and blinked. Li came beside Baldwin and they both gaped.

'You're just full of surprises today, aren't you?' Bradley said, taking him into a hug.

'It's been a strange day,' Marshall said.

Baldwin, who had said nothing during the entire exchange, pointed to the case. 'A gift from Grunner?'

'You could say that,' he said, returning the flask back to the case.

'It's his research?' Colonel Baldwin asked.

'Yes,' Marshall said, nodding.

Baldwin handed over the collection of files he was holding. 'Add this to it, it's all the files I have on what we've done here. Where is Grunner?'

'Let's just say, he'll not be joining us,' Marshall said, turning to Li. 'Lieutenant, gather as many supplies as you can. Boys, go help him.'

'Is he dead?' Bradley asked.

'Yes.'

Bradley smiled. 'Good. Did you kill him?'

Marshall stared into his eyes. 'Yes, I did.'

Colonel Bradley put his foot down and tested it. 'That's incredible. What was that?'

'A gift,' he said. 'From a friend.' He put up his hands and cut off their questions. 'We need to get the hell out of here.'

Keeney and Sarah came through the door with water. When Keeney's eyes found Marshall's, he dropped what he was carrying and went over and embraced him. 'Where the hell have you been,' he yelled. Before Marshall could answer, he hugged him again.

Sarah said, 'I'm confused. Do you need the water or no?'

Husk shook her head.

Colonel Bradley put his shoe on, then clapped his hands. 'Happy reunions can wait until we're out of here. Time to move, people. We'll head through the command centre and outside. It's mid-afternoon, so we'll be clear to get to the hangar.'

General Marshall looked around them. 'I don't know about anyone else, but I'm ready to leave this god-awful place.'

Colonel Bradley put a hand on his arm. 'I'd like to know how you survived.'

'The author of my story has a sense of humour, I think. I can't explain it. Call it fate, a higher purpose, I don't know... however you look at it, it just wasn't my time.'

'Nor any of ours, it seems. Although, I seem to recall you saying you didn't believe in all that higher-power nonsense?'

Marshall chuckled. 'After what I've seen. I think I'm ready to change my opinion.' He turned to the others. 'Let's go.'

The journey they took through to the first level was uneventful. Ira Baldwin led them along the mezzanine floor and up into what should have been a busy command centre. They stopped as they looked at the heavy doors that lead to the outside. General Marshall shooed them forwards, but stopped when Baldwin remained.

'Come on,' he said. 'No time for dillydallying.'

Lieutenant Colonel Baldwin shook his head. 'I'm not going.'

They had stopped behind Marshall.

'What?' General Marshall said, stepping forward. 'Don't be silly now.'

'Bill, take Sarah with you. Make sure you tell them what happened here.'

'You can tell them yourself, Ira.'

He shook his head. 'I let this happen. I have to fix it.'

'Fix what?' Bradley yelled. 'Everyone is dead.'

'Go,' he said.

Sarah moved forward, but Husk held her back. 'No, please, I want to stay.'

'Sarah,' Baldwin said, 'Go... have a life, put me and this nasty place behind you.'

Sarah burst into tears, and Husk held her, rubbing her back.

Marshall met his eyes. Baldwin smiled at him. 'If you'd been in charge, I imagine things would have turned out very differently.'

'Why don't we talk about that on the plane?'

'I'm responsible for what happened here. I'm the one who blindly followed orders and allowed that German to carry on, knowing... knowing what he was doing to the people here, to my son...' He smiled. 'It's time for me to set things right.'

'Damn it, Ira. This isn't the way.'

'It's the only way for me. There's no getting around it, this is my fault. And frankly, I don't think I could live the rest of my life with the guilt. You have all the files. Captain goes down with the ship, right?'

Colonel Bradley stepped forward and touched Marshall's arm. 'Let's go, Bill,' he said.

Marshall shrugged him off. 'Braders, you can't possibly agree with this?'

The two colonels stared at each other. 'Not only do I agree with it, I endorse it. I misjudged you, Baldwin,' Bradley said. 'I thought you were a coward and a fool. I was wrong.'

'No, you weren't,' Baldwin said. 'I was a coward and a fool, but it's nice of you to say.' He turned to Marshall. 'Discussing all this in committee after the fact isn't my style. I'll leave that up to you, General.'

Colonel Bradley smiled, came to attention, and saluted. 'Happy hunting, Colonel.'

'Safe trip,' he said, returning the salute.

General Marshall stepped forward and extended his hand and Baldwin took it. 'You're sure I can't talk you out of this?'

'I'm sure.'

Marshall nodded. 'Then I hope you find the closure you're looking for.'

'I'm sure it'll be explosive,' he said. 'Goodbye, and good luck to you all.'

General Marshall watched Ira Baldwin disappear then turned. 'Well? What are you all still standing there for?' he growled. 'We've got a plane to catch. Move out.'

They headed for the entrance, but Colonel Bradley hung back as Marshall came alongside. 'Brave man, that,' Bradley said.

Marshall nodded, then gestured for them to leave.

CHAPTER TWENTY-EIGHT

It took Colonel Baldwin twenty minutes to make his way to the elevators on level two and down into the subbasement. It surprised him he that he hadn't encountered any creatures along the way, not that it would have mattered either way. Since the one in his bedroom had simply wandered off without so much as a look in his or Sarah's direction, Baldwin concluded the creatures thought as little of him as he did. Apparently, he wasn't even worth murdering.

Colonel Baldwin opened the door and stepped into the room that housed the compound's five thirty-thousand-gallon propane tanks. After a brief pause, he approached one and disconnected the housing, exposing a hose, regulator line, and valve. He pulled off the hose and opened the valve a hair. Movement caught his eye at a window set in a heavy wall, and he watched as the monstrous creatures approached. They were far more humanoid than he remembered. Baldwin moved to the door to seal himself in, but just as he was about to close it, a man stepped through.

'Hello, Colonel,' Bruce Dawson said.

'Bruce? What the hell are you doing? You have to leave, now. And why are you naked?'

'That's a bit of a long story, actually.'

'Well, I have no time to hear it, since you're leaving. That's an order, Lieutenant. Those things out there won't bother you, it's me they want. Marshall and the others are heading to the hangar. If you hurry, you can catch them before...'

'No more orders, Colonel. Not today,' he said, examining the housing. 'You opened the valve already? That's what I was planning to do.'

Baldwin came beside him. 'There's no need for both of us to do this. I thought everyone was dead.'

'Not everyone. I got several groups out before coming here. I imagine they'll have an interesting story to tell.'

'So that just leaves you and me, and those things out there?' Baldwin seemed pleased. 'Bruce, please, you have to leave.'

Dawson put a hand on the colonel's arm. 'You were a little ahead of me, that's all. We both had the same idea.'

'You're really not leaving?'

'You can go, if you like?'

Baldwin smirked as they sat on a step and looked up at the monsters, who were throwing themselves at the window, running tendrils along its edges, trying to find a way through.

'Good luck with that,' Baldwin yelled. 'It's reinforced glass and a solid concrete room. There aren't any holes to squeeze through.'

Dawson chuckled. 'They're clever, they'll figure out how to get in soon.'

'Not soon enough.'

They could smell gas now.

'How long do you think we should wait?' Dawson asked.

'Not long. Probably better do it *before* we asphyxiate.'

'I'd recommend that,' Dawson said with a smile.

Baldwin looked fondly at him. 'I promised General Marshall I'd give him time to get his people out.'

'Yes, I made him the same promise. The remaining survivors should be outside by now.'

'What do you think? Another five minutes?'

'I think so. It only takes one of us. If we both start passing out that's probably the time to do it.'

Colonel Baldwin pulled a pack of cigarettes out of his shirt pocket. 'Smoke?'

Dawson smiled and took one.

'Why are you naked, anyway?'

• • •

John Keeney took in a lengthy breath and let out a contented sigh as they stepped outside for the first time in months. A haze of grey-white clouds covered the sky. The heat and humidity far greater than he'd remembered. He didn't care. He caught Colonel Bradley's smile as he too exhaled away the horrors.

'We made it,' Keeney said. 'We fucking made it.'

'Not yet, we haven't,' the general said, ushering them on. 'Not until we're in the air. Now go.'

'There's a truck, look,' Keeney pointed.

They sprinted towards it. Marshall jumped into the driver's seat and pulled down the visor. A set of keys landed in his lap.

'That was lucky,' he remarked, as he pushed the key into the ignition and turned the engine over. When it spluttered to life, Doctor Husk, Sarah, and the boys got in. Keeney, Li, and Bradley rode on the outside as Marshall drove to the hangar. The exited and Colonel Bradley directed them forward, pointing to the DC-3.

'It's prepped to go already. Get inside, I'll do a visual.'

While Bradley checked as much as he could, the rest of them headed up the steps and boarded. He then ran up and unlatched the steps, and kicked them away.

'Strap yourself in kids,' he said, locking the door behind them. 'This might be a bumpy ride.'

Marshall and Keeney followed him to the cockpit. Bradley sat and ran his eyes around the instruments.

'You sure you can fly this thing?' Marshall asked.

Bradley pulled out a booklet from a pouch on the side of his chair. He was looking at instruments, tapping them, muttering to himself. 'Parking brake set pressure up. Mags off. Mixture... Fuel tank selectors... Props... Throttle, open. Landing gear, latch handle down. Flaps... okay.' He looked up. 'I think I'm ready to give it a go.'

Marshall slipped into the seat next to him. 'What do you need me to do?'

'You know how to read these instruments?'

'No,' he replied.

'John, you did basic flight training, correct?'

'Yeah, but it was a long time ago.'

'Good enough for me. Bill, get the hell out of that seat and go to the cabin. Keep everyone happy while John and I figure out if we can actually fly this bloody thing.'

'I'll just get out of your way then,' Marshall said with a chuckle.

'If you want to do something helpful, check to see if they've got a bar or something. I could really go for a pink gin.'

Marshall laughed. 'Seriously, are you sure you know what you're doing?'

Bradley gave Marshall his best smile. 'John and I have this. We know what we're doing. Go.'

The general traded with Keeney and watched the two men going through pre-flight checks. He stayed with them for a moment longer, listening to their back-and-forth conversation.

'Trims?' Bradley said.

'Set.'

'Pitch?'

'Full fine.'

'Mixture?'

Keeney examined the gauge. 'Auto rich.'

'Fuel...'

When Marshall left, Keeney said, 'You can fly this, right?'

'Me? I was hoping you were flying. Carb heat?'

'Ah... cold and locked.'

'Fuel?'

Marshall wandered to the cabin and found the boys seated by the windows. Kate Husk, Sarah Doyle, and Mike Li sat together in the middle row.

'How's it going?' Husk asked.

'They've got this.'

'Charlie can fly this thing?'

'I hope so.'

Sarah looked askance. 'Wait, what?'

Marshall chuckled. 'He and John know what they're doing.'

They heard the spluttering of engines and the aircraft jolted a little.

'There you see? Seatbelts on everyone,' Marshall said. 'Jake, make sure you lock your brother in, please.'

'Yes, sir,' he said. Marshall smiled at the excited look on Ciaran's face. He climbed into the seat in front and peered over.

'First time in a plane, son?'

'Uh-huh.' He was wriggling against Jake's attempts to fasten him, looking out the window, distracted by everything.

'Well, make sure you stay put.'

'Uh-huh,' he replied.

'He's distracted, General. You won't get much conversation for a while,' Jake said.

'I can see that.'

'General, I'm glad you didn't die.'

'That makes two of us,' Marshall said, smiling.

'Thank you for saving me and my brother, sir.'

'It wasn't just me. You can thank Braders too.'

'I like him,' Ciaran said. 'He's nice.'

'I believe he likes you too.'

'Uh-huh,' Ciaran said, as he stared out the window.

'See?' Jake rolled his eyes.

Ciaran then pointed. 'General, sir. Look. People.'

Marshall ducked down and put his face to the window. To his immense relief and joy, several soldiers were directing people out of the entrance. He couldn't tell how many, but it was a lot more than he expected. A mixture of nurses, military, and civilians.

'Thank you, Bruce,' he muttered, as he continued to watch them escaping.

Colonel Bradley's voice came over the intercom. 'We're taxiing now, as soon as we're out, we'll be up quick. Strap in and stay that way till I say otherwise. Oh, and Kate...'

She looked up.

'...when this is all over. Let's get married.'

Bradley flicked the intercom off.

'That was smooth,' Keeney said, flicking switches and finishing the checklist.

'Well, she hasn't said yes. Gyros?'

'Aligned. She'll say yes.'

'How's the temp of engine one? You think so?'

'Nominal. I know so. Hey, if it were me, I'd say yes.'

'Really? That's lovely, John. Okay, I think we're about ready, don't you?'

He nodded.

Colonel Bradley looked out along the runway. 'We'll use flaps, the runaway's short. Set to one quarter.'

'Set.'

'Okay then. Here we go.'

• • •

Baldwin was feeling light-headed when he looked at his wristwatch and nodded. 'I think that's long enough, don't you?'

Dawson stood. 'They should have reached the hangar by now.'

'That's far enough away, don't you think?'

'More than enough.'

The monsters had moved to the door and were forcing themselves against the outer seal.

'Told you they were clever.'

'You seem to know a lot about them,' Baldwin said, staring at the door.

'I'm just good at reading these things.'

Dawson put the cigarette into his mouth.

'Here,' Ira Baldwin said, 'let me light that for you.'

In an empty corridor on level three, a door opened. Heinz, who'd been waiting for Grunner for what seemed like days, finally poked his head out of the doorway. 'Hello?'

• • •

Colonel Bradley throttled the props and the aircraft picked up speed. When the speedometer hit around the fifty-knots mark, he applied a little forward pressure to stop the tail from lifting. As they picked up speed, he could feel the aircraft was ready. Without looking at the gauge, he gave a gentle pull and her nose lifted.

'Oh, this is too much fun,' Bradley said, laughing.

As they lifted, an enormous explosion came from the compound. The fireball reached almost to the aircraft and the blast rocked them. General Marshall went to a window. They were high and he could see the debris reaching as far as the airfield. A plume of smoke replaced the fireball they'd all witnessed.

'What happened,' Husk said, coming beside him.

'An explosion. It destroyed the compound. Looks like the entire thing collapsed.'

She put a hand on his shoulder. 'Fitting. Enough people died in it, now it's a giant grave.'

'Indeed. Check on the boys, I'll see if the galley has anything to eat or drink.'

'Okay,' she stepped into the aisle. 'Bill?'

He followed. 'Hmm?'

'Thank you,' she said.

'What are you thanking me for?'

'Oh, you know. For not dying.' She kissed his cheek.

'So, what's your answer?'

'To what?' Doctor Husk raised an eye, smiled, and went to check on the boys.

Marshall chuckled as he returned to the cockpit.

'You saw that?' Marshall asked.

'I don't think we could have missed it. Well, except Braders,' Keeney said.

'Been a little busy, old boy,' he said. 'What d'you think happened?'

'I think someone blew up the compound.'

'Good for Ira,' Bradley said, slapping his knee.

'I hope there was no one left alive in there,' Keeney said.

Marshall put a hand on his shoulder. 'Just as it went up, we saw a number of survivors who'd made it out safe.'

Bradley smiled. 'I am happy to hear that.'

'Me too,' Keeney said.

'Bill, we'll level off at eight thousand feet, that'll put us above the clouds. With any luck we might get a glimpse of the sun.'

'That would be nice,' Marshall said, as he they ascended into the thick clouds.

When they were almost at altitude, the clouds continued to obscure their view of anything through the cockpit window. Keeney checked the dial. 'Seven and a half thousand feet.'

'Damn,' Bradley said, frowning. 'I thought we'd be out of the clouds at seven. Looks like we'll be flying on instruments for a while.'

Keeney flicked a couple of switches. 'Where are we heading, exactly?'

'That's an excellent question. Any idea, Bill?'

'North.'

'Why not south?'

Marshall leant on the back of his chair. 'I don't think the monsters care for the cold.'

'Nor do I,' Keeney muttered.

Any further discussion was cut short as the aircraft's nose broke through the clouds, and their eyes were met with the bright yellow glare of the sun. The general put a hand on both Keeney and Bradley's shoulders. They all stared out at it in wonder. An indicator light flashed. Bradley frowned, then he grabbed the headphones. 'That's the bloody radio,' he said, pulling them on.

'Mayday, Mayday, this is Delta-Charlie-Three-Niner. Is anyone receiving, over?' They held their breaths, then a crackle broke the silence.

'Delta-Charlie-Three-Niner, please identify yourself?'

'We're a group of survivors attempting to locate any US armed services. We have a US VIP aboard.'

'Hold on, Delta-Charlie-Three-Niner, I'll redirect.'

They waited then the radio light flashed. 'Delta-Charlie-Three-Niner, this is Alpha-Golf-Two-Zero-One, identify yourself and your position.'

'Alpha-Golf-Two-Zero-One, this is Colonel Charles Bradley, British intelligence. I have General William Marshall and his aide, Captain John Keeney, on board. Current position, err, somewhere above the clouds over Maryland heading north... I think.'

'Delta-Charlie-Three-Niner, please confirm you have General William Marshall with you?'

'That's affirmative.'

There was an interminable pause. 'Tell him the president sends his regards.'

'I will do that. We need a place to land. And you should know, myself and Captain Keeney are learning as we go. Neither of us have flown anything like this before, over.'

'Understood, Delta-Charlie-Three-Niner. Not advisable to land in US territory, continue north, we'll give you instructions along the way. How is your fuel?'

'We're full. But my check card tells me I have a fifteen-hundred-mile range.'

'You need to refuel, so we'll work something out. We'll redirect you to a safe zone in Canada. How comfortable are you with a landing?'

'I got her up. I'm sure I can get her down again.'

'We'll talk you through it before then. Pilots will meet you once you're down, and they'll bring you the rest of the way. You'll have coordinates soon. In the meantime, I have a message for Captain Keeney. Message reads: You're late.'

'He heard you, who is the message from?'

'Major Bobby Rogers. Stay on your current heading.'

Bradley winked at Keeney. 'Roger, Alpha-Golf-Two-Zero-One, waiting coordinates and instructions. Delta-Charlie-Three-Niner, out.'

Colonel Bradley took off the headphones and turned to Keeney. 'Bobby got himself an oak leaf while we were away.'

John Keeney exhaled, and colour filled his cheeks. Marshall gave Bradley a look. It was one he knew well. 'John, you have control. We're straight and level. I'm off to see my future wife.'

Keeney took control as Bradley exited his chair. The colonel stretched, then headed away.

'What if she says no?' Marshall called after him.

'Then I'll marry Sarah,' he yelled back.

Marshall slipped into the pilot's seat. Keeney set his eyes forward.

'John?'

'It's okay, General. I know what's coming.'

'You do?'

'Yeah,' he said with a thin smile. 'I lied on my application. You have a duty to report it.'

Marshall looked through the cockpit window then sighed. 'I've treated you poorly. I let myself down and I let you down too.'

Keeney blinked a few times. 'Thank you, sir. But it doesn't excuse...'

'Oh stop. It was a childhood issue that re-emerged under extreme stress. And we've just survived a terrible situation without you having any reoccurrence. Someone recently told me, some secrets are worth living for. We will not discuss the matter again, understood?'

John Keeney nodded. 'Yes, sir.'

Marshall left his seat. 'You're a wonderful man and I'm proud to serve with you. I'm giving you a field promotion to major.'

Keeney beamed. 'I don't know what to say, sir. I'm honoured, thank you.'

'You earned it.' General Marshall squeezed his shoulder. 'We've come a long way since Washington, you and I. Back then, when this all started, I was so tired.'

'And now?'

General William Marshall smiled. 'Now? I feel alive. Why don't you get your friend Bobby on that radio and tell him your news?'

THE END

ABOUT THE AUTHOR

Christopher D. Abbott is a Reader's Favorite award winning author and a writer of crime, fantasy, science-fiction, and horror. He has a background in human behavioural studies and psychology and loves quirky characters such as Rodney David Wingfield's Inspector "Jack" Frost, Agatha Christie's Poirot, and Sir Arthur Conan Doyle's Sherlock Holmes.

Described by *New York Times* Bestseller Michael Jan Friedman as "an up-and-coming fantasy voice", and compared to Roger Zelazny's best work, Abbott's Osirian series brings a bold re-telling of Ancient Egyptian mythology and presents a fresh view of deities we know, such as Horus, Osiris, and Anubis. He weaves the godlike magic through musical poetry, giving these wonderfully tragic and deeply flawed "gods" a different perspective while increasing their mysteriousness.

Abbott is a keen musician and has written a number of songs—he also likes to get out and play as often as he can. He also volunteers his time to support Chase Masterson's Pop Culture Hero Coalition, a non-profit organisation that champions overcoming bullying and social injustice. He lives in CT. You can contact him at:

Info@cdanabbott.com

cdanabbott@gmail.com

and find him online at:

www.facebook.com/cdanabbott

www.twitter.com/cdanabbott

https://www.instagram.com/cdanabbott/

and at his website:

www.cdanabbott.com

Lieutenant Wilson is found dead at Reardon House, Dartford Kent.

But was it a suicide or a murder?

When Inspector Hargreaves of the Kent Constabulary seeks Sherlock Holmes' aid in uncovering the truth, Holmes and Watson become embroiled in an investigation leading to the heart of Westminster. Possibly to the Crown Herself. Who is Sir Henry Wilburton? What is his connection to the late Professor Moriarty? Holmes must weave a dangerous path if he is to reach a successful conclusion. But with war a possible outcome of failure, the stakes are as high as they can get.

Available on Amazon & Barnes & Noble: